NEW YORK TIMES BESTSELLING AUTHORS

LINDSAY McKENNA

& JOAN JOHNSTON

SHADOWS FROM THE PAST
&
HAWK'S WAY: FARON

HARLEQUIN®

PLEASE RECYCLE · THIS PRODUCT IS RECYCLABLE

ISBN-13: 978-1-335-58009-2

Recycling programs
for this product may
not exist in your area.

Shadows from the Past & Hawk's Way: Faron

Copyright © 2020 by Harlequin Books S.A.

Shadows from the Past
First published in 2009. This edition published in 2020.
Copyright © 2009 by Lindsay McKenna

Hawk's Way: Faron
First published as The Cowboy and the Princess in 1993.
This edition published in 2020.
Copyright © 1993 by Joan Mertens Johnston

This edition published by arrangement with Harlequin Books S.A.

For questions and comments about the quality of this book,
please contact us at CustomerService@Harlequin.com.

Harlequin Enterprises ULC
22 Adelaide St. West, 40th Floor
Toronto, Ontario M5H 4E3, Canada
www.Harlequin.com

Printed in U.S.A.

CONTENTS

Lindsay McKenna is proud to have served her country in the US Navy as an aerographer's mate third class—also known as a weather forecaster. She was a pioneer in the military romance subgenre and loves to combine heart-pounding action with soulful and poignant romance. True to her military roots, she is the originator of the long-running and reader-favorite Morgan's Mercenaries series. She does extensive hands-on research, including flying in aircraft such as a P3-B Orion sub-hunter and a B-52 bomber. She was the first romance writer to sign her books in the Pentagon bookstore. Visit her online at lindsaymckenna.com.

Books by Lindsay McKenna

Shadow Warriors

Running Fire
Taking Fire
Never Surrender
Breaking Point
Degree of Risk

The Wyoming Series

Out Rider
Night Hawk
Wolf Haven
High Country Rebel
The Loner

Visit the Author Profile page
at Harlequin.com for more titles.

SHADOWS FROM THE PAST

Lindsay McKenna

To the ladies of Quilter's Quarters, Cottonwood, Arizona
(www.quiltersquartersaz.com).

Thank you, Mary Beth Grosetta, owner,
for teaching me how to quilt. And to all the wonderful
staff who are quilting queens in their own right:
Carla Armstrong, Karen Crowder, Jody, Joy Albanese
and Sherri Morstman.

And to the incredible Tuesday Group ladies who come in
every Tuesday and create comfort quilts for the poor,
the sick and infirm. Connie Hanks, Dorothy Esper,
Eileen Crandall, Jeanne Bollen, Judy Bishop,
Mary Beth Grosetta and Vivian Raines—you rock! Your
compassion and care for others is truly inspirational.

CHAPTER ONE

IT WAS TIME. As she sat at her bedroom table in Montana, Kam Trayhern's hands grew damp. Outside her window, the May dusk turned a lush pink and orange above the Douglas firs surrounding the two-story Montana home of her adopted parents, Morgan and Laura Trayhern.

Now that she'd returned from a harrowing trip to Africa, she had to face the rest of her life, starting with her birth. Kam lifted a folder marked Tracy Elizabeth Fielding. She opened it and smoothed out the papers inside with trembling hands. She shouldn't be so emotional about this. But she was.

Her gaze fell upon the black-and-white photo that had haunted her for years. The edges were stained and darkened from age and damage from the earthquake that had hit Los Angeles twenty-eight years earlier. A marine dog handler and her golden retriever had found

Kam and her biological mother in the debris of their destroyed apartment complex. That day, Kam's mother had died but she had lived, thanks to that marine, Callie Evans. Kam had been taken to Camp Reed on the Marine Corps base for treatment of her minor injuries.

Kam turned on the desk light to get a better look at the old photo. Just like that the dusk within the room disappeared, but nothing could make her nightmares disappear. She had to face facts. Morgan and Laura Trayhern had adopted her when they discovered she had no family. Her mother had been an orphan and there was no trace of her father. At the time of the quake, many records, memories and photos had been lost—forever. All Kam had from the apartment was this photo. It had been found in her mother's purse.

The photo showed her mother, Elizabeth, with black curly hair like her own, standing with three men. She wore a white lab coat for a Los Angeles veterinary convention. Another vet stood next to her, smiling toothily for the photo. The note on the back identified the veterinary convention. A businessman in a dark gray suit stood on the other side. Kam's gaze drifted to the third man, the tallest one, to the left of her mother. He looked like a cowboy with his black Stetson. His weathered square face, a mustache and narrowed eyes spoke of the harsh elements, most likely from ranching.

How many times had Kam looked at this photo and wondered if one of these three men were her father? Kam frowned and peered more closely at the man standing with her mother. She felt an instinctive churn of her gut as she looked almost longingly at the cowboy. He stood out from the others. Taller than all of them, he was built lean, like a wolf. His face was darkly sunburned, deep creases and laugh lines showed at the corners of his eyes. Everyone in the photo was smiling except him. And her mother was caught looking in his direction. Was this a secret look of love?

A lump formed in Kam's throat. Of course, her adopted father, Morgan, had turned over every stone to find her biological father. After all, Morgan was in the security business at the highest levels of the government with his super-secret Perseus and Medusa companies. No one in the outside world knew what he did for a living. As a cover, Morgan had created a real-estate front to hide his real reasons for being in Phillipsburg, Montana. His secret offices were located deep below the basement level of the turn-of-the-century Victorian house. Kam had been raised in a two-story cedar home not far from the office.

Morgan had promised Kam to find every possible scrap of information on her mother, and over the years, he had. The questions remained: Who had fathered her? And why hadn't that man ever come forward to claim her? These questions cut like a knife. Because she owed Morgan and Laura everything, Kam had waited a long time to approach them about seeking her biological father herself. She simply did not want to hurt them. But now she couldn't put it off. She had decided to take a hiatus from her professional photography job as a stringer for several global newspapers and magazines. This way, she'd have the time and energy to conduct her search. And her parents had to know her plan.

Kam wiped her damp hands on the sides of her jeans. How would they react? Again, her gut tightened with fear. Would they be angry? Throw her out of the house that she had called home for twenty-eight years? Oh, it was true that she was a globe-trotter and had come home only about once a year since turning twenty-one, but still... Kam dreaded the possibility that they would kick her out of their lives.

And then, where would she be? Without any family. Her mother had been an adopted child, and the people who had adopted her were dead along with whatever memories and information they had. It was the worst kind of ending for Kam—to be an orphan of an orphan. What had she done to be a lost spirit in this lifetime? Kam believed in reincarnation, believed that her soul would never die, but that it would return lifetime after lifetime into different bodies to learn how to become a compassionate and spiritually enlightened human being.

Two of the few items retrieved from Elizabeth's destroyed apartment had been a book on Buddhism and one on reincarnation. These books were now dog-eared from being read so many times. Kam had wanted to adopt her mother's views on life and, to a degree, she had. Consequently, her beliefs were different from those of the Trayhern family. They didn't mind nor did they try to force her into their belief system.

It was time. Now was the time to focus and not dwell on the past. As scared as she was, Kam knew she had to initiate the search and conquer this fear. Why should she be afraid anyway? She was wise and worldly thanks to her career. Many times, she'd gone into war-torn and ravaged third-world countries to bring people's suffering and needs to the world's attention. Her photos had garnered her many awards over the years and she'd made more than enough money to take time off to hunt for her real father.

Taking a deep breath, Kam glanced down at the

watch on her wrist. The family would sit down to dinner at 7:00 p.m., as always. She'd arrived three days earlier from her last assignment in Africa. Her mother, Laura, was throwing a party for her this weekend. Her brother Jason and his wife, Annie, and their children lived nearby and would attend. Kathy, one of the fraternal twins, had just married raptor rehabilitator, Sky McCoy. They, too, would be at her return celebration dinner.

Knowing her father would be home by now, Kam decided to talk with him first. Morgan always had a glass of red wine and relaxed from the day's pressures before dinner in the airy library. Standing up, Kam rubbed her knotted stomach. Above all, she didn't want to upset Morgan and Laura. They were the last people she ever wanted to hurt. Torn because she loved them deeply, she sighed.

Kam picked up the photo and headed downstairs. Classical music wafted through the cathedral roof of the cedar home. She smelled basil and knew her mother was probably cooking up a pesto sauce to go with some Italian dish. If only Kam had an appetite.

Her father sat in the study surrounded on three sides by floor-to-ceiling shelves of books. He was in his favorite burgundy leather chair reading. Her heart blossomed with a fierce love for this man. Never had he or Laura ever treated her as anything but their treasured daughter. He lifted his head and smiled with welcome as she entered the room. She noted he was graying at the temples, but his hair still gleamed black beneath the stained-glass lamp suspended above him.

"Hi, Dad," she greeted, her voice hoarse and wavering.

"Kam. Well, are you finally caught up on sleep and out of the jet lag?"

She forced a smile she didn't feel and brought up an upholstered burgundy stool. "Yeah, I think I've left Africa behind."

Morgan closed his book and gave her an assessing look. "Is something wrong? You seem upset."

"I could never hide a thing from you, could I?" She managed a strangled chuckle. Her hands shook slightly as she nervously held the picture between them.

Morgan took a sip of his wine and placed the glass back on the cherry lamp table next to his chair. "No," he murmured, giving her a softened look. "What are you holding?"

Kam was forever surprised by Morgan's keen alertness. He always knew when something was on her mind. "What? Oh this…" Her mouth grew dry and the fear amped up so much that she felt nearly suffocated. She held out the photo to him. "Dad, you remember this picture they took from my mom's purse after I was rescued?"

Frowning, Morgan studied the photo. "Yes, I do, Kam." Softening his tone, he added, "What have you decided to do?"

Kam cleared her throat. "Dad, I think that one of these men might be my biological father." She rushed on when his brows raised. "I know this probably sounds silly and far-fetched but my gut instinct tells me this. I—I want the chance to find out. I want to take the next year off and run down the leads."

Nodding, Morgan rested his elbows on the arms of the chair and clasped his hands. "It's time, Kam. Laura and I were wondering when you would begin the long, hard journey to try and find your father."

"You did?" Her voice sounded thin and stretched. Heart pounding furiously in her breast, she lowered her eyes. "I don't want to hurt you, Dad. Or Mom. I—I know this has to be painful for both of you."

"Baby girl," Morgan whispered, reaching out to her, "we expected you someday to try to locate the man who made it possible for you to be in our life." He gave her a quick squeeze on the shoulders and released her. "You're human, Kam. Every person wants to know who their mother and father are. You're no different." He tousled her short hair. "Frankly, we were concerned because you didn't seem to want to go on that journey. We know you wear your heart on your sleeve. And we know how sensitive you are toward all living things. We felt you just hadn't built up enough of a desire to go after him yet. I'm glad this moment has come, Kam. For you."

Blinking through sudden, hot tears, Kam absorbed Morgan's quick embrace. It was filled with such love and caring. "I—I just don't want to lose you two."

"You won't ever lose us, Kam," Morgan assured her, his voice growing raspy.

Kam searched his blue-gray eyes and saw tears. "You've given me so much. You are so generous, kind and caring…."

"And we'll always be that way with you, Kam. When you love someone, that never changes. Time only deepens love. And that's how we feel about you. I'm sure Laura will be glad to hear your plans."

Just like that, Kam's heart stopped racing and she felt more at peace. "So, you really think Mom will be okay with this?"

Morgan chuckled and sat back in his chair. "If I know her, she'll want to help you find your birth father. Listen to me, Kam. All we want is for you to be happy. We know how much it means to have those few items from your mother's apartment. Parents are bedrock for a child. They tell you where you came from, what kind of person loved you enough to have you. And now, you need to find your birth father."

"He's never come to find me…" Kam choked. Tears blurred her vision for a moment. "You don't know how many nights I lay up there in my bed wondering why he never came to see me. I—I have had so many nightmares about this, Dad. That he didn't want me…"

The words were terrible to say. To admit. Kam thought them often, but to say them out loud was like having a weight sit on her that she could no longer avoid or dodge. She saw Morgan's face twist with concern.

"Kammie, don't go there. At least, not yet. What if he didn't know about you?"

"I've run through that scenario," Kam admitted. "But if that was so, why didn't my mother contact him? Tell him she was pregnant with me? Why didn't he return to her life and take the responsibility?"

Shrugging, Morgan said gently, "We won't know those answers until you find him and confront him."

She pressed a hand to her chest. "I just get so envious of people who know who their birth moms and dads are. I ache inside because I don't. I just feel this huge hole in my heart and there's nothing that can really fill it except to know who my father is."

"I know," Morgan whispered, a catch in his tone. Reaching out, he squeezed Kam's hand. "One step at a time, baby girl. When we have dinner tonight, let your mom know what you want to do. I'll bet she can help."

Nodding, Kam clung to his hand. Morgan Trayhern was a giant in the military and spy business. His reputation was one of respect, integrity and admiration. This man, who was so powerful, was also her dad, the man who had raised her with nothing but love. Kam knew how lucky she was, and, as she sat there clinging to his grip, she understood that her biological father would never meet the stature of this man.

LAURA AND MORGAN sat with Kam after the dinner table had been cleared. Having just finished dessert—Napoleons that Laura had made from scratch—they regarded the photo. Fragrant coffee steamed nearby in white ceramic mugs.

"I've looked at this photo before," Laura told her daughter, as she took a sip of her coffee. "You know what drew me?"

"What?" Kam asked, excited that her adoptive parents were proactive on her decision.

"See that bolo tie that cowboy is wearing?"

Kam looked closely. There was a handsome sterling-silver bolo tie, oval in shape, with an elk head on it. The antlers spread from the middle to the top of the bolo. "Yes."

"I've often wondered about that bolo tie. Whether it was a hint," Laura said.

"Plus," Morgan added, "a long time ago I had my assistant research the veterinary convention and we got the names of two out of the three men in that photograph with your mother. The one we don't have is the cowboy on the end. Maybe he wasn't really attending the convention but was there because of your mother. Or maybe their records are incomplete and he was a convention guest."

"I know," Kam said, frowning. "The dairy and beef convention was held annually in Los Angeles. Mom was a veterinary researcher and she was one of the speakers." She pointed to the two men in the photo. "We know the guy in the business suit was a sales rep for a testing lab and the other one was a scientist who worked with Mom." Her gaze drifted back to the un-identified cowboy. "My gut just tells me he's the one. I can't prove it, but I know it."

Laura patted her hand. "Women have that strong in-tuition. We know without knowing why we know what we know." She grinned over at Kam.

Laura's touch made Kam feel steadier and stronger. "So, all we have to go on is a bolo tie. I've wracked my brain on this for years trying to figure out what the bolo tie might mean, Mom. There's no writing on the bolo tie to say it was this ranch or that. No leads."

"Maybe we need to look on Google," Laura said. She had been a military researcher and writer in the Penta-gon for years before she'd met and married Morgan, and she hadn't lost her knack for research. "I know you've been looking for the image on the Net without success."

"I've tried many times before but nothing comes up," Kam said. "Images are always being added and I keep hoping you'll find something on it."

"Because you're not a researcher," Laura said, smil-ing. "So now, let me show you some of the tools I use now that you're ready to find him."

Kam rose, excited. She knew her mother was an ace

researcher. Not only that but she'd waited for Kam to be ready in her search. "Dad? You want to come?"

Morgan shook his head. "No, you two go ahead. There's not much room in that makeshift office you moved into your bedroom," and he smiled.

Understanding, Kam got to her feet. Laura picked up her coffee and they went up the stairs to her room.

Typing in the two words as she and Laura sat close to one another before the laptop, Kam saw a slew of listings from an archival Web site that Laura used. She quickly strolled through the possibilities and then went to the next set of ten. For the next hour, Laura went through decades of images on the site.

Finally, when Kam was losing hope, Laura gave her a smile.

"Look at this," Laura said, pointing a finger at one entry. "Elkhorn Ranch, Jackson Hole, Wyoming." She clicked on the link and immediately a Web page for a dude ranch came up.

Kam gasped. "There's the elk symbol from his bolo tie!" The exact symbol from her photograph was emblazoned in the upper left-hand corner. Her heart started galloping once more.

"Hmmm," Laura murmured, running her finger over the pad to get the pointer to the left in a column. She clicked on About Us.

Kam saw a multigenerational family portrait. Her breath hitched. In the back, the tallest figure standing in the middle of the family was the man in her photo, only older. Graying at his temples, he still wore a handlebar mustache and a black Stetson cowboy hat. His long arms were wrapped around his wife and an older woman. Two teenage children sat in front of them. An ache built in her chest. "His name is Rudd Mason," she read out loud in a hushed tone.

"And he owns this dude ranch," Laura rapidly read below the family portrait. "Wife is Allison Dubois-Mason, children Regan and Zach. The other woman is Rudd's mother, Iris Mason."

"It says he owns a fifty-thousand-acre family ranch surrounded by the Grand Teton National Park," Kam murmured, rapidly devouring the rest of the information. "He runs an organic beef herd and sells nationally to restaurants and food stores who want the clean meat."

"Iris Mason sounds like a real interesting woman," Laura noted, tapping her finger to the paragraph below. "She's a herbalist and sells her flower essences worldwide." Laura glanced over at Kam. "Remember how much you love gardening? You even loved weeding."

Kam nodded. Her favorite thing growing up had been helping Laura plant, weed and grow the vegetables in their huge garden out back. "If Rudd is my father then Iris could be my grandmother. That's probably where I got the gardening gene."

"Anything's possible," Laura said. "There are so many questions yet to be answered. Rudd's obviously got a family. What if he had an affair with your mother and his wife never knew about it? Or you?"

Mouth quirking, Kam whispered, "I was already thinking that myself."

Patting her hand, Laura said, "One step at a time. Look, there's a help-wanted page." She clicked on it.

Kam's eyes widened. "Wow, look at this, Mom." She put her finger on the screen. "Caregiver wanted with medical background to attend elderly person at the ranch. Must be an EMT or paramedic or registered nurse."

"Good thing you're a certified EMT," Laura said, giving her a quick smile. "Maybe you could be hired and just go in and check them out?"

"I have cold sweats at the thought of walking up to Rudd Mason and saying I'm possibly his daughter and can I get a DNA test to prove it," Kam admitted.

"I know. I've often wondered how you would handle that," Laura confided. "It's got to be scary for you."

"It is. It's my biggest fear. What if I walk up to this man and say, 'Hey, I'm your daughter. Did you want me in your life? Do you even know I existed? Will you let me into your life? Do you love me? Did you ever love me?'" Shaking her head, Kam felt tears coming to her eyes. Looking down at her clasped hands in her lap, she said in a wobbly voice, "Oh, Mom, I'm just so scared."

Placing her arm about her, Laura whispered, "I know you are. Maybe if you tried to get a job there, it would help answer some of your questions on your own. It would give the Mason family time to get to know you, too, before you sprang the big news."

Nodding, Kam admitted, "It's a coward's way out, I know, but I just don't have the courage to go up to him at this point. For all I know, he's not my father. Just a cowboy who was at the conference who met my mother and by chance, got into this photo just because he was at their booth at the time it was shot."

"It could be that simple," Laura acknowledged. "If you could gain his trust, it might make it easier for you eventually to approach him."

"That's what I was thinking." Kam wiped her eyes.

"I just wish I had the gumption it took just to call him up or write him an e-mail."

Laura shrugged. "You could. But what if he knows you're out there and doesn't want this blown up because of his family? Maybe there are family dynamics in play we don't know about. And maybe going in as a hired person at the ranch would give him an opportunity to get to know you over time. And if he is your father, then a lot of the way is smoothed because he will know you. It will lessen the shock of finding out you're the lost daughter coming back to the family. At least he'll know you to be a decent, kind and intelligent person."

Kam closed her eyes and hung her head. "What would I do without you two? It has taken me so long to work up to this, and now you're helping me once again."

"Kammie, all we want is for you to be happy. We feel like your life has been on hold because you haven't wanted to investigate your origins. We've seen you walk away from several developing relationships. We felt that because this basic, fundamental question had not been answered yet, you couldn't commit to one."

"You're right about that." Kam looked up and then over at Laura. "I don't want to fall in love with a man and have a child who doesn't know about my life and background. I don't *ever* want my child to go through what I'm going through, Mom."

"We understand," Laura said, patting her shoulder. "This is a good step to take. Just remember that Rudd Mason might not be your father, though he's the most obvious lead right now. And we may not ever know who your real father is...."

"I can't even go there, Mom. It just hurts too much." An intense sadness flooded her. "If I can earn Rudd

Mason's trust and situate myself into his family as a caregiver, that's as good as it gets for now. Maybe after this, I'll sit down and talk to him privately about who I really am."

"I hope he doesn't feel hoodwinked by you coming like a wolf in sheep's clothing," Laura said. "That's the real caveat in your approach, Kam. He may think you sneaked into his family to cause problems."

"I thought of that, too. There just isn't an easy way to do this, Mom. No matter how I break the news, it'll be messy."

"Well," Laura said comfortingly, "apply for the position and send the e-mail. See if you can get hired. If you get hired, I'd take that as a sign from the universe that this is the way you should go."

Kam watched as Laura stood up and pulled the second chair out of the way so she could sit in front of her laptop. "This is scary, Mom."

"*Life* is scary, honey," Laura said, patting Kam's shoulder. "But life demands we step up to the plate and just do it. No one said it was easy. Now, get going on that e-mail and we'll go from there."

With a mixture of fear and excitement, Kam did as instructed. She had to start her new journey somewhere.

CHAPTER TWO

RUDD MASON MENTALLY crossed his fingers. He sat behind his ranch office desk on the north side of the sprawling single-story log dwelling, hoping against hope. Would this be the right caregiver for his mother? He'd gone through five already. His mother, Iris Mason, was a tour de force, and none of them could cope with her. Glancing up at the clock, whose face was surrounded by a series of elk antlers, he noted that Kamaria Trayhern would arrive in an hour for her interview.

Outside, the May sky was moody with clouds that had drifted across the majestic Tetons on the south side of the fifty-thousand-acre ranch. The typical May weather brought a mix of fronts, delivering below-freezing temps, only to rebound to the sixties during the day. Snow had finally melted around the dude-ranch portion, and his wranglers were busy with last-minute finishes, painting and repair on the ten cabins that would house their clientele.

Rudd nervously moved his work-worn fingers across his red handlebar mustache, now sprinkled with gray. At fifty-five years old, he didn't think much about the gray at his temples, either. His red hair was cut short and mostly hidden beneath his beat-up black Stetson. His wife, Allison, continually chided him about wearing the hat inside the house, telling him he should remove it since it was the gentlemanly thing to do. Well, he was a cowboy, from the bloodlines of trappers who had discovered this area and eventually settled it long before the pioneers had arrived. His blood was connected to the pulse of the earth where he'd been born. It felt good to be so deeply rooted when most people never knew much about their family history. Such ignorance was unforgivable in Rudd's mind.

Watching out the window of his corner office, Rudd felt a frisson of tension. Few applicants had responded to his ad to care for his ailing mother. Jackson Hole, Wyoming, wasn't exactly Grand Central Station. In fact, just the opposite—it was out in the middle of some of the most beautiful landscape and mountains the U.S.A. had to offer. But not much city, that was for sure. Would this woman, Kamaria Trayhern, be a city slicker in disguise? Unable, like the others, to adjust to ranch life and his mother's pace? Her résumé was interesting and, as an EMT, she'd be perfect for his mother's needs. What was Kamaria really like? Only a face-to-face meeting would tell the tale. Fretting, Rudd tugged at his long handlebar mustache and waited the long hour.

KAM UNCONSCIOUSLY RUBBED her tightened stomach as she drove slowly through the sleepy Western town of Jackson Hole, Wyoming. The sky was cloudy and threatened rain. Maybe snow? Here and there on her way up to the small town that was the gateway to the Grand Teton and Yellowstone national parks, Kam had seen patches of snow across the rolling green hills. She crawled along at twenty-five miles an hour in the early-afternoon Monday traffic. The town seemed clean, neat and very Western. She had stayed at the Wyoming Inn of Jackson Hole on the main drag and been treated like royalty. Not only had the staff provided her with a delicious breakfast but they had gone out of their way to help her with directions to the Elkhorn Ranch.

She'd found many quaint establishments off the four-lane highway. One that caught her attention was Jedidiah's Restaurant, which, she'd been told, served the best sourdough pancakes. Kam loved sourdough and made a note to herself to go back real soon.

As she climbed the hill out of town, Kam was not prepared for what she saw at the top. On the left the dragon-teeth Grand Tetons emerged. Wreathed in winter snow, their cragginess evident, the mountain chain resembled the sharp scales on the back of a sleeping dragon. The mountains soared upward out of the flat plain, which made them even more dramatic and spectacular. The beauty of the early afternoon was enhanced by a line of thick, fluffy white clouds scudding across the sharp peaks like soldiers on a march.

To her right was a long rolling valley. The *Hole* in Jackson Hole was an early trapper word that meant valley. Kam spotted many herds of elk who were leaving their wintering ground for the higher reaches of the hills and mountains that surrounded the valley.

The friendly staff at the Wyoming Inn had told her that as many as ten thousand elk wintered in this long, wide valley just outside of town. Now that spring had come and the snow melt at the higher elevations was in full swing, the herds were leaving their valley digs. They would go to their homes high above that were covered with thick stands of willows, deciduous trees and pines.

The four-lane highway narrowed into two lanes. The beauty of the Grand Tetons kept calling to her. Kam wanted so badly to stop and park off to the side and photograph the majesty of these incredible mountains. But not today. She had an appointment to keep for an interview. She wondered idly who would conduct her interview. An office manager? From what Kam could find out from the staff at the Wyoming Inn, this was the largest ranch in the state. Plus, her research had told her that the Elkhorn Ranch was one of the most popular dude-ranch destinations, as well.

Moose Junction came up. It was one of the entrances to Grand Teton National Park. Kam sped on by the turn. The junction looked enticing and Kam longed to make that right turn and put on her back-pack and hiking boots and take off with her camera in hand. The beauty of the area was overwhelming and deserved to be captured in photos. According to all the warning signs along the highway, moose were prevalent in the area. Kam had never seen one. Wyoming wildlife was all around her and she smiled a little. This was the first time she'd been to this state and she was beginning to realize how much she'd missed by not visiting it sooner.

In the back of her mind she never stopped wondering if Rudd Mason was her father. All she had was a photo, a memento of her mother's life before the quake. Mason might have been at the right place at the right time. For all she knew, this trip might be a big waste of time. Did other orphans or adopted children go through this pattern of fear and questioning? *They must.*

Frowning, Kam pushed strands of her wavy hair off her brow. Lucky for her the weather in Wyoming was very similar to that back home in Montana. She wore a conservative dark brown wool pantsuit with a tasteful white blouse beneath the jacket. Her mother had given her a strand of pink pearls when she was twelve years old. Kam had loved pearls ever since she could remember. They were her favorite gem. Touching them briefly, Kam felt Laura's steadying presence. On her thirteenth birthday, her adopted parents had given her a pair of pink pearl earrings to go with the necklace. She wore them today, maybe for luck in her interview, or maybe it was a way to have Morgan and Laura close to her on one of the most important days of her life.

Up ahead, Kam noted a huge sign indicating that Elkhorn Ranch was a mile away. The bolo-tie symbol stood out in the carved-pine rectangular sign. Fear shot through Kam and she gulped unsteadily. Her hands tightened on the wheel. All her sense of inner peace fled. The sign might as well have read: *This is your life. Are you ready for it?* That's how she felt deep inside. What if Rudd Mason really was her father? What if he recognized her? The questions pummeled at Kam until she felt like a badly beaten-up boxer in the last round of a fifteen-round match.

The asphalt road stopped where the turnoff for the

Elkhorn Ranch began. Two pine poles sat on either side of the road with a sign running across the middle: Elkhorn Ranch. There were elk antlers on either side of the sign, anchored into place with unseen wires or bolts. The road was rutted and still muddy from recent rains. She had rented a Toyota Prius and now wondered about the wisdom of the choice. The car had a very low clearance and some of the ruts looked a lot deeper than it could handle. Well, too late. Somehow she had to crawl down the long, wide dirt road.

Weaving around so that she wouldn't bottom out, Kam tried to take in some of the scenery. The sides of the road were fenced. The wire on the left was a good ten feet high, and considerably thicker than that on the right. In a bit, Kam saw why as a herd of shaggy buffalo, numbering close to one hundred, foraged on the green grass. Here and there, newly born buffalo calves raced around like roadsters. Again, she wanted to stop and take photos, but she didn't dare give in to that need.

On the right, as she approached the horizon line, Kam noted hundreds of white-faced Herefords. Buffalo on the left. Cows on the right. Kam recalled that Buffalo carried some disease that could infect cattle, but it seemed that the owners of the ranch kept them well separated. She wondered why there was such a large herd of buffalo. Coming over the slight hill, Kam gasped and stepped on the brake.

Below her on a gently rolling road stood a sprawling ranch. Men rode on horseback, some of them herding groups of cows to other pens, others walking with brooms and buckets toward a row of small cabins below the main area. There was a single-story ranch house made of pine logs and plaster. The structure must easily have been ten thousand square feet. The ranch house seemed to have been built in sections over time. The sheen of the timber contained color changes, which indicated a gradual build. As Kam eased her foot off the brake and allowed the Prius to amble down the slight incline, she wondered just how old the structures were.

A bright red two-story barn on her left appeared to be the center of activity. Kam spotted cowboys holding a line of several horses waiting for the farrier to put new iron shoes on the animals. Two dogs, a yellow Labrador and a golden retriever, bounded around the group, tongues hanging out of their mouths as they frolicked. In front of the ranch house sat a huge garden surrounded with six-foot-high cyclone fence with bird netting over the top. The rich, black soil had been tilled and furrowed but she didn't see anything growing. No one would plant until June for fear of frost in areas such as this. In this valley, she'd read, there were only sixty days a year above freezing. That was tough on any gardening activities. Still, her photographer's eye absorbed the neatness of the garden that surely fed a huge group of people. It was easily two acres in size.

Cottonwoods stood in a semicircle around the conglomerate ranch, their yellow-green leaves just starting to emerge after the hard Wyoming winter. Behind and to the south of the ranch was a delightful brook that reminded her of a lazily moving snake across the valley. Kam wondered if there were trout in it, something that Wyoming was famous for. Her heart started to pound in earnest as she eased into the parking area. Tires crunched the gravel. A number of hitching posts were scattered around the area.

A sign at the main ranch entrance said Enter Here.

Okay, she would. Kam got out and slid the leather purse strap across her shoulder. The May breeze was warming. Sunlight poured down strongly, lifting the coolness from the air. Fingers tightening around the strap, Kam was locking the car when she heard someone riding at a gallop and turned. A wrangler raced by. She took in his dark blue shirt, sleeves rolled up to his elbows, leather gloves on his hands. He wore a red bandanna around his throat and a tan Stetson low across his eyes. The gray horse was long and lanky, probably part thoroughbred. Still, the man's squinted eyes had briefly met hers, and she had felt a sudden, unexpected leap of her heart. But this wasn't fear. He was terribly handsome in a raw, natural way. Under any other circumstances, Kam would have given this guy a second look, but not now.

Grimacing, she turned and walked with determination up the steps to the front door of the Elkhorn Ranch. The dark green screen door had been recently painted and didn't utter a sound when she opened it. Someone had paid attention and oiled it. The inner door was wide open, and she stepped into the immaculate, pine-floored hall. To her left was a sign that said Office.

Taking a deep, final breath to try and steady her fraying nerves, Kam turned into the office. Behind the counter Rudd Mason was sitting at a blond oak desk, frowning as he read some paperwork. Kam stood staring. This man was tall, probably six foot four and about two hundred and thirty pounds. His face was narrow, nose hooked and skin deeply tanned, weathered and lined from living so long in the elements. His hair was red! Kam swallowed her shock. Flaming red hair peppered with some silver throughout the strands. He wore his hair short but what got her attention was that elegant red handlebar mustache. Rudd Mason looked like he'd just stepped out of the 1860s from the OK Corral gun-fight. Still so much like the man in the photo.

If she hadn't been so nervous and afraid, Kam could have appreciated the man's simple cowboy garments: jeans, a checked red-and-white long-sleeved shirt, a blue bandanna around his throat. When he lifted his head to see her standing there, his turquoise-blue eyes narrowed.

"Afternoon, missy. Might you be Kamaria Trayhern?"

Her skin shivered with excitement. Rudd's voice was deep and the drawl took away some of her angst. "Yes, sir, I am. Are you Rudd Mason? The owner?"

He gave her a curt nod. "I'm him." He gestured for her to come around the end of the counter. "Come and sit here next to me. I'm glad you could make it. Any problems with the flight? Nowadays, I never fly. Such a hassle."

Kam smiled. She liked his straightforward demeanor. He stood waiting for her, the epitome of that old cowboy custom of being a gentleman. His hair was plastered against his skull and his black cowboy hat, stained with sweat around the band, sat on the desk next to his pile of papers.

"Thanks. And my flight from Billings was uneventful, thank goodness."

"Can I get you anything to drink? Cup of coffee? Tea?"

At least he was pleasant, Kam thought. "No, thank you. I ate lunch in Jackson Hole just an hour ago. I'm fine." Kam sat down and kept her purse in her lap, hands across it. She watched him settle back down in the wooden chair, which creaked under his full weight. Rudd picked up a yellowed mug and lifted it in her direction. "Well, I'll take a cup of joe anytime someone offers it to me." He took a long sip and set it down in front of him. Rummaging around, he found her résumé and put it on top of the stack of papers.

"I liked your qualifications. You've got EMT certification, but I see you aren't with the fire department. Usually, most EMTs are."

Kam squirmed beneath those assessing blue eyes. "I'm a photographer, Mr. Mason. I do a lot of work overseas in areas where there aren't many hospitals. I decided to get certified as an EMT a long time ago in case it was me who got hurt in the middle of nowhere."

"I see...." He smiled slightly. "You're a gal with some brains in your head. Ever used your EMT skills?"

At least he appreciated common sense. Kam felt her hammering heart slow down a tad. She liked Rudd Mason. He seemed very laid-back, easygoing and able to communicate. "Yes, sir, I have. Usually on villagers. I never had to use it on myself."

"You ever work with older folks, Ms. Trayhern?"

"Old as in...?"

"My mother, Iris Mason, is eighty-two. She's the one who needs taking care of. She lives here with us." He waved his hand in the direction of the rest of the ranch house.

"I've dealt with villagers in Africa and Eurasia who were very old," Kam said. "And I used my EMT knowledge to help them. I think I put in my résumé that I had never actually been a caregiver."

"Right," Rudd rumbled, "you put that in here." He

poked at the paper. "You get along with the elderly okay?"

"I think I do. In my business as a photographer I meet all kinds of people of all ages and nationalities. I try to be a good listener and keep my own stuff out of the way."

"Humph."

A lump began to form in Kam's throat. She saw Mason frowning and studying her résumé again. Struck by how lean and scarred his brown hands were, she began to understand how much this man battled the harsh elements of this state.

"Ever deal with a cranky senior?"

When he lifted his head and nailed her with that dark look, Kam gulped inwardly. "Well, uh, anyone can get cranky from time to time."

"My mother is headstrong, opinionated and stubborn, Ms. Trayhern. You can't sweet-talk her, and once she's got her mind made up, nothin' is gonna change it."

"Oh, I see. *That* kind of cranky." She saw the left corner of Rudd's mouth twitch upward.

"Yes, missy. The doctor tells her she has high blood pressure and she won't take her medication. She's already had a TIA, a mild stroke, but she won't take the medicine to lower her blood pressure so she won't get another one."

"Ouch," Kam murmured sympathetically. Clearly, Rudd Mason was worried about his mother, but he seemed helpless to get her to change her mind.

"Yes, 'ouch,'" Rudd dryly agreed. "My mother is a tough ol' buzzard. She's lived on this ranch since she married my father, Trevor, at age twenty. My father's dead now, but she runs this family ranch in his stead."

Kam nodded. "A true matriarch."

"You could say that."

His dry sense of humor rubbed off on her, and Kam met his slight grin beneath the mustache. There was nothing to dislike about this man so far. Kam wondered if she should just blurt out her real reason for being here. He seemed to be the kind of person who could handle any adversity. Something cautioned her not to rush. Still, the words ached to leap out of her throat and pass her lips. She longed to scream out, *I'm your daughter!* Maturity won out and Kam sat, mute.

"My mother is the boss," Rudd told her. "She's sharp, but the mild stroke has addled her memory somewhat. She's got arthritis and sometimes needs help getting around. Iris loves to drive, but her license got yanked by a local judge about a year ago, thank God. If he hadn't done that, she was bound to have an accident that killed her or some other person. You'd be expected to drive her wherever she wanted to go."

"That wouldn't be a problem."

Rudd assessed Kamaria. "You a city slicker?"

"Uhh...no. I'm a country girl. Why?"

"Humph."

Just what did that mean? Kam almost asked but decided against it.

"You got a young man in your life?"

"Not presently. My life as a photographer was pretty much on the go. I didn't have time for something like that."

"Humph."

She blinked once. He scowled and put on a pair of bifocal glasses to study her résumé again.

"You like gardening?"

"I love it. My parents have a huge garden, certainly not the size of the one I saw at the side of your home, but my mother and I raised a lot of veggies over the summer."

"How about flowers? You like them, too?"

Kam grinned. "Who doesn't like flowers?"

"That's what I always thought, but you'd be surprised," Rudd muttered. He made some notes out in the margin of her résumé. "I'm curious about why a photographer would suddenly want to become a caregiver."

Kam licked her lips and said carefully, "I've been on the move since I graduated from college, Mr. Mason. I'm twenty-eight now. I've been kicked around this globe and seen a lot. I guess I want to have a life. I don't want to lie awake half the night scared out of my wits, wondering if some rebel is skulking about to behead me. Or, that I'll contract malaria or yellow fever and die alone out in the bush." Kam shrugged. What she said was the truth, but not all of it. "I figure I'll continue to do some photography and make a little money on the side as a caregiver. It won't interfere with my job here."

"Your nesting phase, as my mother would say."

"Pardon me?"

"Nesting. You know—settling down. You've been a tumbleweed rolling all around the world and you're tired. You want to settle down and sink some roots like the rest of us."

"That's another way to put it," Kam agreed. She liked his cowboy insight and use of colorful Western slang.

"Iris is unique," he began, leaning back in the creaking chair, his hands resting on his hips. "My family came from a line of trappers who first discovered this area in the mid 1800s. My great-great-grandfather,

Rudyard Mason, married a Blackfoot gal by the name of Buffalo Woman. This ranch became his home. He claimed it and worked it and eventually owned the land outright long before Yellowstone or the Grand Tetons were made into national parks."

He tugged at his mustache. "It seems that each Mason man married an Indian woman, so we have a lot of that in our blood to this day. My mother's father was a full-blood Crow. Her mother was white. Iris lives close to the earth and practices Native American ways. That's her garden out there." He pointed in that general direction. "She also has flowers that she grows in and around the ranch. Her company is Tetons Flower Essences, and she sells what she makes around the world. My mother spends from dawn to dusk with her plants and loves every second of it. I'm happy she's happy. With her brain addled by the stroke, she'll be needing someone to help her with the packing, shipping and making out bills to customers. Your job as her caregiver would be a lot more than that. I need a person who is very flexible, who loves nature, who can deal with a cranky woman who gets her back up every once in a while, but who can appreciate her passion for life."

Kam swallowed hard over the fact that this fascinating woman could be *her* grandmother. What a rich gift that would be. Fighting back tears, Kam blinked several times and whispered, "I'd love doing anything to help her, Mr. Mason. I love the earth, too. Gardening is a healing meditation to me."

"Humph. Iris says the same thing. Says that when she gets out weeding in that garden of hers, any bad feelings she carried out with her just go back into the ground. She always feels better afterward."

Never had Kam wanted a job more than this one. Something about Rudd Mason struck a chord so deep. "Mrs. Mason sounds like a dream come true to me."

"Plenty of people around here consider her an ongoing nightmare."

Kam noted Rudd scowling, his gaze off in the distance. Who wouldn't love a senior like Iris? "Maybe a person who didn't work in a garden might not understand," Kam said forcefully, "but my experience is that gardeners are some of the most peaceful, calm and centered people I've ever known."

Rudd chuckled. "I hear you, Ms. Trayhern. There's folks I'd like to throw into a garden and not let them out until they got it, but that ain't gonna happen."

Kam watched him as he looked up at the ribbed pole ceiling of the office, as if considering something. She had to be bold. "I'd really like this job, Mr. Mason. I believe I could get along very well with Mrs. Mason."

"Call her Iris," he said finally, glancing over at her. "She hates standing on protocol. And she loves her first name, Iris. Her parents named her an Indian name that means Iris Blooms in the Morning. It fits her. My mother is the backbone of this ranch, and she made it into what it is today alongside my father. She's worked hard all her life. She's got arthritic knuckles to show for it, too."

As she heard the pride and love in his voice, Kam hoped he would speak to her in such a tone someday. It all hinged on this job. Gripping the leather purse, she waited for his decision.

"Okay, Ms. Trayhern, let's give you a whirl. First, you gotta meet Iris. She will be the one who decides whether or not you stay or go. Fair enough?"

A shock of relief shot through Kam. "Fair enough."

"Okey-dokey," he said, unwinding and standing. "Let's go find Iris. Chances are she's out back in her greenhouse with her flowers."

Joy mixed with dread as Kam followed him out of the office and down the hall. Her heart hammered again and she wondered if Rudd could feel her nervousness. She tried to steady her breathing and contain her excitement.

CHAPTER THREE

"IRIS, I WANT you to meet Kamaria Trayhern."

Kam smiled as she approached Iris Mason, who sat on a stool in front of her baker's table. In her hand she held dark, rich soil that she was putting into a small clay pot. The woman was about five feet six inches tall with short silver hair that seem to glow around her head like a halo. Her blue eyes were lively and sharp. Kam could easily see the Native American features in her deeply wrinkled, copper-colored face.

"Hello, dearie," she said, holding out a long, lean hand caked with soil.

Kam didn't hesitate but grasped her hand. "Hello, Iris. Just call me Kam. What are you planting?"

Iris chuckled and released her hand. "Not afraid of a little dirt, are you?" Kam took in the woman's dress. She wore a T-shirt covered with a white blouse and a very old denim jacket adorned with Indian beading on the back.

Rudd stood behind his mother, hands on his hips as the two women conversed.

Kam knew he watched and assessed their interaction. However, Iris was the one in charge. "I love gardening. Mr. Mason said you had a huge plot and I got excited. I grew up with one about half the size of yours in Montana."

"Maybe we got lucky, son?" Iris quipped, looking up at him and grinning.

"I hope so, Iris," Rudd rumbled good-naturedly.

Iris gave Kam a keen, long look. "Ever since my head decided to get slightly addled, my son has been trying to fix me up with a babysitter. I've chased all of 'em off. I'm only eighty-two and I'm not in diapers—yet."

Chuckling, Kam enjoyed the feisty elder and hoped they were related. Iris was small but mighty. She kept putting soil in each of the six pots in front of her. Several packets of flower seeds sat on the table. "I hope you won't see me as a babysitter, Iris. I'll be here to help you when you need it. Otherwise, I'll stay out of the way. How does that sound?"

"Oh, you mean you aren't going to tail me around like a proverbial shadow, waiting for me to stroke out? You aren't going to jaw me to death for not taking a high blood pressure pill? Complain that you're outside too long with me in the garden? Whine about pulling weeds?"

Kam grinned. "No, ma'am, I won't. I grew up in the wilds of the Rocky Mountains. My mother always had a huge garden and I loved weeding it. We froze and canned everything we grew. My mother believes in living organically off the land."

"You're a healthy-looking specimen, I'll give you that," Iris said, raising her thinned, arched silver brows. She twisted a look up at Rudd. "Since you insist upon me having a babysitter, this one looks hopeful compared to the others you've dragged kicking and screaming in here."

Kam noted the relief on Rudd's weathered features. He touched his handlebar and smoothed it between his thumb and index finger. "So you'll give Kam a whirl, Iris?"

Shrugging, the old woman eyed Kam slyly and winked. "Oh, I might just do that, son. Why don't you fetch Wes and let him know I need to go into Jackson Hole later for a few things from the feed and seed store? Kamaria can ride along and get used to my routines."

Hands slipping off his hips, Rudd nodded. "I'll do that, Iris."

"I can get my bags. Just tell me where I'll be staying," she said to him.

"Oh, you'll be right across the hall from me, Kamaria. A nice suite with a lovely bedroom," Iris said. "I made the quilt you'll see on your bed. And the curtains, too. The other room is an office and living room. I think you'll like the suite," Iris said.

"I'm sure I will." Kam watched Iris open up the first packet of seeds. "After I get my bags in the suite, would you like me to come out here and help you?"

Iris shook her head. She looked at the watch on her thin right arm. "Are you hungry?"

"No," Kam said, grateful for the woman's consideration. "I ate before I drove out here."

"Rudd, you need to tell Hazel that we have one more for dinner tonight."

Kam saw his face go tight, his eyes flash with shock.

"Iris? You never wanted your caregiver to eat with the family before."

"Well, I do now," she snapped, giving her son a look of finality. Iris poked her finger into the soft soil and then dropped in two seeds and patted more soil over them.

"I'll tell Hazel," he said abruptly, then turned to Kam. "Come with me. I'll show you where your quarters are located."

Kam felt the tension between mother and son. One moment there was warmth and then, just as suddenly, it was as if a storm had arrived. Iris seemed to be smiling over some secret known only to her as she focused on her seed pots in front of her. Rudd appeared suddenly nervous and began to twist the ends of his handlebar. What was going on? There was no way to tell. She'd just have to wait and find out.

"Meet me out front at 2:00 p.m.," Iris called to Kam. "Wes will take us into town. I can fill you in on a lot of things at that time."

"Of course," Kam murmured. She smiled at Iris, said goodbye for now and followed Rudd out of the large, airy greenhouse. The glass panels were set into a steel frame. Across the roof, thicker glass handled the snow's weight during the winter. Some of the panes were louvered to allow fresh air into the area. Everywhere Kam looked small pots of young, green plants sat on every available space. Iris obviously started her garden in here early so she could get a leap ahead for the June planting time. Kam knew from experience living in the Rockies that the growing season was short. Iris was smart and got around that by starting her veggies in the greenhouse.

As she followed Rudd down the immaculately clean concrete floor toward the ranch house through a screen door, Kam smiled to herself. She liked Iris a lot. Her next adventure would be with this guy called Wes who was Iris's driver. One by one, she was meeting the people who made this beautiful ranch what it was. In so many ways, Kam felt at home. The only question left to ask was whether this was her real father and grandmother—or not?

"HEY, SHERIDAN," THE ranch manager called at the opening to the main horse barn, "Mrs. Mason wants you at the main house."

Wes was unsaddling his big gray gelding when he heard Chappy Andrews's booming voice echo down the concrete walkway between the airy box stalls. Bolt, his ten-year-old gelding, a mix of quarter horse and Thoroughbred breeding, stood quietly in the cross ties in the center of the barn. Wes had just taken off the saddle, brushed him down and was getting ready to let him out into a nearby pasture filled with spring grass. Lifting his head, brush in hand, Wes called back, "Okay, I'll be right there."

What now? He'd seen that blue Toyota Prius hybrid come crawling down the hill. After working with a bunch of cows and newly born calves in the pasture, Wes was hurrying to grab a bite to eat before Hazel, the cook, refused to let him in the bunkhouse kitchen between meals. He'd galloped past the parked car but liked what he saw as the driver had emerged from it. Wes figured she was the next applicant for the caregiver's job.

Unsnapping the ties from Bolt's halter, Wes turned the tall, rangy gelding around and led him out the end of the barn. A small corral nearby, containing several cow horses, was used by the wranglers during the day. The sun was warm and felt good across his shoulders. Bolt whinnied anxiously to a group of horses who eagerly munched on newly sprouted grass.

Smiling, Wes opened the latch on the gate and released Bolt's halter. The gelding galloped into the pasture, silver tail held high as he hurtled toward the small waiting group. Horses were herd-oriented animals, and Bolt would slow down and pretty soon have his nose to the ground munching away. *Horse heaven.* Wes grinned wider as he watched his favorite cow horse slow and then drop his long, thin neck to grab at the grass. If only his life was this simple. But it never had been for him.

After closing the gate, Wes took off his elkskin gloves and tucked them in his belt. He walked back to the barn to put his gear in the tack room, unbuckled his chaps and hauled them off from around his hips and legs. Even though Rudd Mason had four-wheel ATV vehicles to herd the cattle, Wes preferred being in a saddle with a good horse under him. And he was thankful that his boss gave him that choice.

Once he finished his duties in the barn, Wes knew that Iris wanted to go to town. She did every day unless the dude ranch was in session, and right now it wasn't. He always enjoyed the crotchety old matriarch even though she was hated by Rudd's entire family. Iris was not tactful nor was she tolerant of fools. Wes liked those attributes in her.

He took long strides across the graveled ground and resettled the tan cowboy hat on his head. He made sure his dark blue shirt was tucked neatly into the waist of his Levi's. He kicked off the worst of the mud and crud his boots had picked up, wanting to look somewhat presentable. Iris didn't like sloppy-looking cowboys working for the Elkhorn. He didn't, either. Rudd might be the day-to-day boss running this huge operation, and Chappy was the field boss, but Iris was the actual owner and creator of this viable and robust ranch. At eighty-two, the matriarch was the brains of the operation despite what Rudd's Hollywood wife might like to think.

As he took the steps up to the office, Wes removed his hat and kicked his boots on a hog-hair brush anchored to the porch. This kept most of the mud and dust and manure out of the house. Feeling happy for no discernible reason, Wes entered.

"There you are!"

Iris stood near the entrance to the sitting room opposite the office. She was dressed in her fringed buckskin jacket, a pair of cranberry slacks, a pink sweater and the beat-up straw hat that rarely left her head. It had a chunk missing from the brim where a horse had taken a chomp. Iris said it gave the hat character. He smiled and nodded.

"Hi, Iris. We going into Jackson today?"

"Yep, we are." Iris motioned for him to come into the sitting room. "Come here, I want you to meet my latest babysitter."

Wes moved into the large room, admiring the white lacy curtains on all the windows. The room was filled with turn-of-the-last-century oak furniture over a large and century-old oriental rug that covered part of the blond oak floor. And then he saw her.

This was the woman he'd noticed emerging from her car. Now, as he drowned in her large blue eyes, his heart thudded, underscoring how her beauty affected him. Her slightly wavy hair was short and black like a raven's wing. Her oval face, high-set cheekbones and olive complexion made him think she might have some Indian blood. Even better, he liked her full lips that made him think of lush tulips in bloom.

"Wes Sheridan, meet Kamaria Trayhern," Iris told him with a cackle.

Wes moved forward, his hand extended toward the tall, lean woman. She was dressed casually but tastefully in a dark brown pantsuit that emphasized her natural carriage, her head held high. "Hi, I'm Wes. Welcome to the Elkhorn Ranch, Ms. Trayhern."

The moment his hand slid into hers, Wes felt his world had been rocked. Her hand was warm and firm. He saw her eyes widen momentarily and those soft, petal-like lips part. Yes, she was definitely eye candy.

"Call me Kamaria or Kam," she responded a little breathlessly.

Reluctantly, Wes removed his hand from hers. "Kamaria? That's an unusual name. What does it mean? Is it Native American?"

"No, it's African," Kam said. "My mother chose a Swahili name for me."

Iris nodded, properly impressed. "Our family has plenty of Native American blood in it and we always gave our children meaningful names. So what does Kamaria mean in Swahili?"

With heat tunneling up into her face and two pairs of

interested eyes on her, Kamaria said, "It means beautiful, like the moon." She didn't know why divulging this personal piece of information made her feel so vulnerable, but it did. Iris's eyes gleamed with satisfaction. And Wes seemed awed by the information.

"You are a pretty-looking little thing," Iris agreed. She glanced over at Wes and whispered in a conspiratorial tone, "You see, Wes? Here I thought she was Indian like us. The color of her skin? Her broad face and high cheekbones?"

Kam moved tensely. Iris was getting too close to her family situation, the fact she'd been adopted. Kam didn't want to go there with them just yet. "How did you get your name, Iris?" Desperate, Kam shifted focus back to them and away from her. Right now, she felt like the proverbial bug under their collective microscope. And, if she was honest, she found Wes Sheridan devastatingly handsome. He was lean and just a little bit dangerous to her. There was no wedding ring on his left hand, either. Maybe it was his wide-spaced eyes, their gray depths and large black pupils that held her in thrall. Or, maybe it was his square, broad tan face that drew her. As her gaze flitted from his straight nose to his mouth, she felt hot and shaky inside. Few men had that kind of effect on her.

"Oh, I got named early on by my mother," Iris told her. "I had a deep love of irises. And that's how I received my name." Iris motioned toward the east side of the ranch building. "I've got about fifty different types of irises planted out there. Pretty soon, they'll be coming up and you'll see."

Wes smiled. "We have a standing joke around here,

Kamaria. If it's early June, we know where to find Iris—in the iris beds."

Kam laughed politely, noticing more how Iris beamed up at the tall, athletic cowboy. The red bandanna around his throat only emphasized the proud breadth of his shoulders and the well-sprung chest beneath his blue canvas shirt. In his belt was a leather sheath with a knife, along with well-used leather gloves. Indeed, Wes Sheridan was a stud of a man. And she felt her body respond to him whether she wanted it to or not. Kam cautioned herself against relationships. Her only reason for being here was to find her father. Until that was settled, Kam couldn't get involved.

"Let's go, young 'uns." Iris lifted her hand and shooed them out the door. "Wes, I need you to drop us off at the feed and seed store. I gotta get some items."

"Yes, ma'am," he murmured, going to open the front door for them. As he held the screen wide open, Iris went through first and then Kamaria followed. For a moment, Wes swore he could smell her feminine scent. Was she wearing perfume? She seemed like a no-frills type. There was a naturalness to Kamaria Trayhern that Wes liked a lot. Maybe too much. She seemed very confident in herself and he liked that, too. But she wasn't pushy like his ex-wife, Carla, had been.

Releasing the door, Wes hurried down the steps to the white Chevy Suburban and opened the passenger door for Iris. He helped the woman negotiate the high climb into the front seat, and, once she was in, he opened the door behind for Kamaria.

"Thanks," she said, climbing in. The inside of the cabin was warm and snug. Sunlight lancing through the darkened windows made it pleasant on the cool-ish May day. Kam watched Wes as he walked around to the driver's seat and slid in. He had an unconscious grace, almost as if he were boneless. As Kam sat in the back, the vision of a wolf sitting on a rock watching the world came to her. Wes seemed as one with the land and moved with it naturally. If he was arrogant, it didn't show. No, he was quite gentle toward Iris, and Kam sensed he liked the elderly lady. Iris liked him, that was for sure.

As Wes backed the big Suburban out of the parking area and headed up the dirt road to the main highway, Iris was constantly touching his arm and chatting away. The big, wide SUV negotiated the muddy tracks a lot better than her Prius had, but then, Kam told herself, the Prius was not an SUV. She bet this big hog of an SUV got very poor gas mileage in comparison to the fifty miles to the gallon her trusty Prius hybrid gave her.

In no time, they were in Jackson and parked at Hardy's Feed and Seed Store. Iris climbed out with vigor from the Suburban before Wes could come around and open her door. Kam was out, too, and following Iris. The midafternoon was a tad warmer in the town, Kam noted. There were a number of ranchers in pickup trucks getting feed for their stock. It was a busy place.

"I need some peeps," Iris told her as they walked down the creaky wooden floor between two aisles. "I'd told Chappy there was a sly ol' red fox getting my hens. He needed to repair a tear I saw in the fence, but he didn't assign a cowboy soon enough. That fox got in my henhouse and killed ten of my best girls." She shook her head and made a right turn to the corner.

"That's sad," Kam said. "I hate to see anything killed."

Iris grunted. She led Kam to the corner where heat

lamps were suspended and about a hundred fluffy yellow baby chicks chirped away. "Listen, you live in the natural world with life and death. We're all gonna die some day." She stopped and placed her hands on top of the board that surrounded the area to keep the peeps warm and protected from any cooler breezes. There were plenty of feeders and water bowls for the young chicks.

Kam joined her and enjoyed the little babies. "I've seen life and death in Africa and Eurasia," she said. "It's still hard to accept."

"At my age, you do because you don't have a choice." Iris chuckled as she eyed the milling chicks. "I come from tough stock. My grandmother lived to be a hundred. It's the Indian blood in us. They knew not only how to live on the land, but how to care for it. We lost all these things when Columbus came here, the bastard."

Laughing softly, Kam enjoyed Iris's honesty. If this was her grandmother, Kam would love to have her in her life. Suddenly, she felt very lucky. Iris was a hoot. Wes was—well, damned good-looking, very quiet, introspective, but sensitive to the needs of others. And the romanticism of him being a hard-working cowboy didn't hurt, either. Kam had always been drawn to men who challenged nature on a regular basis.

"How many peeps are you going to get, Iris?"

"Hmmm, probably thirty." She looked up and pointed toward the office on the opposite side of the feed store. "Go get Susan, the office manager. She always helps us."

Nodding, Kam walked toward the office. Most of the people in the store were rugged cowboys. The lifestyle in Wyoming seemed to keep everyone fit. There was plenty of walking, riding, fence-building and hay-moving. She spotted Wes over in the cattle feed section. He was taking down one-hundred-pound sacks of grain as if they were featherlight. He looked masculine and strong, and her heart fluttered again.

Tearing her gaze from him, she went into the office and found Susan. Together, they got the items for Iris to pick out her chicks.

Iris tittered indulgently as she chose her thirty peeps. Some weren't as plump or as large as others, but Iris left the scrawnier ones behind and chose only the healthiest among them. This was a woman who missed nothing. Kam liked learning from Iris by simply watching her.

Kam put the box of chicks on the backseat beside her. Wes had the rear of the Suburban open and carried sacks of grain over his shoulder with ease. He could have slammed the grain sacks down on the floor of the SUV, but he didn't. He saw Kam putting the box of chicks on the seat and gently placed the grain inside. Kam liked that about him.

"Don't want to shake up the peeps?" she called, smiling at him. His face gleamed with sweat and it made his gray eyes look even more arresting. Flat black brows above them emphasized his large, dark pupils. His mouth twisted into a slight grin.

"Iris wouldn't like her chicks upset by earthquakes," he teased, meeting her gaze. Wes was having a helluva time keeping his eyes off Kamaria. The breeze had tousled her hair. Her cheeks were flushed and Wes liked the soft smile across her full lips. That was a mouth made for kissing and loving. Abruptly, Wes redirected the thought as he straightened, took off his hat and wiped his sweaty brow with the back of his arm. After a disastrous marriage to Carla, Wes didn't want to tangle with another woman for a long time to come. And chances were Iris would dump Kamaria just like she did all the rest within a month. So, there was no reason to see Kamaria as anything other than a transient among the Mason family.

"Still," Kam said, making sure the cardboard box was stable on the seat, "it's nice that you realized the situation. A lot of men wouldn't."

Nodding, Wes settled the hat back on his head. "That's true," he said.

"How long have you worked for the Masons?" Kam's curiosity got the better of her. She saw him frown and wondered if she'd gone too far.

"I've been a wrangler at Elkhorn for two years now."

"And before that? Did you always work as a wrangler?"

Uncomfortable, Wes put his hands on his narrow hips. "I worked at the Bar S over in Cody, Wyoming, before that. And yeah, I was born and raised on a ranch." He managed a smile. "I can't see being anything else." Turning, he left the vehicle and headed back into the feed store to retrieve the four other sacks of grain that Chappy needed for the brood mares.

Kam stood simply watching Wes walk away. His grace was confident and smooth. What a hunk of a man. She hadn't come here expecting to be drawn to anyone.

"Now there's a man to be proud of," Iris said, coming up behind her. "Any woman worth her salt would chase Wes Sheridan down and hog-tie him right and proper."

Coloring fiercely, Kam turned to Iris. She was at the door grinning, her blue eyes sparkling with humor. "Oh…"

Iris patted her arm. "That's okay, dearie, you're young, and why shouldn't you salivate after a man like that?"

Kam choked as she opened the door for Iris to climb in. "Where I live there aren't many cowboys. I love the iconic symbol of them. They stand for the rugged independence that made America what it is today."

Strapping herself in, Iris said, "I love cowboys, too. I married one. Trevor was born and raised on the Elkhorn. He was a man's man." She sighed and closed her eyes. "He died too damned young. It was Rudd's wife, Allison, that gave him that heart attack, damn her. I miss Trevor so much. You know we made the Elkhorn what it is today?"

Kam climbed in and kept the door open to allow the breeze to flow through the vehicle. The peeps were cheeping contentedly next to her. She tried to keep the shock out of her voice over Iris's accusations about Rudd's wife. At Iris's upset expression, Kam tried to divert her. "Tell me about how you built the ranch, Iris."

"Trevor was a cowboy through and through. I have the Sight, dearie," and she tapped the middle of her brow. "That was passed on to me through my Native American blood. I saw that whites were spoiling and poisoning our land and water. I saw them poisoning the food we ate. I told Trevor twenty years ago to switch to organic beef. He stopped giving his cattle all those hormone shots, antibiotics and other crap and got the herd cleaned up. I worked with high-end restaurants on both coasts and convinced them that clean beef was the only way to go."

"That was farsighted," Kam said, impressed. She saw Iris turn around and look between the seats at her.

"Not only that, but I got him to buy a buffalo herd and we started selling buffalo meat long before it was popular. That meat is low in cholesterol and lean. Right now, I make five million dollars a year selling our clean beef and buffalo meat to restaurants all over the U.S. We've made a name for ourselves and my husband and me did it all." She scowled. "And stupid Allison kept whining that we were throwing good money after bad as we made the switch. She kept filling Rudd's head with dire predictions that no restaurant owner in his or her right mind would ever buy our clean beef. She'd be snarky at the dinner table and ask who would *ever* buy buffalo meat?" Chuckling darkly, Iris said, "Allison is the kind of person who tells you what you can't do. Not what you can do."

"I see…"

Waving her hand, Iris said, "Anyway, the Elkhorn is known for its clean beef and buffalo meat. Then, I told Trevor ten years ago to start a dude ranch. I saw so many American families losing touch with the earth. If we can't get these families and especially the children back and connected to her, we're going to kill this planet. My dude-ranch idea was not just the normal hayrides and trail-riding, but also providing lots of fun things for the kids to do with nature. For example, we just harvested about twenty thousand acres of timber. We have our own mill and we sell the wood to suppliers. Children can choose to go with the wranglers assigned to replanting the hills with new pine-tree babies. We teach them that everything has to be sustainable. We care for the land and we take, but we give back. Those are Native American attributes and we teach them that."

"I love the idea," Kam said, meaning it. She saw the

liveliness in Iris's eyes and heard the passion in her husky voice. Truly, she was the matriarch of the ranch in more than one way. "Kids do need to be reconnected with the earth. Especially city children."

"Yes, and I developed a program—despite Allison's objections—to pay for inner-city children from all over this country to come here, free of charge, for seven days to work with us and the land. I got several corporate sponsors to pay for their flights and we pick 'em up at the Jackson Hole airport and truck them out here. These are children of all colors and from all backgrounds, all poor, who have *never* seen a horse, much less a buffalo or a herd of cattle. We spend a lot of time teaching them about nature and how to live in harmony with it. My husband, bless him, had faith in me and my Sight. He backed me every time. We were a good team…" Her voice trailed off in sadness.

"How long ago did your husband leave you?" Kam asked her gently.

"Five years ago. He was too young to die. Allison drove him to it," she said bitterly. "She hated us. Rudd had the damned bad luck of falling for her Hollywood starlet background and married her on impulse. When he brought her home to the Elkhorn, she hated it and us."

"That's so sad," Kam said, noting the agony in Iris's eyes and face. "Surely Allison has adjusted to life at the ranch now?" Kam tilted her head and searched Iris's angry features.

"Humph. Never. She doesn't even try," Iris stated flatly. "Oh, you'll meet her soon enough. Tonight at dinner I'm sure she'll be in fine form. You're new meat to brainwash."

"What do you mean?"

"Allison runs Rudd. She's the queen bee. Or she thinks she is. She forgets who I am. I still *own* the ranch." Her lips flattened. "Which is why Allison keeps trying to have a doctor and a judge rule me mentally incompetent. Once I had that mild stroke, she became obsessed with having me taken down."

Frowning, Kam said, "What do you mean *taken down?*"

"Trevor left the ranch to me in his will. If I'm ruled incompetent and need a power of attorney—that's Rudd—then the ownership is transferred to him and Allison. I know her. The bitch wants to dismantle and destroy everything that Trevor and I did to build this ranch into what it is today. She'll sell it off. She keeps nagging at Rudd to get me to sell off five thousand acres so a developer can come in and set up condos. She keeps telling him that we'll make millions. But we make millions now, the right way. I told her I don't want a bunch of condos on our ranch. It will pollute the water system. I don't want more people out here. If I wanted city life, I'd have moved to the city. I don't want five thousand people on one-acre lots to deal with. But Allison is riding Rudd about this all the time. Any opportunity she gets, she sticks it to me about the development."

"But she can't do anything about it because you own the ranch, right?" Kam said.

Iris gave her a triumphant look. "That's right, dearie. As long as the ranch is in my name, and I'm alive and kicking, I can keep the vision for this ranch alive and viable. The day I die, this ranch is going to hell in a handbasket because Allison runs Rudd. He can't say no to her and gives her anything she wants. Never mind her two spoiled children, my grandchildren. Humph!"

Kam sat back digesting all the information. Clearly, she had walked into a hornet's nest. Iris turned around as Wes shut the back of the SUV. The look he gave Kam was warm and inviting. The slight smile on his mouth made her go hot with longing once more. And then, as quick as the look was there, it was gone.

They drove back to the ranch, and Kam began to dread the family dinner tonight. What would happen next?

CHAPTER FOUR

IRIS OFFICIALLY DECIDED to hire Kam as her caregiver. It was a relief. Kam had overcome one obstacle, one of many. The tension leading up to the family dinner became her focus. Her upbringing as a Trayhern hadn't prepared her for this family, which seemed built on politics, intrigue and power struggles. Where was the love between them?

Kam sat at Iris's elbow while Rudd was at the head. The rectangular maple table was covered with an old-fashioned hand-crocheted white cloth across its gleaming surface. Hazel, their chef, had her assistant, Becky Long, a smiling young woman, help serve the meal. The plates were blue and white and Iris told Kam that she and Trevor had bought them shortly after their wedding. They were used to this day, a sign of her love for him.

Above the table hung a massive elkhorn display with

lights. No matter where she looked, there were elkhorn tables, chairs and lamps. Soft classical music, the same kind that her mother Laura loved, played softly in the background. That was Iris's doing, too. She proudly informed Kam that at one time, she'd played classical piano. After trying to break a horse, she'd broken her hand and had suffered a fracture that prevented her from going on to a career in piano. Kam wondered how such things would steer a person's life. If not for the finger fracture, Iris would have never stayed in the Wyoming area to meet Trevor several months later. They had met, fallen in love and begun this ranching empire. Kam's respect for the elder Mason grew by the hour as Iris let her into her inner world of business and personal information.

The crystal water and wineglasses were old and hand-cut. Kam felt as if she'd stepped back into the 1870s of Western America. It was comforting to her in one way because she loved antiques. The rug on the blond oak floor beneath the massive table was from Turkey, Iris had told her. It had been bought by Trevor on a business trip to the Middle East shortly after their were married.

Everything that Kam could see had a history. Had importance to the Mason family. Her heart swelled with incredible emotion as she sat with her hands in her lap quietly waiting for the rest of the family. There were three empty chairs. Becky stood near the kitchen door, a frown on her round face.

Rudd kept looking up from his place at the head of the table toward the entrance.

Kam could see annoyance in his features although

she suspected that he was trying to hide it. Iris, however, was not so cloaked.

"I'm eating, Rudd. I'm hungry." Iris took a soft, warm sourdough biscuit from the basket at the center of the table. "If they can't be on time, I'm not waiting for them!"

Giving her a pained look, Rudd said nothing. He tried to smile but failed. "Kamaria, if you want to start eating, go right ahead. Sometimes, my family arrives late. We don't want the food to go cold."

Kam nodded and took a biscuit. She slathered butter, hand-churned from their dairy-cow herd, across the fragrant, steaming surface. Iris proudly told her they had sourdough starter a hundred years old. Kam knew her mother Laura just loved baking with sourdough starter. She made a mental note to ask for a jar of it and transport it back to Laura, who would be thrilled.

"Starting without us?"

Kam looked up at the dripping, husky voice at the entrance. A woman in her mid-forties, her hair dyed blond, stood there with her hands resting imperiously on her thick hips. *She was dressed like a Hollywood goddess,* Kam thought as she put the biscuit down on her plate. This had to be Allison Dubois-Mason. She was short and shapely, her breasts as ample as her hips and thin-waisted. She had the coveted hourglass figure from a bygone era. Her blond hair was coifed and swept up on her head and glittering diamond earrings and necklace set it all off. Her green eyes were heavily made up and Kam thought the false eyelashes looked more like caterpillars crawling across them. Her rouge was too bright, making her resemble one of those Kewpie dolls at carnivals.

"Come in," Rudd said, standing. He moved around to the chair at the opposite end of the table. Pulling it out, he waited for his wife to approach. "Allison, I want you to meet Kamaria Trayhern. We've just hired her as caregiver to Iris. Kamaria, this is my wife, Allison."

Kam nodded in the woman's direction. She walked like a queen gliding down an invisible red carpet. The dress she wore was out of place for this rugged Western setting. It was a ball gown made of gleaming gold silk that showed off her considerable cleavage and swathed around her ankles. Her heels were a good three inches high and Kam winced inwardly. The woman obviously didn't care about her feet.

Kam felt the glare from the mascara-framed green eyes. It was not a welcoming gaze at all and her gut tightened.

Halting at the chair, Allison flashed daggers at Rudd.

"And just what is *she* doing at our table? Hired help does *not* eat with us. *Ever*."

The venom seemed to drip from her mouth like acid. Kam started to rise.

Iris clamped a hand over her arm and stopped her.

"Stay right where you are, Kam," Iris growled. And then, the senior shot a poisonous look at her daughter-in-law. "Since when do you care who sits at this table, Allison? On most nights, we wait a half hour for you to appear. Your children never show up. Regan's too busy to sit down with us, and Zach has his head in computer games. So don't go getting high and mighty saying who can or can't be at our dinner table."

Laughing liltingly, Allison waved her bejeweled hand toward Iris. She batted her eyes at Rudd and smiled. "And here I thought you were the boss, Rudd."

She sat down with aplomb and Rudd pushed the chair toward the table.

Iris glared at Allison, "Maybe you need reminding that I'm the *owner* of this ranch, Allison, and I'm not dead yet. Until I am, I'm the one who decides who will have dinner with us or not. Rudd has nothing to say about this and you know it."

Allison took her white linen napkin and smiled fully. Becky came over and poured her some red wine. "Oh, you never allow me to forget that you're the boss, Iris."

Kam watched the maid pour the red wine and thought that blood had been drawn symbolically between Iris, the matriarch, and Allison, the upstart. What a group! She couldn't believe the rage behind the words of the two women. It made her evening meals with her parents in Montana look alien in comparison to this family.

Iris said nothing. Becky gave her a pained look.

"Miss Iris? Should I serve dinner? Or wait?"

Iris addressed Allison. "Are Zach and Regan comin' or not?"

Shrugging, Allison said, "They're busy."

"Would have been nice to let Hazel and Becky know ahead of time," Iris growled. "They aren't slaves to do our bidding around here."

Kam couldn't believe the drama around Allison. Gulping, she realized that if Rudd was her father, this woman was her stepmother. Not exactly a great package. And nothing like Laura, who was the epitome of grace, good manners and kindness. Kam searched the woman's heavily made-up oval face to see if she could find generosity or kindness. She could not.

"Please serve the meal," Rudd requested of Becky.

"And thank Hazel in advance for her help in makin' our dinner."

Kam found Rudd's sensitivity toward others positive. Becky rushed out of the room, through the swinging oak door. Shortly, she came back with squash soup, which smelled wonderful.

"Now this," Iris told her, pointing to the yellow soup in front of her, "is from my garden last year, Kamaria. Hubbard squash from last fall's crop. The best squash in the world to give a nutlike flavor to soup. Hazel always puts on bacon bits and tops it with a tad of sour cream. Makes for a wonderful beginning to our meal."

Kam waited until Rudd picked up his soupspoon and then she followed suit. "Are you going to plant Hubbard squash in your garden this year?" she asked Iris. The soup tasted heavenly. The salty bacon enhanced the nutty flavor of the squash. The sour cream melted and swirled in the golden contents and reminded her of an abstract painting. It was a beautiful presentation.

"Absolutely," Iris gushed, excitement in her voice. "In fact, I'm going to add another squash this year, a Lakota squash. This kind has orange and green vertical stripes. Some of my friends tell me it has the same firm consistency as Hubbard. You need a good, meaty flesh for a good squash soup."

"Good to know," Kam said, finishing off her soup. She glanced over at Allison who seemed bored, her soup untouched.

"Just because Ms. Trayhern is here you trotted out your squash soup. You know I hate squash, Iris," Allison said defiantly.

Rudd sighed. "Allison, Hazel always cooks one soup

a day and you know that. And we have squash soup at least once every two weeks."

Kam could feel Rudd's concern that his wife's petulance would ruin the festive atmosphere. Iris slurped down the soup with relish and seemed content, her appetite clearly in place. Kam felt she had to speak up. "I thought the soup was wonderful, Becky. Thank Hazel for me. I'd love to get this recipe." She almost added that her mother would love to have it. She certainly didn't want them to get entangled in her family background. At least not until the time was right.

"Thank you, Kamaria," Becky said, adroitly moving around the table and removing soup bowls. "Hazel loves to have feedback on her meals. She wants to make people smile over her creations."

Iris smacked her lips, drank a bit of her red wine and patted her mouth with the white linen napkin. "Now, that's a great start to a great meal, Kamaria. You see? Food like this is a special treat and I can see you appreciate it."

"I do," Kam said. "At home, my mother uses all the veggies from her garden to cook with, too."

"Oh," Allison groaned, shooting a look at Kam. "Don't tell me you're into gardening, too?"

"Yes, ma'am, I am." Kam felt the only way to deal with Allison, who wanted to be queen bee, was to treat her with respect.

Allison sighed. "Well, Iris, this will be your first caregiver who loves gardening." Then she looked at Kam. "You know, every caregiver we've hired has left a month after arriving here."

Iris gave Allison a narrow-eyed look. "And I wonder why?"

Kam felt the tension sizzle between the two women.

"No, Iris," Rudd rumbled, "let's not go there. I want a peaceful meal for once. Kamaria is our guest. Can we table some of our conversations at least for tonight?"

Kam saw the faces of the three players. Iris looked incensed. Allison became smug. Rudd appeared frazzled, as if playing the referee between two boxers. Of course, with the dissension here between Allison and Iris, Kam could see how the family dynamic drove off previous employees.

Becky brought out a small garden salad drizzled with buttermilk dressing. The portions were small and she was glad.

"I'm leaving for L.A. tomorrow, Rudd. My friends are throwing a party at the Beverly Hills Hotel and they want me to attend." Allison smoothed her hair and affected a matter-of-fact tone. "I'll be gone for five days."

Rudd nodded and handed Becky his emptied salad bowl. "Is Regan going along?"

"Probably. She hasn't made up her mind yet. You know she has that Goth boyfriend in Jackson Hole." She smirked. "I'm trying to pull her away from that slovenly thing. I checked on him and his parents are truckers. Trash, Rudd. Regan needs to understand she has to get into her own class and not go to the belly of the whale for friends or relationships. It's so frustrating!"

Kam glanced over to Iris, who shook her head in dismay.

"No one is trash, Allison," Iris shot back. "Classism didn't build this ranch, you know. A lot of people worked untold hours. Truckers are very important people to us. And I've found them to be more than honorable folks. Charlie and Rose Burger do a lot for the poor of that town. He's with the Elks and she's with the So-roptomist Club. They raise a lot of money for the needy. I don't see them bein' called trash by the likes of you."

Kam gritted her teeth and stared down at her salad bowl. Did they spar like this at *every* meal? Iris took no prisoners, but then, Allison seem to delight in dropping bombs to goad the old woman. Conversation like this was murderous to sit through, Kam decided.

"Regan's boyfriend, Justin, is a good enough boy," Rudd said. "He's hard-working, Allison. Charlie and Rose raised him right."

Allison sniffed. "I just don't want our daughter hanging around with the likes of him. She's better than that. I'm hoping she'll meet an actor to marry."

Iris snickered. "Oh, yeah, that's right—marry an egotistical monster who can't do without bright lights, fawning people and a bunch of hangers-on. Right."

Allison glared at Iris, then looked down the table at Rudd, as if to say silently that he should protect her from his mother's acidic comments.

Rudd did nothing but scowl, and spread butter across a warm biscuit.

Kam remained silent. How lucky she had been to have Morgan and Laura as parents! Their dinner table was full of lively conversation, searching talks, excitement about things each family member was doing—never this kind of nastiness. First of all, they would not have allowed these types of personal attacks at the dinner table. Secondly, this was a place to meet and talk and catch up on what everyone else was doing. She wiped her mouth with the linen napkin and thanked Becky as she came by to pick up the bowl.

"Hollywood is much more than that, Iris," Allison

sniffed. She saw Becky coming with the main course and halted her tirade.

A delicious stew was placed in front of Kam, along with some freshly steamed asparagus bathed in cheese sauce.

"Now, Kamaria, this is our own buffalo meat," Iris crowed proudly. She swept her hand down toward her plate. "Do you know I've got a Web site where we sell our bison products? Allison said going online was a bust but I proved her wrong," Iris gloated and grinned over at Allison, who pointedly ignored her. "We make five hundred thousand dollars a year off Internet orders from folks around the world. Isn't that something? I might be old, but I sure like the gizmos we have at our disposal for marketing and advertising on the Net. You on the Net at all?"

Smiling, Kam swallowed her food. "Yes, I am. I'd love to see what you've done with your Web site, Iris."

"My geek guy, Tom Courtland, takes care of my server in Jackson Hole. He's a peach. I give him fresh veggies and fruit from our orchard every year. Of course, he's well paid for what he does and he's endlessly creative. I've asked Tom to bring a computer into your suite tomorrow. Then you and I can have some fun."

Kam warmed to Iris even more. She was passionate, unafraid to try out new things and was obviously inventive in her businesses. "I'd love to sit down with you, Iris."

"She's the geek in our family," Rudd said, smiling. "I don't care for the darned things. Never could warm up to them. Can't hardly use my cell phone, but I'm forced to in today's world."

Kam understood his complaint. "A lot of people are turned off by computers."

"It's the e-mails," Rudd complained.

"Well, I told you to hire an office assistant who could field all the e-mail requests for information on our dude ranch," Iris chastised him. "But you won't do it. Sometimes I think you like to be miserable, Rudd. Just getting a young person in there for at least the summer dude-ranch time to help you seems like a better way to go. Instead, you sit in that office fuming and cursing under your breath as you use two fingers to try and type out a message."

Kam tried to squelch her chuckle but couldn't. "Hey, my sympathy is with Mr. Mason," she teased Iris. "A lot of people are ham-handed when it comes to computers. Not that I'm a geek, but I practically grew up using a computer."

Giggling, Iris nodded. "And some people just don't want to learn new tricks. My son has a stubborn streak. One of these days when he's bald after pulling out what's left of his hair, he'll see the wisdom of hiring an office assistant."

Rudd grinned. "I don't want to go bald, Iris."

"Well, then, let me put out feelers to the employment office in Jackson and let's see what I can scare up for you."

"Maybe it's time," he agreed. "Besides, I'm better served dealing with daily ranch life. I hate the office."

"Not much of a saddle to sit in, is it?" Iris quipped with a laugh.

Shrugging his broad shoulders, Rudd smiled sheepishly. "No, it isn't."

Allison shook her head and rolled her eyes again.

She'd played with the food on her plate. "If you'll excuse me…"

"You've barely eaten a thing," Iris said.

"I like keeping my svelte figure. If Hollywood calls asking me to fly in to try out for a part, I can't look fat."

"Hazel made a special dessert tonight," Iris said, ignoring her response. "Your favorite."

Groaning, Allison rose with grace and placed her napkin on her plate. "Thank you, Hazel, but I simply can't do it." She turned and left the room.

Kam took note that Allison didn't deign to look at her or say, "It was nice to meet you," or anything else. She had a gut feeling that the woman didn't like her and would just as soon see her leave the ranch in a month.

"Son? I think you hit pure gold when you hired Kamaria. I'm pleased as punch."

"I'm glad, Iris. She seems a good fit for you. I just hope she wants to stay for more than a month."

"Why would I ever want to leave after a month?" Kam asked politely. Based on the family drama, she knew the answer.

"Your predecessors just didn't seem to fit into our laid-back ranch lifestyle," he said uncomfortably.

"Actually," Iris said darkly, "Allison chased all of 'em off. She'd just as soon see me die of a stroke and be out of the picture so she can take over."

"Iris…" Rudd protested, frowning. "That's not so. Allison does not want to see you die. And I really don't think she chased off the other caregivers."

Snorting, Iris said, "Well, I know better, son. And you're just gonna have to take my word for it." She cut Kam a sharp look. "You seem pretty smart. And you seem to see through people quickly. I'm sure you'll ask questions before jumping to conclusions if Allison starts stirring the pot again."

"Of course I would," Kam reassured her. She saw Becky coming around to pick up their emptied plates. "I work for you. My only focus is you, Iris. You and your health. That's why I'm here. Mr. Mason made it clear that I was to be with you most of the time."

"And you'll help me plant and weed the garden?"

Grinning, Kam said, "Wild horses wouldn't stop me from helping you do that."

"Music to my ears," Iris sighed, giving her son a beaming smile of pure pleasure.

Rudd smiled. "Mine, too," he told Kam, gratitude in his tone. "I think you're going to fit in well here, Kamaria."

"Call me Kam, if you want," she told them. "Most people do."

"Kam it is," Rudd said, raising his head to see Becky coming out with dessert.

Patting her arm, Iris said, "Tomorrow is a bright new day around here with you being on board. I have a nice feeling about you, Kam. You're fun to be around, you're prudent and you're a good judge of character, unlike some of the family."

"Thanks, Iris. I'm really looking forward to being here." Kam felt a warmth in her heart toward the older woman. Iris was a kick-butt, take-names-and-no-prisoners kind of lady, but she had values, morals and integrity, too. In contrast, Allison was a woman in a mask, playing a part. At least Rudd and Iris were real, down-to-earth people who weren't narcissistic. Kam figured she could avoid Rudd's wife most of the time. Or, at least she hoped she could.

"Tomorrow afternoon," Iris told her, "I want you to take a ride with Wes and start familiarizing yourself with the Elkhorn Ranch. Sound exciting?"

"Yes, it does. I love riding horses."

"Ah," Iris sighed, "yet another plus in your column with me. I have a black Morgan mare that I ride almost daily. I'll tell Wes to assign you a nice horse that you can use as your own. I often ride out into the hills to gather my flower essences and you can tag along."

"Sounds great," Kam murmured. Her heart skipped a beat. *Wes.* She gazed at Iris whose features looked perfectly innocent. And yet, Kam knew this woman had acumen when it came to evaluating people. Did she see something between her and Wes? Could she be aware of how Kam's heart beat a little harder when she saw that lanky, wolflike cowboy? Tomorrow was going to be an exciting day for her in many ways, Kam suspected.

CHAPTER FIVE

WES SHERIDAN FELT antsy as he waited for Kam Trayhern at the main stables. Why? Not wanting to look too closely at the reason, Wes reminded himself that his ex-wife, Carla, was enough of a deterrent to getting involved with another woman. Carla had been an alcoholic and he'd blindly walked into the marriage, completely ignorant of her disease. Even though his father was an alcoholic, Wes didn't detect Carla's symptoms until a year into their marriage. Suffice it to say, he had a knack for choosing the wrong women. Even though Kam Trayhern strongly appealed to him, Wes was certainly not going to allow her into his heart. Not a chance.

Besides, he ruminated, standing at the entrance to the horse barn, Kam probably had a steady relationship with some very lucky man. Then, she really would be off-limits to him. Wes found himself hoping like hell she was engaged. He spotted Kam skipping down the steps of the ranch house.

In vain he tried to ignore the way her jeans fitted her long, beautiful legs. She'd traded in her sensible Echo shoes for a pair of newly purchased cowboy boots so that she could ride. In the May afternoon, her short, slightly curled hair glinted with blue highlights. There was such excitement in her features as she spotted him. She eagerly waved.

Wes lifted his hand but without the same exuberance and joy. She was just too damn pretty for him. The way she moved her tall, lithe form, the way that pink T-shirt fitted her and outlined her small breasts—it all conspired against him. Kam wore a red bandanna around her throat and it only enhanced the elegant lines of her neck. In her hand was a tan Stetson cowboy hat. He wondered if Iris had given it to her as a gift. Wes was glad that Kam and Iris were getting along. That was a good sign. He sincerely loved Iris because she was a no-nonsense, down-to-earth woman who had always made positive and healthy decisions for the ranch.

Frowning, Wes thought of his father, Dan Sheridan, who owned the Bar S in Cody, Wyoming. Because of his alcoholism and his refusal of intervention, the once-prosperous cattle ranch was in decline. Just like his father. There was nothing Wes could do about it. He had tried over the years, only to be angrily rebuffed and eventually disowned. That had hurt then as it did now. Wes tried to redirect the thought but it did no good. He watched Kam's approach, melting inwardly over her sparkling blue eyes. She was a salve to his wounded spirit.

"Hey," Kam called gaily, "you got a horse for me, Wes?"

An unwilling grin tugged at the corners of his mouth as she plunked the cowboy hat down on her head. "I think I do. Chappy told me you were a beginning rider, but that you'd ridden off and on when you were a kid."

The friendly nicker of horses in box stalls echoed down the wide, concrete aisle between them. The May breeze was gentle and invigorating to Kam. What was there not to be joyous about? She was with Wes, who was too handsome for words. Kam had been looking forward to this moment. "Yes, as a kid I rode, but my big sister Kathy was really the horsewoman. She had a horse and every once in a while I'd get to sit in the saddle as she led him around. I'm a *real* amateur, Wes. I hope you got me a nice, gentle, slow-moving horse."

"I think I have." He turned and motioned her to follow him down the aisle. "Let's see how you and Freckles get along."

Kam absorbed his powerful masculine nearness. "Has anyone ever told you that you walk like a wolf on the prowl?"

Startled, Wes glanced over at her. "Why...no."

Laughing and embarrassed, Kam held up her hands. "It must be me, then! Don't pay any attention to my creative meanderings. As a professional photographer I see things differently than most people. When I noticed you walking yesterday, you had such an easy grace that you reminded me of a wolf. That was a compliment, by the way." She laughed nervously.

Wes found himself charmed by Kam's innocence and the way she saw her world. Just as abruptly, he yanked himself from her spell. "Well, I've been called many things in my life, but never a wolf. Thank you."

Halting at a box stall on the right, Wes opened it and took the halter of a small pinto and led him out to the cross ties. After he quickly hooked the horse's halter into the metal panic snaps, the gelding stood quietly between them. "This is Freckles. He's a mustang, very small but tough." Wes ran his hand over the paint's brown-and-white body near the withers. "Chappy thought Freckles would be ideal for you. He's fifteen years old, savvy about things and will keep you out of trouble on the trail if you'll let him." Ruffling his hand through Freckles's chestnut-and-white silky mane, Wes added, "Freckles is used for the kids who come here to the dude ranch over the summer. He's one of our safest horses because he was a wild mustang as a youngster. Mustangs are a lot smarter because their wild nature is close to the surface. For instance, if you're riding down a trail and he spots a rattlesnake, he'll stop in his tracks and won't move. He'll let you have the time to look ahead of him to spot the snake. Some horses will bolt. Others won't even see the snake and will step on it or get too close and get bitten. But Freckles won't."

Kam nodded and moved to where Wes was resting his hand on the horse's withers. Freckles had big brown eyes set in his small, short head. She liked the alert look in them. Running her hand down his smooth, silky neck, she said, "He sounds perfect. I'm glad he's not a real tall horse. I have this fear of falling and killing myself. At least if I fall off Freckles, it's a short trip to the ground." She grinned.

Wes nodded. "I'm sure Chappy can set up some riding lessons for you when Iris gives you time off."

Patting Freckles, Kam marveled over the patterns of chestnut and white across his body. "He's beautifully marked, Wes."

Standing opposite her, the mustang between them, Wes was glad Freckles was where he was. It would be too easy to reach out and graze Kam's hand as it rested on the horse's neck. No, he had to keep his hands off Kam. "Yeah, he's what they call a Medicine Hat mustang. They have a very special set of markings." He showed her the brown color across the top of Freckles's head. "You see this brown that looks like a hat over the top of his head and ears?"

"Yes."

"That's called a Medicine Hat pattern. The Native Americans valued a horse with this bonnet because it had powerful medicine. Many of these marked mustangs were kept as breeding stallions to the Native American herds. Iris has a Medicine Hat stallion named Lightning Bolt. She started a mustang-breeding program on this ranch about forty years ago. We have a paint mustang herd that's internationally known. Iris sells Medicine Hat babies all over the world."

"She's an amazing woman," Kam said. "What foresight to save a valuable animal and its genetic line."

Wes nodded. "Believe me, you'll find Iris the heart and soul of Elkhorn Ranch." He walked to the tack room and found a blanket and saddle. Coming back, he set them on the floor and quickly brushed Freckles. "This is what you'll do before riding him. A horse needs to be well-brushed." He took a hoof pick from his back pocket. "You need to clean his hooves and pick out any stones or stuff that might be trapped inside the clefts of his hoof. Let me show you how."

Kam came over and watched Wes pick up one of Freckles's front legs. He held the horse's pastern in his large, rough hand. Their heads almost touched as Kam observed him expertly pulling out debris from the two clefts on the hoof. His masculine scent dizzied her, acting like an aphrodisiac.

"See?" Wes said, allowing Freckles to set that leg down once more. He could feel Kam's warmth, she was that close to him. Gulping, he handed her the hoof pick. "Your turn. I'll guide you in cleaning his other three hooves."

Wes's fingers were rough and Kam's hand tingled as he dropped the hoof pick into her palm. "Right. Okay, here we go." She walked to the other side of Freckles, patted him and said, "Be kind to me, Freckles. I'm a rank beginner."

Once again, Wes stood within inches of her as she lifted the mustang's front leg. He took her hand and repositioned it so that Freckles's hoof was cradled comfortably in her palm. Just the act of touching her sent a thrill through him. "Okay, now you can clean his hoof," Wes told her, his voice slightly off-key. Would she notice how she affected him?

"Good work," he praised. "Now, watch how I move beside Freckles to lift his back leg. You always stay close to the horse. Should one kick, they won't have the arcing power to really hurt you if you're close to them. The farther you stand away from them, the more they can injure you. Now, Freckles is not a kicker, but any horse under certain circumstances might become one. If threatened they will automatically kick to defend themselves. Stay close, put your left hand on his rump to let him know where you're at. Keep the left side of your body in contact. Then, gently run your right hand down his hock here to his pastern just above his hoof."

Kam watched Wes with avid interest. In no time, he had Freckles's rear leg up and the hoof resting on his left thigh just above his knee. "You make this look easy," she said with a smile.

Wes allowed Freckles to stand on all four feet. He backed off and let Kam replace him. "It's easy once you get the motion and contact with the horse. Go ahead, give it a try."

To his surprise, Kam managed it perfectly. She was a fast learner, there was no doubt. Soon, she had both rear hooves cleaned and started to hand the hoof pick to him. He held up his hand in protest.

"No, you keep it. A cowboy *always* has a hoof pick on his person. When you ride out there, a horse can pick up a stone that will make him lame. You'll have a pick in your saddlebags, dismount and lift each hoof until you locate the stone and dig it out. Then, you and your horse can continue a nice trail ride together."

Her hand tingled once more as his grazed it. Hungrily, Kam absorbed his touch. The doors to her heart flew open as she drowned in his dark gray eyes. He seemed like a man of absolute integrity, someone who could be perfect for her. She wondered how a woman wouldn't have snapped him up already. Then again, what did she know? Wes could have a wife or a girl-friend. Sometimes men didn't wear wedding rings but were still married. How she fought the direction of her thoughts. Above all, she was here to see if Rudd Mason was her father. Again, she scolded herself for getting so distracted. No way could she get entangled in a re-lationship with Wes. No way...

After teaching her how to saddle and bridle Freckles, Wes took her on a tour around the main ranch area. He rode his big, rangy gray gelding, Bolt. Compared to the shorter Freckles, Bolt was a giant with a much longer stride. The mustang, however, kept up a brisk walk to remain abreast of the other horse.

Sun poured like liquid gold around Kam as Wes took her over to the small rental cabins. They were neat and clean, each one having red, pink or white geraniums planted in boxes along the front windows. The yards were grassy and neatly cut.

"We have ten families a week reserve these cabins during our dude-ranch session. The season starts June first and we go through the end of September," Wes informed her as they rode toward a large corral nearby. "Iris and Trevor created a lot of different programs for the families. Some are environmental, some are day rides and others are hikes in the hills north of here. The kids aren't forced to ride if they don't want to." He grinned and resettled the hat on his head. "We don't allow video games or computers at the ranch. When they come here, it's about reconnecting with the earth and nature, not the wired world."

"How do some of the kids react to that?"

"Well, the city kids feel naked and deprived at first," Wes said, meeting her smile. "But after a while, other activities help them forget the loss."

"I imagine kids from the country are less shocked over this situation?"

"Oh yes," Wes murmured. He tried not to look at her but it was impossible. And every time he did, he felt a tug in his heart. "Of course, Zach Mason, who is seventeen, is a video-game freak."

"I haven't met him or Regan yet," Kam said, riding close as they approached the wide arena filled with sand. "Iris said Allison's children don't take an interest in the ranch. I think she's very sad about that."

"Yeah," Wes said grimly as they halted at the pipe corral, "Iris had hoped that Allison's children would want to walk in Rudd's footsteps. She was hoping to see the ranch passed on down through the family line." Wes shook his head. "Rudd loves this ranch and he'll see it prosper and flourish. Iris has left him a long-term plan for the ranch after she dies and he'll follow it."

"But if Rudd dies?"

Shrugging, Wes hooked his right leg around the saddle horn and dropped the reins on Bolt's neck. "I don't know what will happen. The way Rudd's will reads, if he dies, Allison takes over. And after she dies, the ranch goes to their two children."

"Ouch."

"Yes," he sighed. "It isn't a positive outcome and I think Iris is really stressed out about it. She's tried to get Zach interested, but he has other things on his mind. He's not very social and stays in his room most of the time."

"That's not good, either," Kam agreed. "Yesterday, neither Regan or Zach showed up at the dinner table."

Wes nodded. "I've heard Iris grouch about it often enough to know that those kids don't show up much."

"In my family, the dinner table was a special place to reconnect and find out what everyone was doing."

"You're lucky to have had that kind of upbringing," Wes said. "Not many families nowadays even have dinner together."

"What about your family, Wes?" Kam couldn't stop

her curiosity. Oh, she knew Wes's official duty was to show her around. Whether he wanted that duty or not, she didn't know. Because she was drawn to him, Kam took advantage of the situation and probed into his personal life.

Wes unhooked his leg from around the saddle horn and placed his toe back into the stirrup. His conscience ate at him over her question. He wasn't proud of his family and talking about it hurt. Funnily enough, Wes found himself *wanting* to share the details with Kam. The caring look on her face, the way her lips were parted, told him that she was sincere in asking him the personal question.

"Let's just say that my father is an alcoholic, Kam. I grew up in a pretty dark and unhappy environment. I have two younger siblings, a brother and sister. We each left the ranch at eighteen to get away from my father. My mother, Anne, is a teacher over in Cody, Wyoming, and I don't know why she stays with him. I just can't understand it."

Kam's heart twisted. She noticed the sadness in his gray eyes and heard it in his low tone. Suddenly vulnerable, Wes was no longer the confident cowboy. Instead, he turned into the haunted little boy who was confused by his alcoholic father's actions toward him.

Not thinking, Kam reached out and laid her hand on his forearm. Instantly, the lean muscles beneath the denim shirt tensed. "I'm so sorry, Wes. Alcoholism is a terrible disease. I've seen it destroy families if the person doesn't get help."

"Well," Wes muttered, feeling the warmth of her touch on his arm, "my father doesn't think he has a problem."

How much Kam wanted to slide her arms around him. His shoulders had slumped as he'd shared his dark secret. "Many alcoholics won't admit they have a problem. I'm sorry it's destroyed your family in so many ways." In that moment, Kam realized, once more, how lucky she had been to have been adopted by Laura and Morgan. She'd had one of the best childhoods compared to most of her friends. Out of tragedy, she had bloomed fully in a family who loved her, not like Wes.

Unable to tear his gaze from hers, Wes thought he saw tears in Kam's eyes. And then, they were gone before he could confirm it. Whatever was happening between them was magical and was pulling him toward her at a fast rate of speed. The horror of his ex-wife's alcoholism resurfaced in his thoughts. When he'd first met Carla, she'd been similar to Kam, all warmth and giving. Only a year later the monstrous symptoms became exposed. His trust in women had been permanently broken. Was he being tested again with Kam? He'd learned his lesson and he was damned if he was going to make the same mistake twice. Who knew what demons and secrets Kam Trayhern had?

"Well, nothing in life is always cherries, as Iris says," Wes said. Breaking the warm connection that strung palpably between them, Wes raised his hand toward the arena in front of them. "This is where we teach families how to take care of a horse, pick its feet, brush it, saddle and bridle it. Iris and Trevor felt that by working around the horses, families would get the message of responsibility. They take care of the horse assigned to them. They go to the box stall, lead their horse out here to the arena and do their morning care with their mount."

The moment was gone. Kam silently lamented the

lost intimacy. She enjoyed talking with Wes. He seemed so solid and reliable despite his terrible childhood. Biting back more questions, Kam knew she'd have to wait until another time to discuss anything personal with Wes. She shouldn't want to. But she did. Iris was like a port in the storm of Rudd's family. Wes offered her the same comfort.

Kam was beginning to understand that the fairy-tale world of Elkhorn Ranch wasn't all it was cracked up to be. She was such an idealist, and that frequently got her into situations where she was disappointed. Somehow, Kam was going to have to weather the storms within the family by hanging in until she could inform Rudd why she was really here. And somehow, she would have to sort out these new feelings for Wes.

CHAPTER SIX

ALLISON TRIED TO calm her nerves. She stood in front
of the well-lit bathroom mirror in her suite. Rudd had
already gotten up and left. He always got up at dawn
and that was fine with her. Eight o'clock was her official waking time and never a minute before. How she
hated ranch life, but what was she to do?

Taking her eyeliner, she carefully outlined her large
green eyes. Again, her nerves jangled. It had been two
weeks since the arrival of the new caregiver, Kam
Trayhern, and Allison was unhappy with her. What
she didn't like was the fact that the old lady, Iris, was
smitten with the young woman. Why should she be?
Finishing off her left eye, Allison devoted all her attention to lining her right eye. In the past, Allison had
been able to drive off each caregiver within a month.

Lips compressing, Allison finished and reached for

her mascara. In her late forties, she had long, beautiful lashes. The face-lift and wonderful Botox had made her look as if she were in her late thirties. In order to be on the Hollywood market, she had to maintain youth. Today, she would fly from Jackson Hole to Cheyenne and then to Los Angeles. There was an audition for a bit part in a television series that her agent had managed to land. She would read the script and pray to God that she'd get the part. It had been so long since she'd worked and she was desperate for a part. She didn't care how she got it.

All her life, Allison had dreamed of being a star. She'd left school at sixteen, escaping poverty on Chicago's east side. She'd left her mother, Clarice, behind and taken a new name. Allison never looked back and threw herself on the mercy of Hollywood in order to fulfill her dream. Now, decades later, she was still fighting.

Frowning, she put her mascara away.

Time to get dressed. The flight was at noon, and she was right on schedule. Allison walked over to her walk-in closet. One thing she was thankful for: she knew the producer of the show. Having navigated Hollywood for so long, she was acquainted with the players. Moving down the long row of dresses, Allison chose a tasteful Riller & Fount plum sheath and a metallic Ferragamo belt was the perfect accessory. She already had on a pair of strappy turquoise Manolo Blahniks. Perfect. She'd look like a queen. The dress showed off her svelte five-foot-nine-inch figure. Long ago, she'd had her breasts enlarged. No Hollywood actress would ever get a second look without huge breasts and an eighteen-inch waist.

"Mom?"

Turning, Allison eyed her daughter, Regan, at the door. "Come on in, sweetie."

Regan wore jeans and an orange T-shirt, her red hair back in a ponytail and her blue eyes heavily made-up. "Hey, Mom, when are you leaving for that casting call?"

"In about an hour. Why? Change your mind and want to come along?" She was so proud of Regan. At twenty-eight, she would soon be a famous film director. She was bright, beautiful and everything that Allison had not been at her age.

"No, I've got a party to go to tonight with my friends in Jackson."

Sniffing as she withdrew the dress from the closet, Allison whisked by her daughter. "Oh, Regan, how can you be around those Goth friends? They're nothing like you!"

"Mom, don't go there," Regan sighed. She followed her mother to the bathroom where she slipped on her clothes. Leaning casually on the doorjamb as her mother dressed, she said, "I love my friends. I don't care if they're Goths."

"You can't possibly love anyone who goes around looking like a vampire, Regan. You're *better* than that! What are you going to do when you go to film school next year?"

Frowning, Regan crossed her arms. "I don't know, Mom. I feel torn. I don't want to leave my friends. And every time I think of leaving you here at the ranch, I get butterflies in my stomach."

Allison patted her daughter's arm. "Darling, you have the world in your hands. I had nothing at your age. You have money, you have an impeccable pedigree through your father and me and you are destined for greatness in Hollywood. Getting into USC is a coup and you know that. We're so proud of you." She leaned over and kissed Regan on her unruly red hair.

"I'd much rather be a star like you," Regan muttered.

"No, you wouldn't," Allison growled in a husky tone. She shifted and moved her dress around, finally pleased with her efforts. "You're going to USC to learn how to make movies. That is a much more powerful position, trust me. As an actor, you're always at the mercy of producers and directors. I don't want you to go through what I did to attain my stardom."

"I guess…"

"You love filming! You've produced the shows at your high school and college. You're a natural, Regan. I know you got the Hollywood gene from me. But I want to see you funnel your creativity into a superior role."

Regan started to brighten a little. "I just got done with the final edit of my new movie for the Sedona Film Festival."

"Good!" She patted Regan's arm as she moved by her and back into the bedroom. "I must see it when I return."

"You can see a copy of it. I have to send it by carrier to the officials of that festival."

"That's fine." Allison picked up her cream-colored ostrich handbag and slid her feet into the narrow, three-inch heels. "There. How do I look?"

Regan smiled. "You look beautiful, Mom. Like the star you are."

"Thank you! Now, go fetch Wes. He's to take my bags to the SUV and drive me to the airport." Looking at the slim gold Rolex watch on her slender wrist, Allison noted she was right on time.

"I'll go get him," Regan called, leaving the room.

Standing alone, Allison scanned their suite. She hated Wyoming. In order to stay in the business, she had to be in Hollywood. Once she got there, she'd go to her new rental apartment in Studio City. Her agent was working to get her other readings for other shows. Allison would schmooze directors and producers to use her for bit parts. It hurt to know that she'd never be considered for a big part again because of her age. With a soft curse of frustration, Allison shrugged, put it all behind her and clicked imperiously out of the room. Hollywood was waiting.

Iris watched Allison get into the SUV with Wes Sheridan's help. With Kam at her side, she was in her iris patch alongside the ranch house.

"There goes the Queen of Mean," she told Kam.

"What?" Kam was on her hands and knees putting fertilizer on the iris rhizomes. Clumps of brown, damp leaves were pulled away from the roots to expose and feed them.

"Allison Dubois," Iris muttered. She shook her dirtied glove finger in the direction of the parking lot. "Allison thinks she's a movie star." Snorting, she added, "And now her agent has gotten her a reading for some bit part in a television show."

"Will she get it?" Kam asked, pulling a handful of compost from the sack sitting between them.

"Doubtful. Allison is almost fifty. And Hollywood is for young things. I don't know why she doesn't give up chasing that rainbow." Iris got back down on her knees a few feet up the line of plants from Kam.

"Was she a star at one time?" Kam wondered. Her

run-ins with Allison had been few and brief. It was obvious she was disdainful of Kam and felt she was a lowly servant instead of an equal.

Digging around the rhizomes and pulling last year's leaves from the earth, Iris said, "She never made it. Oh, she'll tell you she had bit parts, but they were in B movies and that was it. There's a lot to Allison that is secret. I've never trusted her. And I don't know why my son fell for her."

"She's beautiful," Kam said, patting down the compost over the slightly exposed rhizomes. "Men seem to fall for beautiful women instead of women like us. Not that we're ugly or anything, but we're attractive and natural."

"Humph. Allison won't even come out of her suite in the morning unless she's got a pound of pancake on that Botox-filled and lifted face of hers. I can't stand seeing her in full Hollywood glamour around here. A ranch is no place for someone who wants to wear thousand-dollar designer dresses and three-inch-high heels." Lifting her gloved hands out of the soil, Iris showed them to Kam. "Allison would *never* think of getting her hands dirty. Nor would her spoiled children."

Kam laughed and sprinkled more of the rich, black compost down the line of irises. "I think I've seen Regan four times since I got here. She doesn't seem much like her mother and maybe that's good. I hear from Rudd that she's due to go to USC to learn film-making? That's pretty awesome."

"Yes. Regan has her mother's airs because Allison brainwashed the girl. Regan is not a bad person, just distorted by her mother's ambitions. It's taken her a while to figure out what she wants to do with her life."

Straightening, Iris put her hands on her hips. "Regan does show a real talent for movies. She's going to send her first film to the Sedona Film Festival. I'm hoping she wins a prize or at least an honorable mention."

"That sounds fantastic," Kam agreed. "And she's only twenty-eight. What a career she has ahead of her. It seems like she's leaning toward the film industry instead of wanting to go the vanity route."

Iris watched as the SUV turned around in the gravel parkway and left. "Allison is definitely vain and full of secrets. I never did trust her. She keeps Rudd wound around her little finger like a mindless slave. He doesn't see her like I do. She's set her children against him, and she isn't respectful of him. That makes me angry."

Kam recalled that first night here, when she'd had dinner with the family. It had been the only time, but it was an unpleasant experience, with Allison drawing blood wherever she could.

"That's sad," Kam said. "I'm glad I eat my dinner over in the dining area." Indeed, Kam enjoyed socializing with the ranch staff. There were cowboys mixed with the cooking and cleaning staff. They were a great bunch from interesting backgrounds and all loved working for the Elkhorn Ranch.

Kam ate three times a day over at the staff dining facilities and liked it even more because Wes often showed up for meals. Sometimes, they ate together, but most often he was gone because of his duties as second in command; Wes worked directly for Chappy around the ranch. Still, Kam looked forward to the possibility of seeing him. It was far better than sitting at the family table.

"I can barely tolerate Allison at dinner," Iris grumbled, getting back to work on her flower bed. "I don't know why she thinks that because she's had bit parts it makes her better than everyone here."

"Maybe she came out of a rough background. Sometimes people who have to scramble to become famous or successful can become like that." Kam wondered out loud.

Iris nodded, her mouth thinning. "I've done a lot of research on her background. When Rudd came home with Allison on his arm, glowing like a Christmas light, I got suspicious. He'd attended a huge dairy and beef cattle conference out in Los Angeles about twenty-eight years ago. Allison had been an 'actress' at one of the stalls hyping a veterinary product. I remember him calling and telling me he'd found the woman of his dreams." Snorting softly, Iris took a handful of the compost that sat between them and sprinkled it across a few more cleaned-up rhizomes. "He said he had fallen in love with her at first sight."

Kam tried to swallow, but she couldn't. "A conference in Los Angeles?" That was where her photo had been taken. But Rudd was not with Allison in the picture. He was with her mother, the veterinary researcher. Mind spinning, Kam couldn't understand what had happened. Did Rudd connect with her mother, then meet Allison shortly after? Which woman had he really loved? Had Rudd met Allison and forgotten about her mother? Kam rested her hands on her thighs, bewildered. "Iris, you said you did some background research on Allison?"

"Yes, I did." She took her trowel and gently scraped the soil around the rhizomes. "Rudd was like a hormonal teenager with her." She gave Kam a narrow-eyed look. "And it's no secret that there's a casting couch in Hollywood and Allison had quite a reputation. I had a private eye do some poking into her past. She came from a broken family in Chicago. Her mother and father never married. He was a drug dealer and her mother was into meth. Allison got smart and ran away at sixteen for Hollywood. I'll give her credit—she never got into drugs that I could tell. Her drug of choice was fame, and she did what she had to do to get into movies or television shows."

"Sounds pretty awful," Kam agreed, suddenly feeling compassion for Allison. She saw the anger banked in Iris's eyes, however. Given her daughter-in-law's background, it had to be hard for Iris to trust that Allison had Rudd's best interests at heart. What a tangled mess!

"Every time Allison goes to Hollywood, you know what she does?" Iris said in a harsh whisper, her silver brows knitted.

"What?"

"She sleeps around. The private eye told me so."

"Oh, dear," Kam choked.

"And my son is blind, deaf and dumb."

Kam felt the banked rage in Iris's tone. "And she does this why?"

"To try and pick up crumbs of parts so she can stay in touch with la-la land."

"I'm so sorry," Kam said, reaching out and touching the old lady's slumped shoulder.

"Why couldn't he have married someone else? A fine woman with values, morals and integrity? Why did he have to marry this monster?"

Shaking her head, Kam felt her heart squeeze with

anguish. If Rudd was her father, this was a mess for her, as well. "Does Rudd know this?"

"Of course not," Iris grated. "I want to protect my son, not cleave open his heart with an ax! He just wants to make Allison happy and if that means she flies out to Hollywood for a month at a time, well, he's more than willing to pay that price. Allison is usually gone six months out of the year. She spends every winter in Los Angeles. She hates the snow and cold here in Wyoming. Rudd is always depressed when she leaves. I never miss her. We have wonderful family dinners without dissension and bickering when she's gone. Even Regan and Zach are well mannered. What does that tell you?"

Kam got up and moved to the other side of Iris to work on another patch of the long line of flowers. "Is she close to her children?"

"Oh yes. The big mama bear protecting her cubs, that's for sure." Iris snorted and raked the soil around the rhizomes in front of where she was kneeling. "Zach is utterly spoiled. She dotes on the kid. He's not a bad person, just disconnected from the world at large."

"Regan seems pretty well-adjusted, though," Kam said. She raked the leaves off the iris bed and put them in a nearby bucket.

"Rudd and Regan have a good relationship. More than Allison, he noticed her interest in movies and film. It was my son that bought her a camcorder when she was nine, and then she began filming. When he saw her interest in making movies, he supported her every inch of the way."

"I'm glad that Regan is close to him. Rudd seems like such a natural father, wanting the best for his children."

"He's a pussycat," Iris fumed. "Any woman can wind

him around her little finger! I was hoping Rudd would marry a woman from the land. Someone who loved nature, animals and the earth, who would give me grandchildren who love those things, too."

Again, Kam's heart squeezed. If she was Rudd's daughter, then Iris had part of her wish at least. But she could say nothing. Not yet. "Do you think children ever grow up being what their parents want them to be, Iris?"

Iris sat up and pushed away strands of silver hair that had drifted across her brow. She smiled a little. "Now, how did you get so wise for someone so young?"

Feeling heat in her face, Kam shrugged. "Maybe because I was tripping around the world and seeing a lot of different things, Iris. I don't really know."

"Your parents raised you right. You're levelheaded, you support yourself and you have morals, value and integrity. Unlike Allison. If Rudd didn't have the strong influence over Regan that he has, I'm afraid she'd end up being just like her mother. Rudd has tried to interface with Zach, but he's locked up in a mental tower within himself. No matter what my son has tried to do to connect with that boy, it hasn't worked."

"Zach doesn't like ranch life?" Kam wondered.

Snorting, Iris got back to work on the bed. "That kid is moody, sullen and barely squeaks through school with Ds."

"Has Allison tried to get him unglued from his computer games?"

"No. She's never been what I'd call a 'real mother' to her two children. If not for Rudd and myself, those two would be orphans within a family, that's for sure.

I saw Zach as a young boy just wither and go inside himself when his mother was gone for long periods."

"So Zach never got nurtured," Kam suggested.

"Right on," Iris said. "Of course, how could Allison nurture anyone? She was the offspring of two druggies who didn't have a clue about being good parents. She didn't know how. I can't blame her, but I also don't forgive her for not *trying* to be a parent to Regan and Zach."

"I think she tries, doesn't she?"

"Oh, in her own way, she does," Iris admitted darkly. "I should thank my lucky stars she's not a drug addict. Trevor and I wished more for Rudd. After we adopted him, we wondered what kind of person he'd turn out to be. What kind of woman would he marry? How many children would he have? It was so exciting to us to dream for him."

"Rudd is adopted?" Kam gasped.

Iris smiled as she patted the soil. "Yes. Didn't you know? I would have thought Rudd might have mentioned. Then again, most men are private about these things." She sat up. "I was infertile. We wanted children. We went to an orphanage in Cheyenne and put through adoption papers for him. We were never sorry we did that. He's just been the most wonderful son to us."

Swallowing hard, Kam watched Iris. The old woman's face was wreathed with happiness and contentment. Rudd was adopted! She had been adopted! Mind spinning, Kam wondered what synchronicities of life played out here.

"Rudd is our son. In my will, I leave everything to

him. He's more than met our expectations. I know he'll do his best to carry on our dream for this ranch."

Kam rubbed her brow as the shock waves rolled through her.

"The only fly in the ointment is Allison. I just can't understand it. Why couldn't he have met a fine, up-standing woman who had good character?"

He did, Kam almost blurted. For a moment, she wanted to take Iris to her suite and show her the black-and-white photo of her mother and Rudd. But what would that accomplish? No, she had to wait. Confu-sion swirled through her like a muddy, flooding river on a rampage. Kam knew she needed time to digest this shocking piece of information.

"Do—do you know anything about Rudd's back-ground?" Kam hoped she wasn't being too nosy.

The expression on the matriarch's face remained placid. "Rudd's father abandoned him. His mother died shortly after having him. He was taken to a foster home, which was where we caught up with him. His mom, Sally May Thornton, was a schoolteacher in Cheyenne. His father, Patrick Hanlon, was a truck driver. He signed over all rights to us. The man just wasn't cut out to be a parent. He liked his big rigs, his freedom, and he just never wanted to be tied down."

"Is Rudd in touch with his biological father?" Kam asked, her voice strained.

"No. Rudd tried to reconnect with him, but he didn't want anything to do with him. It was heartbreaking for him and for us. We never hid the fact that we'd adopted him. We supported him trying to find his birth father when he was old enough. It just didn't work out."

"Is Rudd okay with how it's turned out now?"

"I think he is. Of course, losing your birth parents is going to put a hole in your spirit, no matter what," Iris said softly. "We've loved Rudd fiercely and he's returned it tenfold to us. But we aren't his biological parents. Which is why I kept a very detailed photographic album of his life. I wanted him to know what he was like when he was a baby, a youngster and a teen growing up with us. I take lots of photos of Rudd doing his stuff. And he got so he'd carry a camera with him whenever he had to go out of town on business. He'd always bring back photos for the albums."

"I'd love to see those albums if you ever want to share them with me, Iris."

"Oh, heavens, yes! You're the first caregiver ever to want to know about my personal life. We'll have tea this afternoon and I'll start with the earliest albums and work forward. Would you like that? We can do this daily until we've gone through all of them."

"Yes, I'd love to do that," Kam whispered. And what would she find? Her heart squeezed in fear and hope.

CHAPTER SEVEN

"GRANDMA, I *HATE* making these stupid flower essences with you every spring," Zach mumbled. He slid off his bay quarter horse and onto the flower-strewn hillside.

"Humph," Iris said, already off her golden palomino, Pal.

Kam glanced over at Wes, who had accompanied Iris on her first big flower-essence trip. He said nothing as he gathered up the reins, placed them around the saddle horns and hobbled the four horses so they could eat the rich spring grass. Kam took a large, lidded plastic box from Wes. Zach was sulking and angrily kicking at the grass around his feet. The boy was seventeen, about six feet tall with acne covering his face in red, pimply splotches. His hands were shoved in the pockets of his low-slung army-green cargo pants.

"Young man," Iris said, going over to him, "you have

ridden out here with me every year since you could remember. You used to love to come out here and help
me. You know this is good for you, Zach. A little fresh
air, some sunshine…" Iris pointed to the clear blue May
morning sky. "A little exercise is *not* going to hurt you."

"There's nothing to do out here," the boy complained, ignoring his grandmother. "There's no Wi-Fi
signal, either. I wish you'd put up a big Wi-Fi unit here
at the ranch. You have the money."

Iris smiled at her grandson, patting his arm sooth-
ingly. "Come on, come and help me."

Sighing heavily, Zach stuck out his lower lip and his
shoulders slumped. His brown eyes matched the color
of his unkempt straight hair. He pushed his thin fingers through his hair and grumbled, "Oh….all right."

They had ridden about an hour from the ranch in a
northerly direction. The area consisted of many rolling
green hills dotted with colorful wildflowers. She had no
idea what Iris would do next and was curious. Wes remained nearby after making sure the horses were taken
care of. The four animals grazed eagerly below them
on the hill, swishing their tails, contented.

Trying to ignore Wes and his quiet masculinity, Kam
knelt opposite Iris. The older woman spread out a small
white cotton blanket and then placed several items from
the box onto the spread. "Talk me through what you're
doing, Iris," Kam said, hands resting on her thighs.

"Well, isn't it nice that someone around here is interested in making a flower essence?" Iris said rather
loudly. She twisted her head toward Zach, who stood
about six feet away, sulking.

"I'll go look for the flowers," Zach mumbled, scuff-
ing away and going down around the side of the hill.

"Thank you," Iris called, smiling. She pushed back her straw hat. "Let me show you what to do."

As she tried to keep focused, Kam felt more than saw Wes come and kneel down on the other side of the blanket. He took off his hat, wiped his brow and settled it back on his head. No matter what he did, the effect rippled through Kam like a soft spring breeze across a pond. Barely meeting his gray eyes, Kam felt her heart leap as he shared a hint of a smile with her.

"Iris is a good teacher," he said, taking off his leather gloves and tucking them into his belt.

"Indeed I am," Iris responded, chuckling. "When Wes came here two years ago, he sort of took over Zach's job. My grandson feels this activity is beneath him now." She held up a clear custard glass. Ten of them were stacked on the spread. "Kam, when you make a flower essence you always want a clear glass bowl to work with."

"Why?" Kam wondered.

"To allow the sun to shine through the clear glass and clean water where the flower is floating. If sunlight lanced through a colored glass, then that color is impregnated into the water's memory and that's not good. If you have, for example," and she pointed nearby, "this beautiful red-orange Indian paintbrush, a colored glass would add another color we don't want. Clear glass deals only with the unique color of the flower. We want only that energy. We have sixty frost-free days here in the area, so wildflowers sprout fast in late May through late July. Some are tough enough to endure the frost and paintbrush is one of them. We're about a week early as most flowers don't start blooming until June, which is right around the corner." Iris frowned. "But our dude ranch opens up on Memorial Day, and Wes won't be able to help me after that. Which is why we're out here a few days early."

Kam observed the tall, red-orange flower that looked like a stalk with a red flame on top. Or, perhaps, she imagined, it looked like a redheaded person who had stuck their finger in an electric socket and their hair was standing on end. She chuckled to herself, then glanced up as Iris gently touched the wildflower. "That's a beautiful flower. What do you do with it, Iris?"

"Well," Iris said, taking a small bottle of water and pouring it into the custard dish until it was about half-full. "We must mentally introduce ourselves to this plant spirit first. The water I'm putting in here is reverse-osmosis water. You never use fluoridated or chlorinated water to make a flower essence because you don't want anything impure in the nature of the water."

"You said you talk to the spirit of the plant?" Kam asked.

"Remember, I'm half–Native American. My mother and grandmother raised me to know that *all* things have a spirit. And that we should always be respectful of nature. Every spirit has a name and a personality, just as humans do. I'm going to move over to this paintbrush, mentally introduce myself to it, tell it my name and ask its permission to take one of its flowers to make an essence. The plant spirit can tell me no. If it does, I go off to find another one and start the process all over again." She moved to the plant. "Usually, the plant nation loves humans and will surrender a life to them as an act of compassion and love."

Kam watched, fascinated, as Iris pulled out a pinch of yellow cornmeal from an old leather pouch pinned on the waist of her jeans. Iris sprinkled the cornmeal over the plant.

"What is that for?" Kam asked.

"We always give the gift of cornmeal to a plant we want to work with," Iris explained, tightening the cords on the pouch. "Just as humans introduce themselves to one another with social patter and a handshake, this is the way we approach a flower. Cornmeal is sacred. The corn mother feeds all her relations. By giving this paintbrush a gift of cornmeal, I show it my intent, Kam. Plants know the protocols between themselves and humans. Before white men came to this land, Native Americans always lived in harmony with all our relations. If a woman had to go out and gather onions in early spring, she would find a patch and give cornmeal to the grandmother plant. She'd ask permission of that oldest plant if she could gather her children for food. If the grandmother plant gave her approval, the women would go through a meadow digging up the onions for their village. And if the answer was no, then they go to another meadow hoping to obtain approval from the next grandmother plant."

"I didn't know that," Kam said, impressed. "But it makes sense. I know I used to talk to the plants in my mother's garden."

"Exactly," Iris said, her face bright. "Sure you don't have some Indian blood in your veins, too? Did someone teach you to talk to the plants?"

Feeling heat tunnel into her face, Kam was caught off guard. "I—well, no, no one taught me to talk to plants. I always did because they felt alive."

"And so they are," Iris praised her. "Just think of

them as people who look different is all. Now, I'm going to introduce myself to this paintbrush."

Kam remained quiet, as did Wes. They traded a look and Kam felt her heart open a little more to him. He wore a denim shirt, the cuffs rolled up to his elbows, his darkly suntanned arms showing strength and muscle. Wes worked from dawn to dusk, and it showed on his lean and toned body. Kam had seen why Chappy, the ranch manager, relied so heavily on him. No one worked more diligently or reliably than Wes. Kam had seen too many men who lacked integrity and a work ethic. It made Wes that much more appealing to her. Quietly, she told her heart "no." There simply was no time for a relationship with Wes, even though Iris had mentioned he had no girlfriend. The information made Wes more dangerous to her heart.

"Okay," Iris told them, looking up, "this plant has given her permission for me to snip off one of her flowers." She showed Kam how to use her thumb and index finger to gently and quickly snap off the flower head. "Now, hand me that custard dish."

Kam got up and took it to where Iris knelt in front of the plant. The elder placed the flower head so that it floated on top of the water.

"I'm going to ask the spirit of this plant to put her energy into the water. The custard dish goes next to her body, near her stem. We've got sunlight dappling this area. I'll ask Father Sun to send his energy into the flower and into the water, too. When we make a flower essence, we have to be in a good space within ourselves. We can't be angry or upset. We have to be focused with our heart open to the plant. That way, our energy is one of harmony and love. This is absorbed by the molecules in the water and that helps to create the flower essence."

"It's a lovely way to gather them," Kam said. She gave Iris her hand to help her to stand up after she'd placed the dish next to the paintbrush. "What now?"

"Well," Iris said, dusting off her knees, "I'm hoping Zach has found a few more wildflowers that might be early. Let's go around the hill and see if we can find him. Wes, will you bring along my stuff?"

"I sure will," Wes said, folding up the spread and putting everything back into the large plastic box.

Kam followed Iris around the grassy knoll. It was only ten in the morning, and the coolness of the night had dissipated. There were unseen gopher holes in the grass and Kam remained near Iris as they carefully trod around the hill. In no time, Wes had caught up with them, plastic box in hand. He smiled over at Kam.

"Pretty cool stuff, huh?" he asked her.

"Definitely." She turned to Iris, who was on her right. "How did you find out a particular flower could help someone?"

"I was taught to journey into the plant by my Grandmother Bell. I would ask the plant's permission to do so and then when I journeyed into it, the spirit would tell me how it would help two-leggeds. I would then come out of the journey and write the information down in my notebook."

"That's an amazing process," Kam said. Iris seemed more like a medicine woman than a ranch owner. It was the wisdom gleaming in her eyes, that smile that hovered around her mouth, that told her the elder knew a great deal about nature and her habits.

"Iris, tell Kam what paintbrush is good for," Wes said.

"It helps people with low self-esteem get their confidence back. For example, if a woman has always dreamed of owning her own business but she's afraid, paintbrush will imbue her with confidence and belief in herself to fulfill her dreams."

"Wow," Kam said, noticing Zach down the hill bending over looking at several different types of wildflowers, "that's pretty impressive."

"Yes," Iris said, proudly. "I sell a lot of Indian paintbrush, mostly to women. I get all kinds of positive feedback from them after they take the flower essence for a month or less. I never have to sell them a second bottle. The energy of the flower, its meaning and abilities, are absorbed by the person and they become very confident. They know there's a lot of hard work ahead of them, but at least they believe they can tackle it. That's the first step to owning your dream. Living life isn't for the weak or fearful. It takes guts to grab for your dream and hold on until you accomplish it. Indian paintbrush gives people just that."

"How's that for flower power?" Wes said, obviously impressed with Iris's story.

Zach lifted his head and called up, "Hey, Grandmother, there are violets over here. Just one bloom, though. Kinda early for them."

"That's my grandson," Iris crowed, giving him a smile. "Good work! We're coming," she called.

"Looks like Zach is getting in the mood," Kam said.

"He always does," Iris responded, more to herself. "The hardest part is dragging him out of his room, taking those earbuds out of his ears and getting him outdoors. He's a good boy, just real solitary and introverted."

"Is Rudd like that?" Kam wondered out loud as they moved down the gentle, grassy slope.

"No. He's an extrovert, but typical man. Gets along with people real well, but can't communicate or share his intimate feelings."

Laughing, Kam nodded and caught Wes's grimace. "I have never met a man who could share his emotions except for my father." It was so easy to talk about her adopted family. Kam smiled and said, "I'm with you, Iris. Not many men are able to share their feelings. I wish they would, though."

"My Trevor did, too," Iris said, pleased. "We laughed together, cried together. Whatever touched him, touched me and vice versa. He was a wonderful friend and the love of my life."

Wes gave Iris a gentle look. "I met Trevor many times before I came to work here. He was a fine man, Iris. I'm just sorry he had to leave so early in his life."

Iris lost her smile and her face softened. "Oh, he's with me in spirit, Wes. I feel my darling around me all the time." She eyed him warmly. "And you may believe this or not, but I hear him talking to me, too. He gives me good advice and I listen. In my dreams at night, we discuss the ranch and how things are going. No, he's still here."

"That's wonderful," Kam said, touched by her admission. "I hope I meet a man like that someday." And then she happened to glance up to see Wes studying her so intently she flushed to the roots of her hair. The look in his gray eyes was unmistakable. It was a man wanting his woman—in all ways. Lips parting, Kam wasn't sure what to do or say. Instead, she ripped her gaze away from Wes and paid strict attention to walking down the hill with Iris to where Zach stood.

Heart pounding, Kam lowered her head and watched for the gopher holes so Iris wouldn't inadvertently walk into one. Wes *wanted* her. Clearly. What was she going to do? Why was her body traitorously giving her away? A warm ache pooled in her lower body. How long had she been without a man? Too long. In her globe-trotting line of business, relationships didn't survive. Her whole life was pointed toward finding her father, not a permanent relationship with a man. Somehow, Kam knew that until she could find her father or bring her search to some kind of satisfactory conclusion, she would never find the right man she wanted to marry. It was that important to her to find out about her parents. And nothing less would suffice.

Iris stopped and leaned down. Zach had knelt and cleared away the grass so she could see the tiny violet blooming. "Ah, it *is* a white violet. Nicely done, Zach. What a set of eyes you have! I'd never have seen it with my old pair." She reached out and patted his head gently.

Zach flushed with pride and pleasure. In that moment, Kam could see just how vulnerable the boy was. Maybe his mother's long absences had driven him inward. It was so important for parents to give a child a sense of safety so they could range out into the world with confidence. As she looked into Zach's brown eyes, Kam wondered if he didn't need Indian paintbrush himself to boost his confidence. Or maybe the insecurity came from teenage hormones. Kam recalled her own years as a teen in the Trayhern family. She had gone through periods of wanting to be left alone, to have privacy but she had never hidden from life or her parents.

Zach pulled some of the closest strands of grass away so that Iris could kneel down in front of the little plant. He was careful not to uproot the violet. Iris had taught him well, and he was respectful of the process despite his earlier gripes.

Wes placed the white cotton spread out to the right of Iris and brought out utensils for her to use.

"Grandmother, remember when I was a little kid you used to take me out in late May or early June to pick violets? You'd make violet candy then." Zach smiled wistfully. "It was always good."

Iris settled in front of the violet. Zach knelt down opposite her, his gangly hands covering his long, thin thighs. "Indeed I do. But the last five years you never wanted to do it."

"Maybe this year? I always loved the violet-flower candy."

"Of course," Iris said, giving him a smile. "Just you and me. You know where the violets are thick in another week."

"Yeah, over on Sunrise Hill. There's a nice, wet marshy area and there's hundreds of them."

Kam could see the magic of their connection. Iris had been visibly moved by Zach's unexpected and enthusiastic request. Maybe it was the magic of the flowers. Kam knelt down to the left of Iris.

"How do violets help us, Iris?"

"Violets have a long history of soothing an ailing heart," Iris told them as she sprinkled cornmeal around the plant. "They are for introverts who need to come and live in the world again." She smiled over at Zach, who watched her every move. "Maybe this flower has touched you with her energy, Zach."

He shrugged bashfully. "I dunno, Grandmother."

"How did you find it? With all this grass, it would be nearly impossible to see it."

"Ahh," he mumbled, avoiding everyone's gaze, "I just felt around and then started looking for it."

"You have your father's intuition working in you," Iris said confidently. "Well done! Often, a plant that wants to share something will call to you. Now, it's certainly not in English, but it gently touches one's heart. You feel a tug to walk a certain direction. Is that what you felt?"

"Yeah, I guess it was," Zach said, a bit amazed.

Kam said, "This is incredible. How magical, Iris."

"Oh, believe me, you start working with nature and magic does happen," Iris chuckled.

Kam suddenly wished there was a flower essence for adopted children. She wanted something to ease the hole in her heart. It was too painful not to know the complete story of her origins. She almost voiced her wish but bit down on her lower lip. To ask would give her away, and she wasn't yet ready to confront Rudd. Every time she thought she was ready, a cold bolt of fear thrust down through her and made her stomach ache with anxiety.

"Violet heals the heart?" Wes asked.

"That's right," Iris said, gently picking the white flower and reverently placing it in the custard glass that Wes had partly filled with water. "Heart healer is what I call a violet. She gives introverts a desire to move out into the real world, too. She celebrates life in all its rainbow colors of love."

Glancing up, Kam caught Wes studying her beneath the brim of his cowboy hat. His eyes gleamed with silver, and, once more, she felt herself go hot and shaky. The man could simply look at her and set her on fire. What would he think of her ultimate goal in coming here? Of not being honest and forthright with the Mason family? Her conscience railed within her. There were no easy answers.

Kam still lacked the courage to unveil herself to them. She didn't want to disappoint Iris or Wes. Or Rudd. And she knew they would be disappointed once they found out she was there under false pretenses. Rubbing her brow, Kam felt anxious and unhappy. She loved these people. They were kind and generous to her. Like the salt of the earth, they had no agenda—unlike her.

What was she going to do?

CHAPTER EIGHT

EVERYONE WAS GOING crazy behind the scenes at the ranch in preparation for tomorrow's special Independence Day celebration. Families had reserved cabins for this particular week and the ranch was filled to capacity. There would be an old-fashioned barbecue, square dancing and a live country band out near the cabins. Wes and his crew had been working for days to lay down the temporary flooring and stage for the event.

"Kam? Do you have a minute?" Rudd stuck his head around the door into Iris's office. It was lunchtime and most employees had left for the dining room. She had wanted to tie up a few loose ends first.

"Sure. Hold on, I've got a couple of more pieces of shipping tape to put on this flower-essence order and I'll be done."

He opened the door further and stood waiting for her, hat in hand.

Rudd gazed around the quiet office. "Iris was saying that her orders for flowers essences are up by thirty percent this year. That's a lot."

Smiling, Kam got up from her desk and put the small cardboard box into the mailing bag. "I think my suggestion to promote via YouTube helped."

"I do, too," Rudd said, grinning. "You've been a real blessing to Iris. To all of us."

Kam felt a stab of guilt once more. She didn't like being such a coward. The family that raised her embraced honor, sacrifice and courage for their country through their generations of military service. How did she fit in? Kam forced a smile she didn't feel.

Grabbing her cowboy hat, she said, "What's up?"

Rudd fell into step with her down the hall. "Oh, not much," he said. "Let's go to the office and talk."

Fear suddenly moved through her. Kam knew this was unusual behavior for Rudd. Normally, he was out in the field and not in the office. He'd finally hired an assistant, an older woman in her fifties named Judy Harper. She was a widow and lived in Jackson. Her dynamic energy and intelligence had allowed Rudd to become mostly free of office duties, much to his joy and relief.

Kam followed him into the empty office. Through the window, she could see into the dining room, where guests and workers alike were eating. Everyone seemed happy to be there. She only hoped she could join them, that Rudd hadn't called her in to fire her. She took a seat and waited.

Placing his hat on the desk, Rudd leaned back in the

chair and laced his long fingers across his flat belly. He gave Kam an assessing look. "I just wanted to take time to thank you for being here. My mother has bloomed because of your presence." He shrugged and said, "None of the other caregivers took to Iris. I'm sure my wife helped drive them off, too. We haven't had much success in finding someone who can deal with the strong women in this household…until now. You're different, Kam."

Kam bit her lower lip to stop herself from revealing that Allison didn't like her, either. Allison didn't seem to like anyone. She was insufferably focused on her dying Hollywood career. Allison hadn't gotten the bit part when she'd flown out to Hollywood in May. She'd come home sulking, irritable and angry at everyone. Often, Kam would hear her fighting with her daughter, Regan. Or worse, with Rudd. Their voices would carry through the sprawling ranch house and Kam couldn't help but hear their arguments. She smiled. "I like Iris. I hope I'm just like her when I get to be her age. She's a real role model for me, Rudd."

"It shows. I just wanted to say thank you, Kam. There's just something about you that agrees with Iris. My mother doesn't suffer fools, as you well know, and I've never heard her complain about you once."

"That's nice to know. Thank you."

He studied her, the silence growing in the office. "My mother's blood pressure is down. She's taking her meds instead of fighting everyone about them, and I've honestly not seen her this well or happy since before my dad died. There's magic between you two, that's for sure."

Kam was touched by his words. "Thank you, Rudd.

Every morning I check her blood pressure with my cuff, listen to her heart and make sure her medications are there to take. She's been a wonderful patient from that perspective."

"Well," he said gruffly, "her doctor is amazed at how she's rebounded. She's actually better. I'm happy about that. She's a tough old buzzard and I always hoped her later years would be kind to her. And I believe you've helped make them just that."

Kam saw a sheen in Rudd's eyes, but it soon vanished as the man worked to school his emotions. "Iris is special," Kam agreed quietly. "I feel privileged to be around her. She's taught me so much about gardening. I love the way she sees plants and how they can help us heal. You're lucky to have such a mother."

Rudd nodded and touched his handlebar mustache. "I'm sorry you never met Trevor. He was so much like her. Together they were a pair of dynamos with this ranch. We have happy employees, we're making money and we're doing something good for people and the earth."

"It doesn't get much better than that," Kam said, clasping her hands. Now was a perfect opportunity to speak to Rudd. To tell him the truth. Automatically, her gut tightened and her mouth went dry. Something inside made her keep quiet.

Rudd sat up and folded his hands on the desk. "I just wanted to let you know that I'm giving you a monthly raise of three hundred dollars. You've done so much for my mother in such a short period of time. It's the only way I can thank you and convince you to stay on. I know you're a professional photographer so I've often wondered when you might fly away again."

Shocked by his generosity, Kam's mouth fell open. What a nice boost to her income. But then she knew the ranch was highly profitable. Iris had even confided that it was worth twenty million dollars, a sum that astounded Kam. "Thanks, Rudd. That's a very generous raise."

"I want you to be happy here."

Kam had never hidden the fact she'd been a globe-trotting photographer for top newspapers, television and magazine sources. A week wouldn't go by when one of them didn't call and ask her if she had any photos to sell. She'd done a lot of work photographing the wildflowers with a specialized macro lens and having the pictures loaded to Iris's Web site. Everyone had praised her photos.

"I'm not planning to leave, Rudd." At least, that was the truth.

He tilted his head and leaned back in the chair again. "That's what I don't understand, Kam. Why would a very successful person like you stop doing what she loved? I see you around here always with your camera in your hand shooting pictures. I think taking photos is in your blood, like ranching is in mine. I keep asking myself—why would Kam leave a world she loved to come here?"

Rudd was giving her an opening. Her heart was pounding unrelentingly in her chest and she wondered if he could hear it thudding. "Well, I..." She grew silent. The inner war to blurt out the truth nearly tore it from her lips. Yet, the fear of being rejected crushed her. Not yet. She needed to work up to the truth.

Opening her hands, she said to Rudd, "I did a lot of third-world gigs as a professional, Rudd. I've been to places where there are crises, catastrophes and drama. When I graduated from college, I went directly into the field. I built my name over the years and I got lucky. I was at the right place at the right time and my photos sold."

"I see," he murmured, studying her. "Somehow, you don't strike me as the kind of person who would enjoy seeing constant human suffering and pain."

His insight was startling and an ache began in Kam's heart. She'd had fantasies of her real father being just like this—insightful and sensitive to who she was. "You're right," she admitted. "That's why I quit, Rudd. I—I couldn't stand the children dying, old people suffering or starving to death. I hated the war zones of Afghanistan and Iraq, too. There's got to be a better way than killing one another to solve issues in our world."

Rudd smiled softly. "Iris and I kinda thought those might be the reasons you walked away from your career."

It didn't surprise Kam that Iris and Rudd had discussed her. "I won't ever go back to it."

"But are you happy *here,* Kam? I live in a daily fear of you coming to me to say you're moving on. My mother loves you. She dotes on you. And I can't stand the thought that you might just up and leave."

Oh, if only he knew… And yet, Kam reasoned, if Rudd knew why she was here, would he be so worried? And what if she wasn't his daughter? Would he allow her to stay after knowing she'd come to them like the proverbial fox in the hen house? Kam just couldn't see Rudd allowing her to stay under those circumstances because he and Iris were from the old school of honesty, integrity and high moral standards. And she was not conducting herself in any of those ways.

Kam cleared her throat. "Rudd, I'm happy here. I feel like I've come home." That wasn't a lie. "I love nature. I love Iris dearly. Oh, she has her days when she's crotchety, but who doesn't? And I'm redefining my photography. I've decided to turn to nature, to wildlife and people who live in the elements, instead. I've already sold a number of my photos from just shooting here around the ranch. And the Teton Range is an incredible photographic subject at dawn and dusk."

"Yeah, we live in one of the most beautiful places on Earth, don't we?" Rudd leaned back in his chair and grinned.

Kam nodded, wanting so desperately to bond with Rudd as daughter to father, not as employee to a ranch owner. Yet, if she didn't have the courage to speak up, that was the only connection she and Rudd would share. It wasn't enough, but it had to be for now. "Your ranch sits in one of the most photogenic places I've ever seen," Kam admitted. "And don't worry about me leaving, okay?"

"We're concerned you're not getting enough personal time, Kam. You're with Iris seven days a week and you are entitled to your weekends off. And if you don't like living here at the ranch, there are nice apartments or house rentals in Jackson Hole. We would understand if you'd rather not have the entire family underfoot here. You're a young and beautiful woman who needs a social life."

Watching Rudd struggle to say all those things only endeared him even more to Kam. She could tell he wasn't used to talking on such a personal level. "I'd love

to have my weekends off. It would give me a chance
to drive around and do some serious hiking and photographing not only in the Grand Teton National Park,
but in Yellowstone. As for leaving the ranch for town,
I really don't want to do that." She saw instant relief in
Rudd's weathered features. "As long as you don't mind
letting me stay in that lovely suite, I'm happy here."
Rudd would never know how she enjoyed waking each
morning to the lowing of cattle, the whinny of horses
and the dawn-to-dusk activity a ranch demanded. It in-
fused her with new lifeblood.

"That's good to hear." His voice suddenly grew
hoarse. "You have no idea how much your staying on
means to me, personally. I love my mother very much.
I would do *anything* to keep her happy. Your coming
into our lives is a godsend. If you *ever* need anything,
you come to me, because I owe you. I can't pay you
enough money to be who you are to Iris. All I want for
my mother is to be happy for the rest of her life. Losing
my father still burns in my heart." He looked up at the
ceiling for a moment, his voice cracking. Blinking several times, he finally gazed back at Kam. "I just can't
deal with the idea of her dying someday."

"Because they are all you ever had," Kam whispered unsteadily, tears burning in her eyes. The fact
he'd shared so much profoundly touched her. There was
a trust growing between them daily and it made her feel
hopeful. One day, when the time was right, she would
come to Rudd. Maybe he could forgive her. Searching
his blue eyes shining with unshed tears, Kam felt a kin-
ship with him that transcended her raw fear.

"That's right," Rudd said, coughing. He sat up and
plunked the hat back on his head. "Well, enough of this

maudlin stuff." He managed a crooked grin and rose. "You are greatly loved here, Kam. We just want you to know that. If you need anything, you come straight to me, okay?"

How desperately Kam wanted to walk around the desk and throw her arms around the man who might well be her father. And even if he wasn't, Kam felt as if she'd met an amazing man, a man just like Morgan Trayhern. Instead of being a military hero and in the spy business, he was a cowboy carved out of the harsh beauty of the Tetons. Could she be fortunate enough to have two such men in her life? The thought was dizzying.

As Rudd came around the desk, he awkwardly put his arms around Kam and quickly hugged her. As he stepped back, she saw that his face was red and he looked bashful. "Just a hug of thanks," he told her gruffly. "Be sure to get to the dining room before it closes."

Kam was shaken by his unexpected gesture. "Uh... yes...in a few minutes."

After a quick nod, Rudd left. The front screen door slammed closed, leaving Kam standing behind the desk, stunned. She rubbed her chest in the area of her heart.

CHAPTER NINE

"You can't want her," Wes whispered under his breath as he put the finishing touches to the band's stage. Kam's face danced before him like a lure.

The famous Fourth of July celebration at Elkhorn Ranch was underway. Families who had been coming to the dude ranch for years got first dibs on staying the week. There were always more takers than cabins. This was a joyful, festive time at the ranch and the high energy was infectious. Everyone was happy—except maybe him. If only he could push Kam out of his thoughts and heart. It was a daily struggle for Wes.

After tacking down the red-white-and-blue drape across the bottom of the stage, Wes put the hammer back in his toolbox. Being a cowboy didn't mean he was in the saddle all the time. So much of what made a ranch run was beyond horse and cattle. Something was always breaking and needing repair. In this case, Chappy had asked four of his best cowhands to get the stage ready for the evening's hoedown and concert.

The sun was hot overhead, the sky a clear, light blue. As Wes straightened and looked west, he could see that the mighty, jagged Tetons were nearly clear of any snow on their blue granite slopes. He never tired of looking at them. He never would. They symbolized to him the power of responsibility and shouldering loads as they came his way. The mountains handled it; so could he.

His mind turned to Kam Trayhern—again, as it always did when he had a quiet moment. Wes had buried himself in his work. He tried to be away from the main ranch house as much as possible. Yet, nearly every day, he ran into Kam whether he wanted to or not. Oh, he *wanted* to see her, there was no question. His heart and stupid body responded powerfully to her every time. As much as Wes tried to stay away from Kam, he couldn't escape his torrid dreams of her. Feeling like a man possessed by an opiate, he wondered why and how he was being so powerfully attracted to her. He wasn't looking for a woman right now. Divorce had cured him of that.

As he snapped the metal lid on the toolbox shut, he noticed Chappy working with several other hands to lay down the rubber matting. Large wooden squares would be locked together on it to make the huge dance floor. Beyond that, a number of the families mingled around their cabins because it was nearly noon and time to eat.

Plenty of younger children and teens stood around the area, looking excited about tonight's massive barbecue, music and dancing. They had been taught square dancing, the West's version of ballroom elegance. Yes, it would be a fun night. But not for him.

Gripping the handle of his toolbox, Wes headed toward the barn, unhappy because he and all the other ranch hands were required to attend the hoedown tonight. They would be expected to dance with the guests, and he knew that Kam would be there, too. *Damn.* Normally, he didn't cuss, but he was feeling so anxious about tonight, he couldn't help it. As he stepped across the sturdy rubber matting, Wes was irritated by the fact that he could not stop thinking about her. Her name and face stirred his mind the way a soft breeze stirs the surface of a quiet morning lake. He must be sick if he was waxing poetic about a woman.

"Chappy? Anything else you want me to do?"

Chappy looked up, his hands on his waist. "Go check the sound system. I got Erick, our electric guy, on it. He's in back of the stage and could use a gopher."

Grinning, Wes nodded and turned back toward the gussied-up stage. Erick was a Swede who was in the process of getting his green card to become an American citizen. The young blond man with startling blue eyes and a pale complexion had idolized the West since childhood. He had wanted nothing more than to become a cowboy. Now, he was making that dream come true. Wes knew that being a cowpoke was in one's blood. Not a head trip, but a heart trip.

Swinging around the end of the stage, he noticed Erick down on his hands and knees working with some serious-looking electric cables. A tousle of blond hair dipped over his sweaty, furrowed brow. Only twenty-five years old, Erick would eventually find a girl and settle down into ranch life. Wes only hoped that he wouldn't run into someone like Carla, who had played the spider to the fly and had trapped him.

"Hey," Erick called, "glad you stopped by. I need another pair of hands."

"That's what I'm here for," Wes said, putting his toolbox down.

"This is going to be a great night," Erick said, flashing a smile as he took black electrical tape and quickly wrapped it around several wires. "I can't believe Mr. Mason was able to snag the Coyote Band. They are hot. He must have paid a fortune to get them here. I want to make sure the sound system is perfect."

Wes grinned. "So, you got a girl you want to take to the dance tonight?" he teased.

"No, but I sure like that little filly from the Anderson family." Erick chuckled.

"Ah, Amanda." She was twenty-five years old.

"All I want to do is dance with her."

"She's been eyeing you," Wes said, helping him to wrap several more wires. "I see her watching you when you aren't aware of it." Wes smiled wide as the Swede blushed red to the roots of his hair. He had some acne on his cheeks, which he was very sensitive about. Once he had admitted to Wes that he felt his acne was a turnoff to a woman. Wes tried to convince him to forget about it. And he was glad beautiful, brunette Amanda with the light brown eyes was coming because Erick had come alive under her interest.

"What about you?" Erick said, picking up a six-foot length of plastic pipe. "Who're you taking to the dance?"

"No one," Wes muttered.

"What about Kam? Now, there's a good-looking woman!"

"Don't remind me," Wes growled, bringing the ends of some wires into the plastic pipe Erick was holding.

"Hey, you talk about eyeballing. She's *always* got this wistful look on her face when she sees *you,* Sheridan."

Snorting, Wes felt a surge of desire hit him. "You're full of it, Erick. You're seeing things."

Laughing, Erick guided the wires into the piece of pipe. "No, I'm not. I heard Iris talking to her the other day. She was saying to Kam what a nice catch you would be."

"Great," Wes muttered.

"Aren't you interested in what Kam had to say about it? I was in earshot to hear her answer."

Mouth quirking, Wes pushed the last piece of wiring into the pipe and asked, "What'd she say?"

Erick placed the pipe on the back of the stage and with Wes's help, used duct tape to anchor it to the wood platform. "Kam said you were very good-looking and she couldn't figure out why you weren't married." He chuckled indulgently and gave Wes a teasing look. "Hey, she likes you and you should take advantage! Dance with her." He pointed to the tall cottonwoods that grew on either side of the large stage. "Plenty of places to take her after the dance is over."

"Forget it," Wes muttered.

"Hey, you got to start living again after your divorce from Carla. It's tough living without a woman in your life." And then he laughed. "I ought to know. I'm trying to find one!"

An unwilling grin worked across Wes's mouth as he stepped back to admire their handiwork. "Don't worry, Erick, you'll find someone. Maybe not Amanda, but there are plenty of available women in Jackson."

Losing his smile, Erick said, "Yes, but how many of

them want to be a wife to a cowhand? Not many. I don't make much money or have the security women want."

"The right one will come along," Wes told him, slapping his broad shoulder. Erick was a good six feet two inches tall and built like a bulldozer. He was heavy-boned, strong and looked like a bodybuilder beneath his white cotton shirt and blue jeans. "Just be patient," Wes said. "You've got your whole life ahead of you."

"You're twenty-eight," Erick said, taking off his hat and mopping his brow with his handkerchief. "You sound like you're giving up on ever finding a woman who will want you again."

Wes shrugged. "I just don't want to fall in love with the wrong woman again, Erick. Once you get stung like that, you're gun-shy."

Grunting, Erick picked up the duct tape and the black electrical tape and threw them in his toolbox. "Well, I still say Kam Trayhern is *ideal* for you. She's no alcoholic, that's for sure. I think I've seen her with a glass of wine in her hand twice in the months she's been here. She's single, very beautiful and kindhearted. When Iris *and* Mr. Mason like someone, you know they're quality."

Wes said nothing as he picked up his toolbox. He wasn't about to admit to anyone that Kam seemed perfect in all ways to him. "Iris and Mr. Mason are good judges of character," he admitted. "You want to test the sound system now?"

"Yes," Erick said, walking around the corner of the stage with him. "I've got all the black boxes over there. If you can sit with them, I'll test the mikes on stage."

"You got a deal," Wes said, heading to where the series of electrical boxes and amplifiers were set. He was relieved to get away from talking about Kam with

Erick. The skin along his neck felt charged with electricity. The sensation moved down around his heart and then into his lower body. Trying to ignore it, Wes sat down at the table under the protective tent where the equipment was located. It wasn't unusual during July and August to see thunderstorms pop up because of the Tetons and surrounding mountains to the east. The valley was a place where the unseen down- and updrafts mixed with weather fronts barreling through the area. The consequence was sudden showers, which would dump lots of rain in a short time.

Wes wanted to stay busy. If he was busy, he was less likely to think of Kam. And of tonight…

"YOU LOOK BEAUTIFUL!" Iris crowed with delight as Kam showed off her country-girl outfit. She wore a simple blue gingham dress with several white petticoats beneath it. The dress harked back to the 1950s when square dancing was all the rage. Kam laughed awkwardly and stopped the spin. "I feel a little odd in this outfit, Iris."

"The whole staff is going to be wearing these costumes. You'll fit right in, don't worry. Besides, our dude-ranch patrons really enjoy it." She sighed. "I just loved the 1950s. It was such a wonderful time. There was no road rage, none of the heinous crimes there are today. We had good, clean fun. Oh, we had guys with their hot rods and street racing here and there, but that was all. There were no guns. No drugs. No wholesale killings. It was a time of innocence," she said, waving her finger at Kam.

"I wasn't even around then," Kam said, "but it sounds like a fairy tale compared to today." She smoothed down the soft folds of the skirt. She glanced down at her sad-dle shoes, a combination of brown and white leather. They were very comfortable, which Kam liked since she hoped to spend most of the night on her feet.

She walked over to Iris who was admiring her own outfit. The dress was red-and-white gingham, exactly like her own in every way but color. "Will the cowhands be wearing gingham shirts?"

"Oh, yes," Iris said, pleased. She sat in her suite on a butter-yellow leather couch. "Rudd puts out some money for white straw Stetsons for this celebration every year. Each cowhand gets a new hat and they like that. They cost money but they're worth it because they can handle the wear and tear of ranch life. The hands wear the gingham shirts and also receive a new ban-danna and hat. It's a lot of fun and a small way to thank all of them for their hard work."

Kam nodded and sat down on the arm of the leather chair next to the couch. Her petticoats raised the skirt a good six inches above her knees. Laughing, she tried to tame them but they were starched and thick and wouldn't be laid down.

"These petticoats are something else!"

"Nowadays, they don't exist. We're lucky we have an American factory that will still make them up for us. I loved petticoats, especially the swirl of them around your body when you dance. Speaking of dancing, you have been practicing square dancing with our instructor?"

"Yes, ma'am, I have." Kam grinned as she put her hands over her runaway petticoats.

Iris smiled and sipped her coffee and then set it back on the elk-antler table. "Everyone looks forward to this day. Our guests love coming back year after year. I like seeing their children grow up. It's always interesting to see them change as they go from being children to teenagers."

Groaning, Kam said, "I didn't like my teen years. I was so up and down emotionally."

"Every teen is," Iris counseled. She beamed over at Kam. "You going to snag a dance with Wes?"

Gulping, Kam avoided Iris's sparkling eyes. "I—well… I thought we were supposed to be available to dance with our guests, not the hired hands."

"Oh, that's not a hard-and-fast rule. Wes has eyes for you. Surely you know that by now?"

Yes, she did. And Kam tried with all her might to avoid the handsome cowboy at every turn. But sometimes, that didn't work. Looking over at Iris now, whose face was beaming, Kam wondered if the older woman wasn't trying to play matchmaker. Of course, Iris was the matriarch and Kam had seen her getting other couples together here at the ranch, too. Right now, Iris seemed to have her eye on blond-haired Erick, who was terribly good-looking and a wonderful person. Iris had two women in mind who lived in Jackson Hole. And she had invited both of them to tonight's celebration, but Erick didn't know that. Yes, there was no question that Iris was manipulative—in a good way—when she wanted to be.

"Wes is very nice," Kam began, sounding sensible. "But I'm not interested in a relationship right now, Iris."

"Why in the world not?" Iris demanded, frowning. "You're beautiful, you're single and you're nice. People weren't created to be alone, you know. In the Garden of Eden, God created Adam *and* Eve, don't forget." She wagged her finger over at Kam. "And you shouldn't be alone, either! No one should."

Kam saw Iris's care burning in her eyes, and it touched her deeply. Rudd had been alone and abandoned, and she and Trevor had stepped up to the plate to make a difference in his life. "I'll keep that in mind, Iris," Kam said softly.

"I expect you to dance with Wes tonight, young woman."

Kam rolled her eyes. "I'll try...."

ABOVE THE JAMBOREE, the stars twinkled, and Kam found wonder in the black blanket of the sky quilted with diamonds. The Coyote Band, composed of five young men dressed in cowboy outfits, worked with a caller who led a fast square dance. The floor was filled with happy couples—a mix of Elkhorn Ranch personnel and the ten families who had been lucky enough to reserve this week.

Everyone was in high spirits, the music drifting out into the darkness around the well-lit dance floor. Soft drinks, iced tea and beer flowed for the adults. As Kam stood off to one side, breathing hard after dancing with a guest, she drank deeply of the iced tea in her hand.

All night, she'd seen Wes on the dance floor. He and Erick were the most popular cowboys among the teenage girls. No wonder, she thought wryly; they were the best looking of the bunch. Erick seemed in particularly high demand and she had watched the shy young Swede literally blossom as the night went on. The two girls Iris had invited with Erick in mind were being elbowed out by teenage-girl guests who drooled over the muscular blond.

When the song ended, to her surprise, Kam saw Wes heading directly toward her. Instantly, her heart began to pound. He was without his hat, his short dark brown hair

gleaming beneath the lights. The feral look in his gray
eyes sent a frisson of desire straight from her heart into
her lower body. How badly she wanted to kiss him. She'd
had so many inappropriate dreams about this lone cowboy,
it was no wonder she kept feeling the urge to touch him.

Setting down her cup, she tried to smile as Wes came
up to her. He held out his rough and callused hand toward her.

"Last dance, Kam. How about it?"

His voice was low and sexy, making her heart spring
open as never before. The expression on his face was
that of a man wanting his woman. Gulping, she held
out her hand, her fingers sinking into his palm. As he
led her out on the clearing dance floor for a slow song,
Kam wondered what it would be like to feel his hands
move across her body. The thought was excruciatingly
sweet and filled her with intense yearning.

Wes took Kam into his arms and left just enough
space between them. What he wanted to do was pull
Kam even closer, but with so many onlookers, he wasn't
going to do that. He smiled. "I've been fighting myself."

"So have I." She saw his brown eyebrows lift in surprise. Giving him a nervous smile, Kam admitted, "Iris
has been wanting me to dance with you all night."

"So that's why she was over there so many times
whispering in your ear?" Wes chuckled. Could he tell
Kam how warm and soft she felt beneath his hands? He
touched the small of her back. She had such a strong,
straight spine. There was such pride in the way she
walked and squared her shoulders.

"Iris was urging me to ask you to dance."

"But you never did." Wes looked deeply into her
shadowed blue eyes, the pupils huge and black.

"I—uh…"

"Cat got your tongue?" Wes teased, swinging her around on the crowded dance floor.

"Not exactly," Kam admitted a little breathlessly, her breasts flush against his chest. The heat was instantaneous and she couldn't fight her attraction. She just wanted to get closer. Their upper bodies touched like feathers dancing in the wind.

"Was there a reason you didn't want to dance with me?" Wes figured he deserved a straight answer. If his desire for her was one-sided, then he'd savagely chop off the connection. He wasn't going to pine after a woman who didn't want him. Yet, looking into her eyes, he saw heat like summer lightning. It was the heat of a woman wanting her man. Wes wasn't too young to read that intent in her wide, glistening eyes. And when his gaze dropped to her luscious mouth and her lips parted, he nearly lost his mind. These were the lips he'd dreamt about touching. About taking as his own. What would her mouth feel like beneath his?

It was hard to think at all with Wes this close to her. Kam inhaled his male fragrance. It was an aphrodisiac to her spinning senses. She gazed upon his full mouth quirked in a boyish smile. Wes was a man but he also knew how to play, laugh and have fun. She'd seen it so many times in the past with the guests or the other cowhands. Wes was good with children and they idolized the tall, lanky cowboy. What to say to him? Her heart told her to tell the truth. If she did, she'd be walking into a relationship with him. Kam didn't want to lie to Wes, yet could she trust him with her secret?

As she looked into his stormy gray eyes, Kam felt no deviousness in him. He didn't manipulate people. What you saw was what you got. Plainspoken and honest was only one reason why she liked Wes. Opening her mouth and then closing it, Kam sighed. She felt Wes move his hand lingeringly down her spine, a slow movement that said so much more than words or a look. Every inch of her flesh reacted hotly to his grazing touch. A man-loving-his-woman kind of touch.

Suddenly, anxiety, fear and want soared through Kam. She wouldn't lie. Ever. It just was not in her nature. She felt awful enough as is. And she simply couldn't do it twice. "I really like you, but I'm not ready for a relationship right now." That was the truth.

His eyes flared and then turned feral again. A sweet panic flowed through her as he brought her solidly against him.

Gasping, Kam tried to pull away, but he just kept smiling like a hunter who had cornered his quarry. And then, just like that, he released her. Heart pounding, Kam frowned. Wes allowed her to keep six inches between them as they continued to dance around the floor. "I told you," she whispered, "I'm not ready."

Wes nodded and saw the anger in her eyes. "I'm sorry. It was good news and I just couldn't help it, Kam. I did let you go."

"Yes, you did." Oh, why wouldn't her heart settle down? Wes was treating her like a gentleman. His hand was barely touching her back now. Her other hand, entwined with his, was damp and sweaty. How badly she wanted Wes! It would be one thing if she were a virgin, but she was not. Kam understood the ache in her lower body that she knew Wes could heal. And yet, she refused to lead him on.

As the music began to slow and die away, they halted

on the dance floor. Kam didn't see it coming—one second, Wes was holding her at arm's length, the next, his head was coming down—his lips were upon her mouth.

The ending of the music, the laughter and chatter, all seemed to drift away from Kam. Wes's mouth moved down upon her lips gently, as if asking her to participate. His mouth was strong, searching and, before she could think about it, her lips parted. As his tongue moved slowly across her lower lip, a shiver of anticipation wove through her. His hands remained exactly where they had been before, but his mouth was wreaking a sweet havoc upon her. Warm breath cascaded against Kam's cheek as he deepened his kiss with her. She *wanted* this! And all her arguments and reasons melted beneath the onslaught of his very male, confident mouth. The scent of his aftershave, a lime essence, combined with his maleness. His lips molded strongly against hers, sliding, giving and taking.

One moment he was taking her. The next moment, Wes reluctantly withdrew from her mouth. Kam was so dizzy and shocked that if Wes hadn't been holding her, she'd have fallen. Her knees were weak. The heat and moisture between her legs sent a keening ache throughout her. Gasping for breath, she looked into his hooded gaze. There was no hint of apology in Wes's eyes. Gripping his hand because she felt boneless in that moment, she could only stare, thunderstruck, at his bold move.

And then, Kam saw that very male mouth hitch up in one corner, and he gave her that boyish smile that always softened her heart.

"That's a kiss between us to remind you that I'm waiting, Kam."

CHAPTER TEN

ALLISON SEETHED INSIDE. Who could blame her after such a disgusting display? Wes kissed Kam Trayhern so blatantly out on the dance floor. What could she do but turn away? Something had to be done to get rid of the girl! Kam was getting too chummy with the family. Allison had made quick work of the other five caregivers by paying them off. They'd given lame excuses for leaving. Everyone had a price, even Kam.

The only way to wrest power from Iris, who held an ironclad grip on her affairs, was to work secretly around her. Allison understood strategy and tactics from her years in Hollywood. If she wanted control, she wouldn't get it by being aboveboard and confrontational. No, the only way for her to take the power away from Iris was to add stress to her life. The old witch would break eventually.

Scowling, Allison left the area of the gala festivities as the fireworks began. She heard the celebratory crowd oohing and ahhing, but she didn't care. After entering her suite, she got out of her silly 1950s costume and threw it over the end of her bed. All she wanted was a long, luxurious bath with a glass of champagne in hand. That would help her think best. Rudd wouldn't be coming in until at least midnight and that left her a good hour alone. Time to devise a plan to get rid of Kam Trayhern.

"THAT WAS A heck of a celebration last night," Iris crowed as she sat at her desk the next morning. Kam was at her own desk with coffee in hand.

"It was wonderful," Kam said, noting her own hesitation. She couldn't help feeling confused. Wes had kissed her. The blazing look in his eyes branded her. What was there *not* to like about Wes? He was hardworking, honest and responsible. How many men had she met who were as good? Next to none.

Kam sipped the hot, black liquid and got down to the business of the day. Iris had entrusted her with the banking and accounting duties for the flower-essence business. Iris hated anything to do with numbers. The trust Iris had placed in Kam's hands—the money, the banking and movement of funds—was huge. She knew Iris was having trouble with her eyes and needed help.

"I saw Wes steal a kiss from you," Iris sang out, giving her a big smile. "That did my heart good."

"It was a surprise," Kam admitted, hoping that would end this topic of conversation. It was obvious Iris was a matchmaker at heart and was always trying to pair up her cowhands with women. Iris knew everyone in

Jackson Hole and she delighted in getting young people together. Clearly, Iris and Trevor had had a marriage made in heaven here on earth. So did her own adopted parents. If only she could be so lucky someday and have a dream marriage with a man who respected her, supported her and treated her as an equal. She hadn't found such a man—until now. Wes Sheridan held her heart whether he knew it or not. But now wasn't the time. She couldn't allow him to know how much he affected her.

Redirecting her thoughts, she got down to the business of paying bills. She had full control of a multimillion-dollar bank account and this left her breathless. There was so much money in the business bank account. She had talked to Iris about putting some of it into stocks, bonds, or a place where it could accrue more interest. Iris had shrugged, maintaining she'd always handled the finances the same way. Kam had countered that someone could steal the money because so much was in one account. Why not parcel it out to several accounts and only Iris would have the password and ability to get into them?

No, Iris didn't think that was necessary. The senior wanted to keep things simple. Kam understood, but felt uncomfortable dealing with so much money. Banks had been hacked into before and identity theft was a widespread problem. Still, Iris had to face these demons and protect her money. Maybe Kam could discuss this with Rudd first. He might understand the gravity of the situation and talk to Iris about changing some of her account procedures.

"You know," Iris said from across her office, "Wes is the son of Dan Sheridan. He's the owner of the second-largest ranch here in Wyoming, the Bar S. Did you know that?"

"No, I didn't," Kam admitted, transferring some funds electronically to an online vendor.

"Dan is an alcoholic, unfortunately," Iris told her. "When Wes left two years ago to come and work for us, his father disowned him. Wes was written out of his will so he'll never run his father's ranch. He has a brother and sister, but they won't have anything to do with their father or ranching, either. Wes was the only one who loved ranching. If you ask me, it's a pretty sad state of affairs for him. He's such a wonderful young man, don't you agree?"

Raising her brows, Kam looked over her computer monitor at Iris. In a bright yellow shift printed with sunflowers and green leaves, her hair slightly frizzed but held up on her head with a rubber band, the woman was full of sunshine, and Kam couldn't help smiling over her motives. "Now, why do I feel your matchmaker side coming out, Iris?"

"Humph!"

"I'm sorry to hear Wes has such an awful family life. I can't imagine being disowned." And she couldn't. And yet, when she went to Rudd with the truth, he might kick her off his land, disown her as Dan Sheridan had done to his son. Kam secretly grieved for Wes.

"I know. On his day off, he usually drives to Cody to meet his mother, Anne. He refuses to set foot on the Bar S, so he meets her in town. He talked to me about it one time."

"Oh?"

"Yes," Iris said. "One day, Wes seemed really upset. I kept nagging at him until he came clean. He asked me why his mother wouldn't leave his father. Dan had been verbally and emotionally abusive to Anne all their married life. Wes couldn't understand why she wouldn't walk away. I tried to tell him that women have this thing in them that doesn't like to leave hurt or sick animals. We had a long talk about alcoholism and how Anne is an enabler to her husband. Wes is very clear about what is going on and how the disease has infiltrated the entire family. I guess he's begged his mother to leave, but she won't. Anne's health is declining, and that's got Wes even more worried and upset. There's nothing he can do. I learned a long time ago the only life I could control was mine." She chuckled a little. "And even my life isn't that much under my control. You never know what's going to come out of left field and knock you on your butt."

Wasn't that the truth? "Wes has a really messy situation," Kam said, feeling sorry for him. Again, she felt lucky that her adopted family had been healthy and stable. What must Wes be going through on a daily basis?

"I feel so sorry for him," Iris told her. "There's not much he can do. His father now has diabetes, and yet he continues to drink like a fish. Anne is way overweight and has heart problems and high blood pressure. They're in their fifties and could have a long, good life but I don't think either of them are going to last much longer."

"What happens to the ranch, then?" Kam asked.

Shrugging, she said, "Who knows? The father has written all three children out of his will. It's a real shame. The ranch is profitable and he could make it as good as ours. But he won't get that chance." Then, Iris looked at Kam with intent. "You know, to some women, a man not having money might turn them off."

"Sure. But times have changed. A woman can take care of herself."

"So, the man you love doesn't have to be rich?"

Hearing the sly undertone in Iris's voice, Kam grinned. "You're matchmaking, Iris, and it won't work."

Iris had enough humility to look embarrassed at getting caught and grinned.

"Wes and you would make a beautiful couple. You're both hardworking, you have integrity and morals." Iris's brows dipped. "Unlike *some* people on this ranch."

Kam nodded patiently. "I'm really sorry for what you go through with Allison. Rudd is such a nice man. I can see why you're so proud of him. We don't always marry the right person, you know."

"Humph."

"I think Allison tries, but from what I can see, she really isn't a rancher's wife. She's tied to Hollywood and loves the glamour, the attention and press. Nothing wrong with that."

"But you won't get much of that out here in Wyoming," Iris said, jabbing her finger toward the floor. With a shake of her head, she muttered, "I just don't know what got into him to marry her. And then, eight months later, Regan was born."

"She was a preemie?"

"I guess," Iris said glumly. "She had a few problems, but then she rebounded and has been healthy ever since, thank goodness."

"Your two grandchildren are pretty nice, Iris."

"Yes, they are. You know how I worry about Zach. He can't keep his head in those darn games forever.

"You did a good thing," Kam said, smiling. "Your ploy to get Zach involved was brilliant."

"Well, I had to do something to dislodge that boy from those stupid, violent computer games. Maybe Regan can accomplish what I can't." She winked. "They don't call me the Silver Fox for nothing."

Kam laughed with her. "Let's keep our fingers crossed."

"You must be my lucky touchstone. Good things seem to happen when you're around."

A lucky touchstone. Kam had never thought of herself as lucky for anyone. "If it works, Iris, it's because of you and your plan, not me."

"Oh no you don't." Iris waved a finger at her. "Every once in a while a person comes into your life who does nothing but bring you happiness and good fortune. You're that person to me."

A wave of love hit Kam. More than ever, she wished Iris was her grandmother. "Iris, you've given all that and more to me by just being you."

Chortling, Iris said, "Well, what do you know? We're a mutual admiration society!"

CHAPTER ELEVEN

KAM COULDN'T LIVE with her cowardice anymore. Pressured by Wes's growing interest and her own attachment to him and the Masons, she needed to confront them soon. On a warm, muggy July night, she sat in the living room of her suite and called her family.

"Hello? Morgan Trayhern speaking."

Feeling an instant of relief, Kam cradled the phone between her ear and shoulder. "Hi, Dad."

"Kam! It's good to hear from you. How are things? Last time you called, you were in a real quandary."

Closing her eyes, Kam whispered, "I'm in an even worse one now."

"Oh?"

Just hearing Morgan's deep, soothing voice settled her knotted gut. "Dad, I'm *such* a coward. I can't believe how scared I am. The more I stay here, the more I love

Iris and Rudd. I get along okay with his son and daughter. Allison ignores me and treats me like hired help, but she does that to everyone, so I don't feel picked upon."

"Honey, I know you're scared that Rudd Mason will reject you. Your whole life is hanging in the balance. For the record, you're not a coward. There are just different ways to approach this situation."

"If it was you, Dad, you'd have just walked up to Rudd and told him the truth."

"But it's not me," he said gently.

Kam rubbed her furrowed brow. "Oh, how I wish I was home right now. I have horrible insomnia, and it's getting worse. All I can do is think about talking to Rudd. And then," her voice dropped, "Wes is…interested in me."

"Oh, that cowboy you like?"

"Yes, him."

"What's so wrong with that?"

Kam opened her eyes and stared at the light and shadows thrown about the living room by the single stained-glass water-lily lamp next to the couch. "I feel like I'm leading him on."

"And so that is driving you to talk with Rudd?"

Kam was always surprised at his insight. "Yes, it is. I've made up my mind to talk to him tomorrow morning. He's usually in the office after the rush of getting the dude-ranch guests off for their morning jaunts. It's usually quiet then and he's alone."

"Isn't there a more private place? What if someone comes into the office? Do you really want an interruption?"

"I didn't think of that. You're right."

"Why not invite him out of the office to your suite?

There, you can talk behind closed doors without interruption."

"That's a better idea."

"Just tell Iris that you'll be gone for an hour and let
her know where you are in case she needs you," Morgan counseled.

"Right. I'm so glad I called you, Dad. I'm still scared
to death, but now I don't feel so out of control."

Morgan chuckled. "Listen, this is the most important
moment of your life, Kam. You know who your mom
was. Now, you're potentially looking at your father.
When you're done talking with Rudd, why not give
us a call? We're here to support you any way we can."

A sheet of love flowed through Kam. "Thanks, Dad.
I will. Can you tell Mom that I called?"

"Oh, you can count on that." Morgan laughed. "She'd
beat me within an inch of my life if I didn't tell all."

Laughing with him, Kam sobered. "Thanks. You
know that even if Rudd turns out to be my biological
father, you'll always be my dad."

"Listen," Morgan said, his voice roughened, "we love
and support you, Kam. We always will. We'll be happy
to play whatever role in your life you want. You're in
control here."

"So," Rudd said, smiling and making himself comfortable on Kam's leather couch, "what's this all about?"

Kam sat down in the chair opposite the couch.

She could hear her heart pounding in her ears. In her
hand was the photo. "Rudd, I feel bad about coming
here under the radar," she began in a shaky tone. "And
I want to apologize for that, first of all."

He frowned. "What do you mean?"

As if an invisible hand squeezed off her breathing, Kam got up and handed him the photo. "I think I need to start with this."

Rudd took the photo. His brows moved downward. "This is from a long time ago." And then he looked intently over at Kam. She had paled, her cheeks were no longer flushed. Rudd saw real fear in her eyes, as if she were warding off a blow.

"Do you remember that time?" she asked him quietly, hands damp and clasped in her lap.

"Sort of. I was attending a cattle convention in Los Angeles. That was a time when genetics and cloning were first coming on the scene. I was interested in the process and attended."

"Do you know the people in that photo?"

"I know the man in the lab coat was a veterinary researcher with a gene-based company. And the other guy was a salesman for a pharmaceutical company."

"And the woman?" Kam could barely breathe, her voice sounding strained.

Rudd sat back, still staring at the photo. His mouth twisted faintly beneath his mustache. "I think I need to ask you something first," he began cautiously. Holding up the photo, he said, "How did you come into possession of this?"

The crush of fear settled around Kam. But for once, she couldn't be the coward. "It's a long story, Rudd, but I need to tell you…" Kam began with the devastating earthquake in Los Angeles. As she rapidly covered the events, Rudd's eyes widened. He would look down at the photo and then up at her. Tears pricked the back of her eyes but Kam forced them away as she finished the story. Opening her hands, she whispered unsteadily,

"I came here to find out if you're my father. The only way to know is for you to get a DNA test. I'm really sorry I wasn't more honest and up-front with you, Rudd. I—I'm just trying to find the truth. That photo is all I have of my mom and you're in it. Did anything happen between you two?"

The words died on her lips as she witnessed many emotions move across Rudd's weathered, lined face. For a moment, he closed his eyes, the photo resting in his hand. And then he opened them and stared at her.

"My God," he rasped. "You look just like her...."

Kam gulped.

Rudd quirked his mouth. "I didn't know."

"What didn't you know?"

Rudd looked up at the ceiling, his mouth drawn in a grimace. "I met two women at that conference. One was your mother and the other was Allison."

"I knew Allison was there. Iris told me how you two met."

"Yes, she was a Hollywood starlet hired by this one pharmaceutical company to present their products. Damn it...."

Anguish and anger flared in Rudd's eyes.

"Then, there is the possibility I'm your daughter?" Kam asked.

"Yes," he said, finally. Putting the photo on the coffee table, he rubbed his face. He shook his head. "This is a hell of a shock."

"I'm sorry. I should have been more up-front about it."

"Wouldn't have mattered," Rudd grumbled.

"Will you get a DNA test to prove whether I'm your daughter?"

Rudd nodded. "Of course." Suddenly getting up, he pushed his hands into his pockets and moved tensely around the room.

"This really makes things messy with your wife and children," Kam whispered. "I'm sorry, Rudd. I didn't mean to hurt anyone."

Rudd looked out the picture window at the lush, green valley. In the distance, brown-and-white Herefords grazed contentedly on the spring grass. "I didn't know about you, Kam." Turning, he stared over at her. "I would *never* father a child and then walk away. I was adopted so I know what it means not to have parents."

"I understand," Kam admitted. "You're honest and responsible."

"I am," he said. Sighing, Rudd glanced at his scuffed cowboy boots. "She never contacted me. Your mother never told me she was pregnant with you."

"I don't know why," Kam answered lamely. "The earthquake destroyed most of the stuff in her apartment. She had a diary, but it was nothing but ashes."

"Damn." Rudd clenched his fist and paced around the living room. "I *tried* to call her after I got home from Los Angeles. She never answered my calls. I chalked it up to a one-night stand after that. Allison was chasing me and frankly, I forgot about your mother shortly after that. Less than a month later, we married. When Allison came to the ranch, my life changed. I wish I'd known."

Hearing the terrible regret in his heavy tone, Kam wrung her hands. She watched as Rudd continued to pace like an imprisoned animal in a cage. "I wish I could get inside my mother's head to know what she was thinking back then. I'm really sorry to stir up the past."

Rudd turned toward her, his arms across his chest.

"None of this is your fault, Kam. You're the victim in this."

"I've never felt like a victim."

"I'm glad the Trayhern family adopted you. And I'm glad you had a good home life." And Rudd scowled. "I'll call my doctor today and drive to Jackson and get the DNA test started. I don't want to leave you hanging fire any longer than you have been already. If nothing else, you deserve to know one way or another. And so do I."

Kam cringed, realizing Rudd would have to tell Allison. No doubt the woman wouldn't take kindly to this revelation. She'd probably come after Kam, accusing her of being a spy among them. Yes, Kam deserved that assault. She hadn't been honest from the beginning. "I'm sorry I was such a coward about this, Rudd. I was so scared you'd throw me out."

Rudd sat back down and stared at her. "I'm trying to understand your side of it, Kam. On one level, I know the hell you've gone through. We're more alike than you realize."

Kam nodded, tears brimming in her eyes, and she could no longer stop them. "When Iris told me you were adopted, my gut just knotted. I wondered what the chances were of an adopted boy growing up to create another adopted child."

Rudd shook his head. "If you *are* my daughter, I am so deeply sorry, Kam. I just wish…well," he sighed, and rested his hands across his knees, "I can't go back and change things. All we can do is move forward now."

"And if I'm not your daughter," Kam whispered, "I'm sorry for the trouble that I know this will cause. I realize you have to tell your wife and mother."

"I'd like to wait to tell them, Kam. For now, I want

to keep this between us until I get the DNA test results back."

"Of course," Kam said.

"Thanks for coming to me privately about this," Rudd said. "I appreciate it."

"All I see is that this thing that happened twenty-eight years ago is going to hurt a lot of people. I hate hurting people, but I had to know the truth. You understand?"

"Listen," Rudd growled unhappily, "I went through this with my father, who left me after I was born. I hunted him down, I found him and I confronted him." He rubbed his callused hands together and slid them along his jeans. "It wasn't easy. I was just as scared as you're feeling. I know what you're going through."

Trying to breathe fully, Kam searched his face. "If the test comes back negative, then I'll leave. I don't want to cause you any more pain or discomfort. And I have to try to find my biological father."

Rudd nodded. "I know what you're saying. I had that same feeling and *had* to track down my father. I had to find out why he walked out of my life. It's a wound, Kam. Unless you heal it, it'll keep bleeding you dry every day of your life. I know..."

Kam swallowed hard as tears ran. "I always feel this ache in my heart that nothing and no one can ever fill."

"Well, let's see where we go from here, shall we?" He stood. "As soon as I know about the DNA test, we'll sit down together and go over it with my doctor in town. I assume you have your DNA tests with you?"

"Yes. I'll give you a copy of it to give to your doctor."

"Fair enough," Rudd said. He came over to her and placed his hand on her shoulder.

His hand felt comforting to Kam. Her heart was raw and hurting, yet, Rudd had the decency and understanding to know what she needed—a hand of reassurance. "Life is scary, Rudd. I'm more scared now than before." Kam shook her head and held his gaze. "How can that be?"

"Well, you go from being scared about confronting the person you think is your father to being scared about what the DNA test will reveal. You're still up on the bubble. If I don't reject you, then the test could. And this is all about rejection."

"You're right," Kam admitted. She touched his hand and said, "Thank you. You've made this easy for me. Maybe now my nightmares will go away."

"I hope so, Kam. We'll get through this together." Rudd smiled warmly.

CHAPTER TWELVE

WES SPOTTED KAM walking from the ranch-house of-fice toward the barn. He was about to intercept her to talk with her privately about that kiss three nights ago. His cell phone rang.

Cursing softly, Wes pulled it off his belt. "Wes Sheridan."

"Wes?"

"Hi, Mom," he said, watching Kam walk to the barn. She must be going for a midafternoon ride on Freckles, which was unusual for her.

"Son, your father just had a heart attack. He's in the Cody hospital. It's serious, Wes."

He heard the tears in his mother's trembling voice. "How serious?" he demanded.

"The doctors don't know if he's going to make it or not." She sobbed. "This morning…well…he was ranting and raving like he always does at the breakfast table. And—and he suddenly clutched his chest and fell out of the chair. I didn't know what to do. I called 911 and they got there as soon as they could."

Heart squeezing, Wes turned away from the barn and concentrated on the call. "How can I help?"

"I can't run this ranch by myself. You know your father would never let me into the business side of things. And our last manager walked off two weeks ago. He'd had enough of Dan's abuse. The men are looking to me to tell them what to do and I don't have a clue."

"Have you called Chris and Rachel?"

"I have," she sniffed. "They both have jobs they can't walk away from and they can't help me."

Wes rubbed his mouth with the back of his hand. The warmth of the sun beat down upon his back as he stood by the corral. Most of the dudes were out on their afternoon trail ride. "What's the prognosis?"

"Not good." Anne sobbed and then whispered, "I'm sorry, Wes. I'm in shock over this. Even with him being an alcoholic, I never expected him to keel over from a heart attack. I need someone here. The cattle have to be fed. The horses…"

"Yeah, I get it," he whispered grimly. "Let me talk to Rudd Mason. I'll ask him for a leave of absence. I can't divide myself between here and there."

"I—I know. I'm so sorry to ask this of you, Wes."

Grimly, he rasped, "It's okay, Mom. This isn't your fault. I'll be there as soon as I can. I'll pack some stuff in my truck and take off within the hour."

"Thanks, honey. I hope Mr. Mason won't get angry with you. He won't fire you, will he?"

"No. He's fair-minded about things like this," Wes

said, already walking toward the office. He didn't add that Rudd knew all about his messy family dynamic.

"Thank you again, honey. I have to stay here at the hospital. Dan is unconscious. I need to find out what else can be done for him."

Wes snapped the cell phone closed and settled it back on his belt. Mouth tight with tension, he quickly walked to the office, mounted the stairs and stepped inside. Rudd had just sat down at his desk behind the office counter. Despite his own pain and shock, Wes noted his boss's sad expression. For a moment, he realized Kam had just left the office for the barn. Rudd seemed very upset, to the point where Wes saw tears in the man's eyes.

Wes allowed his boss to compose himself before launching into his new dilemma.

"So do you think he'll recover?" Rudd asked, scowling.

"I don't know." *I don't care.* But Wes didn't say it out loud.

"Of course, go home," Rudd said, concerned. "Will your brother and sister be able to pitch in and help you at the ranch?"

"No," Wes admitted. "They live in Cheyenne and have nine-to-five jobs, unlike me. I'm sure their employers would give them time off, but they are refusing to come to the ranch. It's a pretty bitter situation."

"Yeah, ranching is 24/7," Rudd murmured. "Of course, go home, Wes. Stay in touch and let me know if we can help you. I hope your father makes it."

Nodding, Wes walked out of the office and headed for the bunkhouse where he kept his belongings. On the way, he saw Kam had led Freckles outside the barn and was ready to go for a ride. Turning on his heel, he moved in her direction.

"Kam?" he called.

Kam had just settled into the saddle when she heard Wes call to her.

Wes saw surprise in Kam's eyes but there was a different expression on her face that he couldn't decipher. He forced a smile he didn't feel. Placing his hand on the paint gelding's neck, he looked up at her. She wore her tan Stetson and looked like a rancher's wife. The thought struck him hard. Wes knew instinctively she would make a great frontier woman out here in Wyoming. She had adjusted to ranch life so easily and with such passion. But he certainly didn't see happiness in those bright blue eyes now.

"Wes?"

"This will take only a minute," he assured her.

Kam felt heat rushing into her face. For once, she wished she didn't blush so easily. "Sure."

"I wanted a chance to talk to you…the kiss…about us."

"I did, too," Kam admitted.

"I meant what I said. I'll wait. I like you and I want to see what happens."

Heart thudding, Kam closed her eyes momentarily and then opened them. "I don't know, Wes." She was unable to tell him the truth and it hurt her even more than withholding it from Rudd. His eyes darkened with pain and it was all her fault. But it wasn't fair to let him think there could be a relationship, not with everything up in the air.

"Will you at least tell me why?" he demanded. Boring into her gaze, Wes felt the rest of his world falling from beneath him. All these months, he'd silently pined for Kam and fought himself. Until the dance. Until holding her so close and smelling her womanly scent. All his reserve had shattered in that moment. Kam had looked so beautiful, so alluring that Wes couldn't help but kiss her. And now, he had to hurry out of here and get home to his father's ranch. It was the last thing Wes wanted to do.

"It's just not the right time," Kam pleaded softly.

"I told you I would wait."

"That's not it," Kam protested. "I just can't say much right now, Wes. I wish I could, but I can't."

Suddenly cautious, Wes wondered if Kam had a boyfriend. There was so much he didn't know about her. Maybe she was doing him a favor. "Okay, I hear you. I just wanted to let you know I have to leave the ranch. I don't know for how long." He relayed the news about his father and she reacted.

"Your father? Oh, no, Wes. I'm so sorry...."

"I'm not, Kam. But that's a long story that I've never shared with you," he said grimly.

Kam noted the anger banked in his eyes and heard it in his voice. "Family problems?" she guessed, her voice more gentle. Above all, Kam didn't want to let on that Iris had filled her in on Wes's troubled family.

"Yeah. Plenty of them. Anyway, I don't have time to share them with you right now." Searching her face, Wes said, "Can I stay in touch with you, Kam? Cody isn't that far from Jackson."

"Of course you can," she said, touching his hand as it rested on her mount's neck. "If there's anything I can do to help?"

Her hand was like balm to his shattered heart. "Thanks for asking. I don't know what I'm walking into at the ranch. It's been two years. I appreciate your offer, though." Wes wanted to believe Kam had reached out because she liked him, but he knew better. She had told him in so many words that a relationship wasn't possible. Yet, as a friend, she was offering her help. He expected that of Kam. She was that kind of person. But he didn't want her as a friend. He wanted to pursue a serious relationship with her.

When Wes removed his hand, Kam felt bereft and did her best to hide it. Right now, her life was up in the air and she was unsure what would happen next. "I'll miss you," she admitted. "You're a linchpin around here. I'm sure Rudd will miss you, too. You're his right-hand man next to Chappy."

"I'll miss being here," Wes confided, his voice off-key. Settling his hat more firmly on his head as the breeze picked up, Wes gave Kam an apologetic look. "I've got to get going, Kam."

"My prayers are with your father and mother," she called, as he walked away.

Kam's heart twisted in her chest even more. She longed to talk to someone about how she felt watching Wes disappear into the nearby bunkhouse. He always made her feel special. And his commanding kiss still lingered hotly in her memory. Kam didn't dare tell him how much she'd enjoyed his contact. Not yet. She didn't dare hope that he'd be there when the dust settled.

Turning the horse, Kam nudged her heels into Freckles's sides and aimed him at one of the many trails just outside the corral area. All she wanted was to be alone with her roiling feelings. Tears brimmed in her eyes as she went down the trail. Alone, she could cry—partly out of relief and partly out of fear of an unknown future.

RUDD SAT IN the office with the radio playing in the background. It had been a hell of a day. He'd already driven into town, given Doc Jones the DNA results that Kam had given him and gotten the test himself. Mouth tightening, he wondered at the results. If Kam was his daughter, it would send a shock like a bolt of lightning through his family. He could not disavow Kam. That wasn't right. Guilt ate at his conscience. Unable to understand what had happened, Rudd shook his head. He'd never had unprotected sex and yet, somehow, Elizabeth had become pregnant.

Looking back on that day, Rudd realized how crazy it had been. He'd been drawn to Tracy Elizabeth Fielding immediately, and then, after he'd made a date with her for dinner, Allison had crashed into his life. He hadn't been expecting a Hollywood starlet at the huge convention. Oh, it was true, she was dressed skimpily, like a fishing lure to pull in the cowboys. When Allison had latched onto him after finding out he owned the largest ranch in Wyoming, Rudd had felt flattered. A lot of ranch owners eyed him with envy as she hung herself on him. Flattered and flustered, Rudd had agreed to take Allison out for a drink around four o'clock that day. That was when she got off this gig, she'd whispered in his ear.

Looking back, Rudd couldn't believe what he'd done because it was so out of character for him. He was a gentleman and a hardworking rancher. Being in Los Angeles at this glittering convention was a first for him. Maybe he was starstruck by Allison's flirting and beauty. Maybe his ego got way out of hand, he decided sourly. After drinks at the bar at a nearby hotel, Allison had taken him to her room. He'd had protected sex with her. And then, at eight o'clock that night, he'd had dinner with Elizabeth. She was completely different from Allison, and Rudd had been smitten, spending the night because he'd wanted to.

The next morning, Rudd had left while Elizabeth was sleeping. He had an early plane to catch back to Cheyenne. He'd left a note and his business card, asking Elizabeth to call him. But she never did.

Allison had, however. Over the phone, she'd giggled and told him that she just might drop by unannounced and see him and his ranch. Rudd had believed it was just bedroom talk. But damned if Allison hadn't shown up five days later, dressed like a Hollywood actress and looking good in a tight red dress.

Shaking his head, Rudd looked up across the desk. It was nearly dinnertime and he could see everyone drifting toward the dining hall. He thought back to the day Allison had arrived. After a whirlwind courtship of ten days, they were married by the justice of the peace in Jackson. Eight months later, Regan was born. She had red hair just like him and Rudd fell in love with the little tyke cradled in Allison's arms. For Rudd, it seemed as if he were in some wild, unimaginable dream. His parents had been against him marrying Allison. They didn't understand his infatuation and begged him not to consummate the relationship. A woman who was that hot in bed, who made him feel like a king among men....well, that said it all.

Now, twenty-eight years later, Rudd had seen his marriage slowly fall apart. He couldn't admit that to his mother or anyone, really. Allison had stopped having sex with him shortly after Zach was born. She continued to keep her Hollywood ties, leaving the ranch for much of the winter each year. Oh, she said it was to get gigs in Hollywood, but Rudd rarely saw her in commercials or television shows. He often wondered what Allison did out there but didn't have the courage to ask. Somehow, Rudd wanted to leave that can of worms alone and concentrate on being a good father to his two young children. They couldn't understand why their mother left for half a year.

His life had been a mess, Rudd realized as he looked back over all of it. What if he'd married Elizabeth Fielding? He wasn't sure she would have wanted him, of course. Would their lives have been so different? The worst of it was, they had possibly produced a daughter from that one night together. Nervously tugging on his handlebar mustache, Rudd had a sinking feeling that the DNA test would confirm that Kam was his daughter.

What then? Rudd winced inwardly. He'd have to tell his family. All of them. His stomach churned over the prospect. He'd been adopted and might have created an orphan, as well. His father had abandoned him. Was it a stain on his genes? Rudd had walked away from his child, left her hanging just as his father had done to him. The pain of that realization sunk into Rudd as never before. Intuitively, he knew Kam was his daughter. It was all too clear to him at this point. The father's sins were carried through the son by some strange, unknown genetic predisposition.

Rudd stood and closed up the office. In an hour he'd have to carry this shocking secret, all while sitting down with his family at the dinner table. Under no circumstances was he going to let anyone know what had just transpired until the test came back. When it did, he had no doubt everything in his life would change. Rudd shut off the light and turned on the answer machine for the telephone. In his tightened gut, he prepared himself for the moment when all hell would break loose.

CHAPTER THIRTEEN

"HELLO?" LAURA TRAYHERN SAID.

Kam closed her eyes, relief surging through her. She sat in her suite, the bedroom door closed so that in case someone entered, they would not overhear the conversation. "Mom? It's Kam. I need to talk to you."

"You spoke to Rudd," Laura guessed.

Curling up on her bed, Kam leaned against the headboard. She smoothed out her pink silk pajamas nervously with her hand. "How did you guess?"

"I can hear it in your voice. Are you all right? How did Rudd take the news?"

Kam told her everything. She glanced outside the window near her bed, the darkness revealing a star-sprinkled sky. "Mom, I'm so scared."

"The worst is over," Laura soothed. "Did he take it well?"

"He did but there was so much pain in his eyes, Mom. I couldn't decipher what it was all about."

"Don't try to read someone. Let Rudd tell you what his pain is about," Laura counseled. "We humans are not very good at reading people. And when we think we have read someone, it's usually through the lens of ourselves."

"Yes," Kam said, smiling a little. "I remember. You called it projection."

Laura laughed softly. "Exactly."

"There's more to this," Kam told her in a low tone, feeling her own anguish. "It's about Wes."

"Oh, that young man you like so much?"

Wincing, Kam said, "Yes, him." She filled Laura in on the latest. And then Kam added, "My heart is with Wes. I wish I could just leave and go help him with the ranch. But I can't. Rudd told me when he got back from the doctor's office that it would take a week to get the DNA results back. Maybe even a little sooner. I can't just take off and drive to Cody to be with Wes."

"Hmmm," Laura said, "that's true. You have a responsibility to Rudd, first of all."

"Wes was booted out of his family by his father, Dan," Kam said, sadness in her voice. "Now, Dan's in the hospital and they don't know if he'll recover from the heart attack or not. I keep wondering if Wes will go see him."

"That's a tough call," Laura said. "Will Wes allow his hurt and anger to stop him from saying goodbye to his father?"

"There's no love lost between them."

"I know, but when it comes right down to it, Dan is his father. Whether Dan was a good or bad father doesn't matter. I think the bigger question is, will Wes rise above all the hurt to say farewell? Maybe even forgive Dan? If he doesn't try to make amends with his father, Wes will live with that choice the rest of his life. And that's a hard thing to carry."

"You're always so wise," Kam said.

"It comes from life experience. Sometimes, no matter how much pain a parent has caused a child, one hopes for forgiveness. And in some cases, that doesn't happen."

"I think the broken connection between Wes and his father is permanent," Kam said. "I just wish I could be there to support him. Wes said at one time there were twenty ranch hands. There was a manager, but he quit two weeks before Dan had the heart attack. Now, Wes is going to have to step in and manage the whole place."

"Until two years ago, Wes was under his father's wing," Laura reminded her. "So, it isn't going to be that tough for Wes to fill his father's shoes in his absence," Laura countered.

"Yes, but if his father dies, he's written Wes out of the will. I suppose he's left the ranch to his wife, Anne. But who knows?"

"Then, if that happens, I'm sure Anne will ask Wes to come back and run it since his two siblings can't."

"True," Kam murmured, not having thought of that angle.

"You can always call Wes. I'm sure that would lift his spirits."

Kam brightened at the idea. "I could. But I've been less than forthright about who I am and why I really came to the Elkhorn Ranch."

"That's something you should handle with him in

person, then, not on a phone call, Kam. Especially when he's stressed out over his father. He doesn't need that kind of emotional stuff on top of what has already happened."

"You always did teach me about timing, Mom. How important it is."

"It's *very* important, Kam. Never more than now."

"Speaking of timing," Kam said, looking out into the darkened night. "If I am Rudd's daughter, how is he going to break the news to his family?"

RUDD SAT WITH the results of the DNA test outside the doctor's office. Overhead, a cold front pushed through over the valley, threatening rain. The wind blew in powerful gusts, sometimes rocking the truck. Mouth grim, he stared at the results.

Kam Trayhern was his daughter.

His one night with Tracy Elizabeth Fielding had produced a child. Looking up, Rudd stared sightlessly across the parking lot. Plenty of tourists came to Jackson, which was the gateway to two national parks north of the cow town. People dotted the parking lot like colorfully painted birds in their summer apparel. He watched them smiling and laughing.

My God, what have I done?

His conscience was raw with guilt. Rudd placed the results back into the manila envelope. What was he going to do? Without a doubt, Allison would fly into a royal rage. Not that he could blame her. To have a child out of wedlock, well, he just never saw that one coming. Rudd dreaded the confrontation.

Pushing the hat back on his head, he gazed up at the pregnant dark gray clouds drifting across the town. A few splatters of rain hit the windshield. What would his son and daughter think of him? That ate more at Rudd than anything. Oh, he knew today's generation thought nothing of having a child out of wedlock, but he came from a different time where that was frowned upon. Rudd had always presented himself as an upstanding citizen. He'd constantly told his children to aspire to keep their moral compass even with today's degraded values. Integrity was everything.

Where was his integrity now? How could he face his children with this new truth about his early life? It hurt. He hurt. Rubbing his aching gut, Rudd closed his eyes for a moment. This was a day when he wished he wasn't alive. That thought came and went quickly. Rudd knew he had to do the right thing and take the heat that was coming.

What about Kam? Rudd had been adopted and knew how terrible it felt not to know one's parents. He had known his mother. Kam had never had the opportunity to know Elizabeth because she'd died when her daughter was only three months old. Kam had never known him, her biological father, either. Rudd saw that Kam's life had been a lot harder than his. Like her, he'd lost his mother at birth. The only difference was that Rudd's father didn't want to be a parent. His father had foisted him off to the state to take care of him. Kam had never known anything about her father so she had never felt the pain of a father's rejection.

Rubbing his brow, Rudd thought about the last couple of months while Kam had been at the ranch. Clearly, his mother doted upon her and now Rudd understood why. There was a silent connection between him, his mother and Kam. Iris had instinctively embraced Kam as a granddaughter more than as an employee. These results explained why. Somehow, unconsciously, Iris sensed that Kam was kin. Rudd knew that Allison wouldn't embrace Kam at all. His wife would see Kam as an outsider causing nothing but trouble.

Quirking his mouth, Rudd pulled the hat down on his head and started the engine on his truck. Might as well get this over with, he thought. The longer he let it go, the more he and Kam would suffer.

"YOU'RE MY DAUGHTER," Rudd told Kam in the privacy of her suite. He handed her the test results. The expression on her face was one of absolute joy and it raised his spirits. She sat down on the couch and studied the report.

Rudd took the chair opposite and added, "I'll recognize you legally as my daughter, Kam."

Kam's hands trembled as she stared down at the DNA data. She heard the determination in Rudd's tone. Tears struck her and she self-consciously wiped them away. Looking up, she said in a wobbly voice, "I was so hoping you were my father...." Sniffing, she added, "Thank you. There were a lot of things you could have done instead, but you didn't."

Rudd shook his head and held her tear-filled gaze. "What?" he asked gently. "Turn you away like my real father did me? No, I know what that felt like, Kam. I'd never knowingly do that to anyone. Not ever."

Unable to stop the tears, Kam stood and found some tissues. Blotting her eyes, she went over to where Rudd was sitting. The deep lines across his broad weather-beaten forehead and bracketing his mouth told her the anguish he was experiencing. "The only unanswered question is why my mother never contacted you. She was pregnant with me, Rudd. Why didn't she tell you?"

Shrugging, Rudd felt the pain whisper through his heart. "I don't know, Kam. I wish I did."

A huge sigh broke from Kam's lips. She blotted her cheeks dry of tears. "This isn't easy on anyone. I'm sorry to come walking in here like this. I can see you're suffering." Kam looked at the closed door to her suite. "Are you going to tell your family about me?"

"Of course," Rudd said. He reached out and slid his hand into hers and squeezed it gently. "We'll all get through this, Kam. Don't apologize. You're the victim in this. You're innocent. I'm the guy who did it and walked away. It's my load to carry, not yours."

His hand was rough, firm and warm. Kam absorbed his touch like a starving flower. "Thank you…" was all she could manage to get out of her tightened throat.

Rudd released her hand, stood up and brought his long arms around her. He embraced her gently and patted her on the back. "I'm sorry, Kam. I really am," he told her in a strangled tone. "I didn't mean to leave you out there in the world alone. I know what it's like myself. I almost can't stand that I did it to someone else."

Resting her cheek against his chest, Kam closed her eyes and simply absorbed her father's strong arms, his roughened voice and his awkward attempts to pat her back. Rudd Mason was trying to comfort her. Kam's heart flew open with relief and joy. Wrapping her arms around his waist, she sobbed against his white cotton shirt.

"It's gonna be okay," Rudd murmured. "You have many years of grief and loss to cry out. Just let me hold you, Kam. The pain will work its way out of you."

Kam didn't know how long she cried in her father's arms. Rudd was strong and steady. He held her like the fragile being she was. Finally, Kam lifted her head from his shirt front.

"I got your shirt wet," she mumbled apologetically, touching the material.

Rudd smiled and released her. "Don't worry about it. I have lots of bridges to repair with you, Kam." He held her at arm's length, cupping her shoulders and looking deeply into her blue eyes. "I hope you can forgive me. I promise, I'll try to make up for lost time if you'll let me. I want you to stay here with us. You've already made yourself an important part of this ranch. Iris loves you dearly, and I can see why you and my mother get along so well. Somehow, she must have felt that connection." He managed a wry smile. "Women continually amaze me. Especially my mother."

"Thank you for everything, Rudd." Kam smiled tearfully.

"You can call me Dad, Father, Pop, Pa or whatever you like," he said gravely. "I'll answer to anything."

Touched, Kam gulped and wiped the remnants of her tears away. As Rudd released her, she saw the grief and sadness on his face. Somehow, Kam wanted to lift his spirits. "There's nothing to forgive, Rudd. You didn't know my mother was pregnant. You tried to contact her, but she didn't return your calls. There's no fault here on your part."

"Okay, sunshine." Rudd smiled a little. "Hey, that fits you."

"I like it."

"It just seemed," Rudd said, hooking his thumbs into his belt, "that when you came, Iris perked up tremendously. She's in better health now than I've seen her in the last decade. And I felt happy about having you here, too. Oh, I know you came as a caregiver, but I felt there was something more to you." Shaking his head, Rudd said, "Now, I understand why. When I saw you, my spirit always lifted. No matter what was going on, or how tough the day was or the stresses involved, seeing you did my heart good."

"Thank you for that, Rudd." Kam stuffed the damp tissue into her pocket. "We just need time to adjust."

"Of course," he said, picking up his hat from the glass coffee table. "There's no rush here to call me anything but Rudd. I understand. We have a lot of things to deal with," he warned Kam, his hat dangling between his fingers. "I need to talk with my wife."

Grimacing, Kam said, "I don't envy you at all."

"No, I don't, either. And my children have to know, as well. I have a lot of fences to mend, Kam. You need to understand this is my cross to carry—not yours. I'm hoping my family will take this in stride. I don't know what will happen. But whatever comes out in the wash, just know that none of it is your fault. Don't ever forget that you're the innocent in this." He drilled her with a look. "I expect my mother will be happy. I don't expect my wife will be. Things are going to be upset for a while. Just don't take any of it personally. You got that?"

Kam saw the seriousness in Rudd's narrowed eyes. She heard the warning in his gravelly tone. "I understand."

Heading for the door, Rudd turned. "I'm seeing my mother first. Why don't you take the day off? I've got a lot of explaining to do with the family. I'll drop by and see you tonight. By then, the truth will be out and we'll decide how to ride out any storms this news creates."

Kam saw his crooked grin but heard his apprehension. "I'll be a ghost today," she promised him. "In fact, I can go over to Chappy and ask him how I can be of help around the ranch."

"Thank you. I'd appreciate any help you can give Chappy. Without Wes here, I feel like I'm missing my right arm."

Laughing a little, Kam nodded. "No problem, Rudd."

Rudd grinned a little, opened the door and quietly left.

Kam stood in the swirling silence. Rudd had fully embraced her as his daughter. All the fears she'd had, all the nightmares of Rudd kicking her out and disavowing her, melted away. The relief was sharp and she outwardly trembled, the weight dissolving.

Kam needed to call Laura and Morgan. She wanted to talk to someone who loved her, who trusted her and would protect her private life. As she turned and sat down on the couch, her heart squeezed. Punching in the numbers, Kam felt sorry for Rudd. He was equally a victim in this, too. Oh, she knew he had taken responsibility for everything; but the real truth was that her mother had refused communication with him. Why, Kam realized, she would never know.

Joy threaded through her, deep and sweet. She had a father now. Her birth father. And he loved her. And he wanted her to stay at the ranch. In just a few moments, her entire life had changed dramatically and forever.

CHAPTER FOURTEEN

KAM COULDN'T STAND to wait, so she set to work on a series of photos on her laptop. Chappy had assigned her to design the new ranch brochure, which she could do in the quiet and comfort of her suite. Somehow, she couldn't concentrate. At least she'd called her adoptive parents and told them the news.

Nearly an hour had passed while she sat at her desk before a soft knock came at the door.

"Come in…" Kam turned as Iris poked her head into the room.

"Chappy said I'd find you here working on our new brochure." It was easy to read Iris's face. The woman was shocked.

Standing up, Kam rubbed her hands against her thighs, then gestured to the couch. "Come and sit down. May I get you anything? Coffee?"

Iris smiled and quietly shut the door. "Heavens no." She went over to Kam, gripped her arms and said, "Rudd told me everything." Her voice became strained. "He found me out in the greenhouse with my flowers. I don't know who cried more—me or him." She released her granddaughter's arms and smiled. "Come, sit with me," she urged, patting the leather couch.

Kam sat down next to her. As soon as she did, Iris held her hand. "He told you about my mother, that I'm his daughter?"

"Yes." Iris lifted her hand and pushed several silver strands away from her brow. "This explains so much to me, Kam. From the moment I saw you, I felt my heart tug. I couldn't understand why I had this emotional reaction to you. Now I know why. You're my granddaughter."

Seeing the tears gather in Iris's eyes, Kam choked up. She patted her hand. "And you're my grandmother." Tears leaked from her eyes. "I could never have dreamed of having such a wonderful grandmother like you, Iris."

"You're the grandchild I was pining for. Regan and Zach never took any interest in the ranch, what I was doing or the care of our land. They are their mother's children through and through. Well, now I have a grandchild who is of the land like my son and myself—you."

Kam stroked Iris's hand. "I was thinking about that, too, how different Regan and Zach are from you and Rudd. When I was waiting for the results of the DNA testing, I hoped I was Rudd's child." Kam looked around the quiet room. Outside the picture window, in the distance, the green grass was spotted with Herefords. Taking a deep breath, Kam admitted, "Iris, I feel badly that I came here under false pretenses. Hope got me here, but I just didn't have the courage to confront Rudd directly about this early on. I hope you can forgive me." She searched the other woman's eyes.

"Listen, I know what Rudd went through when he was a young man. We never lied to him about his origins. But we also saw the hole in his heart from not knowing why his father had abandoned him. He spent several years, off and on, tracking him down. Trevor and I understood why Rudd had to do that. There's a drive to know who you are, where you came from and why you are the way you are." She patted Kam's hand again. "And you were on the same quest. I can understand why you came here under cover. Sometimes, when you have a gut hunch, it's easier to just fit in and observe. I don't blame you for taking your time."

Kam nodded. "Thank you for understanding."

"I won't judge you, Kam. I know being adopted can put a terrible burden on the child. Trevor and I cried in each other's arms many nights because we could see how heavy the load was for Rudd to bear. I can't tell you how helpless we felt for our son."

"Yes, that's how I've felt all my life. My adopted parents are wonderful, though," Kam offered. "I hope you meet them, because they are the most loving people I've ever known."

"And they supported you coming here? Following your heart?"

"Yes, they did. I had a lot of talks with them about being here incognito. They knew the guilt I carried over it. I—I just was so scared, Iris."

"You were worried that we'd reject you."

Iris had spoken the words so quietly that at first Kam thought she'd imagined hearing. Looking deeply into

Iris's eyes, however, she saw that the older woman understood as few ever would. "Yes, that's the real fear
I carried in here," she said, touching her heart. "I was
afraid if I asked Rudd to give his DNA to compare it to
mine, that he'd get angry and turn me down. Especially
given the history with my mother."

"Rudd admitted something I want you to hold secret,
Kam." Iris shook her head sadly. "Rudd fell hopelessly
in love with your mother at the convention. He said he
felt poleaxed the first moment he laid eyes on her. That
was why he'd spontaneously asked her out to dinner.
Rudd's a real shy, conservative type. He's not likely to
march up to a woman and make such a date. Then, at
this same conference he met Allison. She was dancing
to music at a chemical company booth that had hired
her as a 'starlet.'" Mouth thinning, Iris continued, "We
all know Allison was never a starlet. She lives that de-
lusion in her head, but she never made it in Hollywood,
and, like a lot of young women trying to beat down that
door, she took gigs at conventions to make ends meet."

Shrugging, Iris said, "I feel Allison chased him all
the way home after that convention because she knew
he was a very rich rancher. She saw money and security in a man like Rudd."

Kam couldn't put her shock and regret into words.

"Allison didn't marry Rudd because she loved him,"
Iris said, derision in her tone. "And my son is one of
those people who believes what he is told. Allison,
twenty-eight years ago, was a very beautiful and sensual young woman. She used her body and her sex to
trap him."

"Did you ever talk to Rudd about Allison and the
reasons she wanted to marry him?"

"Oh, yes." Iris released Kam's hand and sat back on the couch. "In some ways, I'm afraid we drove Rudd into Allison's arms. We told him she was a gold digger—a woman who only wanted his money and his security, not him. He refused to believe us, of course. It became such a bone of contention between us that Rudd ran off to Las Vegas and married her."

"That's so sad," Kam whispered.

Iris added, "And wouldn't you know? Eight months to the day after Allison ran off and married Rudd, she had Regan. Having a baby that soon after her marriage to Rudd was a way to make sure the marriage wouldn't end up in divorce. Rudd is one of those old-fashioned men who believes that once he marries, it's forever. Doesn't matter how rough it gets or even that he made a mistake in his choice. He'll stick it out to the bitter end."

Kam's eyes widened. "Has Rudd considered divorcing Allison?"

Iris shrugged again. "Not at first. Rudd was blinded by her beauty, her sensuality. He'd never been chased by a woman like that." Waving her hand, Iris said, "Out here in ranch country, you just don't meet that many women, and the ones you do meet sure aren't glamorous."

"Don't you think she loves him?"

"Not a chance," Iris insisted. "Allison used Rudd's money to further her career in Hollywood. As soon as she had Regan, she got herself back into shape and took off for Los Angeles. Trevor and I practically raised Regan and Zach. And though I don't like it, I accept that neither of them cares about the Elkhorn. Remember, I am the owner of this ranch. Then, after my death, it's turned over to Rudd. Over the years, Allison has been trying to find out what changes I've made in the will."

Frowning, Kam said, "What do you mean?"

"Allison wants not only Rudd to own the ranch, she wants my will to give Regan and Zach equal shares when I pass on."

"I don't understand. If Rudd gets the ranch when you pass on, why would Allison be pushing for that sort of thing?"

"Precisely," Iris grunted. Raising an eyebrow, she said, "If Regan and Zach each get a third of the ranch, with Rudd inheriting the last third, from Allison's perspective, she and her children are secure and taken care of because they would own the bulk of the ranch. Above all, Allison is power-minded. In her world, that kind of adjustment in my will would be perfect for her and her children."

"I've just never thought of wills or legal entanglements."

"No, you aren't the type that would," Iris said. "You were raised in a loving, stable family. From the sounds of it, your adopted parents are financially well-off. You were raised in security. You *are* secure. For Allison, finding security is *everything*.

"She's been a constant burr under my saddle about this. She hates me because I maintain ownership of this ranch. She wants Rudd to own it and run it, not me, but I'm not giving up control until I take my last breath. And Allison knows that. She's done everything she could to get rid of Trevor and me, and she succeeded with my Trevor."

Startled, Kam said, "What do you mean?"

"Allison is devious. She manipulates. She tries to

sow seeds of anarchy in our family. Trevor disliked her intensely. You know he died of a heart attack?"

"Yes, I do."

"That was thanks to Allison. When I was in town one day, she found Trevor out in the greenhouse. She laced into him about her children not being named in our wills. When I came home, Trevor told me of their huge fight. And then, that evening, he had a heart attack and died. I know the fight he had with her caused it." Bitterness leaked into Iris's tone. "My wonderful Trevor was hunted and circled by Allison the way a coyote circles the sheep he wants to kill. I swear, at his funeral, Allison was smiling. I could see it in her eyes, the way her mouth was twisted into this grotesque line at the corners. As I stood opposite her at the grave site with the minister speaking, I saw her smile. Once. When she didn't think I was looking. But I saw it, Kam. And I knew—"

"I'm so sorry," Kam whispered, reaching out and gripping her hand. "I just haven't seen that much of Allison."

"No, you've been lucky. She's been gone most of the time you've been here. But that's going to change shortly. Rudd is talking with Allison right now. You need to prepare yourself. She's going to see you as a direct threat to her children."

"*Have* you written them into your will?" Kam wondered.

"Of course not! I made that very clear to Allison after Trevor died. She's been trying to be nice to me, to sweet-talk me into doing it. I let her think I did it already just to get her off my back. Once she has you in her sights, Allison can make your life *very* miserable until you give her what she wants. She's perfected nagging to a high art, believe me."

"I didn't know any of this."

"Humph. Now that you know what kind of toxic family situation this really is I wonder if you think it's worth it all. I rue the day Rudd married Allison. I have wished thousands of times he'd see her for what she is—a gold digger. But he won't. Not ever."

"To do that," Kam agreed, "would be to admit you've made a mistake for the last twenty-nine years of your life."

"Right." Iris sighed and looked up at the white-painted ceiling above them. "I often wonder if I could admit to such a thing if it was me and not my son in this position."

"Iris, I'm no better than Allison. I sneaked in here, too."

Iris held up her hands in protest. "Whoa, now. Yes, you did come here incognito. But you confronted Rudd about why you came here. Allison was never honest. We all use subterfuge at some time in our lives. You and Allison couldn't be more different. I hope you see that."

"When you put it into that kind of framework, I do," Kam admitted.

"One thing's for sure," Iris warned Kam in a heavy tone, "now that Allison knows your connection to our family, she will see you as a direct threat."

"Why? Because of the will?"

Rolling her eyes, Iris muttered, "Of course! It's all about money for her and you might take what she considers her property."

Kam sighed. "I don't need anything, Iris. Just getting to know my father and family is the only gift I could ever want."

"You're his daughter, all right," Iris said.

"She's not wrong to want that security," Kam said.

"Technically speaking," Iris said, "you're right. But what if Rudd wants to leave you a piece of the ranch?" Iris peered at Kam through narrowed eyes. "Do you understand the dilemma now?"

"I just don't think like that, Iris. But yes, I do see your points."

Getting up, Iris smoothed out her wrinkled canvas apron. "You need to watch your back," she said softly.

Kam walked Iris to the door and opened it for her. "Thanks for welcoming me into the family, Iris. You can't know how much this means to me."

Opening her arms, Iris embraced her granddaughter warmly and touched Kam's cheek. "I'm so happy about this. You have no idea. Now, maybe the Elkhorn Ranch has the future Trevor and I always hoped for. I'll see you later. And be ready for Allison's wrath."

CHAPTER FIFTEEN

WES ANSWERED HIS cell phone. He was out at the corral where the wranglers were unsaddling their mounts for the day. "Hello?" He thought it might be his mother and his stomach automatically tightened.

"Wes? It's Kam Trayhern. How are you doing?"

Her voice was instantly soothing. Wes hooked his boot up on the lowest rung of the pipe rail and leaned against it. "Kam. It's good to hear from you. I'm sure Rudd told you what happened." He couldn't keep the surprise and happiness out of his voice. Since coming back to his father's ranch, he'd missed her most of all.

"Yes, he filled me in. How is your father?"

Grimacing, Wes said, "He's in a coma. The doctors don't expect him to live. There's too much heart damage and his kidneys have shut down. It's just a matter of time they said. Seven days at the most."

"I'm so sorry," she murmured. "How are you holding up?"

He laughed a little and watched the cowhands leading their unsaddled horses to the nearby barn. The sunset sky was a shell-pink color with long wisps of high clouds. "Scrambling. Trying to learn everything in three days."

"I'm sure it's all a shock. How is your mom?"

"Struggling. She's staying with my father at the hospital full-time. I'm taking over and trying to understand the rotation of everything that the cowhands have to do here. My father had a manager but the gent wasn't very organized. And then he fired the man two weeks before his heart attack. I have to try and figure it all out as I go along. The hands have been decent about it and helped me out." Although Wes was at the ranch, his mind and heart were with his father whether he wanted it that way or not. The bad blood between them was an open wound constantly digging into his chest. No matter what he did through the day, that pain, that loss, ate at him.

"That sounds daunting."

"It is. But I'm not entirely ignorant. Two years ago, I was helping him run this place. A lot of stuff is coming back to me and I should be able to handle it all." Wes felt his heart thumping hard in his chest. He missed Kam. He had ached to hear her voice and absorb that special warm look she gave him.

"That's a good thing." And then, she hesitated. "Wes, I miss you. I know we didn't get to talk much about what happened between us. I wanted to, but I was scared." And then Kam managed a soft laugh. "I still am, but I felt you deserved to know."

He felt her reaching out to him. It sent a wave of heat and longing through him. Wes said, "I'm scared, too, Kam. I never expected to be interested in a woman while I worked at the Elkhorn Ranch. I don't know why, I just didn't. I miss you, too. How is Iris?"

"Oh, she's fine. Better than ever, in fact."

"I think it's because of you."

"Maybe…"

"What're the chances of you driving up here for a visit one day soon?" he asked. Wes knew he was taking a risk by being so bold, but he missed Kam.

"I'd have to check with Iris, but I'd love to come up."

"Why don't you ask her and then call me back? It would give me some down time just to be with you, and I could show you the ranch I grew up on." Any reference to his childhood still hurt, especially given his father's condition. Wes wondered what his mother would do once Dan died. He'd left everything to her. Would she ask him to come back to run the ranch? Wes thought his mother would, more than likely, will the ranch over to him. Still, it pained him that his father had erased him from his life.

"Okay, I can do that, Wes. I'll talk to you soon."

Smiling a little, Wes felt a lot less lonely than before. "I'll look forward to it, Kam. Say hello to everyone for me."

"I promise I will. Goodbye, Wes."

KAM SAT THERE with the cell phone in her hand. Staring out at the dusk, the high pink cirrus clouds beautiful across the valley, she felt torn. Just getting to talk to Wes, to hear his low voice, lifted her spirits. What was Rudd going through with Allison? Would he talk to Regan and Zach, too? It was clear that Rudd took full responsibility for the situation. Iris had been right—he was a throwback to the days of gallantry, a gentleman who did the right thing. In her eyes, her birth father was a knight in shining armor for his integrity in this matter. Rudd could have disowned her just as Wes had been disowned by his father. There were so many things Rudd could have done, but had not. He did the right thing for the right reasons. Her father was a decent man and that buoyed Kam as little else ever would. Wes was made out of the same cut of fabric. Maybe that was why she was so drawn to him.

Kam rose and moved restlessly about the room. The desire to get out, to get some fresh air was overwhelming. The cooks and help in the dining room always needed an extra hand and Kam could keep herself busy there. Right now, the pressure and tension in the ranch house was just too much for her. Grabbing her cowboy hat, Kam left her suite.

The hall was empty and quiet. She looked down the well-lit corridor to Allison and Rudd's suite, four doors down and opposite hers. She heard no screaming. Nothing. How she hoped Rudd and Allison were having a quiet, mature discussion about her. Maybe this situation wouldn't erupt into a big family drama. Kam headed out of the house and over to the dining hall.

"I can't believe this cockamamie story, Rudd!" Allison leaped off her white leather couch and paced the room, arms stiff against her chest.

Rudd watched his beautiful wife all done up in white linen slacks and a ruffled emerald-green blouse. She paced like a ravishing caged mountain lion. "I'm sorry, Allison. Sorry that this happened, but it's my mistake and I'm the person who has to own up to it. Kam is my daughter."

Turning on her high heels, Allison snapped, "Are you dead sure, Rudd?"

"The doctor confirmed it with the DNA test, Allison. She is my daughter."

"Damn you!" Allison shrieked. Her hands flew into the air. "How *could* you do this to *me?* I've been faithful and loving to you for twenty-eight years! And then, out of the blue, this girl shows up here to our ranch and says, 'oh by the way, I'm your daughter.'" Allison pressed the palm of her hand to her brow. "This is like a bad movie, Rudd. I swear to God it is!"

Rudd winced as she shrieked. Allison had her moments, he knew. And when she was really upset, she was a drama queen on a par with any great Hollywood movie star. "It's no movie," he told her heavily. "It's real life."

Nostrils flaring, Allison glared at him. "And what do you propose to do now?"

He shrugged. "Kam wants to stay here. I want her here, too. She loves the ranch. She loves Iris."

"Oh, and I suppose Iris already knows about your monumental screwup?"

"Yes, she does. And she's fine with Kam being my daughter."

"She would be!" Allison fumed, pacing once again. Her mind raced over the many elements of this shocking problem. Screaming at Rudd would only make him more defensive and set in his ways, Allison knew. Trying to tame her rage, she muttered, "And Iris accepts Kam as your daughter?"

"Of course. Why wouldn't she? DNA tests don't lie, Allison."

"Stop rubbing salt in my wounds, Rudd. I'm angry enough about this." She stared across the room at him, her hands balled into fists at her side. "So, now, you have three children, not two."

"That's right," he said, leaning his elbows on his thighs and studying his work-worn hands. "I just worry about integrating Kam here with Regan and Zach. I want them to get along, to love one another."

Snorting softly, Allison sat down on the couch and crossed her legs. She stared across the oak coffee table at Rudd who sat tensely on the white leather stuffed chair. "You can't *force* people to love one another, Rudd." She raked him with her gaze. When he was nervous, he would stroke the ends of his mustache, which he was doing now.

"I know that. I'm just hoping that they will eventually accept Kam as a family member."

"And so Kam trumps our two children?"

Rudd shot her a look of warning. "What do you mean she trumps Regan and Zach?"

"I had two children by you, Rudd Mason. *They* deserve this ranch when you die. *Not* Kam. *That* is what I'm getting at."

Brows lifting, Rudd stared at her in shock. "I haven't even thought about that, Allison." But then, Allison would, Rudd realized belatedly. Her eyes flashed with anger.

"Has Iris changed her will because of this?"

"I don't know. We really didn't discuss that side of things, Allison. Iris just found out about this an hour ago. If you're so concerned about it, why don't you ask her?" He opened his hands. "Kam is now a part of our family. How Iris reacts to her or what she does about it in her will is her business, not mine or yours."

Nostrils flaring, Allison surged to her feet. "Well, it damn well *should* be your business, Rudd Mason! We have two children between us. *Legitimate* children, I might add." She stormed around the coffee table, the click of her heels sharp against the cedar floor. Jamming her hands on the hips, she leaned over him. "You need to set this right, Rudd. Kam is *not* a full family member. Kam comes from you, not me. She's an outsider claiming inheritance on a ranch she's not been raised on or helped build."

Rudd almost said Regan and Zach hadn't lifted a hand to help build this ranch, either, but he didn't. Nor had Allison aided in the ranch's prosperity. She escaped every chance she got. Those facts would only throw gasoline on the fire burning between them right now. Compressing his lips, he growled, "I have no say over how Iris conducts her legal business and you know that. Iris *owns* this ranch, in case you forgot."

Allison pushed a curl off her bunched brow. "Oh, I haven't forgotten that for one second, Rudd!" Walking swiftly around the couch, she moved to the picture window and wrapped her arms around her chest. "Your mother has run this place forever. All you do is work for her. You might as well be a hired hand. It's wrong that she doesn't turn the ownership of the ranch over to you. She's not doing much of anything except surviving and hanging on to the end, now."

As he slowly unwound from the chair, Rudd felt anger move through him. He stared at Allison's pouty profile. Her full lips were set. "We are a ranch dynasty," he reminded her. "We have a one-hundred-and-fifty-year history here in Wyoming through Mason men and women. The ranch has always been passed on to the next generation after the deaths of the previous one and you know that. Until Iris passes on, she is the owner. I have no problem with that, but you do. And I can't figure out why, Allison. You get everything you ever wanted. Our children want for nothing. This is a good life for all of us."

Allison refused to look at Rudd. This argument was as old and dead as their marriage. "I don't like Iris being boss!"

"She's a good manager, Allison." Sighing, Rudd shook his head. "And she's been nothing but good to you and our children. Iris and Trevor made this ranch what it is today. She's earned the right to own it, don't you think?"

Twisting her lips, Allison muttered, "Her time is *past,* Rudd. You're fifty-five years old. Don't you think it's time that you were the owner of the Elkhorn?"

Rudd shook his head. "Allison, I just don't understand this argument. Our names are in her will. When Iris dies, we'll be the owners."

"Yes, and Iris has said that Regan and Zach will be given a piece of the ranch after she passes. Now will Kam be added to that list? Will the land given to our children be *less?* Can't you see Kam wants to steal land that belongs to *our* children?"

Rudd struggled to keep up with his wife's emotional tirade. "I have no idea what Iris will do."

"Well, you should. Go to her and tell her not to give Kam *anything.* She's your daughter out of wedlock. She is not a true child of this ranch."

"Allison, I'm not going to my mother about this. If you think it's that important, you go and talk to her. I'm okay with whatever way Iris views Kam. If she doesn't want to give her anything in that will, I'm fine with that. If she does, I'm fine with that, too."

"Well," Allison snapped angrily, "someone needs to protect *our* children, Rudd. Damn you for being spineless." With that, Allison marched off, no doubt to plead her case with Iris. Rudd went to prepare himself for the night ahead.

EVERYONE WAS ORDERED to show up for dinner. Iris had backed Rudd on that request at least. He sat at one end of the table and Allison sat at the other. Iris sat with Kam, and Regan and Zach were on the opposite side. The whole family now knew Kam was Rudd's daughter.

Becky Long moved quietly around the table with bowls of gazpacho. Like a shadow, she disappeared through the door, leaving the naked tension in the dining room.

Rudd scanned the table. Hands on either side of his soup bowl, he said, "I'm making an official announcement tonight. Kam, as you know, is my daughter. From now on, she'll be eating with us. I'm hoping that after the shock of all of this subsides, we can learn to get along like a family." He turned to Kam. "I want to welcome you to our table, Kam. I'm glad you're here."

Iris patted Kam's hand. "I'm glad she's here, as well." Iris then looked pointedly at Allison, who was sulking.

"Welcome, Kam," Allison said in a low voice.

"Thank you," Kam murmured. She could see Allison's face was flushed with latent fury banked in her eyes.

"Regan?" Rudd nudged. "Welcome your sister."

Regan lifted her lip. "Sorry, Father, but Kam is a *half* sister." Regan stared defiantly across the table. "I don't have to like you, Kam, but I do have to be civil."

"Fair enough," Kam said. She saw Zach grimace and stare down at his bowl.

"Zach?" Rudd said.

"Yeah, well, whatever," the teen mumbled. "I hate these meals, anyway. I'd rather eat in my room."

Rudd glared at him. "You're in there ninety-nine percent of every day. The least you can do is share one meal with your family. Now, welcome Kam."

Lifting his head, Zach muttered, "Welcome."

"Thanks, Zach." Kam felt the weight of the tension across her shoulders. This wasn't a happy family gathering. Three were against her. Two were for her. Well, what did she expect? How would she feel if she was suddenly told out of the blue that she had a new half sister?

Looking around and meeting everyone's gaze, Kam said quietly, "I can't imagine how shocking or hard this is for each of you. I feel like I should apologize, but Rudd said I shouldn't. I hope over the coming weeks and months that we can get along. I don't expect you to like me or love me. Those are things a person earns over time. I hope you will give me that time."

Regan snatched up her spoon and sipped the soup. Zach sighed and looked up at the ceiling. Allison glared at Kam, her hands clenched into fists on either side of the white bowl. Kam wondered obliquely if Rudd's wife wanted to strike her or her father. She wasn't sure.

Iris picked up her soupspoon. "Kam, everyone here is going to be giving you the time you need." She looked directly at Allison.

"Well, of course, Iris," Allison trilled, giving her mother-in-law a smirk. She picked up her flatware. "This is a bump in the road. I'm sure everyone will strive to get along."

"Nice to hear," Iris said in a grumbling tone.

Kam couldn't wait until dinner was over. It seemed to go on forever. The salad was pretty to look at, but she had no appetite. She noticed Zach ate the soup with relish, pushed the salad away and drank one can of soda after another. When Tilly brought in the main course, leg of lamb rubbed with rosemary, Irish potatoes and curried carrots as a side dish—he didn't touch the food. Zach was pathetically thin. Now, Kam knew why.

She noticed Regan shooting her stabbing looks from time to time. Kam forced herself not to respond to the glares from her half sister. Regan sank her teeth into the succulent lamb as if she were biting into Kam.

Allison kept up a drone of patter enough to bore anyone to sleep. Rudd's wife ran table discussions like a control freak. Everything was about Hollywood, a director, a movie or a friend of hers who was in a television show. Kam kept her head down, eyes on her food and remained mute. Right now, she needed to understand the family dynamic, not blunder into a situation and make things worse.

Dessert was fresh strawberries from Iris's garden slathered with whipped cream. Kam forced herself to eat them because she knew Iris was proud of her home-grown produce. In fact, all the vegetables at dinner tonight had come from her garden last season. Iris canned over a thousand jars of veggies and fruits each year.

When coffee was served, Regan and Zach politely excused themselves, as did their mother. That left the other three at the table with the fragrant Colombian coffee scenting the air. Kam saw the strain on her birth father's face and her heart went out to him. Even though Rudd had stressed that this was not her fault, she couldn't help but feel responsible.

Iris sighed. "That was wonderful lamb, Rudd. There's nothing like growing our own meat, veggies and fruit. It gives me a deep sense of satisfaction."

"I agree, Mother. How do you think things went tonight?" Rudd asked after sipping his coffee.

"They were all on good behavior," Iris responded. "We can't expect them not to be upset, but in time, I'm sure things will settle down."

Rudd glanced over at Kam. "Thanks for taking the high road on this tonight. You could have gotten upset by Regan's anger, but you didn't."

"I feel for all of them," Kam quietly confided. "I try to put myself in their shoes and ask myself how I would feel."

"That's a good thing to do," Iris chimed in, smiling over at her. "That's called practicing the Golden Rule— do unto others as you would have them done to you. Or some such thing. You know what I mean."

Kam laughed softly. "Yes, I do. My belief system stresses compassion and understanding. I always try to extend that to everyone." Kam shrugged and added, "Most of the time it works and sometimes it doesn't."

"It's called being human," Iris said. "No one is perfect."

"Least of all, me," Rudd muttered, staring down at the steaming coffee in the cup before him.

"Son, you didn't know," Iris began, frustration in her tone. "Sometimes, things are meant to be no matter how careful we are. Kam was meant to come into this world." She patted Kam's hand. "And we're *very* glad you are here. Don't ever think for a split second that you aren't wanted, because you are. Always remember that Rudd and I love you."

CHAPTER SIXTEEN

KAM FOUND WES on horseback over in one of the larger corrals. He was busy herding Herefords into a chute for their vet check. The morning sunlight was bright through threatening clouds.

How she had looked forward to seeing him! Iris had given her a couple of days off, and now Kam needed to confess to Wes. He had to know the truth about her being Rudd's daughter.

She wasn't sure what she was going to say. It wasn't exactly good timing either with Wes taking over his father's ranch. Maybe she could alleviate some of his pain. At least, he would understand why she'd been so hesitant. As Kam pulled up and parked near the corral in her Toyota Prius, Wes looked in her direction.

He lifted his hand and smiled broadly, his teeth starkly white against his sun-darkened skin.

Instantly, Kam's heart beat harder as his smile warmed her like sunshine after a hard storm. How handsome he looked sitting astride a buckskin gelding, sweat running down the sides of his weathered face. Wes gave orders to another cowboy in the dust-laden corral with him and turned the gold quarter horse with the black mane and tail toward the gate. Kam walked forward to meet him.

Wes dismounted and tied his horse to the top pipe rail, then opened the gate. Taking off his hat, he wiped the sweat off his brow, shut the gate and faced her. Nothing looked as beautiful as Kam Trayhern coming to meet him. Her white T-shirt and jeans lovingly detailed her long, long legs and shapely hips. The heaven-sent sight of her in her Stetson, cowboy boots and a red bandanna around her neck, was enough to make Wes forget the pressures on his life.

Wes grinned. "You look like a real cattle rancher. It's like you've lived this life forever."

As heat soared from her neck into her face, Kam met Wes's sparkling gray eyes. Strands of dark brown hair were plastered to his brow. "That's a nice compliment." Kam couldn't help herself. She leaned forward and kissed his cheek. While shocked at herself, she had no time to think about her impulse. She did notice the look in Wes's eyes, as if he couldn't wait to get her alone. "How are you doing?" she asked, a little breathless as she quickly stepped back to create some distance.

Wes settled the hat back on his head and Wes grinned. "Fine, now." He pointed to a nearby red truck with the tailgate open. "Let's get something to drink. Always smart on a day like this. We're vet-checking the herd to make sure there's no cuts, abrasions or infections. Something we routinely do, but a lot of hot, dusty work. If Dr. Evans finds any problems, I asked her to use a natural antibiotic product like calendula instead of drugs. They use the same thing over at the Elkhorn. My father uses hormone shots and I think that's wrong. I'm going to sell off this herd and start all over after he's gone. We're going to go organic like the Elkhorn."

"Your father is against raising organic beef?"

Nodding, Wes halted at the tailgate and handed her two tall paper cups. A twenty-gallon plastic dispenser contained iced tea. "Yes. I tried for years to get him to change his attitude. I saw the meat market moving toward unvaccinated and non-hormone beef about ten years ago. He laughed me off and told me my ideas were crazy."

Hearing the regret in Wes's tone, she watched as he took off his gloves and tucked them into his belt. "How many cattle does he run here?" In a smaller cooler were ice cubes, along with a green plastic bottle of lemon juice and a can of sugar. Kam helped herself and put some ice cubes into his cup. Wes put each cup beneath the spout of the large tea dispenser.

"Five thousand head," Wes told her. "He has the second-largest ranch in Wyoming next to the Elkhorn," he said, adding a squirt of lemon and spooning sugar into the cup. After stirring his drink, he leaned against the edge of the tailgate and watched the action in the corral.

"That's a *lot* of cattle," Kam said, sipping her tea. The clouds of dust that rose in the corral were moved by a slight breeze away from the bustling area. She took a deep breath and quietly asked, "What's the latest on your father?"

Wes took a gulp of his drink before answering. "He's dying. My mother asked the hospice to come in, and they are making sure he's comfortable."

"And she's with him?"

"Always."

Wes frowned and drank the rest of his tea. "I know I didn't talk much about my family when I was over at the Elkhorn with you, but it's a mess. My brother and sister who live in Cheyenne refuse to come and say goodbye. My mother is upset, but she doesn't understand."

"I know a little about alcoholism," Kam admitted quietly, sitting on the tailgate next to Wes. "I had a photographer friend whose mother had the disease. It wasn't pretty."

"No," Wes said grimly, turning to get some more tea, "it's not. My father would whip us with a belt when he was drunk. He's what they call a mean drunk. We lived in fear of him drinking because we knew he'd come hunting us down."

"Didn't your mother try and stop that abuse?" Kam heard the alarm in her voice. She noticed Wes scowl as he fixed his tea.

"No. Frankly, he beat up on her until us kids came along. And then he focused on us and not her."

Anger stirred in Kam. "A mother's duty is always to protect her children."

"Yeah," Wes sighed, leaning against the tailgate and sipping the iced tea, "you don't need to tell us that." He rubbed the sweat away from his left temple. "That's why none of us will go see him to say goodbye. There's nothing but anger and hard feelings toward him. My mother doesn't get it. I doubt she ever will. She's codependent and an abuse victim and refuses to break out to get healthy like we have."

"You have a lot of hard decisions to make," Kam said, giving him a tender look. For all the hardness in Wes's face, there was anguish in his gray eyes. He might talk tough about his father, but something told her that he needed to say goodbye to him. That wasn't her call. Kam couldn't even imagine his experience because she had been raised in such a loving, healthy family compared to Wes and his siblings.

"They figure he'll die today," Wes muttered. "My brother and sister will be going to support my mother this evening at the hospital."

"Maybe that's best," Kam said. "Death can be a release for everyone involved. For the person who is dying as well as those who are left behind. My friend went through that with his mother. She got liver disease after all those years of drinking. I saw him suffer through those last six months with her and the terrible toll it took on him. When he came back to work, he had aged five years."

"Yeah, it will do it to you," Wes agreed, watching the activity in the corral. Most of the herd had been pushed through the chutes. Soon enough, they would be released back to the green pastures that surrounded the huge ranch. Wes glanced over at Kam. "You look preoccupied. Anything going on at the Elkhorn?"

This was her chance. Kam realized that Wes would not be going to the hospital to see his father. And he was okay with that, as much as a son could be with his father dying. Sensing he was in a stable place despite the crisis in his own family, she decided to tell him everything.

"Wes, do you have about an hour of time? I know you're busy here."

"No, that's fine. The number-two hand is going to handle the rest of this herd going through for the vet-check." He got off the tailgate and pointed to the sprawling ranch house. "Let's amble over to the front porch. There's a swing there. We can sit and talk."

Kam rose and walked at his side. She felt nervous and her stomach fluttered. Wes's response could go one of two ways: he could feel duped or he could understand why she'd gone undercover. She could only hope for the best.

"Have a seat," Wes invited, taking off his hat. He placed it on the wooden table next to the arm of the cedar swing. The seat was old and worn, but had been lovingly kept in shape with yearly repairs, sanding and a coat of varnish. Soft green cotton cushions lay across the wide swing. Kam sat next to Wes, their elbows grazing one another. "So, what's the latest gossip from the Elkhorn? I miss being over there."

"We all miss you," Kam said, placing her empty cup on the table. "Rudd and Iris speak of you daily, Wes. They really wish you were back, but they do understand your situation."

"Do you miss me?" Wes held her startled gaze. He missed the hell out of Kam. More than he could ever let her know. Even now, the spot on his cheek where she'd placed a peck still tingled. For a moment, his heart had lifted out of a dark hole. Somehow, even in one of the worst periods of his life, with his father dying, Kam was able to pull him out of his seething emotional cauldron.

"Of course I miss you," Kam said, surprised. And then she held up her hand. "When I get done telling you what has happened, you might not feel the same way, Wes."

Surprised, he murmured, "Okay, what's happened?"

"I'm not who you think I am," Kam said, hesitating a little before launching into the complete story of why she had appeared at the Elkhorn Ranch. She watched his face, noted his surprise and then shock over her admissions. When she was finished, she drew in a ragged sigh. "So, you see, I'm not who I said I was. I feel guilty about sneaking in and I've apologized to everyone about it."

Rubbing his jaw, Wes asked, "How did Rudd and Iris handle this news?"

"Wonderfully," Kam admitted with a slight smile. "They said they understood."

"You know Rudd was adopted?"

"I do."

"That's probably why he understood what you did. What about Allison?"

Grimacing, Kam said, "She's not happy about it from what I can tell. At dinner one night Allison accused me of being sneaky and underhanded. I agreed with her that my choices weren't stellar, but that I was too afraid that I'd be rejected out of hand otherwise."

Wes leaned back and studied Kam. "So, you're Rudd's daughter. That's really funny because I kept looking at you two and thinking you had to be somehow related."

Kam's eyes widened. "You did?"

"Sure." Wes laughed. "Because first of all, you look a bit like him. Secondly, you have the same body build. And best of all, you're easygoing and sensitive like he is. Did you notice little things like the fact you two liked pickled eggs and beets? I saw you two chowing down on them like there was no tomorrow at that dude-ranch picnic. Not everyone likes pickled food, you know."

"I didn't even realize that," Kam said, amazed at his alertness. What's more, she was relieved at how well he was handling her news.

"And you both have the same hand mannerisms. Rudd is always throwing up his hands when he gets frustrated. You do, too. Looks like they are definite family traits."

"You really do notice little things, don't you?"

Losing his smile, Wes looked out beyond the porch. The grass was lush, the white picket fence freshly painted for the year. Colorful columbines grew in profusion inside of it. Their colors reminded him of a rainbow. "When you have an abusive and violent parent, you become hyper vigilant. In my early twenties, I started having nightmares. My father stopped beating up on me at age seventeen because I fought back. I broke his nose and that ended up with him coming after me. My brother and sister had already left. They couldn't take the beatings and I don't blame them. I have an aunt and uncle who live in Cheyenne and they agreed to take them in until they were eighteen."

"How awful for all of you." Kam reached over and slid her hand into his. Wes gently squeezed her fingers. For Kam, this touch meant the world. Wes had accepted her story and choices. Now he was opening his heart to her.

"I stayed because I was the oldest and my mother needed me," Wes said. "When I went to see Doc Jones in Jackson and told him about these nightmares, he diagnosed me with post-traumatic stress disorder. Doc took the time to explain it all and he made me realize that every time our father came after us, we thought we might die. And when you think you're going to die, more adrenaline and cortisol shoots through your blood."

"I didn't know," Kam murmured sympathetically and continued to hold Wes's hand. It was warm and strong. She could feel the calluses created by his ranch work. Gazing at his profile, she could sense his grief. How she wanted to hold him and make him feel safe. More than ever, she understood him not going to say goodbye to his dying father. The love between son and parent had died a long time ago.

"I don't go around sharing my childhood with most people," Wes admitted, his voice low. Managing a tight smile, he held Kam's tender blue gaze. "Only with you, Kam. There's something about you that just makes me want to spill my guts." Managing a wry laugh, Wes squeezed her hand. "I hope you don't mind."

"Not at all," Kam said. She wanted to do more than hold his hand. The expression on Wes's face tugged at her heart.

"So now that you know you're Rudd Mason's daughter, what are you going to do?" Wes asked her. He released her hand, because if he didn't he was going to draw Kam into his arms and kiss her until they melted into one another. A powerful wave of desire slammed through him, but now was not the time. Not yet, at least. Wes knew he had to get past his father dying, the funeral, seeing his brother and sister and finding out what his mother wanted to do about the ranch.

"Rudd asked me to stay. So did Iris."

"Is that what you want?"

Kam nodded. "It's kind of hard for me right now, Wes. All my life, I've been a tumbleweed photographer tripping around the world. I kept an apartment in San Diego, but I was there for maybe a few weeks at a time and then I'd be off to another crisis somewhere in the world to take photos." Shrugging, Kam frowned. "I'm not sure what I want to do right now. I want to stay and build ties with my father. And I dearly love Iris."

"But Allison and her children are making it rough for you?" Wes guessed and saw from her reaction that he'd hit the mark. Just like her father, Kam disliked dissension. Who didn't?

"They are, but I'm hoping that will turn down in volume as everyone gets used to me being around."

"Wise choice," Wes said. "Do you miss traveling the globe and being at the center of hot spots?"

"Yes and no," Kam replied. The gentle movement of the swing seemed to make it easier to admit these truths to Wes. Deep down, Kam knew she could trust him with her life. And no man, other than her adopted father, had made her feel so protected. "As I kicked around the globe, I used to wonder if I was trying to find my father. Maybe he was born in whatever country I was visiting. I felt so empty, like a part of me was missing. My adopted mom, Laura, told me that sometimes people like me are vagabonds because we're trying to find our roots. This analogy rang true for me."

"Now you have roots," Wes said softly. "The real question is—do you want to stay rooted in one spot for the rest of your life? Or will you choose something in between? You have a lot of choices."

"Sometimes I think you're inside my head," Kam said, smiling warmly at Wes. "Those are the very ques-

tions I'm asking myself right now. I feel the only answer is to stay at the Elkhorn. I've been searching for
my birth father all my life, and I've just found him. I
really like him, Wes. I used to have so many dreams
about what he might look like, how his voice would
sound, what he would do for a living...." She opened
her hands and laughed.

"Does Rudd fulfill your dreams?" Wes wondered.

"Oh yes," Kam said. "That one photo of Rudd at the
cattle convention spurred so many dreams of my father
being a cowboy. I didn't dream of him owning the largest spread in Wyoming, of course. For me, his galloping on a horse, looking tall and strong, was enough."

"Rudd is all of those things. I've enjoyed working
under his management style. It's been different from the
way my father bossed his cowhands. Rudd has taught
me a lot." Looking over at the corral where all the hands
worked with the Herefords, Wes added, "And I've come
back here and used all that knowledge with them."

"Does it work?"

"Yeah. They were used to my father screaming and
cursing at them. Everyone likes me better." His mouth
crooked into a grin. "Rudd has been a great teacher."

"I like him so much," Kam admitted. "All that love
I had in my heart that I'd held on to for so many years,
is just spilling out toward him and Iris. I feel so lucky!
And Iris is the perfect grandmother for me."

"Yes," Wes chuckled, "like two peas from the same
pod, as they say. Iris isn't the easiest person to be
around. She's a crusty, independent pioneer woman who
built that ranch with her husband. Those two were a
force to be reckoned with. Everyone in Wyoming knew
them," Wes said with a smile. "And you and Iris could

be sisters of a sort, Kam. That's how well you get along with one another."

Kam laughed. "I love Iris so much. She's taught me a lot about life, business and going after my dreams." Losing her smile, Kam admitted, "Iris gave me the courage to go to Rudd and tell him the truth. She told me one day how scared she was about turning their herd into organic meat production. I asked her why she was scared. She said because it meant the possibility of losing a lot of cattle without vaccinations. And then, she just looked me straight in the eyes and told me that no matter how scared I got, always to go forward. That the truth of the situation would prove itself sooner or later. Her courage to confront her own fear helped me. For that, I'll always be grateful."

"I hope you shared that with her."

"You bet I did."

Nodding, Wes said, "Good. Then that means you're going to be around the Elkhorn for a while longer."

"Yes." She saw a strange look in his eyes and couldn't decipher it at all. Right now, both their lives were upended in different ways.

"Good," Wes murmured. "Because I want you to stick around."

CHAPTER SEVENTEEN

ALLISON WAITED IMPATIENTLY on a little-used back street in Jackson Hole. She sat in her silver Mercedes and tapped her fingers on the leather covering the steering wheel. The day was bright and sunny. Behind her, major construction on the street stopped a lot of tourists from ambling into the area, which is what Allison counted on. She wanted this meeting to go down without gawking onlookers. Or witnesses.

Shade trees lined the street. Luckily, the last house was a block behind her and beyond the ongoing construction. This street was out of the way and she could have her meeting without prying eyes nearby. Not that there weren't plenty of Mercedeses in Jackson Hole. There were. Jackson was a little-known place where the rich and famous lived. It was a well-kept secret except for the pricey cars always seen about town. Outsiders didn't have a clue. Movie stars from Hollywood had second homes here, and that suited Allison. Jackson was just one more connection to the Hollywood business she stubbornly clung to.

A sharp tap on the passenger-side window snapped Allison out of her thoughts. A man in his forties with a neatly clipped black beard entered the car and sat down. He wore casual clothes and looked like one of the many tourists visiting Jackson. Nothing about him stood out.

"It's about time," she muttered, looking at the eighteen-carat-gold Cartier watch on her wrist.

"By my watch," he said, holding up his thick, hairy wrist and glancing at his gold Rolex, "I'm right on time." Grinning over at Allison he said, "Maybe you're a little nervous?" He held out his large, square, well-manicured hand. "André Jenkins at your service. I was contacted by our mutual friend who said you needed my professional services."

Allison glared and then quickly shook his hand. "Allison Mason."

"What work do you have for me, Ms. Mason?"

Allison pulled a thick envelope from the glove box and handed it to him. The man had a slight European accent. Perhaps French? Swiss? She knew little of this man's background. "Mr. Jenkins, in there is a picture of the woman I want you to get rid of." Allison stared at the profile of the man. He didn't look like an assassin, but when he opened the manila envelope she saw him focus like a predator stalking his next victim. Jenkins intently studied the photo, then he carefully counted the one-thousand-dollar bills. Nervously, Allison tightened her lips as she watched him. Her nerves stretched to the breaking point.

"Very good," Jenkins finally said, "just as I requested. Fifty thousand dollars in one-thousand dollar bills. That way, there is no way to connect us. Have you hired my type of services before, Ms. Mason?"

"No, I have not."

"Ah. Very well, let me tell you how I work. As a professional, I remain undercover. André Jenkins is not my real name, but I have all the identification to go with my pseudonym. Cash is harder to trace. Although the numbers on it can be tracked, I doubt you have any reason to do that."

"I certainly have not written down any of the numbers."

He tapped the envelope in his lap. "And did the bank raise any eyebrows over you asking for fifty thousand dollars?"

"I have six bank accounts and four of them are in various places in Los Angeles. I took a little from each one. No one said anything. As long as I withdraw less than ten thousand dollars from each, it doesn't raise any red flags."

"Very good," he said, giving her a pleased look.

Allison shivered. The man's narrow blue eyes were pale with huge black pupils. Again, that sense that he was a stalker and predator washed through her. "The money won't be traceable. My husband knows nothing of my four bank accounts in Los Angeles. It's money I put away for whatever I want. And I can account for the twenty thousand in the two accounts he knows about. There won't be a problem."

Nodding, the man held up the color photo. "And this is whom?"

"Her name is Kam Trayhern." Grimly, Allison said,

"She's an interloper in my family. My husband, it turns out, had an illicit affair with a woman twenty-nine years ago. And this woman," Allison growled, jabbing her index finger at the photo, "who claims she is my husband's daughter, just walked into our lives four months ago. Unfortunately, DNA has proved her right."

"Ah," Jenkins said. "So, she lives with you?"

"Unfortunately, yes."

"And how do you want her killed?"

Allison scowled. "How the hell do I know? That's your job."

Holding up his hand, Jenkins said, "I merely meant, do you want her taken out at the ranch? Or somewhere else?"

"I don't care!"

"You should. Once I kill her, there is going to be a police investigation." Looking around, he added, "And, because you live here, no one knows better than you how an accident can occur. What might be an accident you could expect on the ranch?"

Allison thought for a moment. "She rides her horse out on the trails leading into the mountains near our ranch."

"Alone?"

"Yes."

"Good. And are there places along this trail where I might hide?"

"Many," Allison said. She felt panicky for a moment. She'd never hired a hit man before. No doubt she was doing the right thing, but she didn't want to be caught and jailed for having hired Jenkins. "I can draw you a map of the trails."

"Good. But even better is if I were to come to your

ranch in disguise. I have other identity papers with me to go undercover."

"You could be a last-minute dude-ranch guest. I could arrange the paperwork in the office. No one would think anything of it."

"That would work," Jenkins said. "I will show up as Thierry De Bourdeille from Paris, France. That way, I will see Kam Trayhern, know who she is, watch her habits and movements to get an idea of where I could terminate her."

The word *terminate* made Allison shiver. Swallowing hard, she whispered in a thin voice, "Good, I'll put you in as a last-minute guest under that name. I know next week there are three slots available. No one will suspect a thing."

"No, they won't." Jenkins drilled her with a look. "And under no circumstances do you approach me, talk to me or appear to know me. Do you have any duties with dude-ranch guests?"

"No, I don't. I'll avoid you completely, don't worry."

"Good. I'll make myself at home for that period of time. After I 'leave,' I'll get what I need to take her out. By that time, I should have a good idea of her habits, what time of day she goes for a ride and where she rides. When is hunting season here?"

Allison saw where he was going with the question. "Elk and deer season start in October. This is August."

Shrugging, Jenkins said, "Well, there are always poachers. You have elk and deer on your ranch?"

"All over the place. Moose, also."

"Good. I could use a hunter's bullet so that when they perform an autopsy, they'll say it was a poacher hunting elk out of season but that the bullet went astray and killed her."

"And how will I know when you've done this?"

"You won't. She'll just turn up missing some evening when she's supposed to be back at the ranch for dinner. I'm sure your husband will send out a search party. Her horse may come galloping back to the barn without her. If that occurs, they'll know something happened to her." He smiled. "But they won't know what until they find her. How many people know the trails she takes?"

Allison shrugged. "I don't really know. Usually, Iris gives her permission to have her afternoons free. I usually see Kam ride off every other day or so."

"I can track where she goes easily enough."

"So you really know how to track?" Allison inquired.

"Ms. Mason, in my business that is a presumed skill. I'll know the print of her horse's hoof and follow it unless she's in a lot of rocky terrain."

"The trails are all earth, not rock," Allison said. She felt lighter. Happier. Obviously, Jenkins—or whatever his real name was—knew his job. "How soon can you do this?"

Shrugging, he said, "Depends upon many variables. I'll choose a trail and make sure no one else is around. From there, I'll take my shot. Weather plays a part, as well. I'll use a silencer so that the sound of the shot won't be heard unless someone is within twenty feet. And that won't happen."

Allison nodded in approval. "Then, this is goodbye, Mr. Jenkins. You've got the money. You'll get paid the other half when Kam is dead. I'll send it from my L.A. banks to your off-shore bank account in Bermuda." Of course, Jenkins already had three of her major credit cards in case she didn't pay up afterward. Allison would make sure he got the money transfers instead. She wondered how anyone would renege on paying this hard-looking man with the lifeless eyes. In her imagination, Allison saw the hired assassin stalking and killing her if she didn't make the final payment.

"Excellent." He held out his hand to her. "Nice doing business with you, Ms. Mason."

Taking his hand, Allison felt fear as well as exhilaration. She hoped that within the next two weeks, Kam Trayhern would be out of her life—once and for all. Then, she and her children could settle down and be safe from the threat of the latecomer. Iris wouldn't change her will, which was all Allison cared about. Never did she want her children to suffer the way she had in order to survive. Obviously, she would even kill to protect them.

Jenkins departed like the shadow he was. Allison sat for a moment, her hands trembling. Compressing her lips, she started the Mercedes and turned it around. As she took another street to avoid the construction zone, she craved a stiff shot of whiskey.

She *had* to put a hit on Kam. Iris liked her far too much. It was obvious the old woman doted upon the interloper. Hands opening and closing on the steering wheel, Allison could feel the dampness collecting in her palms. Her heart beat like a runaway freight train. What had she done?

Turning onto a main road, Allison felt suddenly suffocated. She pulled over in the parking lot of a fast-food establishment, turned off the engine and gave in to the shakes. She rubbed her brow and looked at the blue sky and sunshine pouring down upon the town. Everywhere she looked, she saw tourists. They walked and laughed as if they didn't have a care in the world. She felt angry and jealous of them.

Allison tried to justify what she'd just set in motion. It wasn't like her to kill. Oh, she'd fought plenty of tough battles, that was for sure. She'd traded her body untold times to agents, directors and producers. Allison was used to horse-trading to get what she wanted. Hiring a hit man, however, was way out of her normal world-view. And now there was no turning back. She had no way to contact Jenkins. The phone number she'd been given was that of a throwaway cell phone. She'd paid the money, things were in motion and no longer within her control.

Some of the shaking abated as she convinced herself this was the only thing to do. Allison was damned if she would let her children go without money and security.

With a sigh, Allison turned on the engine again so that the air conditioning cooled down the interior of the car. From her poverty-stricken origins, now she sat in a silver Mercedes, married to a man worth millions of dollars. The security she'd wanted so badly was finally hers. Tears came to her eyes and she quickly blotted them away. She could not cry. It would ruin her mascara.

The tears felt hot behind her tightly closed eyes as Allison willed herself not to weep. Crying got her nowhere.

Lifting her head, she looked around. The quaking in her stomach had stopped. She felt calmer. Allison drew in a ragged breath. Well, logic was on her side and she clung to it. Kam Trayhern was a direct threat to everything Allison had tried to build to insulate her children from the harshness of life. A part of her was sorry it had to be done this way, but Allison knew that Kam wasn't about to leave her newfound father. The woman had been searching for Rudd all her life. And no way would Allison have her children jilted out of their rightful inheritance. Not ever...

CHAPTER EIGHTEEN

"KAM?" RUDD CALLED from the office desk. He'd seen her coming down the hall.

"Yes?" Kam stopped at the counter. It was 6:00 a.m. on Friday, the last day for this group of dude-ranch guests. On Sunday, there was major cleanup to get ready for the new group coming in that afternoon. Placing her elbows on the counter, Kam smiled over at her father. A frown furrowed his brow. He held the phone in his hand toward her.

"It's Wes. He wants to talk to you."

"Oh?" She had just visited him yesterday. The memory of his kiss and their talks were still vivid. "What's wrong?"

"He tried your cell and didn't get you."

Kam took the phone and stood next to her father. "Hi, Wes."

"Hi, Kam. I tried your cell but it wasn't working."

Groaning, Kam said, "The battery is dead, I'm sorry. What's wrong? You sound upset."

"My mother just called me from the hospital. My father died."

Heart plummeting, she whispered, "I'm so sorry, Wes. Is there anything I can do?"

"Yes, if you have time, could you be here?"

"Hold on, I'll ask Rudd. I'm here at the desk." She put her hand over the phone and relayed the sad information. "Do you mind if I spend the next two or three days with Wes at his ranch?"

"No, go ahead," Rudd said, compassion in his voice. "Just let us know the name of the mortuary and we'll send flowers. And let us know when Dan will be buried. The least we can do is show up for the funeral."

Kam nodded and got back on the phone. Her heart ached with grief for Wes. What would it be like to be disowned by one's father? She couldn't fathom such an act by any parent toward their child. Did Dan Sheridan ever realize how much Wes was suffering beneath that curse? Well, it was too late now. She knew Wes would need help.

"I'll pack my bag and be up there as soon as possible," she promised him in a low tone.

"Sounds good," Wes said, his voice roughened with emotion.

"Are you sure you can do without me around here?" Kam asked, handing the phone to Rudd.

"Go help Wes. He and Anne will need it." With a shake of his head, he added sadly, "Dan Sheridan was a drunk all his life and now Wes has to clean up after him. Anne Sheridan will collapse under the weight of it all, and without Wes, that ranch will fall apart."

Kam didn't disagree. She absorbed her father's tall, lean form. "I'm sure glad you didn't disown me," she said quietly.

Rudd looked up at her and smiled. "That wouldn't ever happen, Kam." He reached out and took her hand and squeezed it gently. "I know we have a lot of ground to make up with one another, but we're going to sort it all out."

Gripping his hand, Kam felt new tendrils of love blossom toward this man. He looked tidy in his denim cowboy shirt, his jeans and scuffed boots. Kam couldn't imagine Rudd Mason in any other kind of clothing. "Thanks, Rudd. That means a lot to me."

"This is a time of upset and chaos for many people. Wes lost his father. Anne lost her husband. I've gained a daughter. Change isn't always bad." He grinned, trying to push away the somber feelings. "Get going. Wes needs you."

Yes, he did, Kam realized, aching to get to him as soon as she would manage. Her new family would be having breakfast at 8:30 a.m., late for a ranch that counted on every daylight hour to complete chores, but Allison had laid down the law. She needed her beauty sleep and refused to get up any earlier. This time, she would miss the family meal, though she couldn't say she was sorry about it.

As she hurried back to her suite along the hall shining with incandescent light from several wall sconces, Kam walked quietly so as not to disturb the rest of her sleeping family. She hurriedly packed a suitcase and carried it out to her car.

Iris was outside the ranch office door, pulling on her gardening gloves, when she spotted Kam. "I just heard what happened from Rudd. Will you give Anne and Wes our condolences? We'll be coming to Cody for Dan's funeral."

"I will, Iris," Kam said, closing the trunk.

Her grandmother came over to stand near the driver's door. "You okay? You look pretty grief-stricken yourself by the news."

"Just shaken more than anything. I guess I didn't think he'd go so soon."

"Death claims us all," Iris said sympathetically. She reached out and patted Kam's shoulder. "I'm glad you'll be over there for the next few days to help them get through this. Do what you can, where you can. It's the little things that help out, like cleaning up the dishes, cooking meals, vacuuming the floor, dusting and stuff like that. May not seem like much, but your world comes to a roarin' halt when someone you've lived with all your life suddenly dies."

"You know that better than anyone," Kam agreed, a catch in her voice as she noticed the woman's grief over losing Trevor. Was it possible to find that kind of deep, lasting love? Wes was that kind of man: loyal, true and enduring. Instinctively, Kam knew that. But so much stood in their way right now. "I'll take your condolences to them."

"Stay in touch, all right? Because if Anne or Wes need anything, we'll be there for them."

"Sounds good," Kam said. She waved goodbye, climbed into the car and backed out of the driveway. As she turned and drove down the road, the sun edged over the horizon. She had to admit it, she felt a fierce, undeniable love for Wes. What did the future hold for them? Her own family situation was tentative right now.

Allison didn't like her and her two half siblings ignored her. In many ways, Kam was no better than an intruder. Iris and Rudd had told her not to feel that way, but when three other people were giving her dark looks and snubbing her, how was she to feel? Driving off the dirt road and onto the asphalt highway, Kam was grateful to have some alone time to try to answer those questions.

Her mind spun with confusion. Wes had to deal with his family's ranch, which meant he might not return to Elkhorn. Kam couldn't imagine Wes walking away from his mother or her plight, nor would she expect him to.

Whatever happened, her life felt upended. The commute soothed her nerves and, as she drove north through Grand Teton National Park and into Yellowstone, she absorbed the volcanic scenery. She would go through the mud volcano area, turn east and eventually leave the famous geyser park. Cody was roughly fifty miles outside the east gate to Yellowstone. On her way, she saw herds of buffalo scattered across lush landscape. Fog lay across one meadow and elk seemed almost ethereal as they grazed the summer grass. When she neared creeks or rivers, Kam had to slow down because some areas teemed with moose. The seven-foot tall animals were so huge that if a collision occurred both animal and driver could die.

Even with the distraction of the mountains, the forest and the wild animals, Kam's thoughts kept returning to Wes. She ached over his loss. She couldn't get to him fast enough.

"How are you doing?" Anne Sheridan asked her son as she entered the ranch house. Placing her black leather purse on a small table in the foyer, she attempted a smile.

"I'm okay," Wes said, giving his mother a warm hug. "How are you?" The hospital was only about ten miles from their ranch, which was good news. At least she hadn't had a long drive to add to her stress. Searching her small oval face, Wes noted the dried tearstains on her cheeks. His mother always wore some makeup, but today even that couldn't cover her grief. How she could love a man like his father was beyond Wes.

"In one way, I'm glad it's over," Anne told him in a quavering tone. She smoothed her pink blouse and re-arranged it around the waist of her dark blue slacks. "At least he's no longer suffering."

Wes bit back a response. He wanted to say, *and we aren't, either. We're free of the bastard.* But he didn't dare. He had no desire to hurt his mother any more than she hurt already. And clearly, she was. "Kam is coming to help us the next three or four days."

"How kind of her," Anne murmured. She looked around the quiet ranch house. "I think I could use some help. I—I just can't seem to put two thoughts together. I'm misplacing things…"

"I've got everything under control here," Wes gently assured her, placing his arm on her shoulder. "Why don't we go to the kitchen table and sit down? Did you have a mortuary picked out for him?" He couldn't even say the word *father*.

As she walked down the hall, Anne placed her arm around his waist. Eastern sunlight flooded out of the kitchen. "No, I didn't."

"I've got all the info," Wes told her. "The other day when I was in Cody at the feed and seed store, I stopped by several of them. I have their brochures on the table. I'll take care of it."

Anne gave her son a grateful squeeze, and walked into the kitchen. The smell of coffee was welcome after the sterile odors of the hospital. On the table was a small stack of brochures, paper and pens. "You're so organized, Wes," she told him as she sat. "Are Chris and Rachel coming?"

"I've been on the phone with them," Wes admitted, pouring coffee and setting the mugs on the table. "With their jobs, they can't come here to the ranch to help. But they want to know the name of the mortuary and they'll be at the burial services to support you." He knew his younger siblings hated Dan Sheridan even more than he did. He wondered if his mother realized they were coming because they loved her—not him.

Relieved, Anne closed her eyes for a moment. "I'm so glad," she whispered unsteadily. Opening them, she watched Wes sit down at her elbow. "What would I do without you here?"

"Mom, all you need to do is hire a good foreman. He can run this ranch better than…" He snapped his mouth shut. He was well aware of his father's will and what it said—his mother got everything, which was fine with him.

"There are so many decisions to make," she whispered, dabbing her eyes with a tissue.

Wes could barely stand to see his mother crying, but now she was better off in his mind. No longer was Dan Sheridan telling her what to do and when. Or keeping her out of ranch business when she should have been immersed in it. His mind ranged back to Rudd and his mother, Iris. She and Trevor had trained Rudd from boyhood to run their ranch. Dan should have done the same thing, but he hadn't. "Look, whatever you decide, you know us kids will go along with it, Mom," he told her gently, laying his hand over hers, Wes saw her try to smile, but failed.

"Thank you. I—I know you children and your father never got on. I—I'm a part of that. As I sat there with him dying in the hospital, I reviewed my own life." She squeezed her eyes shut. "I've failed you children. I'm so sorry. So sorry…"

"Mom, don't go there right now," Wes pleaded hoarsely. "Let's just pick out a funeral parlor. One day at a time, okay?" He couldn't help but be shocked over her admission, and felt some of the weight melt off his shoulders. His mother had always defended Dan to the three children. Maybe dying provided clarity for those left behind. His mother was a teacher and that's all she knew. And right now, looking into her teary eyes, Wes wondered if she wanted the ranch at all. The thought struck him—would she sell the ranch? All he could do right now was address the brochures. One thing at a time.

He wanted—needed—Kam at his side. Just knowing that she was on her way gave him hope as nothing else could. In a few hours, she would be here—at his side. Where she belonged.

CHAPTER NINETEEN

WES WAS OUT on the front porch when Kam drove up. Finally. He wanted to jump for joy. He quickly settled his Stetson on his head and walked out to where she'd parked, beneath a group of shady cottonwoods. Some of the cowhands were busy at the barn corral branding new calves. His other hands were out checking on the various herds.

As he watched Kam climb out of her hybrid car, he realized just how much he needed her. How he envied the peacefulness evident in her face. Obviously, she was in a good place. Was this what happened in a healthy relationship? When one partner went down, the other would support him through the trying times? Wes didn't have any decent role models to be able to know for sure.

Kam turned and flashed him a warm smile.

"Hi, stranger," he said, his voice suddenly hoarse. As

he approached Kam, he noticed she wore her usual jeans and a dark green T-shirt with an orange flower pattern. Her short black hair ruffled in the breeze. She wore no makeup but she didn't need a thing to look beautiful.

Kam heard the strain in Wes's voice. Marred with grief, his eyes glittered with tears. Her heart twisted as she watched him struggle. What was it about men that made them afraid to cry? Afraid to feel? It didn't matter. She rushed into his arms. Kam embraced him and buried her head against his neck and shoulder.

"I'm so sorry, Wes," she whispered, holding him. His arms tightened strongly about her, and then he relaxed, as if surrendering to her womanly strength. They stood in one another's arms, holding and comforting. Kam could only hear the pounding of their hearts beating in unison. His breath grazed her cheek.

Wes groaned as he felt tears squeezing out of his tightly shut eyes. He did not want to cry! With Kam's soft body against his, all of the walls he'd built to remain strong dissolved. A sob like a fist punched up his throat. He gulped hard to stop it, struggled and then felt a gush of tears down his cheeks.

"Stop fighting," Kam said urgently, holding him even tighter. "Go ahead and cry, will you? It's all right, Wes. You've been through so much…."

She understood, somehow made it safe for him to unleash those emotions. The tears flowed freely. All Wes wanted right now was the safe harbor of Kam's arms, her body against his and her soft breath against his neck. He allowed his anger and grief to manifest themselves through his tears. Wes could not recall how long it had been since he'd last cried. When his father had disowned him two years ago, it had done nothing but fill him with rage and confusion. He'd never cried. Not until now.

"Shhh, it's all right," Kam whispered, sliding her fingers through his short, dark hair. With long, gentle stroking motions, she slid her hand from his neck, across his tense, shaking shoulders and followed the deep indention of his spine. Wes was strong and proud. Kam knew that. And she was sure the tears he shared were a rare occurrence. She could count on one hand how many times she'd seen her adopted father cry. And when he had, Laura had held him. Now, she was holding Wes. Maybe a man needed a woman to hold him. It was an act of love and care. Love? Just when had she fallen in love with Wes? As she stood gently rocking him, Kam thought back to how her feelings for him turned to more than just friendship. Obviously, the kiss on the dance floor hadn't helped matters. Ever since, she hadn't stopped thinking of him on an intimate level. It must have. She pressed small, soft kisses against his neck. Kisses meant to heal him, to take away some of the pain she felt trembling inside him.

Though he seemed reluctant, Wes eased away from her. With an embarrassed swipe of his hand, he washed away the evidence of his tears. Moisture beaded on dark brown lashes, and he studied her in the lulling silence. His gray eyes were dark and muddy.

"Oh, Wes," she whispered, framing his face with her hands. Leaning forward, Kam kissed the tears on his cheeks away. And then her mouth drifted into his. She felt him tense for just a moment, his fingers gripping her hard. And then, he took her commandingly as his lips moved roughly against hers.

Kam had never been kissed like this. Her entire

world spun. She melted beneath his fiery, searching embrace. The sounds of birds singing, the rustle of cottonwood leaves dissolved. Her heart almost leaped out of her breast with joy. Kam moaned in response to the wonderful feelings Wes evoked within her. His mouth was strong and hungry. But so was hers. How long had she dreamed of really kissing Wes? Almost nightly, Kam realized as their mouths clung greedily to one another. His tongue glided gently against her lower lip as if to invite her inside him. Even though his kiss scorched her, Kam felt him monitoring her every reaction. Wes did not want to hurt her with his intensity.

Finally, Wes slowly separated from Kam. Inches away from her, he stared into her wide, flawless eyes. Wes released her shoulders and framed her face.

She swallowed hard and whispered, "That felt so right…." His dark eyes were stormy and filled with hungry desire—for her alone.

Wes could barely breathe and his pulse raced. His lower body was hard with need. Pushing a few wisps of black hair off her brow, he managed, "I don't know why it happened, but I don't care."

Closing her eyes, Kam breathed deeply. His fingers brushed her temple. Oh, how she longed to feel his long, callused hands range across her body. When he released her and stepped back, she opened her eyes. They stood so close to one another. Her hands ached to embrace him once more. But now was not the time.

"Tears are healing," Kam told him in a low, unsteady voice. "Thank you for trusting me enough to cry. You needed to, Wes. There's so much pressure on you."

Wes took another step away because if he didn't, he would grab Kam and drag her into the house, to his bedroom, and make love to her. "I don't remember the last time I cried, Kam. Thanks for being there."

Kam smiled reassuringly even as he created more space between them. How rugged and handsome he looked in his jeans and dark blue long-sleeved shirt with the cuffs rolled up to just below his elbows. His boots were dusty, showing how he worked even during the death of his father. She made a motion toward the house. "Is your mother home?"

Wes drew in a ragged breath and hitched his hands upon his narrow hips. "Yes, she is." He told her what had transpired since his mother had come from the hospital. "Right now, she's in her bedroom sleeping."

"I don't blame her," Kam said sympathetically. "She must be so sleep-deprived from her watch over her husband." She knew Wes never referred to Dan Sheridan as his father. Still, Kam trod lightly, not wanting to add to his pain. Sooner or later, Wes would have to deal with his father's death, his anger against him, the years of hurt. Reaching out, she squeezed Wes's hand and released it.

"What can I do around here?"

Wes raised the hat off his head, wiped his brow and then settled it back down. "I can use all the help you can give me. Can you cook?"

"Sure, I love to cook. What else can I do? Have you contacted the mortuary?"

"Yes, I have. But I need to talk to the cemetery."

"I can take care of those details."

"That would help." Wes looked toward the barn. "We've got a thousand head of newborn calves that need to be vet-checked. We've got four hundred six-month-old Hereford calves that need branding. I'm up to my hocks in work right now. This came at a really bad time."

Kam understood enough about cattle ranching to know some of his pressures. "Okay, I'm not so good with a lariat," she teased with a grin, "but I can do phone calls, send out notices, cook, clean and wash."

Wes smiled back. "That sounds great, Kam. Thank you. My mother is…well…you'll see. Just give her space, okay? She's not herself right now."

"Grief has its own way with us," Kam said, following him through the gate and down the cobblestone walk of colorful cream, red and black stones that led to the ranch-house porch.

"My mother will probably sleep until noon."

"I'll have lunch ready for the three of us," Kam said briskly, opening the screen door and walking into the house. The hall was dark, unlike that at the Elkhorn. She saw a lot of dust, some spiderwebs in the corners, and the floor needing a good sweeping and mopping. Soon they were in the kitchen.

Unlike the hall, the kitchen was large and airy. Kam turned to Wes. "My home away from home."

"I'm glad you're here," he told her quietly, his voice gritty. "I'll get your luggage and take it to the third door on the left down the hall. That's my sister's old bedroom. You can make yourself at home in there."

Heat coursed through Kam over the veiled intimacy in Wes's tone. "That's fine. Just drop my one bag in there and get me the cemetery info. You can go help your hands with the branding." She saw the banked desire in his gray eyes and felt needy. Her mouth tingled wildly over their kiss. From his darkly tanned face to his tall, straight form, Kam wanted Wes in every way.

"Sounds good." Wes reached out and touched Kam's reddened cheek. "I know this isn't the time or place, but we need to talk when this funeral is behind us."

The trailing caress of his finger sent wild sensations across her flesh. "Yes, we need to talk."

Nodding, Wes went into the other room and gathered up the information on the cemetery. He placed the file on the square wooden kitchen table. He was relieved not to deal with the details of his father's death. The sooner this was over, the better.

Wes left to go help his men with the branding duties.

THREE HOURS LATER, Kam had lunch ready for Wes. Fresh from her nap, his mother was sitting at the table, drinking coffee. The two women had chatted amiably while Kam fixed them a lunch of grilled cheese sandwiches, three-bean salad and potato chips. Kam was just finishing up when he walked in.

"You're up," Wes greeted his mother at the kitchen entrance. He hung up his dusty hat on a nearby wooden peg, then went over to kiss his mother's forehead.

"I am." Anne smiled at her son who sat opposite her. "And I met Kam, who is a dear."

Wes poured himself some coffee from a percolator sitting on a hot plate. "She's all that and more," he agreed. "Kam, this smells wonderful. Thanks for fixing lunch for us."

Heat coursed across Kam's cheeks. "You're welcome." After placing a sandwich on Anne's plate, Kam retrieved the other two for Wes and herself. Once everyone was served, she took a breath and sat down. Right off, she noticed Wes was still sweating from his work outdoors. At noon, the temperature was plenty high and made branding dusty work, hard and hot. She saw that he'd tried to brush off most of the dust from his clothes before entering the house. Before she got too caught up in him, she handed Anne the bowl of chips. "If this isn't enough to eat, let me know."

"Oh, this is fine," Wes said as he heaped the three-bean salad onto his plate. "What do you think, Mother? You okay with this lunch?"

Anne smiled but it was filled with sadness. "What a wonderful meal, Kam. Thank you so much for coming here and helping us out. I'm afraid I'm not much use right now."

Reaching out, Kam touched Anne's hand. "Under the circumstances, don't be hard on yourself. I love to cook. I'm a little rusty at it, but I don't think I'll poison any of us."

Anne laughed a little and picked at the food.

It was obvious the woman was too upset to eat. Wes, on the other hand, ate voraciously. The work of the cowboy was physical, and Kam knew these men built up huge appetites. Anne gave her son half her sandwich and he thanked her.

"How's branding going?" Kam asked.

"Good. The boys know what they're doing and that means everything," Wes told her between bites. He finished off the salad and put another huge helping on his plate.

"I don't know what I'm going to do," Anne said in a low voice to her son. "With Dan gone, there's no one to run the ranch."

"I can stay and help," Wes told her. "I think the best thing to do is hire a foreman, Mother. You need someone who can run this operation while you continue to teach."

Nodding, Anne wiped her mouth on a paper napkin and returned it to her plate. "Do you know how to go about doing that?"

"Yes, I do," he said. "In fact, we have someone over at the Elkhorn Ranch, Braidy Adams, who is wanting to stretch his wings and get out from under Chappy. He's more than capable of handling this ranch, Mother. Do you want to speak with him?"

Anne's brow wrinkled. "Oh, honey, I wouldn't know what to ask." She gave Wes a pleading look. "Couldn't you do that? Bring Braidy over here and see if he's interested in managing this place?"

Wes smiled. "Not a problem. I'll do it early next week after the funeral is over."

Kam saw Anne's eyes turn grief-stricken. Tears gathered and she sniffed. "Anne? Would you like to sit in the living room for a while? I could bring you some coffee or tea."

"No, no," the woman said, trying to smile but failing. "You two young ones sit here and finish your lunch. I'm just a little overemotional. I think I'll go for a walk outside and see how my flowers are getting along."

Wes stood up and pulled his mother's chair away from the table. When Anne rose, she glanced over at Kam. "I think after I go for a short walk, I'm going to go back and lie down. I'm still very tired."

"Of course," Kam said. "I'll take care of everything here so don't worry." Anne seemed like a ghost with deep, dark circles beneath her gray eyes. Her face had once been beautiful, no doubt, but now, it was obvious that a lifetime of stress had aged her. Kam began to understand why Wes felt the way he did. She saw the worry in his eyes.

They ate in silence for a few moments before Kam spoke up. "All the funeral arrangements are in order. Your brother and sister will be there, along with Rudd."

Wes gave her a warm, grateful look. "I can't do without you, Kam. You've taken a major load off my mother."

"She looks so worn-down and fragile."

"She is," Wes growled, finishing off his sandwich. "Dan made her that way. You stuck around him and that's what he did to you—bled you dry emotionally and then destroyed you."

Kam couldn't respond. What was there to say? Right now was not the time to delve into the wounds his father had created in him. "I'm sorry," she murmured, meaning it.

"Pretty soon, it will be over. All I want to do is get my mother the help she needs and then go back to the Elkhorn."

"Really?" Kam raised her head and stared at Wes. For whatever reason, she had thought he might remain in Cody and leave his job at the Elkhorn.

Shrugging, Wes said bitterly, "There's nothing here for me. My mother now owns the ranch. I don't want to stay here. I want my own life."

"I see...."

Wes cleared his throat and added, "Besides, you live at the Elkhorn now."

A feeling of warmth flowed through Kam and she clung to his narrowed gaze. "I'm glad you're coming home," she whispered.

CHAPTER TWENTY

"WELCOME BACK," RUDD told Kam as she entered the ranch office. The sun slanted brightly behind her as she came through the screen door. It was Thursday and the funeral had taken place yesterday. Giving Rudd a hug, Kam smiled tiredly.

"Glad to be back."

He released her and went around the counter to his desk. Piles of paperwork waited for him. "The funeral went well yesterday. Kinda sad that Anne's two young ones came only to support her, not say goodbye to their father, but I do understand." He hooked his hat on a wooden wall peg and sat down.

Leaning against the counter, Kam saw the group of dudes in the corral mounting horses for a morning ride. "I hope in time they'll deal with their anger with their father."

Rudd nodded. "In a situation like that, we can't know how a person feels. The fact they didn't cry or show any emotions tells me they're pretty well injured by the family dynamic."

Grimacing, Kam agreed. "Where's Iris? I need to go take her blood pressure and see how she's doing."

"Out in the greenhouse as usual," Rudd said, turning on the computer at the desk.

Kam took advantage of the quiet moment. Usually, someone was coming or going from the office. She leaned her elbows on the counter. "Rudd, would you be offended if I started taking my dinner out with Wes in the dining hall?" Wes was going to give Braidy Adams a chance to be foreman for a month to see if he was a good fit. That allowed Wes to return to the Elkhorn Ranch.

Brows arching, Rudd glanced up. The corners of his mouth hitched slightly upward. "Wes will be back in about an hour. I'm glad he's coming here. So," he murmured, giving Kam a intent look, "you and this young man have some kind of feelings for one another?"

"Yes, we do," Kam hesitantly admitted. She peered down the hall toward the main family area. The suite doors were open sometimes and she didn't want to be caught talking about this matter within earshot of Allison or her children. "I don't want to cause trouble by not being at dinner at night but—"

"That's good news. Wes is a fine man, a hard worker. Why not invite Wes to our family dinner, then?"

"Rudd, things are tense enough at dinner right now with me at the table with your family."

"*Our* family, Kam. And yes, I'm aware my wife and my son and daughter aren't exactly pleasant, but I think with time, that will dissolve. I've talked with Allison several times about it. She's promised to try and be more civil."

Kam appreciated Rudd's efforts but knew Allison ran all over him. It was Rudd's nature to try and please his wife and although he was a good manager with people, he was a pushover with her. "I don't want to add fuel to the fire, Rudd. Thanks for offering to let Wes join us, but for now, I don't think it's a good idea."

Rudd shrugged. "I don't disagree. And I do understand. Go eat with Wes over at the dining hall. I'll miss you." He smiled fondly at her.

"I'll miss you, too, but I get to see you all day long everywhere else," she said, relieved.

"Iris won't be happy about this."

"I know," Kam said, frustrated. "I'll go talk to her about it."

"She'll deal with it. She's a tough ol' buzzard." Rudd chuckled.

"No question. I'll get started on my daily activities unless you have something else you want me to do."

"Nope," Rudd said. "As soon as Judy relieves me here at the desk, I'm out with a group of my hands working on that riding trail over in the Twin Hills area."

Kam was familiar with the Twin Hills, basically two large mounds of earth rising up out of the green pastures. The trail between them had been partially washed out by recent thunderstorms and needed repair. Rudd and his men had been working to widen it, fill in the deep trenches where the horses had plodded over it for years. It would make riding smoother and more of an enjoyment for dudes. A number of horses had stumbled on the weathered trail, and Rudd didn't want any accidents. This type of work, she discovered, went on constantly at the ranch.

Lifting her hand, she said, "I'll see you at lunch." She would still spend two times a day at the family dinner table. Luckily, Allison didn't always come to the 8:30 a.m. breakfast and Zach never showed up for it. Regan did come fairly often, but she simply gave Kam the silent treatment, which was fine with her.

As she went to the screen door, Rudd called, "I'll let Wes know that you're joining him at dinner."

Kam grinned back at her father. "Thank you, Rudd. I'm glad you understand."

Rudd winked. "He's a fine young man."

"Thanks, I think so, too." Kam's heart lifted as she skipped down the wooden steps. The sun was peeking over the mountains in the east and shining brightly. The morning was a clear, clean blue and the Wyoming sky seemed to go on forever.

Wes had asked her to eat with him at night. During the day they were so busy at the ranch, they wouldn't get to see much of one another. This way, he told her, they'd have a sit-down dinner during which to chat about the day together. Kam thought it was a wonderful idea. As she walked toward the greenhouse, Kam's steps were light. She felt as if she were floating on air.

"Well, there you are!" Iris crowed with a smile as Kam entered the greenhouse. "I sure missed you! How are you?"

Kam saw Iris was sitting at her baker's table with several flowers floating in transparent custard dishes. These were new flowers that had just bloomed and she was making fresh mother tincture for the coming year. There would be many orders for them. Taking a green apron, Kam pulled it over her head and tied the sash around her waist. "I'm fine. A little tired from all the tension over at Anne's ranch."

"It's hard but rewarding work," Iris said. She wiped her hands on her own green apron, worn today over pink slacks. "That was a nice funeral for Dan. Too bad his kids were so grim-looking. But I can understand their feelings toward their father. I'm just happy they were there for their mother."

Sitting down at the end of the baker's table, Kam pulled out her stethoscope and blood-pressure cuff from the metal locker against the wall. She rolled up Iris's left sleeve.

"Dan Sheridan was a messed-up person, Iris. Wes told me his brother and sister just couldn't deal with him or what he'd done to them over the years. At least they came to be with Anne." Kam wrapped the cuff around Iris's arm and listed for the heartbeats. She was pleased and removed the cuff. "You're normal."

Iris grinned and pulled down her sleeve. "Of course."

"You'll live to be over a hundred," Kam teased.

"With you around, I know I will." Iris pushed some silver strands away from her face and frowned. "About the Sheridan children. Parents can either make or break you. Those kids have a lot of hurt to work through over time. Wes is hurting."

"Yes, he is," Kam agreed, her heart breaking over the whole situation. She relayed how she and Wes would be sharing the dining hall instead of the family table. A sly smile crept onto Iris's lips.

"Why that smile?" Kam asked with a laugh.

"Oh," Iris said, mixing fruit brandy with some of the

mother essence. "From the moment I saw Wes give you that *look,* I knew."

Kam flushed. "What look?"

Iris wrote the name of the flower, along with its Latin name on a white label and stuck it on the bottle. "A look a man gives a woman that he's falling in love with." She looked straight at Kam. "*That* look."

"Oh…" Kam was at a loss for words.

"Well, you do have feelings for him, don't you?" Iris demanded archly.

"I guess I do…"

"Why so hesitant? You haven't talked about any past relationships. As you're my granddaughter, I need to know all." She reached over and patted Kam's cheek.

It was so easy to talk with Iris, though Kam was still adjusting to having a grandmother. She was truly blessed.

"I just—well—the men I met as a stringer photographer kicking around the world, I wouldn't give you two cents for. I wanted a man like…my adopted father, Morgan Trayhern. Someone who was steady, loyal, loved his family, worked hard and tried to do the right thing." She shrugged. "No one is perfect. That I know. But Morgan brought integrity to the way he leads his life. That's the kind of man I wanted to marry."

"Rudd's that kind of gent, as well," Iris said, twisting the black plastic lid onto the amber bottle and setting it aside. "He's of strong moral fiber, knows right from wrong and, like Morgan, tries to do the right thing. He doesn't always, but who among us does?" Her eyes twinkled. "That's what makes us painfully and wonderfully human—the mistakes we all make all the time." She reached for another custard dish and placed a funnel over an eight-ounce amber bottle. Picking up a clean square of muslin, she poked it down inside the funnel. "Rudd and Morgan sound an awful lot alike."

"They are," Kam said eagerly. "And I hope that soon my adoptive parents will come out here to meet you and Rudd. That would be a dream come true. I really think you'd like them."

"I'm sure I would. Look at you." Iris carefully poured the mother essence from the custard dish into the funnel and muslin. "Wes is from that same cut of cloth. But I don't have to tell you that." She slid Kam an arch look that said it all.

Chuckling, Kam removed the funnel from the bottle after Iris was done pouring the contents. The used muslin went on a small pile. Fresh, clean muslin was used on every mother essence and never twice. The used funnels went into a box and would later be washed.

"He's a good man," Kam murmured. "I just don't want to rush things, though. Wes is going through hell right now. His mother needs a ranch foreman and he's got enough to deal with. And so do I." She gave Iris a loving look. "I just found my father and grandmother. I'm going through huge changes, too."

"Well," Iris told her briskly, "you have time. Wes is staying here, and spending your dinners together is a real good idea."

"I'm glad you understand," Kam said, relieved.

"Who wants to sit at dinner with Allison glowering?" she snorted. "I tell you, Kam, it's hard for me to stay quiet about how she's treating you. And those two kids are taking their cues from her. They should treat you with respect."

Reaching out, Kam squeezed the woman's darkly

tanned arm. "Now, we don't have to worry about it, do we?"

"You still have breakfast and lunch with us," Iris reminded her.

"I can handle that," Kam assured her. "Things will settle down. Eventually, there will be a truce between Allison and me."

"Don't bet on it," Iris growled. She sat up and placed her hands in the lap of her apron. "Once Allison decides you are her enemy, it stays that way. I'm her enemy, but she knows I own this ranch. To her, you're nothing."

Kam sighed. "I know…and I feel badly about all of this."

"It's not your fault, Kam. Rudd and I love you, and we're the two people who count." Iris gripped Kam's fingers. "Just be careful."

"I will."

"Good!" Iris released her hand and stood up. She took off her apron and set it on the table. "After lunch today, I want to go to the Twin Hills area. Chappy told me he saw some of my wildflowers in bloom. I'm going to fill my saddlebags. Want to come along? I'll bet Freckles would love to get a trail ride in."

Laughing, Kam stood up and set her apron on the table. "I'd love to!"

ALLISON PEEKED THROUGH the pink curtains of her suite. She saw Iris and Kam riding off in the direction of Twin Hills. Was André Jenkins out there? Did he see Kam? Would he follow her? She fumed because there were no forthcoming answers. Allison dropped the curtain back into place. After smoothing out the wrinkles in her cream-colored linen slacks, Allison nervously touched her fuchsia blouse. She rearranged her chunky gold necklace and sighed out of pure frustration. She hated not having control. It left her feeling like a victim, just like when she was sixteen, before she'd run away from home. As she paced the large living-room area, she clenched and unclenched her fists.

All week, Kam had been in Cody to help Anne and Wes Sheridan adjust after Dan's sudden death. Damn the bad luck of Sheridan dying the week her hit man was here. Today was Thursday, and Saturday was the last day André would be here disguised as a dude-ranch guest. This was the first opportunity he'd had to shoot Kam. Was Jenkins aware she was riding out now? Should she try and find the hit man and tell him? *No.* Halting in the living room, Allison tasted bitter rage. He'd outright ordered her never to approach him, talk to him or let anyone know that she had any connection with him.

Would Jenkins know about this trail ride? She ran her hand across her blond hair, stiff with hair spray and began pacing again. Iris was with Kam. Jenkins had said he'd only kill Kam Trayhern if she was alone. In Allison's fondest dreams, Iris died and got the hell out of her way. The old woman was the matriarch and until she died, the ranch was hers and not theirs. Damn the old bitch, anyway.

Her eyes falling on the liquor cabinet, Allison felt her nerves jangling—a good dose of vodka would calm them. Never mind that it was only nine in the morning. She took a cut-glass lead-crystal tumbler from the cabinet, grabbed the bottle and opened it. After throwing in some ice cubes, she splashed in some liquor.

Allison feared what would happen after Kam was

found dead on a trail. Rudd was deeply attached to his new daughter already. Would they suspect that a stray bullet from an out-of-season hunter had struck Kam? Or, would they suspect foul play and have the local police begin an investigation?

It was the second thought that shook Allison up and made her nerves shriek as never before. Once she gulped down the vodka in quick swallows, Allison set the glass back on the smooth, golden surface of the oak sideboard. Standing there, her hands splayed out across the top, she closed her eyes. Her greatest fear was that the police would discover that she'd hired Jenkins to kill Kam. If she was fingered, she'd go to prison. Maybe even get the death penalty. Real fear gnawed her insides. Allison couldn't stand the idea of prison, and yet she had to take this risk. Everything she'd worked so hard to build, her life, her children's futures could go up in smoke because of one stupid girl. Sure, she could go to jail, but she'd see Kam Trayhern in hell first.

ANDRÉ JENKINS SAT high on the north hill, looking down on the trail through the scope of his sniper rifle. He was well hidden by surrounding bushes. Only the dull black barrel of his rifle stuck a few inches outside the bushes. He'd found this ideal site on his first day at the ranch. Now he had to finish his assignment.

When he'd seen Iris and Kam riding out earlier, he knew the time had come. He told one of the wranglers he had a headache and needed to beg off his morning ride. The man had accepted the excuse without question. It was easy enough to saddle his mount and ride off in a circular path to get to the Twin Hills trail. After tying his horse down on the eastern side of one of the

hills, he'd climbed up and over the top. Halfway down
the western side, he settled into his hiding spot. Jenkins knew that if his mount saw or heard the two riders,
he would start whinnying. The hills were so large that
his mount was a good three quarters of a mile away on
the opposite side. It would be nearly impossible for it
to hear the two horses coming down the trail between
the hills. His only possible sound problem was solved
by distance alone.

His rifle sat on a tripod. The sunlight dappled
through the leaves of the area's many trees. After lunch,
a bunch of hands would be out here working on the
trail. That was fine with him. By that time, he would
have killed Kam Trayhern and gotten out of the area.
Iris would ride for help. The ensuing chaos back at the
ranch would be his cover.

The plan congealed in Jenkins's mind. He hoped that
Kam Trayhern would be riding on the east side of the
trail. That way, he'd get a clear shot at her. If she was
on the western side, it became a dicey proposition. He'd
have to wait for a shot because Iris would be in the way.
Above all, he couldn't shoot the old lady.

Mouth thinning, Jenkins waited and looked down
the trail. He'd ridden hard to get here ahead of them
in order to set up. There was a much quicker, shorter
trail to Twin Hills that the ranch hands always used.
The other trail, created for a long, winding, leisurely
ride to the same area, had been created for the guests.
Iris and Kam had taken that trail. And why not? It was
a beautiful cool summer morning and the old lady had
her flower-essence gear in the saddlebags on her horse.
Why not take a nice, quiet walk to enjoy nature?

The minutes ticked by. André knew roughly how

long it would take the riders to get to this point in the trail. What was the problem? Where were they? Glancing back down at his watch, André decided to wait another ten minutes. If they didn't show up, that meant that they had stopped earlier and wouldn't be coming this far. A thin ribbon of frustration niggled at him, but he shrugged it off. As a hired professional, he never got in a hurry. Patience was his greatest ally.

Suddenly, André heard the snort of horses. *It was them!* Looking through the scope's crosshairs, he saw them approaching and cursed softly. Iris was on his side of the trail—bad news. Kam Trayhern rode next to her. *Damn.* Jenkins had been hoping that they would ride single file, but they weren't. This made the shot even tougher. Finger brushing the trigger, he watched them ambling up the trail. Their laughter and chatter drifted his way. The wind was nonexistent, which meant he didn't have to add in windage to his shot.

As they rode closer, André kept his eye on the powerful scope. A surge of power burst through him. Neither woman knew he was here. The horses plodded along, looking for nibbles of grass to grab along the trail, oblivious to his presence. A smile pulled at his mouth. Finger on the trigger of the sniper rifle, he now tracked them in earnest. They were less than thirty feet away. There was a slight curve in the trail and then they would ride past him. As they rode in unison around the curve, André held his breath. Would they break into single file now? The path grew narrow. Instead, they took both horses on one side of the trail to avoid the deeps ruts. *Damn!*

His finger brushed the trigger and then became firm against it. Iris lifted her hand and gestured. Their laughter rang throughout the area. Each time Kam came into view, her horse would work to stay even with Iris's horse. Frowning, André waited. He barely got one-third of Kam Trayhern's skull in the scope. His shot was no good.

Real frustration bubbled up through him as they went around another curve in the trail—and out of sight. Sitting back, he eased the rifle butt to the ground between his spread legs. *Not today.* Getting up, he hurriedly broke down his rifle and tucked it into a rectangular canvas bag that became a large knapsack. The laughter and chatter of Kam Trayhern and Iris Mason grew distant. They were far enough away for André to escape and get back to the ranch.

Disappointed, he quietly moved with a hunter's ease through the underbrush. Another time would have to present itself. It would be impossible to hurry ahead on this hill to try and get another shot. His crashing through the brush would alert their horses. No, he'd tried and failed.

Cresting the hill, the pines towering around him, André spotted his tied horse below. It was far more interested in nibbling at grass than anything else. The backpack was snug and he carefully made his way down the slippery slope, the pine needles slick underfoot. André didn't have many more days as a dude-ranch guest. If that strategy didn't work out, well, he'd stick around and make the hit happen. André smiled once again. The thrill of stalking was nearly as exciting as watching his victims through the scope of his rifle seconds before he killed them.

CHAPTER TWENTY-ONE

ALLISON STARTED WHEN she saw Jenkins ride back into the barn and dismount from his horse. Anxiously, she peered out the window, the curtain drawn back.

Was Kam dead?

A cold sweat popped out on her forehead, and a galvanizing fear raced through her. Not to mention she was woozy from drinking too much vodka. It had done little to tamp down her raw nerves.

How she wanted to run up to Jenkins and ask what had happened. But she couldn't. Jenkins's face had no expression as he handed the horse to a wrangler and walked away, the large, bulky knapsack on his back. Allison knew his rifle was in there. Again, an icy shiver coursed through her. Stepping back, she allowed the curtains to fall together once more.

Arms across her chest, Allison stood torn. She had to

find out! But how? Jenkins had warned her never to approach him. If Kam was dead, where was Iris? They had ridden off together. Had Jenkins killed both of them?

With a strangled cry, Allison clutched at her stiffly coiffed hair. She paced restlessly around the suite, her breathing choppy and adrenaline shooting through her. She wanted to scream. It was one thing to kill Kam. It was quite another to kill Rudd's mother. Oh God, what had she done?

Sitting down, Allison folded into a nearly fetal position on the couch, crying. Right now, she wanted to be anywhere but here. The weight of the world came down on her and Allison sobbed. It was all Kam's fault for coming here.

She couldn't fall apart like this. No one could know anything was wrong. Finally, she wiped her eyes, smearing her mascara. Allison bounded to the bathroom to repair her makeup. As she stared at her pale countenance in the mirror, her hair shoved off to one side, Allison grimaced. She had to stop panicking. Slow down and think. If she went out to the greenhouse, she might find Iris. If she found Iris, she would know whether or not Kam was dead. Or if Kam was dead and Iris was left alive, surely the old woman would be calling in on her cell phone. Cell phones didn't always work in the Twin Hills area, and calls were spotty at best. Rudd had complained mightily about that problem. Any time a dude trail ride went out, the head wrangler always had a cell phone. If there was an accident, then he could make a call to the ranch house and they could spring into action.

Quickly repairing her makeup, Allison tried to breathe deeply and get a solid hold on her writhing

emotional state. The office was down the hall, and Judy
Harper was manning the desk. All she had to do was
casually walk by. That's it. That's what she would do.
If Kam was dead, Iris might have gotten a call through
to the office. She would know, then.

Allison rearranged her hair on top of her head once
more, checked her clothes, tucked in her blouse at the
waist, tinkered with the thin leather belt and then turned
on her heel. One way or another, she'd find out what
she needed to know.

"HOW ARE THINGS GOING?" Allison asked Judy in what
she hoped was a casual tone. There were several walkie-
talkies on the desk, as well as the cell phone and a land-
line that Judy manned.

Looking up, Judy smiled. "Hi, Allison. Everything's
quiet, thank goodness."

"I see." Allison stood there for a moment. Judy was
a brunette and reminded her of the women painted by
the Old Masters of Europe. She wasn't thin as a rail as
Allison was. But then, the woman was an avid hiker
and in surprisingly good shape. As if feeling her scru-
tiny, Judy cocked her head.

"Are you all right, Allison? You look a little pale."

Stung by the observation, Allison scowled. "I'm fine!"
The words snapped between her red lips. She didn't mean
to sound so tense and Judy couldn't see through her plan.
Allison quickly walked out of the office and pushed the
screen door open. Her stomach sank as she saw Kam
riding beside Iris down the Thorn Hills trail.

Allison suddenly felt faint. She gripped the screen
door for support. Heart pounding, she wondered if she
would die of a heart attack. Allison turned on her heel

and went back into the office. Without a word, she swiftly walked past Judy, her heels clicking loudly against the shining cedar floor. Kam was not dead! Somehow, Jenkins had screwed up a perfect opportunity!

Reaching her suite, Allison jerked the door open and slammed it behind her. She paced the suite, her emotions part relief and part fear and anger. Why did she feel relieved Kam wasn't dead? Her ultimate fear was getting caught, and if there wasn't a dead body, no problem. She rubbed her damp hands against her slacks. It would start all over. Today was Thursday. Saturday afternoon, Jenkins would have to leave to keep his cover in place. He had assured her that if he couldn't kill Kam in that week, he would skulk around and wait without anyone knowing of his presence.

Groaning, Allison halted. She could barely stand the tension of waiting or the terror of Kam dying. Should she tell Jenkins the hit contract was off? No, she couldn't! Fingers digging into the back of the couch, Allison stood paralyzed. No way could she back out of this. And yet, the agony of her decision tore her apart. Allison had suffered a lot of cruelty in Hollywood, but none of it reached this volume of tension and fright within her. None of it.

Glaring around the quiet suite, the lowing of cattle barely heard outside the window, a neigh of a horse in a nearby corral, Allison hated her life. Why hadn't things gone right for her out in Hollywood? She could act, dammit. She'd proven that over and over again in bit parts in movies and television. Oh, she'd never made the big time. She was no A-list actress. Not even a B. Allison knew she was one of thousands who dreamed of breaking in, had got some gigs, but had never caught on with the Hollywood producers and directors.

A sob caught in her throat. Looking around through a haze of hot tears scalding her eyes, Allison clung to the only thing she'd ever been successful at—raising her two children. She worshipped them. A fierce love welled in her chest and her heart expanded with such intensity that she sobbed. No. She had to see this through. No matter what it did to her on a personal level. Kam Trayhern was a threat on so many levels.

"How does it feel to be back here at the Elkhorn Ranch?" Kam asked Wes as they ate in the dining hall. Around them, the noise, the laughter and story-telling going on between dude-ranch guests filled the large, airy cedar room. The wooden picnic tables personified the rough-and-tumble cowboy era.

Kam sipped her tomato soup and watched Wes across the table.

"Good. Really good," he confided, finishing off his soup and setting the bowl aside. He reached for the plate of beef, black-eyed peas and mashed potatoes with thick brown gravy. "It's like night and day. I'm glad to be back."

"What a stroke of luck that Braidy took the job as manager of your mother's ranch," Kam said, savoring this time with Wes. It felt like months since she'd last seen him.

Wes cut into the thick slices of beef. "Mother is very happy with him. He'll provide the leadership the wranglers need. She can go back to teaching and everything will be okay."

"That's right," Kam said. "Soon enough, kids will be starting back to school at the end of August."

Nodding, Wes chewed the succulent organic beef.

As good as it was, just looking at Kam filled his heart. Everything about her was endearing. From her green T-shirt and formfitting jeans to her cowboy boots. Her black hair was always tousled and she wore that red bandanna that she'd been given upon first arriving at the ranch. "Let's talk about us," he said.

Kam smiled and picked up her knife and fork. "Okay. A subject close to my heart." When his gray eyes narrowed upon her, Kam felt heat fly up her neck and into her cheeks.

"I'm glad it is," he said. "I've been doing a lot of thinking about the last week, Kam." He pointed his fork around the dining hall. "I really enjoy doing what I do here. I like seeing people get back to nature and allowing their kids to absorb it."

Kam spoke carefully as she ate. "Do you compare your childhood to these kids' experiences?"

Smiling a little, Wes dug into the mashed potatoes and gravy. "One of the many things I've come to discover about you is your insight into people. Why they are the way they are. Seeing what pushes or supports them. Yes, I see these kids with nice parents who dote on them. I wish I'd had that, but I didn't. Nor did my brother and sister. Maybe, in some ways, I'm living vicariously through the children who come here. I watch the parents and I see the joy and pride in their expressions when their kids are riding, or they're on a hike or they're helping us in some small ways."

"And your father never did that with any of you?"

Shaking his head, Wes said, "Never. My mother was our support. As a teacher, she knew how to engage us and get us working as a team. Dan wouldn't let her near any of the ranching, but she enlisted the help of some of the wranglers and they taught us a lot. Or—" he smiled a little "—as much as we wanted to learn. My brother and sister never absorbed ranch life."

"Don't you think part of their reluctance was due to Dan?" she asked.

Wes sipped his coffee. "I believe it was. When they were thirteen and fifteen, they left for Cheyenne to live with my aunt and uncle, and then they made lives for themselves. They wanted nothing to do with Dan or the ranch. They saw it as a reminder of their suffering and pain."

"But you didn't let that deter you. Why?"

Wes cut the last of the beef and thought about her question. "I don't know. Maybe ranching is in my blood, like it is with Rudd and Iris. I love the land, the animals and wilderness where we live. We're surrounded by nothing but nature, plenty of land between ranches and less population. I'd never make it in city life." Wes chuckled darkly.

Kam scooped up some mashed potatoes and gravy on her fork. "I couldn't, either. I loved my life as a stringer going to foreign countries. I thrived in the wild country. I hated the cities. I would never take any urban assignment."

"Maybe that's Rudd's genes coming through?"

"I hadn't thought of it, but I'll bet you're right," Kam said, a little amazed by his suggestion. She met and held his warm gaze and felt herself melting all over again. Wes could give her that special look and all she wanted to do was kiss and love him—fully. Forever. The thought startled her. She digested the possibility of having a relationship with Wes. Yet, he'd always been silent about his own private life. That had to change.

"Listen, I'm a nosy person," she began, "and I've always wondered why you weren't taken, Wes. You're awfully handsome, you're hardworking and responsible. Those are attributes any woman would kill to have in a man. What happened?"

Wes was finished with his meal and he placed his plate on the green tray at the end of the table. He wrapped his hands around his coffee cup. He told her of Carla and their sordid marriage. The more Wes confided in her about that traumatic time in his life, the sadder the look in Kam's beautiful blue eyes became. When he was done with his story, he said, "So, that's it in a nutshell. I figured I was pretty bad at picking the right woman after that. I knew that sometimes children of an alcoholic parent will choose an alcoholic partner. I did. And I didn't like it or myself."

"You're being pretty hard on yourself," Kam said sympathetically. She set her plate on the tray. Reaching out across the table, she briefly touched Wes's hand. "You married young. What do any of us know in our late teens? I'm twenty-eight and I just shake my head over my ignorance about relationships and the world when I was only eighteen."

"It was a mistake," Wes said, his hand tingling warmly where her fingers had been. Looking around, Wes saw many of the guests were finished and ambling through the dining-hall door. Pretty soon they'd be alone and that was fine with him.

"I've made plenty of my own mistakes along that line," Kam told him. "I guess I was lucky in one way—I never married any of the men that I got tangled up with." She told him about her two relationships and why they hadn't been successful. By the time she was finished, the dining hall was quiet. All the guests were gone and only the kitchen help was still in back. The clinking of pans and dishes was the only sound to penetrate the depths of the deserted hall.

"At least you had the brains to see what was wrong with these two men," Wes told her. "I met Carla, fell madly in love with her—so I thought—and we were married two months later. I didn't give us time to get to know one another. I was such a know-it-all. I thought I understood her." With a shake of his head, he muttered, "I couldn't have been more wrong."

"And that's why you're gun-shy of any other relationship with a woman," Kam guessed.

"Yes." Wes moved his fingers through his hair. Looking around the well-lit room, the cedar shining beneath the lanterns placed above on the rough timber rafters, he said, "Until lately…"

Kam's heart thudded over his words, over the way he watched her. His gruff tone stimulated her and she began to ache. The silence strung gently between them. "I never came here expecting to meet a man that I was interested in," Kam admitted in a quiet voice.

"I never expected to be working here and want another relationship with a woman, either, Kam."

Kam held his darkened gaze as he seemed to look straight through her. "I learned a long time ago to be honest with a man who was interested in me."

"I want your honesty, Kam. You have mine."

"I came here trying to find out if Rudd was my father," she began. "I didn't come here to be so drawn to you."

"That feeling is mutual," Wes said. He felt fear and hope alternately within his chest. Fear that Kam didn't want to deepen their budding relationship. Hope that she would. "I know you're in the midst of a lot of changes. Rudd is your father. You're his daughter. There's plenty of things you two have to go through to reestablish your connections with one another. I understand that. You need time." Wes flexed his mouth. He leaned forward a bit, his gaze on hers. "What I'm trying to say is that I'm willing to wait. You don't need me pressuring you right now. I think we have something special, and I'm smart enough to know that time is on our side and is not our enemy. How do you feel about it? About us?"

Kam reached out and tangled her fingers in his. "I'm very interested in you, Wes. But I'm up to my hocks with my new family. Rudd isn't the problem. It's Allison and her children who are making this a challenge. We all need time."

"So, you want to go forward with us?"

Nodding, Kam felt his fingers tighten around hers. "Very much so, Wes, as long as you know the obstacles."

"I understand." Right now, all Wes wanted to do was kiss her. Her lips were parted and soft. He knew how they felt and he yearned to crush them beneath his once more. But now was not the right place or time. Reluctantly, Wes released her fingers. "I like what we have. I like where it's going," he told her, straightening up. "We'll just take it a day at a time with no expectations."

"I'd like to have dinner with you every night," Kam told him. "This is so special." She looked around and then smiled at Wes. "A good way to get to know one another. Our life stories."

Agreeing, Wes stood up and settled his hat back on his head. "You got a deal, Kam. Come on, I'll walk you home."

CHAPTER TWENTY-TWO

As Wes walked with Kam toward the ranch house, he slid his arm around her shoulders. The evening had turned to dusk and as she turned to look over at him, a soft smile pulled at the corners of her lips. It was her eyes, a velvet-blue filled with such longing, that sent heat and excruciating need through him. Without a word, she folded against him and they walked in silence.

His heart pounded once to underscore the sweetness of her tall, firm body against him. Wes had lost count of how many dreams he'd had about her. He slowed his walk and faced her. "I don't know where this is going, Kam."

"I don't, either, but I don't care, Wes." Gazing into his dark eyes, Kam realized he had shadows from the past, his failed marriage. Her soft words had a gentle effect on his tense expression. Her arm wrapped tightly around his narrow waist. "When I was a stringer over in Darfur I sometimes lived minute by minute. There were times I wasn't sure I'd live to see the sunrise. I'm used to living on the edge, Wes. I don't need promises of forever. I know how precious life is."

His hands cupped her proud shoulders. "I didn't know that. You've mentioned taking photos for big-time newspapers and magazines, but I didn't realize you were in danger." That scared the hell out of him. Wes couldn't believe that as beautiful and gentle a spirit as she was, Kam would place herself in such scary situations. He struggled to understand the depth of her courage. The look in her eyes shone with love—for him. And when her hands moved to his shoulders and that devil-may-care smile came to her lush lips, Wes began to understand the adventuresome spirit that lived and breathed within Kam.

"We haven't had much time just to sit and talk about who we are, where we've been and where we want to go, Wes." Kam watched his eyes but it was the gentle caress of his hands across her shoulders that made her want to melt against him. "I'm hoping that if things quiet down and we have our nightly dinners together over at the dining hall, we will get to understand each other."

"We'll have the time," he promised her thickly. Wes wanted the time. Nothing was as important in his life as Kam, he was beginning to realize. The shadow of his father, his death, had marred Wes's ability to really see her until now.

"Hey, that's not always true. I lived overseas in third-world countries for too long. I know that a life can be snuffed out in an instant by a sniper's bullet. I saw too many people die, Wes. All we have is right now. Not the past. Not the future."

Looking beyond her as the night grew around them, Wes saw the bright lights shining from the many windows in the main ranch house. "I never had to go to war like you. I haven't seen lives snatched away in a heartbeat." He grazed her cheek with his fingers. "And I know you have more of a Buddhist outlook on life. Maybe you got the philosophy because of what you survived?"

Kam felt her flesh ripple with a delicious sensation as his work-worn fingers stroked her skin. "I had many friends die. Sometimes I was with them when it happened. Sometimes, I wasn't." Her brows dipped. "When you see someone shot and they're lying bleeding to death, it changes you forever. I learned the hard way how to live. The past is gone and we can never relive it. The future is unknown." She lifted her hands and framed his face. Their eyes met and she drowned within the tender gray flame. "I've learned to cherish the moment."

Without a word, Kam leaned forward and placed her warm lips against his mouth. Instantly, he relaxed and parted beneath her tentative exploration. *Right now.* That was all that would ever really exist and Kam knew it. Every cell in her body screamed to kiss Wes. His lips swept commandingly across hers, his arms crushing her against him. The instant their bodies met, Kam moaned with pleasure. How she hungered to lie with him and make torrid, nonstop love!

She inhaled his scent, part dust, pine and horse mingled with his maleness. Kam deepened their kiss, and the world ceased to exist around her. All she wanted—

needed—was Wes Sheridan. He was lean, tight, like a coiled spring ready to explode. As her hips deliberately met his, Kam felt his hardness pressing insistently against her belly. The wetness between her thighs increased. If only they could go off somewhere and make love. His mouth stroked fire across her lips. When his tongue slid between them and tangled with hers, a soft sigh rose in her throat. As his fingers threaded through her hair, her skin prickled with pleasure.

The snort of horses from a nearby corral blended with the hoot of a great horned owl in the nearby pines. The cheerful ribbits of the frogs in the stream behind the ranch house added to nature's symphony swirling around them. Wes was an incredible kisser and Kam relished his strong mouth wreaking havoc across hers. Her breasts swelled with neediness against the powerful wall of his chest. She kept seeing herself taking off that shirt and running her fingertips through his dark chest hair. The idea made Kam tremble.

Tearing his mouth from hers, Wes said in a husky tone, "Let's go to the barn. To the loft. No one is there and we'll be alone." Searching her upturned face, Wes wondered if he'd gone too far…assumed too much.

"Yes," Kam whispered unsteadily. "Now… I need you, Wes."

That was all he ever hoped to hear. They turned away from the dining hall, walked past the corral full of horses and toward the huge, shadowy barn. At nightfall, a sulfur streetlamp came on at the apex of the roof, but that was all. Wes didn't want anyone to see them enter the barn so he guided Kam around to the side entrance.

As Kam entered the large, rectangular feed room, she inhaled the scent of the molasses mixed with grain. Wes flipped on the light and they made their way through the room to the exit into the main barn. He shut the light off, opened the door and stepped out. The lamp at the far end of the barn shed just enough light to allow them to see the wooden steps leading up to the hayloft.

Once up there, Kam noticed a small room off to one side. Wes led her over to it, his hand firmly around hers. Opening it, he turned on a light and pulled her inside.

"And here I thought we'd have hay for a bed," Kam teased, looking around. There was a queen-size bed covered with a dark-green-and-white quilt of wedding-ring design. The floor was gleaming pine and the bed frame was made from the same wood. It was a beautiful room, one she hadn't known about. But then, she was still discovering so much about the ranch.

Wes quietly closed the door and smiled. "This is sort of a secret place. Sometimes we get dudes who want to sleep in the hayloft or honeymoon couples. They dream about a toss in the hay." His smile widened. "Of course, if you'd rather use the straw…"

"No, this is fine." Kam laughed, delighted. Indeed, the room was large and smelled of sweet, fresh hay and straw. "This is perfect, Wes."

Wes turned on a small stained-glass lamp that threw off just enough light to make the space romantic. He turned off the main light, then drew Kam into his arms. "No regrets about this?"

"None," she whispered and began to pull apart each pearl snap on his work shirt.

"I need a shower."

"So do I."

Grinning a little, Wes closed his eyes and felt the whisper of her fingertips across the dark hair of his chest. "There's a shower through that door," he said, opening his eyes.

"We'll use it later," Kam told him, pulling the shirt off his upper body. As the material dropped to the floor, he was already pulling off her tank top. The white silk outlined her breasts and she felt the nipples harden. He cupped them in his lean fingers almost with reverence. Leaning down, he closed his lips over one of the nipples.

With a gasp of utter, raw fulfillment, Kam gripped his tense shoulders and swayed unsteadily. The pleasure rippled outward like circles across a pond. Her breathing changed and she felt her lower body explode with heat. Kam wasn't going to be shy about her desire. She eased away, lamented the loss of his lips on her, but she wanted him naked—now. Without a word, their breathing harsh and shallow, Kam undid his belt and unsnapped his jeans.

Wes obliged and sat down on the bed to push off his boots, peel off his socks and get rid of his jeans. As he stood, Kam walked over with a gleam in her eyes that thrilled him. She was like an alpha female knowing her place and wanting her mate. Her fingers slid inside the band of his boxer shorts and she pulled them off him. Standing naked, he felt powerful. He liked the approval in her smile as she assessed him.

"You are beautiful," Kam whispered.

His hardness increased beneath her softly breathed words. To feel her love, her need, nearly overwhelmed him. He had never felt like this with any woman. Walking over to her, Wes said thickly, "Now it's your turn."

Kam laughed and allowed him to lead her over to the bed. He pressed her down upon it and removed her boots, socks and jeans. Her white silk panties were the last to go. Straddling her with his long, firm thighs, Wes pressed a kiss to her belly. With his tongue, he circled her belly button. And then teasingly slid lower.

Moaning, Kam gripped his shoulders. The hot anticipation of his lips drifting downward, his tongue easing into the cleft between her thighs, was too much. The wetness between her thighs built, his warm breath coming closer and closer to that juncture. Suddenly he was there, and Kam groaned. Her fingers dug deeply into his taut shoulders.

Stars exploded behind her tightly shut eyes. Her breath hitched. The strong, warm movement of his tongue exploring her womanhood sent her into a frenzy of need. Almost unable to stand the pleasurable sensation, the driving desire to have Wes inside her was even more powerful. Opening her eyes, panting, Kam rasped, "I need you…"

Without a word, Wes covered her with his long, lean body. Her eyes were wide with hunger, her lips parted, her breathing ragged. He could feel how close she was to a climax. Kam leaned upward, her hands framing his face, her mouth ravenous against his. With a groan, Wes felt her plunge her tongue inside his mouth. Startled, he groaned in response. As his elbows settled on either side of her arched, wanting body, he smiled against her mouth.

Then he moved his hips forward, thrusting into her. Automatically, her legs came around him, drawing him even more deeply into her depths. He felt the scalding heat of her inner body, the tightness that surrounded him and he groaned heavily. Their lips clung together, as hungry as their lower bodies had become. Wes became lost in sensations of heat, wetness, the slickness of their bodies melding and molding hotly with frantic demand. Kam thrust against his hips with an insistence that sent a lavalike explosion cascading through him.

Never had he met such a wild, uninhibited woman. And it made him wild in return. Unable to get enough of her, Wes brought one hand beneath her hips and angled her even more so that he could thrust completely into her. He heard Kam gasp with pleasure, her fingers opening and closing against his shoulders. He wanted to please her, pleasure her. Within seconds, she tensed like an overdrawn bowstring. A gasp escaped her and she trembled violently like a leaf in a mighty storm. Sensing the gripping and releasing around his shaft, he gritted his teeth and his eyes shuttered closed.

As she climaxed, Wes's body grew hot and the violent eruption of his own orgasm coincided with hers. For a moment they hung in a nether world, fused together, frozen and in a waterfall of bliss that took them higher.

Kam tried to catch her breath as Wes sank heavily against her. He was breathing roughly, the warm moisture caressing her face. She wrapped her arms around him as he laid his head next to hers. Her body sang with a brightness she'd never before experienced. Whatever they had shared was pure magic and her body thrummed like a well-played instrument. His hand moved down the flank of her hip, caressing her, letting her know how much he cherished her. When his mouth met hers and he kissed her ever so gently, it brought tears to Kam's closed eyes. He smelled of musk, her body scent. Like an aphrodisiac, she inhaled it and the sweat that made Wes the man he was. The glorious sensations still rippled inside her. Every time he moved his hips, her body responded.

Lifting himself up on his elbows, Wes looked down into her tender blue gaze. He smiled as she smiled. When she threaded her fingers through his hair, he felt his heart widen with a joy he'd never known existed. "You're magic," he told her roughly.

"No, you are," Kam whispered tremulously. She moaned softly as he angled his hips and thrust teasingly into her. To her surprise, he grew hard all over again. But then she wanted him, too. "More," she demanded, drowning in his stormy gaze.

Wes was stunned by how his body had a life of its own with her. "We're wild animals," he agreed against her lips. "I like it...."

Kam closed her eyes, feeling her needy body responding to him all over again. She moved her hips, drawing him deep within her once more. The heat built within her and she smiled. "I like it a whole lot, too. Let's do it again...."

CHAPTER TWENTY-THREE

AN HOUR LATER, they lay exhausted in each other's arms, the colorful stained-glass lamp throwing rainbow-colored patches across the ceiling and parts of the room. Together, they eased off the bed and showered. Afterward, they dressed and left their secret place of love. Kam would always feel that this room was special—for them. They took the stairs and exited through the feed room once more to avoid detection.

Outside the feed-room door, bathed in darkness, Wes pressed her gently against the barn. He looked into her eyes. "I have a past that dogs me but I'm working to be here with you."

Kam slid her fingers up across his shoulders. "We all have ghosts from our past, darling. I know we need time and talking. And especially more of this." She angled her eyes toward the barn. Wes grinned and caressed her cheeks with his roughened fingers. His hands had loved her body into a glowing hunger. His mouth, such a delicious part of his male anatomy, made her hot and shaking once more. Kam wondered if she would ever get over her hunger for him, for his strong, lean body loving her. Whatever the powerful emotions that lay between them, they were binding. Kam felt it in the depths of her pounding heart like an oak tree taking root.

"I don't want to leave," Wes told her in a husky tone.

"I know," Kam said softly. "I wish I could just stay with you all night up there in the barn."

"We'll make sure it happens as often as you want."

She was grateful for his allowing her to make the decision on such intimacy. "We'll have to be careful. I don't want anyone in the family knowing. At least, not yet."

"Right," Wes agreed. "Too much is going on now. We'll be careful."

Giving him a final kiss, Kam whispered, "Hungry?"

He chuckled and pulled her away from the barn. "For you." *Only you.* The words, *I love you,* flew up into his throat. How badly Wes wanted to share them with Kam. But it wasn't the right time. She had to integrate into her new family. His father had just died. Everything was in chaos right now. Kissing her brow, Wes knew he had to wait for a quieter time in their lives. Eventually, the time would come. Looking into her shining eyes filled with the happiness he knew he'd given her, Wes gulped the words back down inside himself. *Patience*—that would be his watchword in the meantime.

Placing his arm around Kam's shoulders, they walked out of the darkness and into the light at the front of the barn. The horses snorted gently and Wes could hear them munching contentedly on their hay. Everything was perfect as they ambled companionably past the corral.

"What's this?"

Kam jerked to a halt, surprised by Allison's intrusion. Her voice held sharp censure and she stood there glaring at them. Because of the nearby ranch-house lights, she could see the older woman's bright red lips twisted into a savage grimace. How much had she seen?

"Taking candy out of the store, Wes?" Allison asked, her tone taunting.

She was dressed for dinner in a pale lilac silk dress with matching heels. The amethyst necklace around her throat went with her dangling earrings. As always, the woman's hair was kept in place with plenty of hairspray that they could smell even from where they stood.

Wes felt anger stir in him as he met the woman's judgmental gaze. "Mrs. Mason. Good evening," he said, his voice low and respectful.

Kam sensed his immediate tension but quietly admired how he didn't take her bait. "I don't know that it's any of your business what Wes or I do, Allison." Since becoming a legitimate member of the family, Kam had held her tongue. But not tonight. She was damned if this harpy eagle was going to start savaging something so beautiful. All her joy evaporated beneath Allison's accusing stare.

Allison lifted her chin imperiously. "Since when, little girl, do you get away with being disrespectful toward me?"

Kam held Allison's glare. The woman looked positively garish in the sulfur light.

"If anyone has been disrespectful," Kam shot back,

"it's you, Allison. We're allowed to be together, and we don't need you poisoning it."

Allison smirked. "Mind your tongue, girl. You might be a part of this family, but you're at the bottom of the totem pole. I'm Rudd's *wife* in case you forgot."

Kam saw the woman's face twist and the glitter increase in her narrowed eyes. Heart pounding, she felt her patience thin to the point where she wanted to fly at the woman and chase her off. Kam had never had these urges before, but Allison now brought out the worst in her. Again, she felt Wes's hand gripping her shoulder as if in a silent warning to say nothing more.

After so many months of Allison's innuendoes and digging remarks, Kam could no longer control herself. "Allison, I came from a family where we respected one another. My adopted mother would never say such awful things to me. My adopted father, Morgan, raised me to have manners. When I came here, I was shocked by your behavior. You rule this place like the queen bee and you expect all of us to bow and scrape to you. Well, that's not going to happen. I will no longer take your snide remarks. If you are going to be nasty, I'll fight back."

"You little bitch," Allison breathed, her fine nostrils flaring. "How *dare* you!"

"All I ask is respect from you and everyone else. If you can't give that to me, Allison, then I'll take you on," Kam breathed, her voice tense.

"You're *nothing*," Allison whispered unsteadily. "You're the offspring of a one-night stand. You have no pedigree. You have no history or family heritage."

Quivering, Kam wanted to lunge at the woman. But then she saw the fear in Allison's eyes. Why would she be afraid? "I'll let my daily walk through life be a state-ment of who I am," Kam told her. "Your assessment means nothing to me. You think everyone is beneath you anyway. You live in a plastic world and you're only with Rudd for six months out of the year. You raised your children. And when they needed a mother, not a Hollywood starlet, you weren't there for them. What does that make *you?*"

With a cry of rage, Allison flew at her.

Startled, Kam froze for just a second. She'd been in too many civil-war situations and had read the woman correctly. She'd been attacked by soldiers intent on kill-ing her. Kam never carried a weapon, but she knew karate. Wes cursed softly beneath his breath and put himself between the women.

"Stop, Allison," Wes commanded in a dark voice.

The woman came to a halt inches from Wes, breath-ing hard. Her mouth twisted into a snarl, her small fists clenched.

"Get out of the way, Sheridan!" she barked.

Kam took a step back. It was something new for a man to stand between her and a threat. Her adrenaline heightened, Kam watched as Wes held Allison's glare. The woman looked like an eagle ready to tear both of them to shreds.

"Allison," Wes said in a low voice, "I think you need to go back to the ranch house. This isn't going any-where. I'll walk you back to the office."

Without waiting, Wes slipped his hand beneath Al-lison's elbow and turned her around. "This isn't the way to settle things," Wes told her in a soothing tone. "When you sleep on it, you'll see the wisdom of walk-ing away. Come on."

Kam watched Wes mollify the angry woman. Looking up, she saw the blanket of the Milky Way spreading like spilled, glittering milk across the darkened sky. Her heart felt as though it was leaping out of her chest. Taking in an unsteady breath, Kam began to walk in order to ease the adrenaline charge in her bloodstream. After circling the corral twice, she slowed down. The trail horses munched on grass hay as Kam hitched one foot up on the lowest pipe rung of the fence. Closing her eyes, she rested her arms on the pipe fence and pressed her head down upon them.

"Are you all right?"

Wes's voice washed over her like a cooling blanket to the heat and anger she felt inside. "I will be. Thanks for stopping her. I—I don't know what I'd have done," she whispered.

"I saw you go into your civil-war mode," he teased grimly. He placed his arm across her shoulders. "It's going to be all right, Kam."

Pushing a few strands off her brow, she sighed deeply. "I should have ignored her but I couldn't. Not anymore…"

"Allison is hard on everyone," Wes agreed. He studied her profile. "I felt you shift. I've never experienced that feeling before with anyone," he told her quietly. "It was as if you were a different person when she attacked you. And I had an invisible cord attached to you to sense it."

Laughing sharply, Kam said, "Now you've seen *my* PTSD side."

"Post-traumatic stress disorder?"

"Yes. That was one of the reasons I quit my job. My adopted father spotted those symptoms in me. He sat me down one night and told me what PTSD does to a person. I took a year off and stayed at home after that. I got help from a therapist and made some inroads into my reactions."

"Well," Wes told her, "when you're about to get killed, anyone would go into that mode, don't you think?"

"No question," Kam murmured, feeling the warmth of his strong hand on her shoulder. She loved how Wes would lift his hand and lightly stroke her back as if he were gentling a fractious horse. She hungered for his touch, his way of calming her. "Morgan told me that he'd had PTSD from all his experiences, too. I asked him if it ever all went away and he said no. And then, he laughed and said that if I were ever in a dangerous situation again, I'd know how to survive. You just saw me face down danger."

Grimly, Wes looked over his shoulder at the ranch house. "I can't believe Allison attacked you. In the two years I've been here, she's been all bluff with nasty, digging comments. I've never seen her do what she did tonight."

"She sees me as a genuine threat to her life," Kam growled. "At least I know what she really thinks of me."

"You can bet Allison is going to tell Rudd, but it won't be the truth."

Kam gazed at Wes's darkened face, noticed the worry banked in his eyes. "What do you think will happen?"

"It will be our word against hers," Wes said tiredly. "Allison has taken being a drama queen to a high art form. She's good at blaming others and never taking responsibility for herself in those actions. Allison will get her way, whatever it is."

Kam shrugged. "What? She'll throw me off the ranch? Rudd or Iris won't allow that to happen."

"I really didn't know how dangerous Allison can be," Wes confided. "She's like a lioness when it comes to her children. It's all about the will."

Kam shook her head. "I could care less about that will."

"But Allison cares," Wes warned her. "I've watched her try to maneuver Iris for two years. The old gal won't budge and she understands Rudd's wife better than anyone."

"That's all I hear from Allison at the breakfast and lunch table," Kam grumbled. "It's always about the damned will. She's constantly making snide reminders that Iris has to give Regan and Zach equal shares of the ranch when she dies. It sickens me."

"God," Wes muttered. "I couldn't sit there and listen to that kind of stuff every day."

"Well, obviously, I can't, either," Kam said wryly, looking up at him. Just absorbing Wes into her heart calmed her.

Wes laughed a little. "She had it coming. It's none of her business what goes on between you and me."

"She's trying to run my life," Kam said unhappily. "Rudd and Iris warned me about her."

"Good thing you stood up to her," Wes told her with a slight smile. He saw Kam's eyes widen a little. "Because Iris and Rudd have lived with Allison for so many years, they're able to disconnect from her verbal attacks. Sort of like water rolling off a duck's back."

"Not me," Kam said darkly. "I grew up in my adopted family respected and loved. We *never* had anything like this going on between any of us, Wes."

"I'm glad you had that experience before you got here," Wes said, meaning it. "You know what's normal. Allison makes this family behave in a twisted way. Rudd won't take her in hand and tell her to stop."

"I've often wondered why Rudd won't talk to her. Your family was abnormal, too," Kam reminded him softly. She reached out and slid her arm around his shoulders.

"It was," Wes agreed, needing her touch once more. "I knew that not all families were like my own. I had friends who had loving families like yours. That's what I wanted when I got married, but that got screwed up by my bad choice."

"Hey, Wes, we all make mistakes." She gently moved her hand up and down his strong back.

"You don't seem to."

Raising her brows, Kam said, "Oh, I have. I just didn't marry any of the guys, fortunately."

"At least there, you had good luck," Wes told her, sharing a soft smile with Kam.

"Maybe," she said, holding his tender gaze. Kam brushed his cheek with her fingertips. The sandpaper quality of it made her skin tingle. "We all make a lot of mistakes, Wes. The deal is to *learn* from them."

Wes kissed the top of her hand and held it. "Maybe I've been too hard on myself regarding my marriage. I'm beginning to see that. I was looking at you through that lens until recently and it wasn't fair to you. Or to me."

Turning, Kam moved into his arms. "Wes, I'm not her and you know that. You're moving out from under that shadow and you're seeing us differently." Touching his cheek, Kam whispered unsteadily, "And I'm glad. I just think you're the most wonderful man I've ever met. I want to continue to explore what we have."

Leaning down, Wes brushed her waiting lips and they parted beneath his. He smelled the scent of earth mixed with her sweet femininity. Her mouth opened to welcome him in and her arms slid around his shoulders, drawing him strongly against her contoured body. *They fitted together,* Wes thought, *like long-lost puzzle pieces that had searched a lifetime for one another.* Where he was hard, she was soft and undulating. A woman's body reminded him of a valley with hills and mountains. How badly he wanted to explore every inch of Kam once more. But the time was not right now.

Reluctantly, Wes withdrew from her soft, wet lips. He looked deeply into her warm blue eyes. In them, Wes saw love. For him. He was glad he could recognize that look. "Listen to me," he told her in a gruff tone, "be careful. Allison is going to take this confrontation and blow it out of proportion. She'll probably do it tomorrow at breakfast, so be prepared."

Kam smiled. "Don't worry, Wes. I promise I won't leap across the table at her when she attacks me. I don't believe Rudd will side with Allison, no matter what her charges are against me."

The words, *I love you,* begged to be torn from his lips once again. How badly Wes wanted to whisper them to Kam. Clearly, love was glistening in her blue eyes. "Well," he managed, "just be careful. I'll make sure I'm around tomorrow morning. I'll send out my assistant to ride the fence line and hang around. I don't trust that woman."

CHAPTER TWENTY-FOUR

ALLISON FOUND RUDD and Iris in the living room. They were enjoying their after-dinner coffee and apple crumb cake in their respective overstuffed red leather chairs. As she stormed into the room, she didn't care that Iris was present. Her heels dug into the bearskin rug. Hands clenched, she marched up to them, breathing hard. Rudd frowned and lowered his coffee cup.

"Allison? What's wrong?"

Feeling as if her eyes were bulging out of her head, she strangled out in a rush, "It's that bitch! I've had it, Rudd!" Taking her right hand, she shoved her index finger down at the floor. "I want her *gone. Now!* I don't care if she's your long-lost daughter."

Iris scowled. Whatever had riled the woman, she was breathing flames from those fine, paper-thin nostrils of hers like a fire-breathing dragon. Taking another bite of her dessert, Iris slid a glance over at her son. Rudd seemed taken aback by his wife's fury. Wisdom dictated it would do no good to react with the same idiotic fervor that Allison displayed. It would only amp up Allison's Hollywood performance. Iris compressed her lips to refrain from speaking.

Rudd set his cup on the mahogany table next to his chair and sat up. "Allison, what are you talking about?"

Pacing in front of the floor-to-ceiling flagstone fireplace, Allison snapped, "That bitch tried to attack me! If it wasn't for Wes Sheridan, she'd have hit me!" Allison jerked to a halt and stabbed a finger at her chest. "Kam was going to strike me, Rudd!"

"Whoa," Rudd muttered, his hands coming to rest on his thighs. "Tell me what happened."

Allison twisted the story to make it sound as if Kam had charged her instead of the other way around. When she was done spitting out the details, she rasped, "I want her *gone,* Rudd. Tomorrow morning! Never to return to *our* home!"

Standing, Rudd twisted the ends of his mustache and faced his red-faced wife. "Allison, you know I can't do that."

"You'd let that bitch strike me?" Her voice went shrill as she eyed Rudd in disbelief. "You'd let her stay here after what she tried to do to me?"

"Did you provoke her in any way?" Iris asked in a quiet tone.

Allison snapped her head toward Iris and glared down at her. "How *dare* you!"

"I'm only asking for the truth," Iris shot back, her voice rising a few notches. She gazed at Rudd, who looked torn and upset. The hatred that Iris had for Allison bubbled close to the surface. She allowed enough of it to be reflected in her tone. "I know you don't want Kam here, Allison. You've made that painfully clear to everyone. You're going to have to mend fences and make peace with her. Kam is my granddaughter. She's not leaving the ranch because I want her to stay, also."

"You are already a grandmother to *our* children," Allison shot back, giving Rudd a frantic look that said: *jump in and side with me.* "Rudd is the father of *my* children!" Allison added in a lethal voice.

Raising one brow, Iris studied Allison. The room had turned cold. The tension snapped tautly between them.

"I won't have Rudd's children savaged by this bastard child! I just won't." Allison stomped her foot, the sound swallowed up in the large grizzly bearskin rug. She stared at Rudd. "They are *your* children by *me*. You have to protect them! What if that bitch decides to go after one of them? What then? Are you going to sit back and let it happen?"

Iris had had enough. "Stop calling Kam a bitch, Allison. She's my granddaughter. And you have no right to savage her like this."

"Go to hell, Iris."

"Allison!" Rudd growled. "Stop this! You're out of control. And none of this warrants your overreactions."

Iris slowly stood up. Her face was set, her mouth grim. She held Allison's steely gaze. "I have a suggestion, son," she said softly.

Startled, Rudd looked over at his mother. She seemed so tense that he wondered if she was going to fly at Allison and tear her apart. "What?" he wondered.

"Tomorrow, take Regan and Zach to the doctor. Get DNA blood tests on them."

Iris watched as Allison's face drained and went chalk-white. She smiled faintly at the woman whose red mouth opened and closed several times without a sound. Her son cleared his throat.

"I don't understand," Rudd said, confused and looking at one woman and then the other. They seemed like two cocks ready to fight, their eyes never leaving one another, their stances squared, the tension brittle between them.

"Allison calls Kam a bastard just because her mother is someone else. Yet, you're her father." Iris lifted her chin to a challenging angle and stabbed Allison with a glare. "And you *dare* to infer that my son is the father of your two children?"

Allison rocked back in shock. "You're a cruel, lying person," she quavered, waving her finger unsteadily at Iris. "You're doing this just to muddy the waters! Kam *is* a bastard! My two children are fathered by Rudd." Her voice cracked. "No one else. How can you even *suggest* such a thing?"

Iris smiled a little. She brushed away a few crumbs that had fallen on her cranberry slacks. Iris had always known that one day she'd play this card. She hadn't known when or why, but she'd known it would be played. "Allison, you seem to place a lot of spit and venom on Kam because she's not 'pure' like your children. You allege they are by Rudd. Well, I'm calling your hand on that. I'm not putting up with any more of your tirades and your hatred of Kam. At least she came to us and revealed her true intentions. She faced the music and owned up to who and what she was." Her voice dropped with derision. "I can't say the same of you."

Rudd tugged on his mustache. "Wait a minute," he

said, holding up his hand and looking at Iris. "What's this all about?" He knew the two women disliked one another intensely. And he knew how hard it was on his mother because Allison was tough on everyone. His wife was never sensitive toward others, only herself and Regan and Zach.

Allison felt her heart pound so damned hard she thought she would suffer a heart attack. The look in Iris's eyes scared her as nothing else ever had. The old woman reminded her of a deadly cobra, her eyes mere slits. And what she read in them turned Allison to ice. How could the old woman know that Regan and Zach were fathered by two different men and not by Rudd? In those heart-pounding seconds, she ravaged her brain to think of a time when Iris might have gotten wind of the truth.

Allison figured her mother-in-law was bluffing to defend Kam. The old dowager knew nothing. Allison had been very careful about the conceptions of her children and ensured she'd had sex with Rudd within a week of each affair. That way, he'd never guess they were fathered by another man. Rudd had never suspected her of cheating. Allison had quietly taken hair samples from Regan's and Zach's brushes and had them analyzed for DNA. In both cases, her lovers were the babies' fathers and not Rudd. She vowed that no one would ever find out. But now, as she studied Iris, she could see the conviction in the old woman's eyes. How much did Iris really know? She couldn't have gotten her hands on the results because they were locked away in a safe deposit box in a bank in Los Angeles only she knew about. There was no paper trail to those DNA results.

"I see no reason to get DNA on my children," she

snapped at Iris. Gaining her former confidence, Allison huffed, "The very fact you'd even suggest such a thing makes you small in my eyes, Iris. I've always respected you, and now, you do this to me in a moment when I need your support."

"Your drama is wasted on me, Allison." Iris looked over at her son who had a drawn expression. The last thing she wanted to do was hurt Rudd. *Damn Allison.* She'd forced a hand that Iris had not wanted to play. All along, Iris had been going to make sure in her will that neither child got ownership of the ranch. Oh, she'd take care of Regan and Zach, but this ranch was too important, too much of her and Trevor's blood had poured into it, for it to go to them. They'd get ample money, but not the land because of the false circumstances that Allison had created.

"Allison, I'd like to talk to you in our suite." Rudd gave his wife a withering look.

"Of course, dear," she said contritely, reining in her anger. There was more than one way to manipulate Rudd. Right now, Allison's focus was on blunting Iris and her damnable demand. Somehow, she had to turn that request around. The look on Iris's face, however, scared her as little else ever could. That old woman was going to have her way. As she turned to leave, Allison thought of asking André Jenkins to take Iris out as well as Kam. She'd be more than willing to pay the price to get the old woman off her back once and for all.

"Stay," Iris told her son as Allison disappeared down the hall.

He nodded. Sitting down on the leather stool in front of where she stood, Rudd asked, "What do you know?"

Iris sat down after placing her hand on her son's

slumped shoulder. "I'm sorry it had to come to this, Rudd. But I'm not going to let Allison push Kam out of our lives."

Sighing, he waited until she'd settled into her chair. Her gaze was like steel and he realized she had information he did not. Was it possible that Allison had borne two children that were not his? The idea was just too much for him to absorb. Oh, he knew Allison was devious. But to lie to him about *that?* To make him think that Regan and Zach were his when they were not? Rubbing his brow, he muttered, "What do you know, Iris?"

She sat there and placed her hand over his. "Son, I'm sorry. So sorry. I had hoped this day would never come." She squeezed his hand and took in a deep, ragged breath. "Do you notice anything about Regan?"

He eyed her pointedly. "Like what?"

"She doesn't bear any resemblance to you, son, except for her red hair. Not her eyes. The shape of her face. Her interest in the movie industry."

Rudd shrugged. "So what? It happens. I can see Allison written all over in Regan's face."

Iris knew this was going to be hard for Rudd. "Look at Kam, son. Do you see resemblance in her face shape to yours?"

"Well, yes I do."

"She also has some of your mannerisms even though she's never lived with you."

"I saw that," he said tensely.

"And Kam loves the earth like you do."

"That's true," he muttered.

"And look at Zach. Do you see *any* of your features, mannerisms or body structure reflected in him?"

"He's tall and gangly, Iris. But at his age, he should be."

Hearing the panic and hurt in his tone, Iris couldn't go any further. She knew more. Much more. "Maybe the best way to approach this is through a DNA test."

He glanced away. "This can't be true," he whispered unsteadily. "It just can't."

Patting his hand, Iris said in a quavering tone, "Rudd, I hoped to have spared you from this. But Kam *is* your daughter. And I can't allow Allison to throw her out on such a trumped-up charge. It wouldn't be right."

Rudd gazed at his mother. His eyes filled with tears and then he fought them back. Maybe she was wrong. "Yes," he rumbled, "a DNA test. That will settle it once and for all."

"Yes," Iris answered him softly, "it will."

ALLISON STOOD WAITING for Rudd. Her heart wouldn't stop pounding. She *had* to stop this insanity! Her mind spun and her emotions were ripped apart. Never in her life had she conceived of Iris knowing her grandchildren were illegitimate, that they were not Rudd's offspring. If that secret were to open up, Allison saw her life's work—to give them what she had never had—destroyed.

Her emotions seesawed between hatred of Iris and an urge to contact André Jenkins to finish off Iris and Kam. The assassin was an end to all her problems. If Iris were dead, she couldn't encourage Rudd to test the children. Her husband was putty in her hands when his mother wasn't around.

The door opened and Rudd stepped in. Allison noted his gray pallor, his eyes like wounded sockets. The man was in pain and for one split second she felt pity. He closed the door and stood there, hands tense at his side.

"Is it true? That Regan and Zach aren't my children?"

The words cut through Allison like a saw and she started to cry. "How can you believe that filth? I bore those two babies from you, Rudd. Your mother is saying those awful things to protect Kam!"

Grimly, Rudd walked toward Allison. When she lifted her face, her mascara running, she reminded him of someone wearing war paint. Her eyes were glittering shards of rage and frustration. Rudd tried to steel himself against her coming tirade. "My mother doesn't lie, Allison."

"Well," she exploded, throwing up her arms, "if that's the truth, then why didn't she tell you this years ago? Why, all of a sudden, did Iris concoct this stupid story? Does that make sense to you?"

Scratching his head, Rudd rumbled, "No, it doesn't." And it didn't. "My mother is a straight talker and so am I." He wondered if Iris had brought up the accusation just to protect Kam. Anything was possible, he decided.

"Yes," Allison said harshly, "but she sure as hell is on Kam's side. Never mind that Kam was going to hurt me, Rudd. The moment I brought her up, Iris sprang into action like a protective old bear."

Rudd couldn't deny her argument. He watched Allison dab at her eyes, but all it did was blotch the black mascara across her blazing-red cheeks. "That's true, she did come to Kam's defense." He looked at her hard. "Kam isn't the type to attack a person, though, Allison."

She rankled beneath his intent, searching stare. She'd never loved him, but was grateful for his care of her children. He wasn't the sharpest knife in the drawer, but he was loving. "Anyone can attack if they're provoked enough."

"Did you provoke her, Allison? You've never been known for being diplomatic."

Allison tried to curb her rage over his insult. "Let's stick to Iris's accusation. She's trying to build a wall between you and me, Rudd. You can't believe her."

"Is she telling the truth?" he asked, his voice wary.

Seeing the fear in his eyes, Allison said, "Regan and Zach are yours, Rudd. I swear to God they are! How many Bibles do you want me to swear on?"

He shook his head. Allison had never considered the Bible a holy book—ever. In fact, she disdained going to church. And she derided those who did. He didn't go regularly, but at least once or twice a month, he attended the Unitarian church in Jackson Hole. Many of his rancher friends went there, as well. Rudd went for the religion as much as socializing. Since his wife was such a social creature, he could never understand why she didn't go with him. Churches did an awful lot of good in a community. Didn't she see that?

"No need to swear on a stack of Bibles, Allison."

She stared at him, her mouth open. "You mean? You believe me?"

Hearing her strident tone, Rudd winced. He felt as though he were caught in a bear trap. Iris never lied to him. Yet, if this was the truth, why hadn't she told him a long time ago? It just didn't add up. He did understand that Kam and his mother were very, very close. The love between them was clear and wonderful. Rudd was delighted that finally Iris had a granddaughter who loved her and the ranch.

"Let's drop this for now," he told Allison. "There's a lot for me to think on."

"I won't allow you to test my children," Allison warned, holding his shadowed gaze. "I just won't, Rudd. Iris is wrong. I'm not subjecting our children to this insane political allegation. Not like this. And not by her!" Allison jammed her index finger down at the cedar floor with a finality that made him cringe.

"I need to read my newspaper," Rudd muttered, walking toward the living room. "I've had enough of this for tonight."

A thrill of victory ran through Allison. Rudd looked defeated. Had she convinced him? Allison couldn't be sure. One thing she knew: she would give André Jenkins a second target to take out. One way or another, Allison was going to protect her children, make sure they got their deserved legacy and give them the security they deserved. And no one—not even Iris—would stand in her way.

CHAPTER TWENTY-FIVE

WES MADE ONE last inspection around the main trail-horse corral near the barn before he hit the bunk for the night. He spotted a shadowy figure hurrying toward the last dude cabin. Frowning, he stopped, unsure of what he'd seen in the darkness illuminated only by the rising full moon. At first, he thought it had been a fox or other creature foraging for a meal.

No, he was wrong, and he squinted into the darkness. To his surprise, it was Allison. And even more shocking, she was dressed in what appeared to be a pair of jeans and a black tank top. He knew her by her stiff blond hair that sat like a helmet on her head. Halting at the gate of the corral, with the horses also watching her stealthy progress, Wes watched, curious.

Allison never came outdoors after dark. She always retired to her suite after dinner. Where was she heading? And why? Stymied, Wes remained stationary and watched her stealthy progress. After using the rear of the barn as a way to cover her movements, she slipped around the rear of the dude cabins. He almost had the urge to call out to her but his instinct told him to stay silent.

To his surprise, she came around the end of the last cabin where Thierry De Bourdeille resided. Wes moved quietly toward the end of the corral to get a better look as Allison slipped up onto the porch. Her knock was so light he could barely hear it. The door opened and the light revealed, without a doubt, it was Allison. He didn't see Thierry. The woman slipped inside and the door quietly shut.

Pushing up the brim of his hat, Wes shook his head. Iris had told him about Allison's affairs in Hollywood. Was Allison having an affair with this guy? Something didn't smell right. Wes turned and headed toward the bunkhouse.

"KAM?" RUDD CALLED.

Concerned over her father's tone, she walked up to the counter of the office and flashed him her brightest smile.

"Are you feeling okay, Rudd? You look a little under the weather."

"I'm okay," he said. "You goin' somewhere?"

"I was going to help Wes. Two of his wranglers are taking the dudes over to the Twin Hills area. I was going to get the box lunches from the dining room and carry them over to the supply horse."

"That can wait for a moment." Rudd sighed and stared into Kam's wide blue eyes. "Allison came in

mighty upset last night. I was wondering what your
side to the story was."

"Oh…that…" Kam gulped before launching into her
version of the events. Rudd's face mirrored surprise as
he listened. "I'm sorry it happened. I was out of line for
what I said to her. It won't happen again."

Rudd looked down at the papers on his desk, his
mind whirling with confusion. Allison had said Kam
attacked her. Now he was hearing that the opposite had
happened—Allison had launched herself at Kam. Wes
had stepped between them and stopped the attack. Who
to believe? Lifting his chin, he searched his daughter's
blue eyes. Rudd never wanted to think that Kam would
lie to him. He didn't like thinking the worst of people
and maybe that was his downfall, he decided. One of
the women *was* lying, either his wife or his daughter.
His heart squeezed with fresh pain. He'd barely slept
last night.

"Do me a favor? Send Wes over here when he's done
with the trail group." Rudd didn't say why but he noted
relief in Kam's face.

"Sure, no problem." She skipped out of the office
and out the door.

Sitting there, Rudd rubbed his face. He'd cut himself
shaving this morning. Unlike him, but he was wrestling
with huge and shocking revelations. Had Allison had
affairs in Hollywood? Had she conceived twice with
other men? The charge leveled by his mother seemed
ludicrous. Allison was right: If Iris had known this all
along, why hadn't she spoken to him about it much
sooner? Why now? There were no easy answers.

The screen door opened and closed. Finally, Wes
stood at the office window. Without preamble, Rudd

asked Wes for his version of the attack that had occurred last night.

Wes wiped his brow, settled his hat on his head, and
did as told.

"Okay, fine, Wes. Thanks," Rudd said when the man
finished.

"Sure thing," Wes said, lifting his gloved hand and
leaving.

The office became quiet. Allison had lied to him.
Damn it, anyway. Rudd felt guilty questioning Kam's
version of the incident. He had relied instead on Wes,
whom he knew would not lie. He'd had two years with
this man and he was as honest as the day was long.
Rubbing his chin, Rudd felt trapped. At 8:00 a.m., there
would be breakfast. And Allison would be there and so
would Kam. And Iris. God, his stomach felt like a tight
knot. He had no appetite.

As he sat there, Rudd wondered again if Allison had
deceived him about Regan and Zach? He'd caught her in
many "white lies" over the years. His mother had never
lied to him that he could tell. Why would Allison lie
about the attack last night? What was wrong with her?
What was wrong with their marriage?

Rudd felt a bitter taste in his mouth and took a swig
of water. The taste didn't go away. Not only was he
miserable, but he felt suffocated. At 8:00 a.m., his office assistant would relieve him. Until then, Rudd had
to man the phones and be here to help the dudes. It was
the last place he wanted to be!

His mind went over the previous night. He'd taken a
shower and gone to bed, but Allison hadn't been there.
Because she demanded her beauty sleep, she was usually in bed long before him. But not last night. Rudd

had fallen asleep alone. Sometime later, and he wasn't sure of the time, Allison had quietly slipped into bed. Oh, he knew better than to try and snuggle up to her. She never wanted to be touched by him. Their sex life had died after the last child was born. Rudd blamed himself. He realized he wasn't handsome or a powerful Hollywood mogul or actor like those that Allison was always gushing about at the dinner table. He was plain. A commoner. Allison had no interest in those things. Rudd knew the truth and it hurt if he thought about it too much. Rudd had consoled himself that they'd created two beautiful children and he funneled all his energy and focus into being their father. The importance in his life was Regan and Zach.

Was Iris right?

Feeling a lump tunnel up through his gut and into his throat, Rudd swallowed convulsively. Oh, God, his whole life had exploded before him. How badly he'd wanted his children to love him, to feel safe and secure. He'd worked hard to provide them everything they'd ever needed. And what if they weren't his? How would they take the shocking news? Rudd worried more about them in this mess than anything else.

Dejected, Rudd forced himself to answer the phone when it rang. It would give him momentary solace and right now he needed the distraction.

"HEY, KAM," IRIS called from her greenhouse, waving for her granddaughter to come.

Kam had helped Wes and two other wranglers get the dudes off for their morning ride that would end in a picnic just outside of Twin Hills. The trails had been repaired and were nice and flat and easy to ride once more.

"Good morning, Iris," Kam greeted as she halted in front of her.

"It is," Iris said, smiling. "I'm avoiding breakfast this morning. Want to play hooky with me?"

Anything to avoid Allison was a gift to Kam. "You bet."

"I've had the cook put some croissants, jam and a thermos of hot coffee into my saddlebags," Iris said with a teasing smile. "I need to ride out to the Twin Hills area. The other day Wes spotted some monkshood in bloom down at the stream. I need that for my flower essences. Want to come along?"

"Awesome!" Kam exclaimed with a whoop. "Let me saddle Freckles. I'll be there in a heartbeat." She leaned over and gave Iris a peck on the cheek. The old woman smiled fully.

"Go on, get saddled up. My horse is ready in the barn. All I gotta do is get my flower-essence bag and I'll join you over there."

ANDRÉ JENKINS WATCHED the chatty women ride off toward the Twin Hills trail. He continued to rock and pretended to read a paperback novel. With a sly look he could see a few wranglers over at the barn. The striking of the anvil by the blacksmith, who forged the horses' new shoes, was the only sound he heard.

After putting down the paperback, Jenkins slowly got up and stretched languidly, all for show. As if he didn't have a care in the world, he stepped into the cabin. He knelt down on a braided oval rug near his bunk and pulled out his dark green canvas bag. He had to get to the barn, saddle his assigned horse and then bring it over to the rear of the cabin. There, out of sight of curious wranglers, he'd shrug into his backpack and mount his horse. To casual observers, it would appear he was going for a ride.

First things first. He had to get his horse and all the activity was over there at the entrance. Would any of the hands watch him? Take any interest in what he was doing? Jenkins thought not because he normally did not go out on rides with the group. Instead, he usually rode alone. The wranglers knew his habits so they wouldn't think anything of him appearing over there now.

WES WAS HOLDING a palomino gelding when Thierry moved like a silent shadow over to the barn. The man wore black as he always did. Wes met the dude's dark eyes and nodded a silent greeting to him. The French-man nodded back but said nothing. He didn't exactly display normal social graces, which made him an odd-ball at the friendly vacation retreat.

Wes pulled his attention back to the farrier and the horse he was holding. Earlier, he'd seen Kam and Iris riding down the Twin Hills trail. Their joy lifted his heart as he heard their shared laughter. There was no question in Wes's mind that he loved Kam. Last night's lovemaking had sealed his heart with hers. Never in his wildest dreams had Wes ever expected to meet such a woman. He only regretted that their time together had been rudely interrupted by Allison.

The bad taste of Wes's divorce from Carla melted away. Kam was everything Wes had ever wanted. And right now, Wes was plotting how to get her away for a couple of days. Maybe a hiking trip up into the Tetons in the back country. There, they could share their sleeping bag and make love, torrid love, with no interruptions.

He was pulled out of his daydreams by Thierry mounting and riding back to his cabin. The man guided his mount around the rear of it. Wes watched, curiosity piqued. About five minutes later, the dude rode his chestnut gelding out onto the trail that paralleled Twin Hills trail. He wore a big, bulging knapsack now. Why hadn't he brought it over with him to the barn? Maybe because it was heavy. Wes had good eyes and squinted for a better look. There was an unusual bulge at the top of the knapsack. Wes swore he saw the barrel of a rifle poking up into the tightly stretched fabric. A rifle? Here? Dudes knew that firearms were not allowed.

Feeling a sense of foreboding, Wes turned. "Hey, Sam, come and hold this horse. I need to check out a situation."

Once the younger wrangler had taken the quarter horse gelding, Wes went into the barn. Bolt was already saddled and standing in the breezeway. Wes debated whether to tell Rudd where he was going. Thierry had been a shadowy figure at the ranch for the past week and Wes hadn't taken to him. They had probably exchanged ten words.

What was the man going to do? Shoot an elk out of season? Bull elks had velvet on their antlers right now, getting ready for breeding season in October and November. Wes leaped into the saddle and walked Bolt out of the barn. He saw the dude take the short cut to Twin Hills that the wranglers always used. It didn't make sense. Wes held Bolt to a slow walk. The gelding wanted to run and pranced sideways. "Easy," Wes crooned to his gray horse. He slid his leather-gloved hand down the animal's sleek, arched neck. Instantly, the horse settled and Wes loosened the reins. Above all, he didn't want Thierry to know he was being followed.

ONCE OUT OF sight of the ranch, Jenkins clapped his heels to his heavily muscled quarter horse gelding. He knew how to ride. The wind flew past as they wove in and out of stands of white-barked aspen. He had to get ahead of the two women on the slower trail, go back to his original sniper site and set up. His targets were about ten minutes ahead of him. With the trail now repaired, he hoped that his shots would be easier.

As he rode, he smiled. Allison Mason had handed him two credit cards and showed him the proof that she'd put the money for the second hit in his offshore bank account. Although he didn't approve of her showing up at his door late last night, he liked the thought of the extra money. Taking out two women would be no problem. But Allison would have a problem. There wasn't a lawman around who would believe both women were killed by an out-of-season hunter's errant bullets. Oh, she could get away with one of them dead. But two people dead? No. He'd tried to argue his point with Allison, but she refused to listen. Not his problem after today.

He urged his horse into a ground-eating gallop across the flat plain. Up ahead, a mile away, were the two hills clothed in late-summer raiment. A choppy breeze came and went. That wasn't good. André would have to compensate for this erratic breeze. Still, as he rode, the thundering of his horse's hooves like music to his pounding heart, André knew that the thickly wooded hills would stop most of the inconstant breeze. It insured a clean shot. Two shots. Two dead people.

CHAPTER TWENTY-SIX

JENKINS TIED HIS horse at the bottom of the hill and climbed upward. The chestnut's flanks heaved with exertion and foam covered his sleek neck after the long, hard ride. The horse's fatigue didn't faze Jenkins as he settled into his sniper position. Around him, the brush protected him from prying eyes. With smooth, flawless motions, he removed the disassembled rifle from the pack and expertly put it together. Once it was on the metal tripod, he tested for a breeze. There was one, and it was inconstant. A bothersome detail but not a big deal.

Peering intently through the scope, he spotted the two riders plodding around a bend in the trail. Soon, they would be in full, unobstructed sight. And soon, they would be dead. The rifle had a silencer so the sound wouldn't carry. All he had to do was be patient. Patience was something he did very well.

Wes pulled Bolt to a halt next to the chestnut quarter horse. He saw the animal was still breathing hard, so that meant that wherever Thierry had gone he'd done so recently. Bolt was trained to ground tie; as soon as Wes dropped the reins, the horse stood quietly. The gelding would not wander, but would wait in that spot for Wes to return.

Squinting as he turned and looked around the quarter horse, Wes spotted what he wanted—tracks. The rain from the night before had made the area muddy despite the grass on the lower slope. The footprint was a male, too long and large for a woman. Leaning down, Wes noticed how the tracks went up to the crest of the hill. The grass at the bottom was lush, but as the shade of the trees covered the ground, the grass disappeared.

Wes walked quietly, following the footprints. If Thierry was here and if he had a rifle to hunt, Wes wanted to catch him in the act. The wranglers with the trail rides always carried rifles as protection against charging moose, grizzly bears or elk. While those confrontations occurred rarely, the possibility that they would made it mandatory that a rifle always be handy. Now, Wes wished he had one.

As he quietly tracked the imprints up the shady slope, his mind went back to the dude. To say the least, he was a strange bird. He never joined the activities, always the loner. Never once had Thierry gone out on one of the many trail rides. Wranglers had told Wes that the man preferred to take off on his own. Had he had the backpack on then? Wes wondered. After dude season was over, it was hunting season and hunters from around the world came to the ranch to try and snag a trophy elk or moose rack. Wes had never had an incident with a dude wanting to take a rifle out to kill game out of season. This was a first.

He slipped silently past a clump of thick brush. He was careful not to make it shake or cause rustling noises. He'd hunted all his life and knew how to track his quarry. The big difference between him and the trophy hunters was that any animal he shot meant meat on the dinner table. Nothing was wasted with the taking of an elk's or deer's life. Wyoming ranchers hunted in season to feed their family. A rack and its height or points didn't mean a thing to them.

Stopping halfway up the hill, Wes listened. He glanced back downward and saw the two horses standing quietly. Keying his hearing, Wes thought he heard two women talking. It had to be Iris and Kam coming down the trail between the hills. Wes removed his hat, wiped his brow with the back of his arm and settled it back on his head. Why would Thierry be here? He had to know this was a highly used trail morning and night for dude rides. If he was a hunter, he certainly wouldn't set up in such a busy area, because wildlife would avoid it at all costs.

Wes searched the shaded and shadowy hillside above him.

None of this made sense. For whatever reason, a deep fear kicked in. Fear for Iris and Kam. That was a silly feeling, of course. But if this guy was hunting, they might be caught in his line of fire.

Wes's heart thudded in his chest. Adrenaline crashed into his bloodstream as reality gripped him. Wes touched the left side of his belt where he kept a six-inch hunting knife in a leather sheath. He studied the brush above him, looking for anything that resembled a man's shape but saw nothing.

Urgency pushed him forward. He followed the vague imprints quickly and tried to be careful about not making any noise. Already, he could hear Iris laughing. It sounded like the two of them were having a good chuckle over something that she had said. Wes tried to breathe silently through it as he dug the points of his boots into the damp soil and lunged forward. It was inconceivable anyone would shoot a rifle when they could clearly hear people nearby. Hunters knew bullets traveled a mile and could kill whatever they struck. Wes's fear suddenly turned to outright terror.

As HE CAPTURED the two women in his sniper scope, Jenkins's mouth pulled into a slight smile. Within the next minute, they would present clear, unobstructed shots. His finger was firm against the trigger. As always, he kept his breathing shallow. A sense of unequaled power soared through him. Neither woman knew that her life would be snuffed out. He felt like God. A slight breeze moved past him and Jenkins frowned, his eye pressed to the scope. The wind came from another direction. He hated this type of weather where one couldn't predict the direction of the wind.

Just thirty seconds more…

His skin became wildly sensitive, his hearing excruciatingly sharp. Jenkins felt more animal than human. These sensations always overcame him seconds before the actual kill. He watched the two women ride side by side, talking animatedly and laughing. They would never know what hit them.

A twig snapped behind André and he started. Should he turn or hold steady on his targets?

Before André could decide, he heard a crashing sound coming through the bush—right at him. Jerking his head from the scope, he turned. Eyes widening, he saw Wes Sheridan flying through the air at him.

Wes slammed into the man full-force. The lunge sent him into the earth. The horror of Thierry's goal fueled Wes's rage. Blown away by the shock, Wes disregarded his own safety in order to save them.

They rolled end over end, the branches snapping and tearing off. As he balled his fist, Wes landed on top of the struggling man. His fist landed squarely on his nose, and Wes heard the crunch of breaking bone. A sense of satisfaction thrummed through him. Blood spurted from the Frenchman's nostrils.

In the next second, the man arced a left fist and it connected with Wes's temple, sending him sideways.

Thierry leaped to his feet. Breathing hard, he glared down at the cowboy. He lifted his foot, pulled it back and sent it outward to catch the cowboy in the rib cage. But Wes moved fast enough to avoid the blow. Off balance from the thrust, Thierry cried out and fell.

Wes was on his feet as the man slipped in the mud. Though his temple throbbed, Wes didn't feel the pain. The adrenaline kept surging through him. Leaning down, Wes grabbed the dude by the collar of his shirt. Just as he thought he'd subdued the killer, Thierry thrust his fist upward and caught Wes on the right cheek. It was just the break the man needed as Wes went down. Before he could recover, Thierry leaped over several small bushes and tore down the hill to his horse.

Shaking his head, Wes got to his feet and staggered.

Bright lights danced in front of his eyes. His cheek ached like fire. Thierry was getting away! Cursing, Wes ran to the crest of the hill. Below, he saw Kam and Iris looking up at the commotion with puzzled expressions. They didn't know what was going on, but at least they were safe. Wes had no time to tell them what had just happened. Whirling around, Wes ran down the hill, zig-zagging around the larger bushes. He held up his arm to protect his face, slipping and sliding down the slope. Below, the dude raced for the horses.

He'd never reach Thierry in time. But then the man tumbled after hitting a slippery spot. The chestnut geld-ing, about a hundred feet away from him, shied, but didn't go anywhere. Wes knew that Bolt wouldn't move an inch. Breath tearing out of his mouth, Wes surged down the hill.

Thierry reached his horse, and the animal backed away, eyes rolling. It wasn't prepared for a human to come charging. Grabbing at the reins, Thierry jerked the startled gelding to a halt. Looking over his shoul-der, Thierry saw the cowboy hot on his heels. In an-other thirty seconds, he'd reach him. Not if he could help it. Leaping into the saddle, Thierry sank his heels into the quarter horse and sent it off to a flying gallop.

Damn! Wes reached the bottom, panting loudly. Bolt's ears were working back and forth, his eyes large. But he didn't move. Wes leaped upward, one hand hook-ing around the saddle horn. He swung himself on board the horse. Bolt took the weight, two steps sideways and then anchored.

Leaning over, Wes grabbed the reins. Without even touching them to Bolt's neck, Wes pressed his right leg against the horse's barrel. Like a cat, Bolt lifted his front legs, pivoted ninety degrees and then took off at a thunderous gallop. Wes managed to slide his boots into the stirrups. The horse's mane stung his face as he leaned low and asked everything of his half Thoroughbred. He had to catch the fleeing Thierry! The horse's hooves pounded down the damp wrangler trail that led around the Twin Hills toward the ranch. As Bolt broke around the first hill, Wes shouted to him. Ears laid back against his head, Bolt knew he was after the fleeing chestnut. He stretched his long, gray legs and rapidly ate up the distance between them.

Wind whipped around Wes as they closed in on Thierry. He saw that the man was a good rider, but as good as he was, he whipped the horse unmercifully to try to escape. In the end, he could not. Bolt was much taller and had longer legs. Plus, a quarter horse was good for a sprint of a quarter mile while Bolt, part Thoroughbred, could easily breeze a mile at top speed.

As Wes drew up on the killer, his mind whirled with questions. Why would someone want to kill Kam and Iris? Who had put this man up to such a shocking deed? Did Jenkins have another weapon on him? Wes was without defense except for his hunting knife. He urged Bolt the last fifty feet to close the gap on the tiring chestnut. The man kept looking around, no fear etched in his face—just a black look that made Wes think this was a paid killer.

As Wes surged toward the chestnut, the man suddenly threw the horse to the right—in front of Bolt.

Wes felt his horse drop its haunches and skid wildly to avoid the coming collision. He gave his horse its head because to saw on the reins at this moment would only unbalance Bolt more. The horse knew what it would take not to tumble headlong into the quarter horse. Wes's heart stopped. Everything slowed for him, as though he was watching an old home movie, frame by frame.

Thierry had made a fatal error. When he'd wrenched his horse's reins to pull him into Bolt's path, he hadn't counted on his horse stumbling into a rut in the road. As Bolt grunted and sat down, literally, on his rear, the chestnut stumbled. Wes sat back on Bolt, giving him his head. Mud splattered all over the place as the huge gray horse skidded to avoid the collision.

Wes felt his horse begin to twist to the left to avoid the falling chestnut. The quarter horse went down five feet in front of them. Thierry flew headlong out of the saddle. Bolt leaned to the left. Wes felt his horse losing his balance. In a swift motion, he got his boots out of the stirrups. He launched out the saddle to the right, hoping to avoid the fall of his horse.

Hitting the ground hard, Wes rolled over and over again. Mud splattered him. He heard Bolt slam into the earth not far away. He stopped rolling and sprang to his feet. Bolt was getting to his feet, shaking his head but unhurt.

In front of Wes, the quarter horse too was getting to its feet, unhurt. The animal was covered with mud. Wes ran around the chestnut and found the killer lying facedown, unmoving. Wes pulled him over on his back. The man was unconscious, chalk-faced but breathing. A purplish lump had already formed on his forehead.

Taking no chances, Wes walked over to Bolt and retrieved some rope from one of the saddlebags. He pushed Thierry onto his belly and brought his hands behind him. No stranger to tying calves for branding,

Wes made sure the rope was snug without cutting off the man's circulation.

As he stood up, he heard the thunder of hooves behind him, and looked around to see Kam and Iris riding hell-bent for leather toward him. Wes walked out to meet them, seeing the concern in Kam's eyes. Iris seemed beyond shocked.

As they pulled their horses to a stop, Iris said, "Wes, what's going on?"

"The man was trying to kill the two of you," he told them grimly. Placing his hand on the neck of Kam's mount, he told them the story.

With a gasp, Iris stared down at Thierry, who was slowly returning to consciousness. "Call the sheriff, Wes. Who would do such a thing?"

"I don't know." Wes gave Kam a long, hard look. If his hunch hadn't led him to follow Thierry, she might be dead. The thought pulverized him. Reaching out, he took Kam's hand resting on the horn and squeezed it. The words, *I love you,* nearly tore out of his mouth, but he swallowed them back for now. The look in Kam's eyes was unmistakable: she was afraid for him.

"I'm okay," he reassured her. Reaching for the cell phone on his belt, he made the call to Deputy Sheriff Cade Garner. By the time he was done, Thierry was sitting up and scowling at them.

Iris rubbed her nose and glared at Thierry. Then she ordered Wes, "Don't call Rudd. We'll tell him once we get there."

Though confused, Wes did as she requested. Normally, he'd call something like this into his boss. Rudd needed to know. Why would Iris ask him not to alert him? Maybe because she was worried that Rudd would be stressed out to know Iris and his newfound daughter had nearly been killed. Understandable. Nodding, he said, "No problem, Iris."

"Let me go," Thierry growled at Wes as he came over to him.

"Not a chance. Get up," Wes ordered tightly, sliding his gloved hand beneath the man's arm and hauling him to his feet.

Thierry limped to the chestnut. Wes helped him to get on making sure he kept hold of the reins. Mounting Bolt, Wes set off, leading the chestnut with the killer on board behind him. Kam and Iris rode beside Wes.

KAM FELT FEAR cascade through her as she grappled with what might have happened only minutes earlier if not for Wes. Who would want to kill them? And what if Wes hadn't followed his hunch about Thierry and the odd backpack he'd worn? Suddenly, for Kam, all the silly notions of not allowing Wes fully into her life disappeared. Hungry to speak with him privately, Kam knew that couldn't happen for a while. Catching Wes's glance, she smiled slightly.

"Dinner tonight?"

"I wouldn't miss it," Wes told her, his voice low with feeling.

ALLISON BLANCHED WHEN she saw Wes, Iris and Kam ride in with Jenkins in tow. Rudd was with her in the office when they arrived. Panic struck her. Rooted to the spot, she watched her husband scowl darkly and stride out the door to meet the returning group. What had gone wrong?

Allison's mind turned a million miles in those seconds. She had to have a plan! If she ran, they would know she was behind it all. Would Jenkins squeal on her? Or, would he, as he had promised, be mute? Did assassins have an honor code that kept them from revealing who had bought their services? An icy fear clutched at her throat as she stood numbly, staring out the door.

She had to do something so she walked jerkily out of the office. As she moved to the door, she saw the sheriff's cruiser arrive. Cade Garner was a tough hombre. He had been widowed two years ago, his wife and five-year-old son lost to a drunk driver. She saw the grimness in his thirty-year-old features. Cade was strict and helped run a tight ship in the county. He was far too intelligent not to be able to squeeze the truth out of Jenkins.

Dizzy with fear, Allison turned and went unsteadily down the hall to her suite. Shutting the door, she sank against it, her hands pressed to the roughened wood. She would deny it. No matter what Jenkins said, she'd deny it. What if someone checked out her credit cards? Cade Garner would overlook nothing. He was wily as a coyote.

Shakily, Allison pressed her hands to her face. Would Rudd believe her? Or Jenkins? Somehow, she had to keep secret the fact she'd hired an assassin. Whatever happened in the next twenty-four hours would seal her fate. Allison was determined to stay above it.

KAM'S WORLD WAS upended three hours later. She was working with Wes over at the barn. The shadows were long through the central part, the breeze cool compared to the heat outside the structure. Since the killer had been taken away, Kam had felt shaky in the aftermath of all the excitement. Wes and she were over in the tack room cleaning the leather bridles as well as the saddles. There was something soothing in sitting quietly with Wes in the airy tack room, redolent of leather. Right now, all she wanted was some kind of fixed routine to calm her jittery nerves.

Wes was working on a saddle when Rudd entered through the open door. The man's face was grim, his eyes reddened, as if he'd been crying. "Rudd?" Wes said, setting the saddle soap and cloth aside.

Taking a deep breath, Rudd regarded Kam, who sat in a wooden chair working on a leather bridle. "The sheriff in Jackson Hole just got done with his questioning of De Bourdeille at the jail facility." The next words were so hard to speak. "The Frenchman accuses Allison of paying him a large sum of money to kill Iris and you, Kam."

Kam's eyes widened. "What?"

"I'm sorry, Rudd," Wes said, his voice hoarse.

Wearily, Rudd took off his hat and ran his fingers through his hair. "Jenkins signed a statement."

"Oh, my God," Kam whispered, her hand going to her lips as she looked at her father. "How awful." Kam couldn't conceive that Allison could put out a hit on them, but it felt like the truth. She saw the devastation in Rudd's eyes.

"The sheriff is sending a cruiser out here to pick up Allison right now. They need her statement."

Wes blinked and shook his head. "I know Allison feels threatened by Kam being here but…" His voice trailed off in disbelief.

"I don't know what to believe," Rudd told them heavily. "Allison is swearing the opposite, that De Bourdeille is lying to save his own skin."

"Son?"

Iris stepped through the door of the tack room. She put her hand on Rudd's arm and looked over at Kam and Wes. "I heard it all. And I need you to know something. The truth has to come out here and now." Her hand tightened around Rudd's upper arm. "I've never trusted Allison. When she had Regan eight months after she married you, I got suspicious. I hired an investigator to find out if Regan had been conceived before she married you." Iris saw Rudd's eyes flare open. It would hurt him so much to tell him the rest of the truth. "My investigator took DNA samples from Regan's and Allison's hair that I provided him with. I also gave him some of your hair from your brush, Rudd. The DNA shows clearly that Regan is not your daughter. I believe from the investigation that Allison had a liaison with a producer named Patrick Dobson. He is Regan's father."

Rudd looked like a broken man, his eyes wide with shock, his face pale.

Iris gently moved her hand to Rudd's shoulder. "It gets worse, Rudd. After that happened, I had my investigator follow Allison every time she left for Los Angeles for six months of the year. She had another long-term affair with a director named Zacharius Blanchard. And she conceived. She was living with him that six months after she left here. She got pregnant a month before she came back to the ranch. Zach is his child, not yours. If you recall, she was insistent that Zach be called Zach. You'd wanted another name."

Stunned, Rudd closed his eyes. He inhaled a deep,

shuddering breath. "I wanted to name him Stephen Trevor Mason in honor of Trevor...."

"Yes," Iris whispered. "But I checked it out and DNA verifies it—neither child is yours, Rudd. It makes a lot of sense to me why Allison could have done something like this."

The room was brittle with silence. Kam stared at her father; the information seemed to have broken him apart. Regan and Zach were not her half sister and half brother after all. Allison had lied and manipulated to have her children inherit property and money they had no legal, moral or ethical right to. "This is all too much," she whispered, touching her brow.

Wes shook his head. "I'm sorry, Rudd. So damned sorry this has happened." He looked at Iris, who seemed to have aged ten years in front of his eyes. Tears streamed down her face as she devoted her full attention to her long, lanky son. Maybe coming from the family of an alcoholic wasn't as bad as he'd thought after all. His heart hurt for Rudd and Iris.

"D-do you think Allison could really do this?" Rudd asked his mother, his voice cracking.

With a nod, Iris whispered, "Son, I think she could do it. Above all, Allison was super-protective of her children. You know how she mentions almost daily that they should be in my will. I haven't put them in there, Rudd. I lied to her to get her off my back about it. I won't have this ranch go to them. It will be your ranch, Rudd. Only yours."

Rudd sat down abruptly on a wooden chair near the door. He put his elbows on his knees and then buried his face in his hands. Iris came over and gently smoothed out the fabric across his broad shoulders. A sob ripped from somewhere deep down inside Rudd. Iris murmured his name and leaned over, cradling him the best she could given her diminutive size.

Kam felt hot tears scald her eyes. Her father was crying over the pain and shock of what his wife had done. She didn't try to stop her own tears. Everything blurred. In the next moment, Wes pulled up a chair and sat down next to her. His arm went around her shoulders. Without hesitation, Kam turned and laid her head against him and cried.

Wes closed his eyes and held Kam tightly in his arms. He didn't know who was crying more—Kam or Rudd. The tack room was flooded with the awful sounds of pain being released. And then, his own eyes teared up and Wes rested his head upon Kam's and let them flow. He hadn't cried since his father's funeral, but as he held Kam, Wes realized that she could have been killed today. He loved her so much it hurt and he hadn't told her as much. When this was over, he promised her silently that he would share his feelings.

Finally, silence returned to the tack room. Rudd thanked his mother in a gravelly voice and sat up, wiping his eyes. He settled the hat back on his head. Looking over at Kam, he said to Iris, "Then she's my only child."

"That's right," Iris said gently, patting his shoulder. "And DNA has proved it."

"Now I understand why Allison was so het up about us wanting to get DNA samples from Zach and Regan." He looked up at his mother. "This explains a lot—now."

"I knew the truth all along. Allison didn't know I knew and had no idea about the P.I. I'd never confronted her with the truth until recently. I was willing to let it be, but when Kam entered your life, things changed." Iris gave Kam a warm, loving look. "Kam, I'm so sorry you had to step into this mess. It's not of your doing and I don't want you to feel guilty about it."

Rudd nodded. "I've been a fool, Iris."

"We're all fools, son. You trusted Allison. You let her go to Los Angeles because you loved her."

Rudd rubbed his face, going over the tragic scenario. "She lied to me, Iris. About the children. My God, how could she do such a thing?"

Iris shook her head. "I don't know, son, but I've already called our attorney. You're going to need him. Ralph Talbot will be out here shortly. In the meantime, Allison has gotten an attorney from Cheyenne by the name of Horton Sanders, and he has told her to say nothing more until he arrives."

"Do the children know?" Kam asked, hurting for them.

"Not yet," Iris said. "Rudd and I will talk to them since they'll never get the truth out of Allison. We have serious decisions to make, the first being where Allison will live. She can't live here after she gets bail. You can set her up in an apartment in Jackson Hole if you want. There's a long trial coming and it's going to be hard enough on all of us."

Rudd nodded. He more than understood his mother's point. "But I want the children to have a home. I love them and I always will."

Iris sighed then smiled raggedly at her son. "Of course. They're going to need a lot of support with what's happened."

"I won't abandon them," Rudd told her. "As far as I'm concerned, they're mine. I'll make sure they have the money, the education and support they need now and in the future."

"I agree," Iris said. She wiped her eyes. "What a day!"

Kam nodded. With Wes's arm around her shoulders she felt more steady. "Just tell me what I can do to help."

"All I need from you, Kam, is assurance that you'll stay here with us. I just found you. I don't want to lose you again," Rudd said warmly.

"I'm going nowhere, Dad." How easy it was to say those words, Kam realized. She saw Rudd's face change and some of the pain disappeared from his eyes. A slight smile hitched the corners of his mouth. "You're my dad," she repeated. "I love you. I don't want to go anywhere. I'll do what I can to help all of you through this…."

Iris saw her son rally. Kam's words were a healing balm on his torn-up heart. Gratefully, she looked over at Kam. The love for her father was evident, and it lifted Iris as nothing else ever could. "We'll get through this—together," she promised them.

Wes eyed Kam uncertainly, then addressed mother and son. "I haven't talked to Kam about this yet, and she can still say no. There's a small house that's empty right now about a mile from here. I'd like Kam and I to live there." He turned and gazed deeply into Kam's glistening eyes. "I love her. And I want to be with her."

"Yes, I'd like that," Kam managed, feeling the intensity of Wes's love. Looking over at her father, she said, "Is that okay with you, Dad?"

Rudd shrugged. "Iris and I have known for some time now that you two young ones were meant for one another. Today's young people live together before they marry, unlike in our day, but I'm okay with that." He looked up at Iris. "What do you say?"

Iris grinned. "Wes, just ask Chappy to get some of the hands to help with furniture and such. We'll take Kam's things from her suite and move them over to your new house."

"Thank you," Wes told them gravely, with a nod. He'd thought Rudd might not go along with his request. He was old-fashioned in many ways, but Wes saw the man wanted his only daughter to be happy. "I'll go get Chappy now." Because tonight, he wanted Kam in his arms and his bed. He could see the devastation in her lovely eyes—the realization that she could have been killed today. And more than anything else, Wes wanted to give her a safe haven against the future. The entire family would have many adjustments to make.

CHAPTER TWENTY-SEVEN

"I CAN'T BELIEVE all that's happened in the last seven days," Kam told Wes. Their bodies still damp, they lay in bed together after making love for the second time that night. The window across from the bed showed dawn chasing the darkness away. Kissing Wes's roughened jaw, Kam nestled her head in the crook of his shoulder.

Wes pulled the sheet up to their waists and then brought Kam back into his arms. Inhaling her womanly scent, the freshness of the earth combined with a sweetness that was only her, he nuzzled her hair. "Allison is going to stick to her story. I knew she would."

"She can't explain away her credit cards or the money pulled from all those bank accounts to pay Jenkins for those two hits."

Wes sighed and felt a contentment he'd never experienced before. "In a jury trial, I'm sure Allison will be found guilty on that evidence. It's just a matter of time."

Closing her eyes, Kam slid her hand around Wes's lean rib cage. The grayness of the dawn slid silently into their bedroom. Every day brought new shocks and surprises. Zach and Regan were reeling from the events. They'd decided to leave the ranch to stay with their mother at her new condominium in Jackson Hole. Kam couldn't blame them; after all, she *was* their mother. "I feel sorry for Allison's children. They're torn up and they don't know what to believe."

"I think when Rudd and Iris sat them down with them and showed them the results of the DNA tests, they could no longer refute the truth."

"It's a tragedy," Kam whispered, her heart aching for Zach and Regan. "I don't know what's worse—not knowing anything about your birth parents or suddenly being told that your father isn't your father. Allison denied each of her children their real father as they grew up."

Wes held Kam gently and kissed her brow. He understood Kam's heartrending words. "I always felt Allison coddled her children and protected them too much. She never let either of them take the hard knocks of life that you need to survive out in this world," he said. "It's going to take time, a lot of time, for them to get right with what's happened."

"I wonder if they'll be angry with Allison?"

Wes threaded his fingers through Kam's soft, dark hair. "In time. It's more important that they create contact with their individual fathers at some point. Rudd's attorney just contacted their biological fathers. Neither of them knew they had a child by Allison." He sighed.

"Now, their lives and the lives of their families are in chaos, as well. Allison's decisions have caused pain for a lot of people."

Kam closed her eyes and felt her scalp tingle beneath his ministrations. "Right now, neither of them seems to want to contact their birth father."

"They're scared Allison will be thrown into prison and they won't have her around to protect them as before," Wes said. He propped himself up on his elbow, his hand moving across the sheet that outlined Kam's hip. "She never created inner strength in them. All they know is to circle the wagons around Allison, who continues to lie to them. Until they can start pulling themselves up by their own bootstraps, they'll hide from the truth."

"Allison was the perfect helicopter mother in many respects and now, her children are going to suffer because of it," Kam said. "I just couldn't believe all her affairs. I'm not a prude, but her way of getting a part is just beyond me. I could never do that."

"Allison was desperate to leave her unhappy past behind."

"We have no right to judge her on that," Kam said quietly, pressing a small kiss to the column of his strong neck, "but what she has done to her children is plain wrong. It's one thing to make life decisions for yourself, but to make them for others and not think about the consequences for them is sad."

"No question," Wes breathed, pressing his mouth to hers. For a moment, the awakening world around Wes halted. This was the sweetest moment he could have except to be inside her, loving her. They'd loved each other to exhaustion tonight without regret. It was as if he could not get enough of Kam, nor she of him. Wes knew this was a heady, wonderful time in their lives. Easing his mouth from her soft, full lips, he looked into her half-closed eyes. "I love you, Kam. I did from the first day I saw you as I rode by on Bolt. When you climbed out of the car, my heart did double-time." He gave her a tender look.

"Me, too," Kam whispered, gliding her fingertips up across his cheek and his temple. "There was just something about you, Wes. Your strength and confidence."

"I feel kind of guilty being so damned happy when Rudd's and Iris's lives are being torn apart."

Sadness filled Kam and she sat up, the sheet pooling around her hips. "I know. I'm walking on air every day and I see the stress, the pain and anguish in their faces. I wish I could do something to lift it off them, but I know I can't."

Wes pulled her into his arms. He loved the warm, quiet strength of Kam's body against his own. "You *are* helping them. Just maintaining a schedule with them gives them stability, Kam. And in times like this, that's what you need—sameness. Fixedness."

"I just hurt so much for them."

"Until Allison is out of their lives, the pain will continue. Rudd's attorney said that if Allison doesn't confess, this will go to trial. I guess it's too much for me to hope she'd do the right thing for once and save this family from more suffering."

"I know," Kam said. She leaned her full weight into his arms and languished against his strong, hard body.

Wes gave her one last kiss. "Let's forget about this for a while and go take a shower together." He got to his feet.

"Perfect." Kam gave him a teasing smile. His hair was tousled, his beard darkening his face. He looked incredibly virile and handsome. Throwing off the sheet, Kam climbed out of bed and took his hand. Together, they walked down the hall to the bathroom. It held a claw-foot tub and a large shower stall. The rest of the house might be small, but the bathroom had been given ample space.

"When we have dinner with Rudd and Iris tonight," Wes told her as they ambled down the hall, "I'm going to announce our engagement."

Brightening, Kam halted. "Really?"

"Sure. Are you game?"

Just absorbing Wes's smile sent a wave of heat through her. She halted and slid her arms across his shoulders. "That would be wonderful! I know that will lift their spirits."

"I'm not doing it for them," Wes growled playfully, kissing her cheek, "I'm doing it for us. I want to marry you, Kam. Make it legal. Real. I want to stay here at the ranch and work. My mother is doing fine with her ranch. She's happy with Braidy as the new manager and things are going right for her, for once."

"It's sort of sad, though," Kam murmured, catching his hand and pressing a kiss to his work-worn fingers. "I feel when your mom writes her will, she's going to leave the three of you the ranch. She'll give you what you deserve."

"I don't care," Wes said, bringing Kam against him. "Everything I'll ever want is right here in my arms, leaning up against me, smiling at me. I can lose everything but not you, Kam. Maybe we could also set a date for our wedding."

"I'd like that," Kam said. "I can contact Morgan and Laura and let them know the date, too. I'm sure they'll come down and help. They need to meet Iris and Rudd. I'm lucky to have two families instead of one."

Nodding, Wes pressed a kiss to her hair. "They both love you. This happy occasion will offset the trial."

"It will," Kam whispered. "Such a positive celebration for everyone."

"You bet," Wes said, smiling at her.

Joy thrummed through Kam as never before. She knew the wedding would probably take place in September, a beautiful time of year here in Wyoming. The colorful fall leaves would have turned and all of nature would bless their union, as well. "I like your plan, darling."

Leading her into the white-tiled bathroom, Wes felt his heart expand until he thought he'd explode with bliss. All his life, he'd lived a life of trauma and stress. Now, with Kam at his side, that seemed like another world—one that he had left behind him. All he had to look forward to was a life with her. It would be a good life, he knew. There would be trials, no question. Hard times. Sad times. But through it all, he knew she'd stand at his side like the courageous woman she was. As he handed her a white fuzzy washcloth to take into the shower with her, Wes gazed down at her flat belly. One day, she'd carry his child. That thought blazed through him powerfully and he felt euphoric. Their child would have a loving father, not an abusive one. And he knew Iris would dote on her great-grandchild. Wes hoped that it would give the senior a measure of happiness that she had long deserved. They would be a family again. A real one with no lies or deception between them any longer.

As he closed the shower door and the steam began to curl and flow around them, he hoped that someday Rudd might meet another woman who would love him for who and what he was. He would hold that thought for the man because he deserved the same kind of happiness Wes had found with Kam.

* * * * *

Joan Johnston is the *New York Times* and *USA TODAY* bestselling author of more than fifty novels with more than fifteen million copies of her books in print. She has been a director of theater, drama critic, newspaper editor, college professor and attorney on her way to becoming a full-time writer. You can find out more about Joan at joanjohnston.com or on Facebook at Joan Johnston Author.

Books by Joan Johnston

Hawk's Way: Jesse
Hawk's Way: Adam
Hawk's Way: Faron
Hawk's Way: Garth
Hawk's Way: Carter
Hawk's Way: Falcon
Hawk's Way: Zach
Hawk's Way: Billy
Hawk's Way: Mac
Hawk's Way: Colt

Visit the Author Profile page
at Harlequin.com for more titles.

HAWK'S WAY: FARON

Joan Johnston

CHAPTER ONE

HE WAS A man who loved women. Blond or brunette, freckled or dimpled, witty or shy, Faron Whitelaw made it his business to discover the facet of each woman that made her uniquely beautiful. Needless to say, women found Faron irresistible. Even if he hadn't been handsome, which he was, they would have loved him for the innate thoughtfulness that always made him give as much as he took. Any woman who passed through Faron Whitelaw's life—whether in bed or out—received a gift that would remain with her a lifetime: the knowledge that she was a very special, desirable human being.

In fact, Faron had never known a woman he didn't like. Until now. At the age of thirty he had finally encountered the exception to the rule. He not only didn't like Belinda Prescott, he was prepared to hate her with a passion. Because, despite the fact he had never laid eyes on her, the woman was personally responsible for turning his life upside down.

"Want some company?"

Faron looked up at his eldest brother from the chair where he sat slouched with a whiskey in his hand. "Not particularly."

Garth snorted. "Too damn bad." He poured himself two fingers of whiskey and took the chair opposite Faron's in front of the stone fireplace. He put his feet up on a sturdy rawhide-covered stool that had held generations of Whitelaw boots. "I can't believe you're making so much out of this."

Faron's gray-green eyes narrowed. His lips twisted into a bitter smile. "You're not the one who just found out he's a bastard."

Garth laughed. "Hell. I've been called a bastard all my life."

"That's how you act. It's what I *am*."

Faron's voice was stark as he asked, "How could Mom have done such a thing? Having an affair with some rich sonofabitch…. Did Dad know?"

Garth's lips flattened. "He knew." He paused and added, "So did I."

Faron stared into his brother's dark eyes, stunned by the realization that Garth had lived for years with this awful knowledge. "How long have you known that I was only half your kin?"

Garth looked away into the fire before he answered. "Since you were born."

"And you treated me like a real brother?"

"You *are* my brother!" Garth snapped. "Nothing's going to change that. Dad's name is on your birth certificate. He raised you. Nothing else matters."

Faron sneered. "You haven't read any of those letters from the widow—my stepmother—asking when I'm coming to claim my inheritance from my *father.*"

"Forget it," Garth advised. "There's plenty of Hawk's Way for both of us. You can stay right here in Texas, and we'll keep on raising and training quarter horses, just like we always have."

Faron shook his head. "I've got a mind to meet Belinda Prescott. The lawyer said she was the one who talked my fa—Wayne Prescott into putting me in his will. Said she *insisted* I get half of everything. Otherwise, I might never have known what Mom…" Faron's voice trailed off as his throat tightened up on him.

He had been feeling too much since he had found out that his beautiful mother had indulged in a tawdry affair with a millionaire rancher visiting Texas from Wyoming and had borne a bastard son. It was a stunning revelation to Faron that he was only related *on his mother's side* to his older brothers Garth and Jesse and to his younger sister Tate. He felt bereft, wrenched from the bosom of his family. An outsider. And it was all that Prescott bitch's fault.

"I never figured the money would mean so much to you," Garth said in a quiet voice.

Faron's gray-green eyes turned cold. "It's a good thing I grew up knowing how distrustful you are of everybody's motives. Otherwise I'd have to stand you up and knock you down for saying that. I'd have given anything not to know the truth. I don't want half that old man's fortune. I just want things to be the way they were."

The way they never would be again.

Garth swallowed half his glass of whiskey. But he

didn't apologize. Faron hadn't expected him to. He began to understand a little better what had made Garth so cynical about women, why his older brother refused to trust the species, let alone love one of them. Faron might have felt the same way himself, if he had grown up knowing his mother had betrayed his father.

Both his parents were dead now. His mother had died giving birth to his sister, Tate, when Faron was seven. His father had broken his neck coming off an ornery bronc when Faron was fifteen. He felt ill equipped to deal with this secret that had been kept from him for so many years.

Faron tried to remember if his father—or mother— had treated him any differently than Garth or Jesse or Tate. But it was too painful to even think about that right now. He was still too shocked. And angry. And frustrated. He felt battered and needed to escape.

Faron played with the frayed seam at the knee of his jeans. "I just want to see the place where my fa— Where *he* came from," Faron said. "I can't explain it except to say that I feel like there's a hole inside me now that needs filling. Maybe I'll find something in Wyoming that'll give me the answers I need."

"Give my regards to Belinda Prescott," Garth said with a caustic smile.

"Your greetings will have to wait," Faron said grimly. "I've got a few things to say to Mrs. Prescott myself."

BELINDA PRESCOTT FELT guilty as sin. She should be in mourning. Her husband of eight years had been buried a mere four months ago. She should be home wearing black and recounting the memories of her too-brief marriage. Instead she was riding the fastest horse in the stables across Wayne's Wyoming ranch, King's Castle, enjoying the early spring sunshine and feeling finally, at long last, *free*. Because for six of the past eight years, The Castle had been a prison and Wayne her jailer.

It hadn't started out that way, of course. She had met Wayne when she was a waitress in a short-order diner in Casper that he frequented. She had worked the grave-yard shift trying to make ends meet, and he had often come in for a midnight breakfast. They had started talking, and one thing had led to another.

Wayne had found out that she was supporting three sisters. He was more than willing to accept a beautiful and youthful bride in exchange for a substantial trust fund for each of her siblings. She and Wayne had each known exactly what they were getting into. Twenty-year-old Belinda had willingly said her wedding vows with a man old enough to be her father. It was a small enough sacrifice to make so her sisters could have better lives.

She had been too young and desperate at the time to realize the ramifications of selling herself—body and soul—for money. In the years since, she had regretted her devil's bargain, but never so much as now, when she was finally free of Wayne and ready to go on with her life. Belinda had given up something besides her youth to marry Wayne—she had lost her innocence. She was no longer credulous, gullible or naive. She would never trust another man. The lessons Wayne had taught were hard, and he had been brutally thorough.

She spurred the mare beneath her into a lope and lifted her face to the sun. She didn't want to remember. But she couldn't forget.

Wayne had been such a gentle husband. At first.

Then his heart had started causing him trouble. He had needed to take medication to keep him alive, and the medication had made him impotent. He had felt less a man and had sought other ways to relieve his frustration. He had begun to gamble. Then he drank to forget his huge gambling losses.

Slowly but surely he had become less gentle and more unreasonable in his demands. His fortune had dwindled until all that was left was The Castle, the land and a few prime head of breeding stock. And a twenty-eight-year-old wife who had learned that sometimes the price of security comes too high.

Belinda pulled the mare to an abrupt stop and wiped tears from eyes that were too blurred to see the grassy prairie around her. Her chest felt leaden—not because of sorrow, but because she felt none. God help her, she had felt only relief when the heart attack killed Wayne. It was difficult for her to look Wayne's mother, Madelyn, in the eye. Because Madelyn truly grieved, and Belinda could not.

At least she had been able to do one good thing. She had convinced Wayne to leave half of everything to his son. If it hadn't been for Wayne's mother, Belinda would have urged Wayne to leave his entire ranching empire to Faron Whitelaw. But Belinda had no money of her own. She hadn't had any trust fund put in her own name when she had married Wayne. He had gambled nearly everything else away. She had to have some way to take care of Madelyn, who had become as precious to her as her own mother.

Over the years, as Wayne had become more cruel, Madelyn had often stepped in to act as a buffer between her son and his wife. Madelyn had been appalled when she caught Wayne slapping Belinda. She had threatened to call the police if her son ever threatened Belinda with violence again. The two women had never spoken about Wayne, but they had shared other confidences, other hopes and dreams. Which was why Belinda had been determined to light a fire under her stepson that would goad him into moving north as soon as possible.

Belinda wondered what Faron Whitelaw would do when he learned the other conditions of Wayne's will. Her brow furrowed in concern. She had to hope that he would want his half of King's Castle enough to do what had to be done. She was counting on it. She was willing to do her part. She only hoped he would be willing to hang around long enough after he showed up to do his.

Otherwise they were both going to lose everything.

CHAPTER TWO

FARON SPOKE SOFTLY as he unloaded the quarter horse gelding from the trailer. He had pulled his pickup well off the highway near a pasture gate. "I know it's been a long trip, Sonny. We're both tired of traveling. Just take it easy, boy. According to that old man at the gas station in Casper we're standing on Wayne Prescott's land. Just be patient a few more minutes until I get you saddled up, and we'll take ourselves a look-see."

The horse nickered as though he understood Faron and stood patiently while Faron brushed him down and saddled him up. It had been a long drive from northwest Texas to northeastern Wyoming. As Faron stepped into the saddle he thought of what the white-haired gent at the gas station had told him about his father's land.

"Mr. Prescott had him a kingdom, all right. Called his spread King's Castle. Miles and miles of the prettiest grassland you ever did see," the old man had said. "That big old house is set off in the middle of nowhere. Near three stories high, made of gray stone, with them little pointy things on the roof like some storybook castle. Even called it The Castle, Mr. Prescott did."

Now, as Faron surveyed his father's domain, he was humbled by its vastness, awed by its richness. On this warm, surprisingly summerlike day in May, blue grama grass and wheatgrass flowed in waves over the rolling hills as far as the eye could see. This was cattle country, but there was a wealth of riches under the ground, as well. Oil. Natural gas. And coal.

Faron gave the horse his head and let him run. He felt the power of the animal beneath him, taking him farther into an untamed wilderness. He urged the animal on, as though by running faster he could escape the oppressive feelings that had haunted him since he had learned the truth about his birth.

It had taken him a week to put his things together after he had told Garth he was leaving. He had received yet another letter from Belinda Prescott asking him whether he was coming. She had sounded desperate. It made him wonder why she was so anxious for him to visit King's Castle. He had unbent enough to tell her he was coming, but he hadn't given her a definite date. His wire had simply said, "I'll be there when I get there."

Faron rode some distance from the highway, until there was nothing to remind him of the civilized world he had left behind. He couldn't believe his eyes when he spied a blond woman riding a palomino in the distance. Horse and rider presented a stunning picture. Her waist-length hair, flying like a gonfalon behind her, was the same magnificent gold as the horse's mane and tail.

He shouted to attract her attention. When she turned her head to stare at him, Faron drew breath with an audible gasp. She was incredibly beautiful. Ethereal. Like some fairy princess. He wondered for a moment if he had conjured her in his imagination.

But the shock on her face was real. And the sound of the palomino's thundering hooves as she galloped her horse away was real.

Intrigued, Faron pursued his elusive golden princess. He dug his heels in and urged his mount to a run. The quarter horse was bred for speed over short distances, and Faron quickly overtook the woman. He grabbed the palomino's bridle and hauled her horse to a stop.

The woman stared at him wide-eyed, wary.

Faron smiled. It was a smile that said, "You can trust me. I won't hurt you. I find you absolutely lovely."

But his elusive princess—who else but a princess would he find on King's Castle land?—wasn't the least bit impressed.

"Let me go," she said in a breathless voice. "Please."

He let go of the bridle but said, "Don't go. Stay and talk with me."

She took her lower lip between her teeth. He could see her distress, the struggle to decide. "We're strangers," she said at last. "We have nothing to talk about."

"If we talk, we won't be strangers for long," he promised. "Please."

"I have to go home."

"What's your name?" he asked.

"None of your business."

"All right, then. No names. I'll call you Princess. You can call me… Cowboy."

He thought he saw the hint of a smile curl her lip, but

she flattened it out damn quick. Faron stepped down from his horse and walked around its head to stand at her side. He tipped his Stetson back and smiled up at her. "I'll help you down."

He didn't give her a chance to object. Before she could say anything Faron had got hold of her tiny waist. He could feel the tension in her as he lifted her off the horse. She met his gaze for an instant with frightened eyes before she lowered her lashes, and he realized that she expected him to take advantage of the situation. Maybe he should have dragged her down the length of him. He sure as hell had wanted to bad enough.

She clearly had a body made for loving. She was nearly as tall as he was. Her head came all the way to his chin, which was surprising because he was well over six feet. She was wearing a long-sleeved man's shirt tucked into fitted Levi's, but both shirt and jeans showed off a figure that was fully feminine. Her boots were well used but expensive, ostrich if he wasn't mistaken.

He had to bite the inside of his cheek to keep from gasping when she glanced up at him again. She had eyes a rare violet color. Her complexion would have earned the envy of a pale pink rose. As he stared at her, stricken by emotions he couldn't name, he saw her cheeks darken to a redder rose.

"I should go home," she said. But she sounded less sure about leaving. She was worrying that full lower lip again with pearly white teeth.

Faron slipped her hand through his crooked arm, took the reins of both horses and started walking toward a meadow of spring wildflowers. "It's a beautiful day, isn't it, Princess?"

He could feel the tension in her, and he kept talking

in an attempt to show her he wasn't a threat to her. At least not yet.

"Tell me about yourself," he urged.

She eyed him from beneath lowered lashes. "What do you want to know?"

"Any brothers or sisters?"

For the first time, her lips curved in a genuine smile. Sweet and kind of sad. "Three sisters."

"Older or younger?"

"All younger. You?"

Faron opened his mouth to say two brothers and a sister, then realized he would have to qualify that— half brothers and a half sister. He frowned. Damned if he would. "I've got two older brothers and a younger sister."

He felt her relax almost immediately. Amazing how having a family made him seem less dangerous. Little did she know. His family was about the most unruly bunch he knew. "What are you doing way out here?" he asked.

She looked off into the distance. "Running from my problems."

He was tempted to make a flippant retort, but her honesty spurred him to equal sincerity. "Me, too."

She looked up at him again from beneath those dark lashes, to see if he was telling the truth. He realized she hadn't once looked at him directly and figured she must be used to hiding her feelings. But from whom? And why?

His lips twisted wryly. "Seems like we do have something in common, Princess. How 'bout if we run off together and leave our problems behind?"

"I can't—"

"Just for the afternoon," he urged. "What do you say? Let's throw our cares to the four winds and enjoy this afternoon together."

He felt her hand tremble where it lay on his forearm. She withdrew it and clasped her hands together in front of her. He could see she was tempted. He wished he knew what to say to push her over the brink. Nothing came to mind, so he just smiled.

Belinda knew she was making a mistake even as she nodded her head yes. She had to be crazy. She was truly certifiable. Imagine agreeing to spend the afternoon with a perfect stranger. She recognized the quality of both his horse and saddle, so she knew he was more than just some drifter. He was wearing frayed jeans, but his Western shirt appeared to have been tailored to fit both his broad shoulders and his lean waist.

But who was he? And where had he come from? She had lived so reclusively at The Castle, he might even be a neighbor from one of the outlying spreads for all she knew. "Are you from around here?" she asked.

"Just passing through."

That was some comfort. "What brings you here?"

He looked off across the prairie. "Just taking a look around. How about you? You live around here?"

She nodded. "Around." She wasn't about to be any more specific than he had been. It was safer that way.

Apparently the Cowboy gave her evasive answer a different meaning because he grinned and said, "So you're trespassing, too?"

"What?"

"Trespassing. On Wayne Prescott's land."

"Oh." Belinda knew she ought to correct his mistaken impression, but that would mean admitting she was Wayne Prescott's widow. Which would mean an abrupt end to her afternoon with the Cowboy. She wanted—needed—to forget who she was for a little while. So she said nothing.

Faron took her revealing blush as an admission of equal guilt. He smiled and said, "Don't worry. I won't let you get into trouble." After all, he owned half the place. If that bitch stepmother of his tried to make trouble, well, he would handle her. He pulled off his worn leather gloves and tucked them in his belt. Then he held out his hand to her. "I feel like walking some more. Will you join me?"

His smile made the invitation irresistible. Belinda's heart was doing a *rat-a-tat-tat* that made her want to press her hands to her chest to slow it down. She forcibly relaxed the knotted fingers she had clasped in front of her and reached out to take his hand. It was warm and calloused like a working man's ought to be. It gave her a feeling of strength and security as it closed around her fingers.

At the same time, she looked up into the Cowboy's unusual gray-green eyes. They were the color of a mountain spruce, wide-set, heavily lashed and crowned with arched brows. There were webbed lines at the corners, etched there by the sun. His nose was straight and angled slightly at the tip, and he had a beauty mark— was it called that when a man had one?—high on his right cheekbone.

She had been terrified when he chased her on horseback, but he had done a good job of allaying her fears. He hadn't touched her in any except the most gentlemanly way. She had noticed his restraint when he lifted her off her horse. On the other hand, he hadn't exactly given her a choice of whether she was going to join him on the ground. She felt certain he wasn't the sort of man to be denied something he wanted.

Nevertheless, she was inclined to accept him at face value. He was an open, friendly and—she would not deny it—handsome man...who knew his way around women. She had been charmed by that ridiculous name he had called her, Princess. And it was telling that he had tagged himself Cowboy, after that chivalrous knight of the Old West.

So what did he *really* want from her? She angled her head and took a long hard look at him.

"Something wrong?" he asked.

"You look familiar somehow."

He grinned. "Maybe I'm the man you've been waiting for all your life."

Her expression sobered. She was waiting for someone, all right, but it wasn't the man of her dreams. Any day now she expected her stepson from Texas to arrive. For a horrified instant she wondered if this stranger with whom she had been flirting could be Faron Whitelaw.

But this man couldn't be Wayne's son. He didn't look a bit like Wayne. Wayne's well-trimmed hair had been almost white blond. This man had coal black hair hanging down over his collar. Nor did his gray-green eyes have anything in common with the cold sapphire of Wayne's. And the Cowboy's forearms, visible where his shirtsleeves were folded up, revealed a warm bronze tint totally different from Wayne's light, easily freckled skin.

Did it really matter who he was? Would it be so awful if she stole an afternoon for herself with a perfect stranger? She had seen the admiration in his eyes, and it felt good. She had found him equally attractive.

He was extraordinarily tall, which was a good thing, since she had been as long-legged as a giraffe all her life. He had the rangy build of a cowboy, long, lean and strong. He had lifted her from the saddle as though she weighed nothing. And she had felt the play of muscle and sinew where her hand rested on his forearm.

Why not join in the Cowboy's fantasy? Just for an afternoon. What could possibly go wrong?

"So what are you running from?" Belinda asked as she strolled with the Cowboy toward the nearby meadow.

Faron left the two horses with their reins dragging. A cow horse wouldn't wander far ground-tied like that, and there was plenty of grass to keep the animals close.

"I think this is only going to work if we leave our problems behind us," Faron said. "We can only talk about good things this afternoon." He stopped and turned to face her. "Agreed?"

"It's a deal," Belinda said.

He lifted the hand he held, turned it over and kissed the center of her palm.

Belinda felt a streak of electricity shoot up her arm. She yanked her hand back reflexively, then laughed to cover the awkwardness it had created between them. "That tickled," she murmured in excuse and explanation.

"Yeah," he muttered back. Faron wondered if she had felt the same charge on her skin as he had felt on his lips. It had been an amazingly strong jolt to his system.

"Let's sit down, shall we?" Belinda dropped to her knees near a patch of large, daisylike flowers. Nearby was a bunch of bright blue lupine. The top of the hill-side was rimmed with Indian paintbrush. "We couldn't have picked a more perfect spot for an afternoon idyll if we'd tried," she said.

Faron's eyes narrowed as he surveyed the country-side. "It is beautiful. It's a shame…"

"What?"

"Nothing." Faron wasn't about to spoil his after-noon by thinking about his father and stepmother. He sat down and realized the ground still held the chill of winter. He pulled off his denim jacket and said, "Why don't you sit on this? It'll keep you from getting cold."

"I don't think—"

Again, he didn't give her a choice. He spread his jacket on the ground, then slipped a hand around her waist and resettled her on the denim. "Thanks," she murmured.

Faron's gallantry won him a rare smile that made his heart skip a beat. "You're welcome."

Belinda immediately began making a chain from the daisylike flowers. Faron stretched out beside her, his head on his hand.

"God, you're beautiful," he said.

Belinda laughed. "Are you always so forthright?"

He felt his body tighten at the sound of her laughter. "I tend to say what I'm thinking."

She looked up at him from under lowered lashes. "Then since we're being honest, you're quite good-looking yourself."

He grinned. "Thanks."

She laughed again. He was so different from Wayne. So carefree. She ought not to be here. She ought to be home, wearing black. Mourning.

"What are you thinking, Princess?"

The Cowboy's voice ripped her from the melancholy that threatened her peace. "What?"

He smoothed the furrows on her brow with his thumb. She had to purposely hold herself still for the caress. It was the first one she had received in so long her skin seemed to come alive beneath his touch. When his fingers trailed into the hair at her temple she leaned away, and his hand dropped back to the grass.

"You looked worried," he said. "I wondered what you were thinking."

"That I shouldn't be here."

"No time for regrets now. We made a deal. Only happy thoughts." Faron sat up and leaned his wrist on one bent knee. "Let's see. What should we talk about?"

"When was the happiest time in your life?" she asked.

"It's all been pretty good," he admitted. Until lately. "I guess I'd choose the day I made love to a woman for the first time."

Faron was both surprised and delighted by the blush that stained her cheeks at his revelation.

"I can't believe you said that," Belinda protested with a laugh.

"I warned you I was honest," Faron said. "It's your turn now."

"The happiest time?" she asked. There was a long silence while she thought about it.

"It wasn't that tough a question, was it?" Faron asked.

She grimaced. "I suppose the happiest time would have been before my parents died, although life was such a struggle on the ranch…" She shrugged.

Belinda could see the Cowboy was about to ask questions she would rather not answer, so she asked, "What did you want to be when you grew up?"

"That's easy," Faron replied. "The best."

"At what?"

"Something. Anything."

"That certainly gave you a lot of room to succeed," she said teasingly. Apparently he hadn't liked the idea of being tied down to any one thing. "Are you the best at something?"

Faron grinned. "I'm a damned good cowboy, ma'am." He leaned back so she could see the rodeo belt buckle he was wearing.

Belinda laughed and realized suddenly it had been a long time since she had done so. "I should have known." She leaned over and traced the writing on the buckle with her fingertips. *Rodeo Cowboy All-Around Champion.*

No wonder he had called himself Cowboy!

Faron held his breath as Belinda traced the face of the silver buckle with her fingertips. It was as though he could actually feel her touching his skin. He wanted her hand lower. His body was doing a helluva good job of imagining all by itself.

He cleared his throat, distracting her attention. "How about you? What did you want to be?"

"I never let myself dream. I couldn't."

"Why not?"

She draped a chain of flowers around the brim of his Stetson. "My sisters and I were orphaned when my parents were killed in a car accident. I was eighteen and had just graduated high school. Dori and Tillie and Fiona were still in school. The ranch went to the bank for debts. I found a job in Casper that paid enough to feed us and keep a roof over our heads. That didn't leave much time for dreaming."

"Let's pretend you're a real princess, and you can have anything you want. What would you wish for?" Faron asked. He laid a handful of flowers he had broken off just below the bud in her lap.

She scooped up the white, yellow and blue flowers and lifted them to her nose to see how they smelled. "I'd wish for a man to love me. And for children. I've always wanted to have children."

"How many children?" he asked in a quiet voice.

"More than one," she said definitely. "I liked having sisters. I grew up knowing I never had to be alone."

"Do your sisters live close?"

"Unfortunately they're scattered across the country. Every Fourth of July we get together. That's the only time everyone can get free."

Which meant she spent the rest of the year alone, Faron deduced.

Her lashes fluttered down to conceal her eyes. "You're not wearing a ring. Are you married?"

"No."

"Do you have a girlfriend?"

"No."

"But you've had lots of them, I suspect."

Faron eyed her askance. "What makes you say that?"

"You're awfully charming, for one thing."

He shrugged. "If you say so."

She smiled. "I do. For another thing, you don't seem in any hurry to…" Her cheeks felt warm. "I don't know exactly how to say this."

"Jump your bones?"

Her flush deepened. "Well, I wouldn't have said it quite that way, but—"

"The afternoon isn't over yet."

She swallowed hard. "Then I'm not safe with you?"

"As safe as you want to be," he said in a husky voice.

His eyes were more green than gray as they sought hers. Belinda was aware of a frisson of desire that began in her belly and spiraled upward. She could feel herself being drawn to him. She had already begun to lean toward him when she realized what she was doing. She jumped abruptly to her feet, scattering flowers around her. "It's getting late. I have to go."

She had already started toward her horse when he caught up to her and grasped her arm, stopping her. "Are you sure you can't stay a little longer?"

Belinda looked at the sun lowering in the western sky. Why, several hours must have passed! Where had the time gone? The Cowboy had cast some sort of spell on her to make her forget who—and what—she was. She would be lucky to get back to The Castle before suppertime. Madelyn would worry if she wasn't home by then. "I have to leave. Really, this has been lovely, but I have to go."

"Where do you live? When can I see you again?"

"You can't!" She hadn't meant to be curt, but she couldn't bear to see the look in his eyes if he ever found out she was a widow, a woman who should be in mourning. "You can't," she said more calmly, but just as firmly.

"Why not?"

"Because…please don't ask me to explain."

"All right."

Belinda breathed a sigh of relief. It turned out to be premature.

"I'll settle for a goodbye kiss."

"What?"

He didn't give her a chance to argue about it, simply pulled her into his arms and captured her mouth with his.

The Cowboy's kiss was like nothing Belinda had ever experienced before in her life. He tunneled all ten fingers into her hair. His lips softened on hers, and his tongue slipped inside her mouth to tease and to taste. For a moment she was quiescent. Then she kissed him back.

Faron hadn't known what to expect when he kissed his Princess. He had supposed from her shyness that he would be tasting innocence. For a few moments he had. But she had pulled him down to a deeper, darker well of desire than he had ever explored with a woman. A well where feelings and emotions were intimately bound with the physical act of love.

He lifted his head far enough to look into her eyes. "Princess?"

Belinda gazed up into gray-green orbs that were fierce with need. She reached up to touch the beauty mark on the Cowboy's cheek, then trailed her fingertips back down to his mouth, which was still wet from their kiss. She traced his lips with her forefinger, then looked up into eyes that had darkened with desire. She raised her mouth and touched it lightly to his. Then her tongue slipped inside his mouth to taste him.

She could feel the restraint he exercised to remain still for her kiss. It made her dare more. Her hands slipped around his neck and her fingertips teased the hair at his nape. She kissed the edges of his mouth and lingered to nip at his lower lip with her teeth. A harsh sound grated deep in the Cowboy's throat, and Belinda found herself answering with a kittenish purr of satisfaction.

He kissed his way along the edge of her jaw to her ear and caressed the delicate shell with his tongue. His breath was hot and moist and sent a shiver down her spine. Then his tongue slipped into her ear, and her belly curled with erotic sensation.

Belinda's eyes closed in surrender as her body swayed toward his. The Cowboy's arms closed around her, pulling her tight against him. She could feel the blunt ridge of his manhood against her femininity. As he rocked their bodies together, Belinda felt her knees give way.

The two of them slipped to the ground together. Belinda was aware of the cool grass beneath her, but it was the warmth above that she found so intriguing. The Cowboy held most of his weight on his arms, but their bodies were pressed together from the waist down, their legs entwined. His mouth found hers again, and this time he was more impatient.

One yank ripped the first three buttons on her shirt free. His mouth was reverent as he kissed the creamy mounds that spilled out of her lacy bra. He freed the bra itself, and his mouth latched on to a rosy crest. When he began to suck, Belinda's whole body arched up into his.

She was desperate to touch his skin, and she pulled at his shirt to free it from his jeans. She tried to unbutton the buttons, but her hands were trembling too much. The Cowboy ripped the shirt off himself, sending buttons flying. Then he pressed their bodies together, flesh to flesh. Belinda made a soft little sound in her throat as the crisp hair on his chest brushed her tender nipples.

"Princess, you feel so good. You feel so right." His hand slid down to unsnap her jeans. The rasp of her zipper coming down sounded loud in her ears. Before she could come to her senses his mouth had captured her breast again. The Cowboy sucked and nipped and sucked again so the sensual tension never let up.

His hand slid down inside her panties, through her feminine curls until he found the tender bud he sought. Belinda nearly came up off the ground as his fingers began to work their magic.

"Come apart for me, Princess," Faron crooned. "Be beautiful for me, only me."

He shoved her jeans down out of the way and unfastened his own. Belinda caught his face with both hands and brought his mouth up to hers.

"Kiss me, Cowboy. Please, kiss me."

She felt his body invade hers at the same time his tongue thrust into her mouth. He was big and hard, and her body arched up to take all of him as he thrust deeply inside her. Belinda heard an animal sound rip from her throat as their bodies surged together. He withdrew and thrust again in ageless rhythm as her hips rose in counterpoint to his.

Her fingernails dug crescents in his shoulders as her body arched up in passion. At the last instant, Belinda tried to fight the pleasure. This shouldn't be happening! She had no right!

But the Cowboy wouldn't allow her to withdraw. "Come with me, Princess. Come with me!"

Then it was too late. Her body began to convulse in wave after wave of unbearable pleasure. She gritted her teeth against the ecstasy that besieged her, holding her prisoner for timeless moments. While she was caught in the throes of passion, the Cowboy claimed her for his own. His cries were guttural as his body arched and spilled its seed within her.

Afterward, they both lay exhausted, unable to move. Belinda was aware of a fine sheen of sweat on his body and the musky smell of sex.

"I want to see you again," the Cowboy murmured as he slipped to her side and drew her into his arms. He was already asleep before Belinda could answer him.

Which was just as well.

Belinda was appalled at what she had done. But she couldn't regret it. What had passed between the Cowboy and his Princess was one brief shining moment when two souls blended into one. They might be strangers still, but they had found something more than physical satisfaction in each other's arms. She would hold this magical afternoon close to her heart forever.

But there was no way she could see him again. He would be horrified if he knew the truth about her. And she would be ashamed for him to find out. She had to escape now, while he was asleep.

She dressed quickly and quietly and led her palomino a short distance away before she mounted him, so that she wouldn't wake the Cowboy. When she was far enough away that the sound wouldn't waken him, she kicked the mare into a gallop and raced back to The Castle.

The instant she stepped inside the kitchen door, she was greeted by her mother-in-law. Belinda plowed a hand through her hair, shoving it off her face, and tried a smile. It failed dismally.

"You're late," Madelyn said. She took one look at Belinda's disheveled appearance and asked, "What happened to you?" There was more curiosity than accusation in her tone.

"I...my horse threw me," Belinda said, brushing at the grass stains on her jeans.

"Your blouse is ripped. Are you sure you're all right?"

Belinda flushed and clutched at the torn fabric. Getting thrown shouldn't have torn three buttons off her blouse. "I'll just run upstairs and change for supper." She hurried from the kitchen and practically ran up the majestic circular staircase that led to her bedroom.

"There's no hurry," Madelyn murmured to Belinda's disappearing back. There would be plenty of time before supper to ask about the love-bruise on her daughter-in-law's neck.

CHAPTER THREE

THE COOL NIGHT air woke Faron. At first he didn't know where he was. It all came back to him in a hurry. As he dressed himself, one thing quickly became apparent. His Princess was gone.

Faron was furious when he realized he didn't know her name or how to find her. Nor could he track her in the dark. Besides, he had phoned The Castle from Casper, and Madelyn Prescott was expecting him for dinner.

He dressed quickly, muttering profanities when he realized half the buttons were gone from his shirt. He would have to change it when he got back to his truck. He took a look at the knees of his jeans and realized it probably wouldn't hurt to change them, either. Not that he gave a damn what the Prescotts thought of him, but he had been taught manners around ladies that were hard to shed.

Faron whistled for his horse, and Sonny nickered a response. The quarter horse hadn't drifted far. Faron mounted up and rode in the fading light of dusk back in the direction of his truck and trailer. There wasn't any chance he would lose his way. He had learned young to look back every so often when he was riding the range to mark his trail. He easily found the landmarks that took him back to the highway.

Faron had gotten directions from Madelyn Prescott, and it didn't take him long to find the formal entrance to King's Castle. If the land had awed him, the house itself—The Castle—left him speechless.

As he stepped from his pickup he couldn't help staring. Light poured from tall, narrow, leaded windows, and there were sconces on the outside stone walls that created an eerie silhouette on the plains. The house did indeed have crenels along the roofline and what appeared to be turrets at the corners.

When he cut the engine a cowhand came from the direction of the barn.

"I'm Toby, Mr. Whitelaw. Mrs. Prescott said I was to take care of your horse," the cowhand said.

Faron backed Sonny from the trailer and watched long enough to make sure the cowhand knew what he was doing before he left his horse in Toby's care.

Moments later Faron found himself on the front steps of The Castle. The three-story gray stone structure had a massive double wooden door headed by a stone arch that might once have been the gateway to a medieval castle. When Faron knocked, the imposing entrance was opened by a tiny, silver-haired lady dressed in black. He found himself looking into a pair of gray-green eyes the same unusual color as his own.

"Hello, Faron," the woman said with a smile of greeting, "I'm your grandmother, Madelyn Prescott. We've been expecting you."

Faron's hat came off at once. He leaned over and kissed the old woman on the cheek. She smelled of lavender powder. Her skin had the softness of the very young and the very old. The wrinkles on her face gave her character, as well as age. Faron felt his throat tighten as he realized this woman was indeed his grandmother. It was true, then. He was a bastard.

Madelyn cupped her grandson's cheek with her hand and searched his features looking for signs of Wayne. There was nothing of her son in Faron, but there was something of her. "You've got the Halliwell eyes, I see."

"If you say so, ma'am," Faron said. "Hope I'm not too late for supper."

"Not at all. Belinda is still upstairs getting dressed. Perhaps you'd like to share a brandy with me in the parlor while we wait."

"I'd be pleased to, ma'am."

"Please, call me Madelyn."

But Faron couldn't bring himself to call his grandmother by her first name. It seemed disrespectful somehow. By what fond nickname would he have called her, he wondered, if he had known as a child that she existed? He had called his father's mother Nanaw, and his mother's mother Gram. "Would you mind if I called you Maddy?" he asked.

Her gray-green eyes quickly misted, and she pressed a fragile hand against her heart. "Why, that would be lovely, Faron."

He frowned when she seemed to have trouble catching her breath. "Are you all right?"

"My health isn't what it used to be. My heart, you know."

"I didn't know. Have you seen a doctor?"

"Oh, yes. I'm afraid in my case it's just a matter of age catching up with me. Come along now. Belinda will be down soon, I'm sure."

As Faron followed Madelyn, he stepped into a world of days gone by—an open drawing room with walnut woodwork, nineteenth century furniture of polished cherry and oak, lace curtains and brilliant chandeliers of sparkling crystal. Two broad stairways formed a sweeping arc leading to the upper floors.

Faron frowned at what he saw only because it represented his father's wealth, which was the source of the current calamity in his life. It was not the setting in which he had expected to find his ogre of a stepmother. It felt too much like a home. He couldn't help but admire the sense of history that was represented in the antique Western furnishings.

Faron and his grandmother had gotten only as far as the stairs when they heard the echo of footsteps.

"That will be Belinda," Madelyn said.

Faron followed her gaze up the stairs. The composed, graceful young woman who came walking down the sweeping staircase was a far cry from the ugly stepmother found in fairy tales. In fact, she was his very own Princess.

Her glorious golden hair, which he had grasped in his fists while he came inside her mere hours ago, was bound up now in a stylish twist. Her sleek black silk dress showed off a lush figure with which he was intimately familiar. A long black chiffon scarf circled her neck and floated on the air behind her. But there was nothing of the wanton woman he had loved reflected in the cool violet eyes that met his gaze.

It would be difficult to say which of the two lovers was more shocked to see the other. It was equally apparent that neither of them was willing to do or say anything in front of Madelyn that would upset the old woman.

"Good evening, Mr. Whitelaw," Belinda said, extending her hand. Her heart was pounding, and she felt as though she were going to faint. When the Cowboy took her hand, he held it longer than he should. His mouth had formed into a smile, but his gray-green eyes looked wintry.

"It's a pleasure to meet you at last, Mrs. Prescott. Please, call me Faron. If you don't mind, I'll call you… Belinda."

Faron's anger had returned with a vengeance. Here stood a woman he had hated sight unseen—but with whom he had just experienced an incredibly passionate assignation. He wanted to ask her why she had made love to him when her husband—his father—was barely cold in the ground. But his lips clamped tight on the question. What they had done was awful enough. He had no intention of embarrassing his grandmother with revelations that would have to be distasteful to her.

Beyond being angry, Faron was hurt. His stepmother had made a fool of him. He had called The Castle from Casper hours ago, so she must have known he was coming. Which meant she also must have known who he was when she had made love with him. No wonder she hadn't wanted to give him her name! How could she have done such a thing?

But despite being angry and hurt, he was also

aroused. The memory of what had happened between them was still fresh, like a green wound that ached when prodded. Even icily distant, she was still his Princess. And he wanted her as much now as he ever had.

Tension lay thick in the air. A powerful current sparked between them, threatening a shock to the first who broke it.

"Come along, children," Madelyn said at last. She led the way to the dining room, which was as richly furnished as the rest of the house. The pine trestle table was at least fifteen feet long. Three places had been set at one end with fine china and silver.

Faron held Madelyn's chair as she sat at the head of the table. Then he went around to help Belinda. Her stomach clenched when Faron leaned over to whisper in her ear and trailed his hand across her bare shoulder. When he spoke, it was his anger she heard.

"It didn't take you long to find some young stud to service you," he hissed. "Did I measure up to my father?"

Belinda's face bleached white.

"Are you feeling all right, my dear?" Madelyn asked.

"I'm a little tired," Belinda said. "I had a long ride this afternoon." She raised her eyes to meet Faron's and realized the second meaning that could be given to her words. His lips lifted in a slight smirk that made her feel physically ill.

Belinda wanted to tell him she was sorry. But she wasn't sorry. What had happened between them had been beautiful. What she really wanted was the chance to explain why she had needed what he had offered. She had been so very vulnerable. It had been so wonderful to allow herself the fantasy of loving and being loved.

Now Belinda was sure Faron Whitelaw had entirely

the wrong idea about what kind of woman she was. She could feel his attraction to her, but it was laced with harsher, harder feelings. The fierce look on his face gave ample evidence that he didn't want to hear what she had to say. And that he was unlikely to forgive or forget what she had done.

When Belinda realized the road her thoughts had taken she was alarmed. Hadn't she learned her lesson with Wayne? Here she was ready to make the same mistakes again! Why should she care what her stepson thought of her? She would never give another man the sort of emotional, physical and economic hold over her that Wayne had possessed.

She ought to show Faron the door. If it had only been herself involved in the catastrophe that threatened, she would have. But there was Madelyn to think of. So she clamped her back teeth together and held her tongue.

Once Faron was seated, an older woman wearing a voluminous white apron began serving dinner. She passed out plates already laden with pork chops, mashed potatoes and green beans. The servant had hair dyed a shocking red and fingernails painted an equally vivid color. When she left the room Madelyn said, "Rue has been with the family forever. Belinda and I couldn't manage without her."

To Faron it was further proof that Belinda Prescott was the pampered Princess he had labeled her. His stepmother sat across from him looking cool and elegant and totally in control. Meanwhile, his body was hard and throbbing from the small caress of her shoulders he had allowed himself. But he would be damned if he'd touch her again anytime soon.

As he ate his dinner, Faron tried to revive the feelings of dislike he had felt toward Belinda Prescott for forcing him to confront his true paternity. But it was one thing to hate a woman you envisioned as an interfering rich bitch, and quite another to hate a woman with whom you've just shared the most poignant physical encounter of your life.

To compound his confusion, the woman he found so attractive was his stepmother. He had been determined not to take anything handed down to him from Wayne Prescott. Now he found there was one thing he wanted very much: his father's widow.

"Did Belinda write you about the terms of the will?"

Madelyn's question jerked Faron from his thoughts. "What?"

"The will. Did Belinda tell you the terms of Wayne's will?"

Faron's gaze swung back around the table to spear Belinda. "No, Maddy, she didn't. She did seem in an all-fired hurry for me to get here."

"Why don't you tell Faron the problem, Belinda," Madelyn said.

"If you came here expecting to inherit wealth beyond your dreams, you're going to be disappointed," Belinda began.

Faron's brows arched. "I heard my father was a millionaire."

"*Was* is the correct word," Belinda said. "King's Castle, including the land and The Castle on it, is mortgaged to the hilt. The mineral leases only provide enough income to cover the taxes, and the worsening economy has left the ranch only marginally profitable."

"So sell the ranch and move into town," Faron said.

"It isn't that simple."

"Why not?" Faron asked.

"If we could sell the property piecemeal, there might be some hope of making a profit and avoiding foreclosure. But Wayne's will stipulates that King's Castle has to be sold all in one piece. Otherwise it gets donated to charity.

"We simply haven't been able to find a buyer willing to take the whole thing—thousands of acres of land, dozens of buildings, farm equipment, the stock, the house—in short, someone willing to buy the losing aspects of the ranch along with the profitable ones," Belinda explained. "I was hoping you might have some ideas about improvements that would make the ranch attractive to a single corporate buyer."

Faron had wondered why his stepmother had gone to so much trouble to have him included in his father's will. Now he had his answer. She needed someone with the right motivation—a promise of half the proceeds—to spend the time and energy putting King's Castle back on its feet so she could make a big killing when it was sold!

His sense of self-preservation warned him to get right back in his truck and go home to Texas. He decided to ask a few more questions first.

"How much money do you have to work with?"

"You mean cash?" Belinda asked. When Faron nodded she said, "There's just enough in the bank for food for us and the stock over the summer."

"Surely there are some jewels or furs you can liquidate," Faron said.

"Oh, dear, no," Madelyn said. "Wayne sold all those things years ago."

"Have you tried cutting the staff for the house and the number of cowboys on the payroll."

Madelyn's eyes twinkled as she laughed. "You've seen the house staff," she said.

"Rue?" Faron asked incredulously.

"We simply couldn't let her go," Madelyn said. "She's almost family."

"And the cowhands?"

"You've met Toby, I presume."

Faron nodded. When Madelyn said nothing more he realized the middle-aged cowboy was all there was. "Who takes care of things around here?" he demanded.

"Why, Belinda does, of course," Madelyn said.

Faron stared hard at his stepmother. That wasn't at all what he had expected to hear.

"I can see you two need to discuss business," Madelyn said. "So I'll just excuse myself and go upstairs and get some rest."

Faron stood and escorted his grandmother to the door of the dining room, sliding the wooden door closed behind her. Then he turned back to the woman who had become his nemesis—and his desire.

Faron stared at Belinda with narrowed eyes. "How bad is it?" he demanded.

She laced her hands together calmly. "It's as bad as you think it is. We're as poor as church mice. If something isn't done to make King's Castle salable, Madelyn and I will be penniless and homeless within the year."

Faron fisted his hands so hard his knuckles turned white. He might have been able to leave Belinda to her fate, but there was no way he could stand by and watch his own grandmother be put out in the street.

"All right," he said. "I'll hang around long enough to help put the place in shape to sell. But as soon as we find a buyer, I'm out of here!"

"No one could want to leave this place more than I do!" Belinda said vehemently. "There are no happy memories here for me!"

"No one forced you to marry my father," Faron snarled. "You made your own bed. Now you have to lie in it. Just don't expect me to join you there."

Belinda's face blanched white. She could feel his fury, his hate and his desire. She had learned from Wayne how to avoid confrontation. It didn't always work, but often enough it had saved her a bruise or a blackened eye. She put those lessons to good use now.

She lowered her eyelids to hide the anger blazing there. She rose and smoothed the front of her skirt with hands that appeared much more calm than they were. In a soft, deferential voice she said, "I believe I'll retire now."

When Faron took a step toward Belinda, her eyes flashed defiance. She would not become a victim, ever again. "Keep your distance, Cowboy!"

He took another step toward her.

"I'm warning you—"

Then it was too late. He had her in his arms before she could turn and run.

"Let me go," she cried breathlessly. "This is wrong!"

"It's a little late for that argument, don't you think, Princess?"

"I didn't know who you were! I never would have…"

"Never would have rolled in the grass with your stepson?" Faron finished for her.

Tears blurred Belinda's vision. She held herself stiff in Faron's arms. "I don't have to explain anything to you."

"No, you don't," he murmured.

The hardest thing Faron had ever done was to let

her go. His body was hard and throbbing with need. It didn't matter one bit that she was his father's widow. But he had to work side by side with her over the next several weeks—or months. It was going to be awkward enough being together every day without knowing for sure that she still desired him as much as he desired her.

"Where do I sleep?" he asked.

Belinda was quivering with relief—or unsatisfied desire. She wasn't willing to examine her feelings closely enough to find out. "Follow me," she said. "I'll show you where your room is."

Once again Faron found himself staring into violet eyes that had turned to ice. He followed her up one half of the curving staircase to a room that might have welcomed some cowboy a hundred years ago. It was furnished sparingly with a maple four-poster, a dry sink, a chest and a rocker. A rag rug covered a small area of the oak hardwood floor. The lamp was electric, but it was Victorian in style.

The connected bathroom had a tub on legs and a pedestal sink. "The linens on the rack are for your use," she said.

Belinda was aware of the confines of the bathroom. She edged her way past the Cowboy and back into the more spacious bedroom. "If you need anything…"

"I'll be fine," Faron said, realizing that she didn't want to spend any more time with him than she had to. "Good night, Princess," he said. His eyes said what he didn't put in words. He wanted her. She was welcome to stay.

Belinda didn't bother to answer. She did what any self-respecting Princess would have done when the dragon started breathing fire. She fled to her room.

CHAPTER FOUR

FARON WAS ASTOUNDED at how much Belinda knew about the business affairs of King's Castle. Unfortunately, the more he learned from her, the more grim-lipped he became. Because things were every bit as bad as she had suggested they were.

"I don't know how you've kept the bank from foreclosing before now," he muttered when he was done examining his father's records.

"Can anything be done to save King's Castle?"

Faron felt his gut tighten as he met Belinda's expectant gaze across the width of the oak rolltop desk in Wayne's study. Even now he wanted her. This morning her golden hair was confined in a single tail that fell over her shoulder, and she was wearing a Western shirt, jeans and boots. She reminded him much too much of his prairie Princess.

He leashed his memories of the previous day and concentrated on the matter at hand. "We can't do it alone," he said. "We'll have to hire some help."

Belinda wiped her palms down the length of her jeans, unaware of the way Faron's gray-green eyes followed her gesture. "I don't have money for that."

"I do."

Belinda frowned. "I can't let you spend your money."

"You can't stop me," Faron retorted. "According to my father's will I own half of King's Castle. If something isn't done, the bank is going to take my inheritance. It's no skin off your nose if I invest my money to save my half of this place."

Belinda's lip curled in a wry smile. "You'll also be saving my half," she pointed out.

"I don't want to see my grandmother put out in the street."

Belinda's smile twisted into something more cynical. "And you have to save me to save her, is that it?"

"Something like that."

"Where do we start?" Belinda asked.

Faron arched a disdainful brow. "We?"

"I presume you have some plan in mind. Things that have to be done. I want to help."

"What is it you think you can do?" Faron asked. He preferred to keep her—and temptation—as far from him as possible.

Belinda's chin came up pugnaciously. "What do you need done?"

Faron tried to think of something that would impress upon his stepmother—he had to keep reminding himself how Belinda had deceived him about her identity—

how very much *work* was involved in restoring King's Castle to its former greatness.

Not one, but several ideas caught his fancy. He reached out and grabbed Belinda's hand and pulled her after him. "Come with me. I want to start with a tour of the ranch, so I can get some idea of what needs to be done." He only got as far as the back porch before he stopped and asked, "Are there enough roads to get us where we need to go, or should we do this survey on horseback?"

Belinda wasn't sure which was worse. Spending half the day on horseback together would remind them both of the events of the previous day. But if she said they ought to drive, she would have to endure an hour or more confined with him in the cab of a pickup truck. The pickup seemed the lesser of two evils.

"It would be faster and more efficient to drive," she said. "But the only pickup I have isn't in very good mechanical shape."

Faron grimaced at this reminder of the state of poverty in which his father had left his stepmother and grandmother. "We'll take my truck. Just give me a minute to disconnect the horse trailer," he replied.

It was strange seeing King's Castle through Faron's eyes. The splendor of the land, which Belinda had taken for granted, he found not only pleasing to the eye, but a definite economic asset.

"The land itself is a selling point," he explained to her. "It hasn't been overdeveloped. The grass is tall and there's lots of it."

She headed him in the direction of the small herd of Herefords that still roamed King's Castle.

"I see you're using a windmill for water," he said as he pulled the truck to a stop beside the windmill tank.

Faron got out of the truck and headed for the windmill, and Belinda followed after him. He leaned his head back and watched and listened as the wind pushed the windmill around.

"It's not running right," he said at last. "You've got a bolt or two loose up top that ought to be tightened."

She put her hands on her hips. "Who would you suggest I send up there to tighten them. Myself? Or Toby?"

Faron recalled the stature of the stocky cowhand, then gave Belinda a looking over that had a blush skating up her throat. "I guess you," he said at last in a taunting voice.

Belinda's eyes went wide. Was he serious? But if he thought she would back off from such a chore, he had another think coming. "All right," she said, pushing her sleeves up out of the way. "What is it you want me to do?"

Faron pursed his lips in chagrin. He had been certain she would defer the job to him. Now he found himself in the awkward position of having to admit that he had been manipulating the situation. He certainly didn't expect a woman to do the kind of dangerous repair job that was necessary.

He opened his mouth to tell her so and shut it again. The challenging look in her violet eyes dared him to admit he was wrong. Before he conceded the issue, Faron decided to see just how far she was willing to go.

He left Belinda and crossed to the back of his pickup where he kept a tool chest. He rattled around in it for a few moments and came back with a wrench.

"I think this is the tool you'll need."

Belinda took the wrench from him, but she hadn't the slightest idea what to do with it. What she was thinking must have shown in her face, because he stepped up beside her and showed her how to adjust it.

"This way tightens it, this way loosens it. You're not afraid of heights, are you?"

Belinda stared at the thin metal ladder that was attached to the windmill. Her eyes followed it what seemed an immense distance into the air. She swallowed and said, "No. I'm not afraid of heights."

"What you're looking for is the bolt that attaches the wheel. Right now the wheel isn't at the correct angle to the yaw axis in the vane."

"What?" Belinda hadn't the vaguest notion what he was talking about.

"You do understand how a windmill works, don't you?"

Belinda wrinkled her nose. "Sort of. I understand the principle of the thing, but not exactly how the pieces fit together."

"Maybe you'd better let me do this." Faron waited for her to concede that he was the one better equipped to handle this job. He had underestimated her stubbornness.

"I can do it," she insisted. "If you'll just explain what it is I have to do."

"That's a little difficult without having the windmill down here where I can point things out," Faron said.

Belinda looked at the ladder. No way could both of them go up it together. "Let me try," she said at last. "If I can't fix it, then you can do the job."

Faron was amazed, but not amused, by Belinda's insistence on climbing to the top of the windmill. "Dammit, woman. It's dangerous to go up there."

"I'm not afraid."

"I am," he muttered. Faron wasn't about to let her endanger her life. "You've proved your point," he said. "You're willing to do what has to be done. Now give me that wrench, and let me go up and tighten that bolt."

"I'm not helpless!"

"I never said you were," Faron retorted. "Now give me the damn wrench!"

Instead, she turned and started up the ladder.

Faron put both arms around her and dragged her back down. Belinda didn't come without a fight. The wrench fell to the ground in the struggle. She kicked and hit at Faron, but he had her from behind and her efforts to free herself were useless.

At last she slumped in his arms.

"Are you done fighting me?" he asked.

"Let me go."

"Are you done fighting me?" he repeated.

"Yessss," she hissed.

Now that he could let her go, Faron realized he didn't want to. His body was way ahead of his mind. It had long since reacted strongly and certainly to the woman in his arms. Faron felt the weight of her soft breasts resting on his forearm. She smelled of soap and shampoo and woman. His hands slid down until his fingertips lay at the base of her belly.

"Faron."

Belinda bit her lip to keep from saying more than Faron's name. Oh, God, she wanted him! She wanted to lie with him, to merge their bodies, to join their souls. But she was not so far gone with desire that she couldn't see the folly of repeating what had happened the previous day.

Belinda covered the male hand on her belly with her own. "We can't do this, Faron. Please. Your father—"

His whole body stiffened. A moment later she was free.

Belinda was afraid to turn around and face him. When she did, she wished she hadn't. There was an awful look of disgust and disdain on his face. The gray-green eyes she had found so fascinating yesterday were slicing shards of cut green glass today.

She stooped to pick up the wrench, thus avoiding his piercing gaze. When she rose, she kept her lashes lowered. She held out the wrench, and he took it from her, careful not to touch her hand. Soon after, he was halfway up the ladder.

"Be careful," she whispered. She shaded her eyes from the sun and watched as Faron made his way to the top of the windmill. It didn't take him long to do what he had to do, but Belinda hardly breathed the whole time he was working. He hadn't been kidding about the danger of the job. A fall from that height would break a man in pieces.

When Faron came down the ladder she stayed out of his way. "All finished?"

"That's all I can do right now," he said. "There's a part missing. I'll have to get a replacement."

"Will it cost much?"

"Always thinking about money, Princess?"

"Don't call me that! Not like that!"

"Why not? That's what you are. A pampered, golden Princess. Living off an older man's money—"

"Stop! Stop!" Belinda put her hands to her ears. "How can you be so cruel?"

"Cruel? Princess, I don't hold a candle to you!"

Faron stalked back to the truck. He was furious with himself for losing his temper, for taking out his sexual frustration in such a—yes, cruel—way. He hadn't realized he was capable of that sort of behavior with a woman. Before Belinda... Hell, that was a lifetime ago. Before Belinda he had been Faron Whitelaw, happily oblivious to the fact he was Wayne Prescott's son. Before Belinda he had known who he was. Now, everything was so damn confused!

"Get in the truck," he said.

"I'd rather walk back to The Castle than get in that truck with you," Belinda snapped back.

"Listen, Princess. Either you get in that truck under your own steam, or I'm going to pick you up and put you there."

Given that choice, Belinda stomped over to the pickup and got in. He stepped in behind the wheel and gunned the engine. The wheels sent dust flying as they headed down the road.

There was a long silence while both of them fumed. At last Belinda said, "I don't think this is going to work. I think maybe I'll just let the bank take back the ranch. I'll go to work somewhere in town to support myself and Madelyn."

"Doing what?" Faron demanded.

Belinda shrugged. "I used to be a short order cook. I could—"

Faron snorted. "Princesses don't flip hamburgers. Besides, you may be willing to give up your half of this place, but I'm not about to give up my half."

"Now who's thinking about money?" Belinda goaded.

"It's not the money," Faron gritted out. He kept his hands on the wheel and forced himself not to put his foot down on the accelerator. "Oh, hell. I don't have to explain anything to you. Just get the idea of giving this place away out of your head. I'm here and I'm staying until King's Castle is sold. Now, if you're through pouting, maybe you'd like to tell me what else I ought to take a look at."

That was just the beginning of a very long day.

Belinda had put in a lot of hours over the past few years holding King's Castle together, but she had never worked so long or so hard without a rest. She marveled at Faron's energy, at his strength, at his tirelessness. But no matter how many jobs he threw at her, she was determined not to be the one who cried mercy first.

It was nearly dusk when he decided they should clean out the tack room in the barn. The small, windowless room that held saddles, bridles and other leather tack was dark and cool. Belinda pulled a string that lit a single bare bulb hanging overhead. She was assaulted by the pungent smells of leather and horses and, once Faron stepped into the room behind her, hardworking man.

"Some of this leather could use a soaping," Faron said as he walked around the room checking stirrups and reins.

"There hasn't been much time—"

"We'll start now."

"No."

It was the first time since the incident at the windmill that Belinda had objected to anything Faron had suggested. He had been expecting her to quit long before now and head back to the house. She had amazed him with her fortitude. And slowly but surely driven him crazy with her presence.

His body had tightened as he watched her lick off a fine sheen of perspiration on her upper lip that he knew would be salty to the taste. As he watched her stoop and bend and lean in jeans that hugged her rear end like a man's hand. As he watched her cant her head and lift that golden hair up off her neck so the ever-present breeze could cool her, whipping tiny curls across petal-soft skin.

He should be glad she had finally given up, glad she would be out of his hair at long last. Perversely, he said the one thing he believed would provoke her into staying.

"Conceding the battle, Princess?"

Her violet eyes flashed with anger. "I won't dignify that comment with an argument. I'm going to get cleaned up for supper. We can start here tomorrow morning."

When Belinda tried to leave the room, Faron spread his arms and rested his palms on either side of the doorway, blocking the way out.

"Please get out of the way," she said in a controlled voice. "I want to leave."

"You surprised me today."

She arched a brow but said nothing.

"I didn't think you'd be able to keep up all day."

She still said nothing.

"I was wrong."

As an apology it lacked a lot. But it was as much of a concession as Faron was willing to make. "There's something I don't understand," he said.

"What?"

"Why would someone who's willing to work as hard as you have today marry a man twice her age for his money? It doesn't fit."

Belinda's face paled. "It doesn't have to. I don't owe you any explanation. Now let me pass." She wouldn't discuss her marriage to Wayne with Wayne's son. She wouldn't.

When Faron saw she had no intention of answering, he took his weight off his palms and leaned back against the door frame, his legs widespread. She could get out, but not without touching him.

Belinda kept her eyes lowered as she tried to skim past him. She had to turn sideways, and the tips of her breasts brushed his chest. She gasped at her body's reaction to even that brief contact.

Faron's response was powerful and instantaneous. Before Belinda could get past him, he clamped his hands on her shoulders and turned her toward him. His arms folded around her, and he drew her close.

"Faron, don't!"

"Do you think I want to feel like this?" he rasped in her ear. "It's driving me crazy, knowing how your skin tastes, knowing what it feels like to be inside you—and knowing that you were my father's wife!"

Belinda pushed at his chest with the heels of her hands. "Let me go, Faron! This is wrong!"

"You didn't think so yesterday."

"I told you, I didn't know who you were yesterday! This situation is awkward enough. Let's not make it worse."

He nuzzled her temple, let his lips trail down to her ear and felt her shiver in his arms. "And this will make it worse?"

Belinda exhaled a shuddery sigh. "What happened between us was—"

"A miracle."

"A mistake. Faron, we can't let this happen again."

Faron heard the desperation in her voice. He felt the same desperation himself. However, he could afford to be patient. He wasn't going anywhere anytime soon. Neither was she.

He dropped his hands to his sides and stood up straight so there was more space between them. "Call me when supper's ready."

She didn't answer him, just made her escape as quickly as she could. Belinda didn't run back to the house, although it took all her willpower to keep her pace to a walk.

How had things gotten out of hand so quickly? She should have known better than to let herself get cornered like that. But she hadn't been expecting Faron to confront her. She hadn't been expecting him to admit that he still desired her.

But she had been right to push him away. There could be no repetition of what had happened yesterday. Under the circumstances it was unthinkable.

Belinda stepped up on the back porch and shoved her way through the screen door that led to the kitchen. In some ways, The Castle was like any other ranch house. Friends and neighbors always entered through the back door which was usually left open, rather than the front. She stopped dead when she saw Madelyn standing in front of the stove, stirring a pot of chili.

"What are you doing in here?" she asked.

Madelyn lifted a spoonful of chili and sipped a taste of it. "Making supper."

"Where's Rue?"

"She's having one of her spells."

That was Madelyn's way of saying Rue was drunk. Once a year, on the anniversary of her son's death in Vietnam, Rue got drunk. How long the "episode" lasted depended on how good a job Belinda did of finding Rue's stash of bottles and disposing of it. "I thought we'd gotten rid of all the bottles."

"She must have had another tucked away somewhere."

Belinda came up behind Madelyn and put a hand around her shoulder. "You should be resting."

"There'll be time enough for that when I'm laid in my grave."

"I wish you wouldn't talk like that!" Before Wayne's death, Belinda hadn't been quite so aware of Madelyn's mortality. Now she worried about the older woman's health. Madelyn's heart wasn't in much better shape than Wayne's had been.

Madelyn turned and patted Belinda on the arm. "I'm sorry, dear. Why don't you sit down and tell me how the day went with my grandson?"

That brought a wry smile to Belinda's face. "I'll make a deal. *You* sit down, and I'll tell you how the day went."

Madelyn handed over the wooden spoon and took a seat on a bar stool next to the woodblock island in the center of the kitchen. "I'm sitting. Talk."

Belinda turned away to stir the chili, which gave her a chance to organize her thoughts. There was no hope for her feelings, which were still in a state of chaos. "He's a hard worker," Belinda conceded.

"Then you two should have gotten along well," Madelyn said.

Belinda shot Madelyn a look over her shoulder. She was a shrewd old woman. Belinda wondered how much Madelyn knew—or suspected—about the tension between her daughter-in-law and her grandson. "We didn't argue much, if that's what you're getting at." Only at the very beginning and the very end of the day. "Faron has his own way of doing things. I just went along with him."

"Go along and get along. That didn't work very well with Wayne, my dear."

"Faron is nothing like Wayne!" Belinda astonished herself with her outburst. She flushed and tried to backtrack by saying, "I mean, they look nothing alike."

"And they don't act alike, either. Is that what you wanted to say?"

"I don't intend to criticize my late husband to his mother," Belinda said.

Madelyn sighed. "Unfortunately, I'm well aware of my son's faults. I hope you won't let what happened between you and Wayne keep you from finding another young man to love."

Belinda dropped the spoon in the chili and turned to face Madelyn. "I hope you're not thinking about matchmaking, Madelyn. Not matching me with Faron, anyway. For heaven's sake, he's Wayne's son!"

"And quite a good-looking young man, if I do say so myself."

"Please, Madelyn. Don't interfere. Things are difficult enough as it is."

"Difficult? How so?"

Belinda grimaced. She should have known Madelyn

wouldn't be satisfied without specifics. But she wasn't going to get them. "We just don't get along."

"It didn't look that way to me last night."

The old woman saw too much. Belinda took a deep breath and let it out. "Suffice it to say that I don't want to get involved with *anyone* right now."

Madelyn was wise enough to know when to let well enough alone. She had said her piece. Not that she wouldn't consider a little manipulating behind the scenes. She would have a talk with her grandson and see which way the wind was blowing.

When the table was set and the corn muffins were just about ready to come out of the oven, Belinda stepped out onto the back porch and circled the triangle hanging from the eave several times with an iron rod. The metallic clang was a sound that cowboys recognized all over the West as a call to supper.

Sure enough, Faron's head and shoulders appeared at the barn door, followed quickly by the rest of him. Belinda knew she should turn around and go back inside, but she couldn't take her eyes off him.

His stride was long and his body moved with an easy grace. His face was hidden by the hat he had pulled down low on his brow. His shirtsleeves were rolled up onto his forearms and she could see the muscles move as he swung his arms in rhythm with his legs. He was almost to the porch by the time she realized he was aware that she had been staring at him.

He stopped with his boot on the first step and tipped his hat back so she could see his face. He was grinning.

"See anything you like?"

"Oh!" She whirled and headed for the door, but she

didn't get two steps before he caught her arm and pulled her back around to face him.

"I wasn't complaining. In fact, I'm flattered. I can't keep my eyes off you, either."

"Faron—"

He laid two fingers across her mouth to silence her. His voice was gruff when he spoke again. "You'd better be careful how you look at me with those violet eyes of yours, Princess. I've got myself on a short tether. Don't you go untying any knots."

His fingers slid across her mouth to her cheek, and then tunneled up into her hair. Belinda found herself caught by Faron's green-eyed gaze. It was a powerful force, the desire in a man's eyes. It made a woman want to give herself up to him. Belinda felt her knees growing weak—nature's method of getting a woman down so a man could couple with her more easily. She was having trouble catching her breath, and her mouth dropped open slightly for more air.

Faron saw it differently. He perceived her open mouth as an irresistible invitation. Faron had always liked parties, and he never turned one down. He didn't now.

His head lowered slowly, and his lips parted slightly to match hers. He paused just before their mouths made contact and took a breath. Belinda felt as though he were stealing the breath right out of her. A soft moan sounded deep in her throat.

His lips were pliant against hers. And urgent. She felt his need as his tongue came searching hungrily for sustenance only she could provide. Her hands seemed to have a will of their own. They latched on to his shirt at the waist, then slid up behind his back and threaded into the curls at his nape.

She could feel the dampness where his hair was soaked with sweat. He smelled of hardworking man, a pungent odor, but one that made her think of his muscles bunching beneath cloth as he hefted a bale of hay. His body was hard where he had it pressed against her hips, and his mouth was hot and demanding on hers.

Belinda didn't want to feel so much. Didn't want to need so much. She felt the trap closing on her and at the last minute realized that she must escape. She yanked hard on Faron's hair, and when he howled in pain she let go and backed away as quickly as she could.

"No," she said. "We're not going to do this."

His eyes were feral, his body taut with need. He could still take her if he wanted to. Her aroused, aching body cried out for fulfillment. She saw him hesitate, torn between taking what he wanted or letting her go.

He whirled abruptly and headed for the sink on the back porch. He turned on the cold water full blast, yanked off his hat and threw it down, then stuck his head under the spigot. She stared as he cooled the back of his neck with the icy water. Then he stood and slung his wet hair back. His hands forked through the tangled black curls, setting them in some kind of order. Then he picked up his hat and settled it back on his head.

Water still dripped from his nose and chin and clumped on his eyelashes. But no signs of passion remained when he looked at her again. "You've got some supper ready for me, I believe."

"Yes. I— Yes." She turned and hurried inside, letting the screen door slam behind her. A moment later she heard it creak as he opened it and followed her inside.

Belinda could hardly believe the gentleman who exchanged witticisms with Madelyn at dinner was the same cowboy who had kissed her senseless on the back porch. Faron was absolutely charming. She could see he was good for Madelyn. He made the old woman laugh and even blush once. Asking him to leave was out of the question, even though it was what Belinda desperately wanted to do.

She urged Faron and Madelyn to stay in the dining room and talk while she cleared the table and washed the dishes. But she could hear everything they said through the open door to the kitchen. She cringed when she heard Madelyn ask whether Faron had ever been married.

"No," he answered.

"Why not?" Madelyn asked.

"Never found the right woman, I guess."

"What is it, exactly, you're looking for?"

There was a long pause before he answered, "I'll know her when I find her."

Belinda smiled. Maybe Madelyn had met her match. Faron Whitelaw wasn't the kind of man who could be manipulated. But she should have known her mother-in-law wouldn't easily abandon her matchmaking efforts. Madelyn's next question left Belinda gasping.

"How do you like Belinda?"

"She's a hard worker."

Madelyn chuckled. "She said the same thing about you. I suppose that's one thing you both have in common. I wonder if there are any others."

Again, that long pause.

"I admit I thought Belinda was, well, a little more pampered than she's turned out to be."

"Wayne wasn't the most considerate of husbands."

Belinda gritted her teeth. She wasn't about to let Madelyn start talking about her marriage. She grabbed the apple pie on the counter and marched back through the open doorway. "Dessert, anyone?"

Belinda kept her expression bland, but she had a feeling she wasn't fooling either of them.

"I love apple pie," Faron said. "I'll take a piece. How about you, Maddy?"

Belinda saw the flush rise on Madelyn's cheeks as Faron turned his smile on her.

"Why, I guess I will join you."

Faron turned that stunning smile on Belinda, and she felt flustered. She dropped the pie on the table and said, "I'll go get some plates and the pie knife."

She turned just in time to keep the two of them from seeing the color race up her throat. This situation was unbearable! She had spent so many years learning to control her emotions, learning to keep what she was feeling hidden, because Wayne inevitably used it against her. All that Cowboy had to do was smile at her and she felt young and foolish again.

And desirable.

Lord, Lord, Lord, he made her feel like he wanted to lick her up like an ice cream cone on a hot Sunday afternoon.

Belinda leaned her forehead against the cool tile wall in the kitchen and took a deep breath. Then she scurried to find plates and a pie server before Faron came looking for her.

She could hear voices again from the other room.

"I'd love to play a little gin rummy," Faron was saying. "Penny a point is fine with me."

"You sure you wouldn't mind?" Madelyn asked.

Belinda could hear the worry in the old woman's voice. Madelyn didn't like being a burden on anyone. She would know if Faron was lying about spending time with her. Belinda heaved a quiet sigh of relief when she heard Faron reply, "Maddy, there's nothing I'd like better than skinning you at gin rummy."

Madelyn giggled. It was a youthful sound and one Belinda couldn't remember ever hearing from the old woman. Had their lives with Wayne been so very grim? It was hard for Belinda to be objective. But hearing Madelyn tonight with her grandson made Belinda wish that things could have been different with Wayne.

She put a smile on her face as she reentered the dining room. "Did I hear you say you're going to challenge Madelyn to a game of rummy?" she asked Faron.

"Yes, ma'am. Soon as I finish my pie."

Belinda served him a piece and set another in front of Madelyn. When she started to leave Faron asked, "Aren't you going to have some, too?"

"I'm not very hungry right now." She kept her lids lowered so Faron wouldn't find out the truth. She wanted to get away now, while she could still think rationally. She didn't want to see him being nice to his grandmother. She didn't want to see him being charming. She wanted to remember who he was and who she was and why any relationship between them other than the legal one resulting from her marriage to Faron's father was a mistake.

"I'm a little tired. I thought I'd go to bed early tonight," she said.

She was unprepared when Faron left the table and

crossed to her. He stood facing her and said in a voice too low to carry back to Madelyn, "Are you all right?"

She felt breathless again. "Yes. I'm fine. Just a little tired."

He put a hand on her shoulder, and she felt the pressure of it deep in the pit of her belly.

"I made some calls while you were having lunch and hired some men to do the heavy labor. There's no reason for you to leave the house tomorrow."

Her eyes flashed up to meet his concerned gaze. "I'll do my part," she said.

"You don't—"

"I don't want any favors from you. I'll see you tomorrow morning."

Belinda jerked herself away and marched toward the spiral staircase. She felt Faron's eyes on her the entire way up to the second floor. When she reached her room, she closed the door behind her and leaned against it.

She felt like crying. Why hadn't she met Faron Whitelaw eight years ago? It was too late now for what might have been. And what made her think things would be any different with Faron? She had learned her lessons from Wayne. Things had been fine with him, too, at first. It was only later...

But Wayne Prescott had never made her feel the things Faron Whitelaw made her feel. Belinda was frightened. And excited. She felt a sort of anticipation for the days to come that she knew was dangerous for her peace of mind. Worst of all was the knowledge that she desired Faron Whitelaw every bit as much as he seemed to desire her.

She had to resist temptation. She had to make herself a regal, unapproachable Princess. Maybe that would keep the Cowboy at bay.

Belinda lifted her chin and focused her eyes on the distant canopy bed with its delicate eyelet covers. It was a bed eminently fit for a princess who had resigned herself to life in an inaccessible, remote ivory tower.

She crossed the room and sat down on the bed with her back stiff and her teeth clenched to still a quivering chin. She had survived a lot over the past eight years. By God, she would survive this, as well.

CHAPTER FIVE

OVER THE NEXT several weeks, Belinda kept her distance from Faron. She conversed with him at breakfast, where Madelyn provided a buffer, and he gave her jobs so she could contribute to the work being accomplished at King's Castle. But nothing she did brought her into contact with Faron.

She marveled at the improvements in the ranch. Fences lost their dilapidated look, buildings got a new coat of paint, windmills began to whir again, machinery had a well-oiled sound. She began to believe that they really might find a buyer for the ranch. And to realize that if—when—King's Castle was finally sold, she was going to miss it.

One of her jobs today was to oil all the hinges on the stalls. Belinda thought she was alone in the barn, so she practically jumped out of her skin when a voice behind her said, "What are you doing?"

She whirled, then expelled a relieved breath. "You scared me half to death!"

Faron grinned. "I usually have a somewhat different effect on women. So what are you doing?" he asked again.

She held out the oil can so he could see it. "I'm doing just what you ordered me to do this morning."

"Ordered?"

"All right, what you *suggested* I do."

He took the can out of her hand and set it on the corner of one of the stalls. "Madelyn sent me to get you. She said she needs you in the house."

If Belinda thought that keeping distance between them had diffused the sexual tension one whit, she was finding out now that she had been wrong. She was aware of Faron from the top of her head to the tips of her toes. "Did she say why she wants me?"

"No. But I noticed there's a lot of cleaning going on in the house. I asked Rue what was going on, and she said we're expecting company."

"My sisters and their families always come to King's Castle to visit during the Fourth of July holiday."

"Now I remember. You said something about that the first day—" He cut himself off. He didn't want to think back to the day he had met Belinda, when they had shared a special moment in time together. He had been trying desperately over the past couple of weeks to treat her like the stepmother she was.

It wasn't working. All he had to do was take a breath around her, and his body surged to life. He had given her things to do that would keep them apart, but once her family arrived they would be forced into social situations together. It would be hell pretending in front of her family that he didn't want her.

"When does your family start arriving?"

"Tomorrow."

Faron took off his hat, forked his fingers through his hair and tugged the hat back on again. "You could have given me a little more warning."

"Why? There's nothing you need to do. Madelyn and Rue and I will take care of everything."

If he'd had more warning maybe he could have figured out a reason to be gone from the ranch during their visit. If he left now it would look like he was running. Faron wasn't the kind of man to run from trouble. Not that he necessarily sought it out, either. But he could see trouble coming.

Still, some good might come of this visit. He would have a chance to ask Belinda's family some of the questions she had refused to answer. "I'm looking forward to meeting your sisters."

Belinda smiled. "It'll be hard not to trip over them, since they'll all be staying at the house."

By sundown the next day Faron realized that Belinda hadn't been exaggerating. Her three sisters, Dori, Tillie and Fiona, had all arrived. Dori had come with her husband, Bill, and three daughters under seven years of age. Tillie was also married. She and her husband, Sam, had two boys, five and nine. Fiona was still single, but she had brought her Abyssinian cat, Tutankhamen, Tut for short.

There were trucks on the floor, dolls on the chairs and screaming children chasing each other and the cat up and down the stairs. When they all sat down to dinner it was chaos.

It reminded Faron of home. Of the days when his mother had still been alive, and he and his brothers had argued at the table while their parents refereed. He felt his stomach twist when he realized that the picture he remembered hadn't been exactly as it had seemed.

Had his father's eyes been sad as they met his mother's across the table? Had there been any hesitancy in the way his father had lifted him up into his arms and held him in his lap? He couldn't remember.

Whatever his father had felt about raising another man's child hadn't been evident in the way Faron had been treated. He had felt loved, had known he was loved. By a woman who had been faithless to his father in conceiving him. By a man who had overlooked the foreign blood that ran in his veins.

He sat back and listened to the children around him and searched for the warm memories he knew he would find.

"Mom, Travis threw a pea at me!"

"Travis, stop throwing food at Peter."

"Dad, make Jennifer stop kicking the table."

"Jennifer, that's enough. Eat."

"Daddy, Trisha spilled her milk."

"I did not!"

"It's all over your dress."

"Is not!"

"Is, too!"

"Is not!"

"Penny! Trisha! That's enough from both of you. Can't we have a little peace and quiet here?"

No, Faron thought. There would be no peace and quiet until the kids had been put to bed. But he didn't mind. And he could see that Belinda didn't mind, either. In fact, the look in her eyes was decidedly soft—and yearning.

He remembered what Belinda had said about wanting children. He wondered why she and his father hadn't given him stepbrothers and stepsisters. Suddenly he was fiercely, selfishly glad that Belinda hadn't borne his father's children. Even if it meant she had no child to hold to her breast during this family reunion. Because he wanted to be the one to give her those children.

Until that moment Faron hadn't realized how deep his feelings for Belinda ran. He had known, of course, that he desired her physically. When he looked at her now it was with the knowledge that she was the one woman he was meant to spend his life with. With a sense of awful frustration he conceded that the unique relationship that had brought them together was equally likely to be what kept them apart.

Faron turned his gaze on Belinda. She had settled Jennifer, the youngest of Dori's daughters, in her lap and was playing patty-cake with the child. The smile on Belinda's face was easily as broad as the little girl's. When Jennifer threw her hands wide, Belinda tossed her head back to keep from getting hit. And met Faron's eyes.

He made no effort to hide what he was feeling. At first her expression softened. She shared with him the joy of holding the baby in her arms. As he continued staring, she lowered her lids and hid those expressive violet eyes from him. But it was too late. He had already seen the need, the desire, the yearning for a child of her own.

"Time for baths," Tillie announced.

"Aw, Mom!"

"Jeez, Mom!"

"I want to play some more."

Faron listened to all the complaints knowing that they were being made in vain. The children's parents slowly but surely herded their offspring up the stairs. He wasn't surprised when Belinda took advantage of the opportunity to escape with them. Madelyn excused herself to check on Rue, who had apparently found another bottle this afternoon.

That left Faron sitting at the table with Belinda's youngest sister, Fiona. Fiona had a pixie face, and from what Faron had seen, a puckish sense of humor. She was blond and blue-eyed, but considerably shorter than her eldest sister. She had a figure that curved in all the right places. If Faron had met her before Belinda, he might even have been interested in getting to know her better.

Fiona picked up her wineglass and walked down the length of the table to take a chair across from Faron. "I guess you and I are the only ones without someone to bathe." She paused and added with a come-hither smile, "Unless you'd like me to scrub your back?"

"No thanks," Faron said, returning the smile.

"Thank goodness."

"Pardon?"

Fiona's smile turned into a grin. "I was just checking. I mean, I saw the way you stared at Belinda all night. You wouldn't be the right kind of guy for her if you were willing to hustle me the minute her back was turned."

"Thanks for the vote of confidence."

"Oh, I'm still not sure you're what she needs."

"And what is that?"

Fiona's blue eyes bored into him. Her hands fisted on the table. "Someone who wouldn't take advantage of her. Someone who would make her happy."

"She wasn't happy with my father?"

Fiona gave an unladylike snort. "Not hardly."

Faron waited for her to say more. He didn't have to wait long.

"Wayne Prescott abused my sister. Oh, not so much physically. Although I know he hit her once or twice. But he crushed her spirit. Or at least he tried. Toward the end Belinda learned to hide what she was feeling, and he left her alone."

Faron felt a rage such as he had never known directed at a man who was beyond his reach. "Why didn't she leave him?"

"I asked her the same question. She said they had made a deal, and she owed him her loyalty."

"What kind of deal?"

Fiona's eyes were bleak. "Belinda sold herself to get the money to take care of us. Me and Dori and Tillie. When she married Wayne he established a substantial trust fund in each of our names. Dori went to UCLA and fell in love with Bill. Tillie married the doctor who put the cast on the broken leg she got skiing in Colorado. I bought a bed and breakfast in Vermont. Belinda got nothing. Except marriage to Wayne.

"Of course, all of us were too young to realize what she was doing when she did it. She told us she was in love with Wayne, and during the first couple of years they got along pretty well."

"What happened then?"

"Wayne started to gamble. He lost big. He took it out on Belinda. He kept her like a prisoner here, wouldn't let her go anywhere. I guess he was afraid she wouldn't come back. If it hadn't been for Madelyn, she probably would have left him."

"What does Madelyn have to do with anything?"

"You've seen them together. Madelyn treats Belinda like the daughter she never had, and Belinda returns her affection. They both tried to curb Wayne's excesses. Sometimes I think if Belinda hadn't been there, Wayne might have taken out his frustrations on his mother."

"Not the best father figure a man could have."

"I'm sorry. I forgot he was your father. But he wasn't really, was he? I mean, someone else raised you. You're certainly nothing like Wayne from what I've seen today."

"The question is whether Belinda sees my father when she looks at me," Faron said.

"I don't see how she could," Fiona said. "You don't look a thing like him. You don't act like him, either. Wayne mostly thought about himself. From things Belinda has told me about you—"

"Belinda talked to you about me?"

Fiona shrugged. "She just told me you were Wayne's son." Belinda had revealed a whole lot more about her feelings for Faron Whitelaw through what she had not said. But Fiona wasn't about to give away Belinda's secrets to the cowboy. She would keep her eyes open over the next couple of days and make her own judgment about whether Faron deserved a chance with Belinda.

"Guess I'd better go see if I can help get things settled upstairs. I'll be down later to help with the dishes," Fiona said.

Faron looked around him and realized everything was still sitting on the table. With Rue sleeping off her latest binge there was no one to handle such details. "I'll take care of it," Faron said.

Thus, when Belinda came downstairs she found the

table cleared, the leftovers put away and Faron wiping down the counters with a sponge.

"You didn't have to do the dishes," she protested. "I would have done them."

"You were busy. I didn't mind. Charlie One Horse taught me how to stack a dishwasher."

"Who's Charlie One Horse?"

"A cross between hired hand, mother and father at Hawk's Way. He kind of takes care of things."

Belinda sat on one of the bar stools at the center island and leaned her chin on the heel of her hand. "When you see Charlie again, tell him I said thanks. I have to admit I'm a little tired."

"You work too hard."

"It was mostly play today. I love having my family around, but they keep things hectic."

"I spent some time after dinner talking to Fiona."

Belinda's lids lowered to hide her eyes. "And?"

"She told me why you married my father."

"Fiona never could keep a secret."

"She's grateful for what you did."

Belinda's voice was bitter as she explained. "If I had it to do over again, I wouldn't. And I won't make the same mistake twice. I'll never let another man do to me what Wayne did. I won't—"

Belinda suddenly realized who she was talking to. Wayne's son. A man it would be all too easy to allow into her life. Would she be making a mistake if she did? Or would things be different with Faron? She wished... she wished...

"Excuse me." Abruptly Belinda stood and headed for the screen door. She shoved her way outside and started walking. She didn't have any destination in mind, she just wanted to get away. Belinda didn't want to think of might-have-beens. She was tired of feeling regret. It wouldn't change what had happened. She had to forget about the past and go on with her life. Alone. That was the safest way, the best way to survive.

Faron stood in the kitchen after Belinda was gone, thinking back over what he had learned about her marriage to his father.

Belinda might have married Wayne Prescott for money, but she had done it from self*less* rather than self*ish* motives. It had become increasingly clear to him that she had bought security for her sisters at a very high price.

Now that he knew Belinda bitterly regretted what she had done, he allowed himself to acknowledge that he had been jealous of her relationship with his father. He wanted Belinda's love unbound by memories of her past. He was grateful to learn that he didn't have to compete with loving recollections of Wayne Prescott. But it had dawned on him this evening that he might have even more difficulty overcoming the damage done by his father's abusive treatment of his wife.

I won't make the same mistake twice. I'll never let another man do to me what Wayne did.

Faron was going to have to prove to Belinda that he wasn't like his father. That he was capable of loving her, of cherishing her, of treating her with the respect she deserved. He had to find a way to convince her that marriage to him wouldn't even remotely resemble her relationship with his father.

There was no time like the present to start.

Faron shoved open the screen door and marched out into the darkness after Belinda. She had already disappeared beyond the light pouring from the windows. He increased his pace and finally caught up to her at the edge of the river that ran across King's Castle.

The North Platte was narrow here, and the shallow water rushed over stones that made up the riverbed. Cottonwoods lined the water, and their leaves rustled in the wind. A zephyr cooled the night air. The cicadas chirped, and Faron heard an owl hoot in the distance. They might have been two people lost on the prairie with no one around for a thousand miles.

Or so it felt.

The moonlight created a glow around Belinda, outlining her so she was easy to find. "Why did you run away?"

Belinda whirled, surprised to find she had been followed. "I thought it was pretty obvious why I left. I was telling my late husband's son that his father was a terrible husband. Not the most proper after-dinner conversation I can imagine."

"But fascinating all the same."

"Why don't you go away and leave me alone? I've made up my mind not to get involved with another man—ever."

Her statement seemed to confirm his fears and left him feeling angry over what he couldn't control. "Are you only precluding marriage? Or do you plan to live the rest of your life as celibate as a nun?"

Belinda crossed her arms defensively. "I don't think that's any of your business."

"There you're wrong. Because," he said in a low, dangerous voice, "you're lying to yourself if you think you can live without love for the rest of your life."

"I don't need a man—for any reason."

"I think you're lying. To me. And to yourself." Faron stalked her now as he had wanted to for the past month. He was fighting for their life together. This time he wouldn't allow her to escape.

Belinda backed away slowly, but for every step she took, Faron took two. She found herself backed up against a cottonwood at the edge of the river with nowhere else to retreat.

Faron laid his palms on the bark on either side of her head and leaned down so they were eye to eye. "I'm not my father. I would never hurt you."

"That's what you say now," Belinda said in a tremulous voice. "But later—"

"Later I'll be the same man I am now. A man who desires you, Princess. A man who wants to cherish you."

It was too much what she had always wanted to hear from a man she cared for, and never had. Belinda's eyes sank closed. A moment later she felt Faron's mouth on hers. Gentle. Tender. Coaxing.

He insinuated his body between her thighs and rubbed himself against her. "Princess, open your mouth for me. Please."

He caught her upper lip with his teeth and teased it, then slid his tongue along the crease of her lips, making her gasp with the pleasure of it. He took advantage of the opportunity to slip his tongue inside, to taste, to tempt her to join him in his sensual exploration.

She put her palms on his chest, intending to push him away, but her fingers curled against the cloth instead, and she pulled him closer. Faron's arms curved around her and aligned them from breast to hip.

"I need you, Princess."

Belinda caught fire in Faron's arms. There was no

denying that she wanted him. And needed him. As the prairie grass needed sunshine. As the flowers needed spring rain. Her knees would no longer support her, and she and Faron sank to the ground together.

Faron made short work of Belinda's blouse, but when he reached under her skirt he found a delightful surprise. "You're wearing nylons."

"I always wear nylons with a skirt."

Faron grinned. "I mean real nylons." His hand slid around the top rim of her nylons and followed the garter belt up to her waist. "It's been a long time since I've met a woman who wore a garter belt."

"So I'm old-fashioned. Sue me."

"I'd rather make love to you."

Faron took his time removing her nylons. By the time he had her garter belt off, they were both having trouble breathing. He unsnapped his shirt and then pulled it off over his head. He unbuckled his belt, but when he reached for the zipper, she was there before him.

She took her time, touching him as she had always dreamed of touching a man. Aware of his guttural groans of pleasure, aware of the restraint he exercised to remain quiescent under her touch. But soon, touching wasn't enough for either of them. Faron finished what Belinda had started, and in moments they were both naked in the moonlight.

"You're so beautiful," Faron said. "So exquisite."

Belinda had never felt so loved, so cared for, so much the object of a man's desire. She ran her hands across his broad shoulders, feeling the play of muscle and sinew. Then her hands slipped up his back and tunneled into his hair. She urged his head down until their mouths met.

It was a kiss of longing. Of belonging. Her to him.

Him to her. It was more than sex. It always had been. It always would be. Something magical, something mystical happened between them when their bodies merged. Their souls meshed, as well.

When at last they lay sated in each other's arms, Belinda didn't feel grateful to Faron for proving her wrong about needing him. She hated him for being right. Because she was afraid to take another chance. The consequences of her relationship with Faron's father were too devastating ever to forget.

She sat up with her back to Faron and began putting her clothes on. "This doesn't change anything."

Faron sat up, but made no move to touch her. "What do you mean?"

"I'm not going to let myself get involved with you."

"You already are involved!" Faron retorted. "You can't pretend nothing just happened between us."

"It was just sex."

"Like hell it was!" Faron was angry. Even though he knew why Belinda was shoving him away, it didn't make the rejection any less painful. He stood and slipped on his shorts, then yanked on his jeans. "I know you had a tough time with my father, but I thought we'd settled all that."

"I can't take the chance you'll turn out to be like him," Belinda said in a quiet voice.

"I'm not—"

"You're an especially bad risk, Faron. After all, like father, like son."

Belinda could see Faron was furious. She waited for a blow that never came. Instead, he sat back down, pulled on his socks and boots, then stood and retrieved his shirt without saying another word.

He wasn't like his father. She knew it. And he knew it. Yet he didn't argue with her. When he was finished dressing he turned to her and said, "I'll walk you back to the house."

"I don't need—"

"Don't argue with me, Princess."

She didn't. She stuffed her nylons and garter belt into the pocket of her denim skirt, stuck her bare feet into her shoes and headed back toward the house.

The house was dark when they returned. Apparently both adults and children had welcomed the day's end. Belinda began to think she might escape to her bedroom without any further confrontation with Faron. She almost did.

At the top of the stairs Faron caught her hand and drew her toward him.

"It was beautiful, Princess. What happened between us was beautiful. I don't know what my father did to you. I don't even want to try to imagine what it must have been like living with him. But I don't intend to let what happened between the two of you interfere with our relationship."

"But—"

He put his fingertips to her lips. "All men aren't like my father. Not even his son. Especially not his son."

He let her go, and she disappeared into her bedroom. A moment later Faron found himself facing Belinda's sister, Fiona. Faron held his breath, waiting for whatever she had to say.

"I didn't mean to eavesdrop. I was looking for Tut." The Abyssinian curled himself around her bare ankles and purred. "I think maybe you'll do for Belinda. I think maybe you'll do just fine."

Faron smiled grimly. "All I have to do now is convince your sister of that."

"You'll manage. Be patient. All it'll take is a little time." She leaned down and picked up the cat, then closed the door, shutting Faron out.

Faron stared down the hall at Belinda's closed door. He didn't have as much time as Fiona seemed to think. With the progress he was making turning the ranch into a showplace, they were bound to find a buyer soon. Once they sold the ranch, he would head back to Texas.

If he didn't get matters resolved with Belinda, he was likely to end up making the trip alone.

Faron clenched his fists in determination.

He would be damned if he'd leave her behind.

CHAPTER SIX

BELINDA MANAGED TO avoid Faron until her sisters left. She knew he was giving her space. Fiona had told her so—and a lot more besides—while they were sitting at the Casper airport. Dori's and Tillie's flights had already come and gone. She was waiting for Fiona's plane to depart.

"You can't judge every man by your husband," Fiona had said.

"What other gauge would you suggest I use?" Belinda demanded.

"Your heart."

"I don't have one."

Fiona laughed. "Don't you wish! You've got one all right. Maybe a little bruised and battered, but it's in there beating away. And if what I suspect is true, beating a whole lot faster whenever a certain cowboy is around."

Belinda was helpless to control the flush that rose on her cheeks. "All right, so I'm attracted to Faron Whitelaw. He's a handsome man."

"And charming."

"And charming. But he's also my stepson."

"A fact that makes absolutely no difference."

"How can you say that?"

"It might be different if Faron had grown up at King's Castle, if you had stood in the role of stepmother and he had been your stepson. But that wasn't the case.

"You know what I think, Belinda? I think the fact Faron is technically your stepson is just an excuse."

Belinda laughed nervously. "An excuse for what?"

"An excuse not to fall in love with him. Which you already half are, if I'm not mistaken."

That nervous laugh escaped again. Belinda lowered her eyelids to hide her expressive eyes, but Fiona exercised the prerogative of younger sisters the world over to ignore her elder sister's tender sensibilities.

"Look," Fiona said. "I say you ought to go for it."

Belinda gasped. "*Go for it?* What kind of thing is that to urge your sister to do?"

"Look, you like the guy, right?"

Fiona didn't wait for Belinda to respond.

"And he likes you."

Again Fiona didn't wait for Belinda to respond.

"So go for it. Give the relationship a chance. Get to know Faron. Let yourself fall in love—I mean, if that's what happens."

"And if nothing happens?"

"Then you're no worse off than you were before," Fiona said philosophically.

Fiona's flight was called. She rose and hugged Belinda, then picked up the cat carrier that held Tut. "Be happy, Belinda. You deserve it. Call me, okay?"

"Okay."

Belinda waved as Fiona turned and smiled over her shoulder. Before Fiona even got to the door, she had met a man traveling on the same flight. Belinda shook her head in disbelief at her sister's easy way with men as she turned and headed for the parking lot. But she used the drive back from Casper to think about Fiona's advice.

Be happy, Belinda. You deserve it.

It was wonderful advice, actually. If only Belinda knew what would make her happy, she would do it. The problem was, Belinda had no idea what she wanted. She had been honest with Faron the day she had met him. She hadn't ever allowed herself to dream. Right after her parents were buried, she had needed to work to support her sisters. After she had married Wayne, whatever hopes she'd harbored had died a sure, if not precisely sudden, death.

So what would make her happy?

A husband who loved her. A houseful of children, with Madelyn nearby, a doting grandmother.

It was all so very simple. The Princess would just fall in love with the Cowboy and live happily ever after.

But as Belinda drove up to The Castle, the old fears rose up before her. How could she be sure things would turn out happily ever after? Was she willing to take the risk of loving Faron? They had been forced by circumstance into each other's company. What if the ranch sold in the next few weeks? Would he leave her behind and return to Texas without another thought of her?

Belinda found Faron sitting in one of the rockers on the stone terrace along the side of the house with Madelyn sitting in the rocker beside him. The sun was just setting, and in the fading light Belinda saw that Madelyn's head was thrown back and she was laughing. Belinda wanted to be a part of that picture.

When she stopped the pickup, Faron bounded down from the terrace, pulled open the door and practically dragged her out.

"Come on and join us," he said. "We're having a glass of tea and exchanging war stories."

"War stories?" Belinda felt the strength in Faron's hand as he gripped her fingers and tugged her along behind him.

And yet she knew how gentle he could be. Surely he wasn't like his father. Surely…

Faron seated her in the rocker where he had been sitting and settled himself on the flagstone terrace cross-legged facing her. "I just finished my war story," he said. "It's Maddy's turn."

"What kind of war story?" Belinda persisted.

"Be still and listen, girl, and you'll find out soon enough," Madelyn chided with a twinkle in her eye. "Now, let's see. It must have been '42, or maybe it was '43. Everyone contributed what he or she could to the War Effort. I did my part. I danced for the USO."

"I didn't know there was a USO in Casper," Belinda said.

"Hush, girl," Madelyn said. "This is my story." She leaned back in the rocker and set it in motion with the toe of her shoe.

"His name was Tommy Neville. He had the bluest eyes and the blackest hair I'd ever seen. We met at the USO. He was a navy flier headed to California, scheduled to ship out to the Pacific. It was his last night at home. He said he wanted to hold an American girl in his arms one last time, and feel the touch of her lips on his—because he might not be coming home."

"What a line!" Faron interjected. "So did you kiss him?"

"What kind of war stories *are* these?" Belinda asked suspiciously.

"Hush, dear, and let me finish," Maddy reproved. "Of course I kissed him," she said with a girlish grin. "What kind of patriot would I have been if I'd let a soldier go off to war without a goodbye kiss?"

Faron clapped his hands. "Good for you, Maddy. Your turn, Belinda."

"My turn for what?"

"We're telling romantic war stories," Maddy explained. "Your turn."

"I… I wasn't dating anyone during a war."

Faron and Maddy exchanged disbelieving looks and then burst out laughing.

"She can't be that naive, can she?" Faron asked Maddy.

"I wouldn't have said so, but maybe she is. Perhaps you'd better explain it to her."

"We're telling 'war' stories about our previous love affairs," Faron said.

"You're exchanging romantic escapades with your *grandmother?*" Belinda asked incredulously. "Whose idea was this?"

"Mine," Madelyn said.

That took the wind out of Belinda's sails.

"So, are you going to play or not?" Madelyn asked.

"I'm not!"

"Chicken!" Faron taunted.

"Coward!" Madelyn accused.

"All right!" Belinda retorted. "You asked for it. You're going to get it!"

"I can't wait to hear this," Faron said, settling back against the short stone wall that edged the terrace.

"Me, either," Madelyn said with a chuckle.

"He had the biggest, brownest eyes you ever saw."

"You like brown eyes?" Faron asked with a frown.

"Shut up and listen," Belinda said. "And he had curly red hair."

"So tell us about the date," Faron urged.

"We spent the whole night together," Belinda said.

Faron's eyes narrowed. "The whole night? Who the hell was this guy?"

"His name was Whitey."

"What kind of name is that for a redheaded man?" Faron asked disgustedly.

"It's a terrible name for a man," Belinda agreed. "But a great name for a Hereford steer."

"A steer?"

Belinda saw the moment when recognition—and relief—dawned on Faron's face.

Madelyn joined Faron's laughter. "I guess she showed us."

Belinda was glad they believed she had told her story as a joke. Because the truth was, there weren't any other men in her life. Not that she was embarrassed to admit to her lack of experience. No wonder she was afraid to take a chance on romantic love. Having never felt the emotion, she wasn't sure she would recognize it if it bit her on the nose.

"I'm going in to see if Rue needs any help," Madelyn said.

Faron jumped up to help his grandmother out of the rocker.

"You'd think I was an old lady," she muttered.

"No, just a lady," Faron said with a gentle smile.

Madelyn shot a look at Belinda as though to say, "You're a fool if you don't grab him!"

When Madelyn was gone, Faron took her seat and set the rocker in motion. Belinda joined him rocking, and the only sound for a while was the creak of the wooden rockers and the occasional lowing of cattle.

"Did you have a nice drive back from Casper?"

"Yes."

"I like your sisters."

"They are nice, aren't they?"

"Was the sacrifice worth it?"

Belinda sighed. "It was a foolish thing to do. Everything turned out better than I had a right to expect."

"Meaning your sisters ended up happy, even if you didn't."

Belinda didn't bother to respond because Faron hadn't been asking a question, he had been making a statement. The two of them rocked quietly, each caught up in his own thoughts.

Faron's sister Tate had called while Belinda was at the airport. It had been one of the most difficult conversations of Faron's life.

"I called Hawk's Way looking for you," Tate began, "because Adam and I want you to be our son's godfather. Garth said you'd gone to Wyoming, but he wouldn't tell me why. He just gave me this number and said you'd answer my questions. So what are you doing in Wyoming, Faron?"

Faron felt a lump in his throat. This is what it meant to be a part of the Whitelaw family. Caring. Concern. Curiosity. But he didn't have the right to play the role she wanted to cast him in without confessing the truth first. "Tate, I—"

She was too impatient to allow him to get a word in edgewise. "Spill the beans, big brother. What's going on up there? I'm guessing there's a woman involved. Am I right?"

Tate had been talking virtually without taking a breath, so when she finally stopped, the silence was awesome.

"Faron? Is something wrong? Talk to me."

Faron realized Garth had left it up to him to decide whether to tell the rest of the family the truth about his birth. For a moment he thought about making up some kind of story to hide what their mother had done. But Tate was a mother herself now. She was no longer a child who had to be protected from the facts of life.

"I'm here in Wyoming to meet my stepmother."

There was an absurdly long silence on the other end of the line.

"Is this some kind of joke, Faron? I don't understand."

Faron heard Tate's confusion, her anger and her fear. He shoved his free hand through his hair. "It's no joke, Tate. Mother had an affair before you were born. I was the result. My real father left me half his ranch in Wyoming. I came up here to...to see this place."

"Am I...?"

"You're legitimate, as far as I know," Faron reassured her. "I guess Mom and Dad got back together after her affair."

"I'm so sorry, Faron."

Faron swallowed over the lump in his throat. "I'll understand if you don't want me to be godfather to—"

"Oh, no! Please, Faron. You *have* to be the baby's

godfather. It's what Adam and I both want. This other…
thing…doesn't change how I feel about you. You're still
my brother, and I love you dearly."

Faron's eyes burned with tears. He wanted to tell
Tate how much her love meant to him but he couldn't
get the words past his constricted throat.

"Faron? Are you there?"

At last he managed, "I'm here, Tate."

"Well, will you do it? Will you be Brett's godfather?"

"I'd be proud and pleased to be godfather to your
son."

He heard a sigh of relief on the other end of the line.

"Everybody's coming to Hawk's Way over Labor
Day. That's not a problem for you, is it? Because if it
is, we can change the day. We need you there."

"I can make it. I might bring a couple of people
along."

"So there *is* a girl involved!"

Faron grinned. "Maybe."

"I can't wait to meet her. What's she like?"

"Goodbye, Tate."

"Goodbye, Faron. And thanks again. I love you. See
you at Hawk's Way. Oh. Wait. Does Jesse know?"

"I haven't said anything to him."

"Do you want me to tell him?"

Faron thought how easy it would be to say yes. "No.
I'll call him. Goodbye, Tate."

"Goodbye."

Faron hadn't waited to make the call to Jesse. It
seemed better to get it over with right away. Jesse was
considerably more philosophical than Faron had expected him to be.

"I'm not surprised," Jesse had said.

"You're not?"

"I'm older than you. I guess I saw more than you did as a child. Mom and Dad…there were some arguments, some hard words. It went on for about a year. Then it suddenly stopped. That must have been when she was having the affair. Their marriage seemed stronger after that."

Faron marveled at how differently his two older brothers had viewed their mother's infidelity. Garth remembered only the hurt. Jesse had remembered the healing. Surprisingly, Faron felt better knowing that his illegitimate birth hadn't split his parents apart, but might even have helped draw them closer together.

Faron had hung up the phone feeling like a huge weight had been lifted from his shoulders, one he hadn't even been aware he was carrying around.

Remembering the two phone calls reminded Faron that he had already set in motion plans to get Belinda to visit Hawk's Way. Now all he had to do was convince her she should go.

"I think you'd like my brothers and sister if you ever met them," Faron said, breaking the peaceful silence between them.

Belinda was still half dreaming and murmured, "Maybe I will someday."

"How about Labor Day?"

Belinda put out a foot to stop her rocker. "What?"

"I got a call while you were gone to the airport. The family is getting together for the christening of my sister Tate's son. I've agreed to be his godfather. I thought you might like to come with me."

Belinda wasn't sure what to think, what to do.

"That's two months from now. Maybe the ranch will sell, and you'll be long gone by then."

"Maybe. Maybe not."

"I couldn't leave Madelyn alone," Belinda said.

"I've already invited Maddy to come, and she's agreed."

"Maddy's your grandmother. She has a reason to come."

"I want you to come, Belinda."

Belinda searched Faron's face. "Why?"

"Because this will be an important moment in my life, Princess. And I want to share it with you."

"I…"

"You don't have to answer me now. Just think about it."

A moment later Belinda was alone. Faron had disappeared in the direction of the barn.

OVER THE NEXT month Faron kept his distance from her. At first Belinda was grateful. She figured he stayed away so she wouldn't feel pressured to accept his invitation. It also allowed her to avoid having to examine her feelings for the Cowboy. However, Belinda soon realized that unless she spent time with Faron, she wouldn't have a chance to find out whether she wanted their relationship to develop further.

So when she got a call from a corporate buyer who wanted to take a look at King's Castle, she saddled her horse and went in search of Faron. She found him working on another windmill on the northern border of the ranch.

"I thought you had hired men to do the manual labor," she said as she stepped down from the saddle.

"This just needed a little fine-tuning. Thought I'd take care of it myself."

Belinda took a moment to admire the man. He had removed his shirt, and his bronzed upper torso glistened with sweat. The muscles in his back bunched as he manhandled the wrench he was holding. He twisted it once more, then stood and threw the wrench into the tool box in the back of his pickup. He pulled a bandanna out of his back jeans pocket and used it to wipe the sweat from his brow.

He seemed to realize suddenly that she was staring at him. Only this time when he met her gaze, she didn't look away. She did nothing to hide her desire. Nothing could have been a more powerful aphrodisiac.

"Why did you come out here?" he asked.

"There was a phone call…" Belinda lost her train of thought as Faron reached out and cupped her cheek with the palm of his hand. He tilted her face up and it seemed the most natural thing in the world to lift her lips to meet his.

Warm. Welcome. Like coming home. She hadn't known she needed his kiss so much.

Soft. Receptive. She belonged to him. He must have been insane to have stayed away so long.

Faron pulled her into his arms, nearly crushing her with the strength of his embrace. He spread his legs and settled her in the cradle of his thighs.

Belinda wondered if this was what it felt like to be in love. She couldn't deny the passion that flared between the two of them whenever they were together. Touching Faron gave her as much pleasure as having him touch her.

It had been too long for both of them. He was impatient, but so was she. Once Faron had her breasts bare under the sunlight, he took his time. He bent his head to kiss her soft curves and then suckled her. Belinda arched into his caresses, and her traitorous knees once more gave way.

Faron picked her up in his arms, but the only shady spot available was already occupied by cattle.

"How about going for a ride?"

He set her back in the saddle, then mounted behind her. When Belinda started to rebutton her blouse, Faron stopped her.

"Don't. I want to hold you while we're riding." Belinda leaned back into his embrace, and Faron's hands crossed around her, cupping her breasts. Faron kicked the palomino into a lope, heading toward the river and the cottonwoods he knew they would find there.

It was the most decadent ride Belinda had ever taken. By the time they got to the river, each of them had aroused the other beyond bearing. Faron slid off the palomino's back and pulled Belinda down onto the ground. He had them both stripped in record time.

The day was hot, but the grass was cool on Belinda's naked backside. Their coupling was urgent, so quick that each offered a quite unnecessary apology to the other.

"I should have waited—"

"I couldn't wait—"

They both laughed, and then hugged each other and rolled to their sides, their bodies still joined. They lay like that a long time, until at last they separated to lie on their backs and stare at the sky through the rustling leaves of the cottonwood.

"So why did you come out to see me?" Faron asked as he nibbled on the lobe of her ear.

"We got a call from a corporate buyer. He wants to take a look at King's Castle." Belinda was close enough to be aware of the way Faron stiffened. It was still a month until Labor Day.

"When does he want to come?"

"Tomorrow."

So soon. Faron wasn't ready to leave King's Castle yet. Over the past month he had begun to see the potential of the place. With a little better management it could become a successful enterprise again. Of course, a woman alone would have a tough time managing, but a couple—a couple could do just fine.

He didn't dare mention to Belinda what he was thinking. She couldn't even make up her mind to take a trip to Texas with him. How could he expect her to consider marriage and a life spent together at King's Castle?

Faron surprised himself with how easily that thought had formed in his mind. Was he really ready to get married? What would his family say when they heard he wanted to marry his stepmother? He could hear Garth now. His eldest brother would think Faron had lost his mind.

But Faron knew if his family met Belinda, they would understand how he had fallen in love with her. Which was why he had to convince her to come to the christening at Hawk's Way on Labor Day.

Now that they knew he had a different father, he wanted them to see that he wasn't going to allow his bastardy to separate him from his family. In fact, he wanted them to see that he had merely extended his family to include his grandmother. He hadn't figured out yet what he would say about Belinda.

"Did you tell the buyer we'd be glad to show him around?" he asked her.

"I told him we'd call him back."

Faron arched a brow. "Was there some reason you wanted to wait?"

"I just thought...what if he makes us an offer?"

"If it's a reasonable offer, we'll accept."

"Do you really want to sell the ranch?"

"Don't you?" Faron asked.

"I guess I do," Belinda said. "But it's been home for a long time. It'll seem strange to live in town."

"Is that what you'd do? Move to town?"

"Where else would I go?"

Home with me to Hawk's Way. But Faron didn't say what he was thinking. It was too soon to tell Belinda the plans he had for the two of them. He didn't want to scare her away.

It wasn't until she had told the story about spending the night with a brown-eyed, redheaded steer that he had realized just how limited her experience with men was. He knew she'd had a bad time with Wayne Prescott. He could understand her reluctance to trust another man.

But if he'd thought his time was short before, it was down to nothing now. Tomorrow. It might all end tomorrow if the buyer made an offer they couldn't refuse. So maybe he should say something to her now, let her know that he didn't intend ever to let her go.

Faron opened his mouth to declare his love and shut it again.

Belinda was asleep.

He lay down beside her and pulled her into his arms. Tomorrow would be soon enough to speak his mind. Maybe the buyer wouldn't want the property. Maybe there would be no decisions to be made right away. He would just wait and see.

CHAPTER SEVEN

"How DARE YOU refuse an offer for this ranch without consulting me!" Belinda raged.

"He offered a quarter of what the place was worth!" Faron retorted.

"I don't care how much he offered. What I care about is the fact that you made the decision without saying anything to me. I should have been consulted."

"Both of us have to agree for this place to get sold. Since I would have refused the offer anyway, it didn't make sense to get you involved."

"Didn't make sense? I can't believe what I'm hearing! That's just the sort of thing Wayne would have said. 'No sense troubling your pretty little head with business.' I own half of King's Castle, and by God, I'll be a part of any decisions that are made regarding this ranch."

Faron realized he had made a big mistake, and

he quickly sought to make amends. "I'm sorry. Next time—"

"If there is a next time!" Belinda put her fisted hands on her hips. "There aren't so many corporate buyers out there that we can afford to refuse an honest offer."

"So maybe we just won't sell!"

"Right! And when the bank comes to collect the mortgage payment what do you suggest we use for money?"

"I've got—"

"I don't want to rely on you to keep this place afloat."

"Why not?" Faron asked.

"I learned how much that sort of debt can cost when I was married to your father!"

There it was again. The comparison of Faron with his father, and it hadn't been a compliment. "I am not my father," he said quietly.

"Could have fooled me," Belinda muttered. "Tyrannical, autocratic—"

"That's enough," Faron said. "I get your point."

Belinda was still quivering with rage. And fighting tears. She had talked herself into believing that Faron was different from his father. His actions today, discounting her opinion and involvement in a way similar to what Wayne might have done, was a deep disappointment. Her romantic bubble had burst, and she was sharply, brutally disillusioned.

"I hope you're not going to use this incident as an excuse not to come to Texas," Faron said.

"I've learned never to make decisions when I'm angry," Belinda admitted. "Maybe when I've calmed down we can talk about where we go from here."

She turned on her heel and left Faron standing alone

in Wayne's study. He leaned back in the swivel chair and put his boot heels up on the rolltop desk.

Was what he had done so wrong? Faron was used to making decisions on his own. Except on major issues that concerned Hawk's Way. Then he and Garth would discuss the matter... As he should have discussed the matter with Belinda, Faron realized.

If the situation had been reversed, he would have been furious if Belinda had made a major decision regarding King's Castle without him. She deserved no less consideration than he would have demanded for himself. Unconsciously he had put himself in the role of caretaker, but it was clear now, if it hadn't been before, that Belinda intended to be nothing less than an equal partner.

Which he was willing to be. Only what he wanted from her was not just a business partnership, but a deeply committed personal relationship.

Faron cursed the father who had so wounded the woman he loved. His recent error hadn't helped matters. Belinda was sure to be less trusting of him in the future. It was going to be a challenge convincing her that she didn't have to worry about repeating the mistakes with him that she had made with his father.

Meanwhile Belinda had retreated to the vegetable garden behind the house where she was on her hands and knees pulling up weeds between a row of snap beans and a row of tomatoes. She wasn't precisely aware when Madelyn joined her. The older woman wore a floppy hat to keep the sun off and gloves to protect her hands. The two women worked in silence for a while, as they had on many another day. It was Madelyn who finally spoke.

"You're going to get sunstroke working without a hat."

"Don't you start treating me like a child. I get enough of that from Faron."

"Oh?"

"He turned down an offer for the ranch without even consulting me. Just like Wayne, he—"

Madelyn's interruption cut off Belinda's tirade before it even got started. "Oh, no, my dear. He's not like Wayne at all."

"It didn't even cross his mind to speak to me before—"

"But he apologized when you pointed out his mistake, didn't he?"

"Yes, but—"

"Wayne would never have apologized. I think you should give Faron the benefit of the doubt."

Belinda dusted the dirt off her hands. "Does that mean you also think I should go to Texas with him?"

"Tell me one good reason why you shouldn't go."

"I've never been beyond the borders of Wyoming in my entire life."

"Land sakes, girl. All the more reason to go."

"I've never been on an airplane."

"Flying is a piece of cake."

Belinda resorted to the real reasons she had reservations about going to Texas. "I'm the widow of the man with whom Faron's mother had an affair. I'm Faron's stepmother."

"When the Whitelaws meet you they'll be just as fond of you as Faron is."

"Faron isn't—"

Madelyn pursed her lips and looked at Belinda across the row of snap beans. "Don't try to deny it. I've got eyes, Belinda, and I'm not too old to see what's right in front of my nose."

Belinda pulled a snap bean and broke it into pieces looking for the tiny beans inside.

Madelyn reached out and put a hand on Belinda's knee. "You're like my very own daughter, Belinda. I only want you to be happy. I think Faron could make you happy."

"If I go to the christening with Faron, it doesn't mean I'm committing myself to anything where he's concerned. I want to be sure you understand that and don't get your hopes up."

"Of course not, dear. I understand perfectly. It would just be a much-needed break from all the work here. A chance for you to get away and see another part of the country."

"That's all I'd be doing," Belinda affirmed.

A FEW WEEKS LATER, when she found herself facing the Whitelaws' antebellum mansion at Hawk's Way, Belinda was having second thoughts. The ranch house was an imposing two-story white frame structure with four twenty-foot-high fluted columns and railed first- and second-story porches. The road leading to the house was lined with majestic magnolias. The branches of a moss-laden live oak draped the roof of the house. It had a majesty every bit as profound as The Castle.

Faron had one arm around her shoulder and the other arm around Madelyn as he escorted them up the front steps and inside the foyer. "This is my home," he told Belinda.

She could hear the pride in his voice. The reason for it was evident in the well-kept, homey furnishings she found inside. There was tradition in this house, oak and pine furniture that had survived the rough and tumble of generations of Whitelaw sons and daughters. An ancient map framed over the mantel delineated what had once been the vast reaches of Hawk's Way in the Texas panhandle.

"It's beautiful," she said. "You must have missed being here these past few months."

Faron was surprised to realize that he hadn't missed Hawk's Way as much as he might have expected to when he left. The reason was obvious. In Wyoming he had found something to fill the hole inside him. He no longer felt the same sense of belonging here since he had staked his claim on his father's land—and his father's wife.

Faron's brothers and sister were arrayed in the parlor with their families. The two babies, Jesse and Honey's daughter and Adam and Tate's son, were sleeping in small antique cribs. From descriptions Faron had given her, Belinda easily recognized the two couples. Honey was sitting in Jesse's lap on a chair in front of the fireplace. Adam and Tate were sitting close beside each other on the couch.

Garth was standing with an arm resting on the thick pine mantel above the stone fireplace. There was another young woman in the room, but Belinda couldn't imagine who she could be.

Faron proudly introduced Belinda and Madelyn to the assembled group. "This is my grandmother, Madelyn Prescott," he said. "I call her Maddy."

There was an awkward moment when Belinda wondered whether Faron's family would accept the old woman. Tate made the first move. She jumped up from the couch and crossed with her hands extended to the older woman. "It's so nice to meet you, Maddy." She gave Maddy a quick, hard hug. Then she stood back and looked to see whether her brother resembled his grandmother. "Oh, my goodness. Faron has your eyes! Come see, Jesse, Garth."

The two large men came forward to greet the old woman and to agree with Tate that yes, Faron and Maddy had eyes the same unique gray-green color. Honey and Adam soon joined them and everyone began talking a mile a minute.

In the confusion Belinda was tempted to sneak back out the way she had come. Just when she thought Faron had forgotten all about her, he raised his hand for quiet. It took a few moments for the commotion to die down.

You could have heard a pin drop when he said, "And this is Belinda Prescott, my stepmother."

"That's the ugly stepmother?" Jesse whispered. His wife elbowed him in the ribs to shut him up.

It was Garth who took control of what could have become a very awkward situation. "I'm pleased to meet you, Belinda."

But Belinda didn't think he was at all pleased. She didn't know when she had ever met such a granite-faced man. His greeting was formal and his manner stiff. Belinda felt like crying. She didn't belong here. She wasn't part of this family in any way, shape or form. When she would have turned and run, a beautiful young woman with long blond hair and widely spaced gray eyes reached out and grasped her hand.

"Hi. I'm Candice—Candy Baylor. I guess you and I are the only two people here who aren't family."

Candy smiled, and Belinda immediately felt better.

"I've been working at Hawk's Way this summer, and I can imagine how you must feel, meeting this rowdy bunch for the first time."

"They are a little overwhelming," Belinda conceded.

"I don't know if you remember me," Faron said, extending a hand to Candy. "I'm Faron." Faron shot a look at Garth as though to say "What's she doing here?" But Garth's face remained stony.

"Of course I remember you," Candy said. "Last time I was here with my father you yanked my braids at the breakfast table."

Faron grinned. "Guilty. Was that only three years ago? You've grown up a little since then."

Garth interrupted, saying, "I think it's time you showed Maddy and Belinda where they'll be staying."

Faron was intrigued by Garth's possessive attitude toward Candy. That was a situation he intended to find out more about later. "Come on upstairs, ladies, and I'll show you to your rooms."

After taking Maddy to her room, Faron led Belinda to hers.

Belinda was relieved to see that she and Maddy were staying on a wing of the house that was separated from the rest of the family. She felt less pleased when she saw that Faron had settled Maddy in a room that was at the opposite end of the hall from hers. She looked at the room next to hers and said, "Who sleeps there?"

"I do," Faron answered.

Belinda turned startled violet eyes on him. "I thought the family was on a separate wing."

"The rest of them are."

Belinda stared at him for a moment. "Faron—"

He leaned over and gave her a quick, hard kiss.

"Don't ask me to move you somewhere else, Princess. I want you close to me."

He didn't plead, he didn't cajole. Just that simple request. Belinda remembered Fiona's advice. And what Madelyn had said. It was time to act on her feelings for the Cowboy. Time to take a chance. "All right," she said at last. "I'll stay here."

She heard his exhaled sigh of relief and smiled inwardly. So, he wasn't as confident as he had led her to believe. Somehow that made her feel better. "Do you suppose there's something I can do to help with supper?"

"As soon as you finish unpacking, come on downstairs to the kitchen, and I'm sure Charlie will put you to work."

"I can't wait to meet the man who taught you how to stack a dishwasher," Belinda said with a grin.

Faron kissed her again, then turned and left her. If he didn't go now, he was afraid he wouldn't go at all.

The chaos in the kitchen seemed familiar to Belinda, who had so recently been visited by her siblings and their families. Everyone was there pitching in to get things on the table except Garth and Candy, who had headed for the barn to check on a mare that was expected to foal in the next day or so.

Belinda was amazed and amused at the contrast between Faron's family and her own. Maybe it was because she had sisters, but there seemed to be a lot more roughhousing among Faron's clan. Even Tate, Faron's youngest sister, could hold her own with her brothers. When Faron threw a handful of potato peelings at her, she responded by throwing an entire peeled potato back at him.

Faron simply caught the potato and tossed it to Jesse, who tossed it to Honey, who tossed it to Adam, who tossed it back to Tate. She handed it primly to Charlie One Horse, who cut it into four pieces and dumped it into the pot of boiling water on the stove. Belinda didn't know when she'd had so much fun making a meal.

It was harder for Belinda to cope with her feelings when she watched Honey and Tate nursing their babies after supper. They sat in the parlor, a blanket thrown over their shoulders in deference to her presence, and suckled their children in full view of the Whitelaw men and Tate's husband, Adam. As though it was the most normal thing in the world for two nursing mothers to be sitting in a roomful of cowboys.

And it was.

Belinda's chest ached with the feelings that assailed her. She met Faron's eyes across the room. For the first time in eight years, Belinda allowed herself to imagine what her life might have been like if she had waited to fall in love and marry. It was a wonderful picture, full of love and laughter…and children.

Suddenly she couldn't stay any longer. She rose as quietly as she could and left the parlor, heading upstairs. She felt, as much as heard, Faron coming up the stairs behind her. She pretended she didn't know he was there, just kept putting one foot in front of the other until she reached her bedroom. Just as Faron caught up to her she stepped inside her bedroom and closed the door behind her.

She leaned back against the door, closed her eyes and listened. She could hear him breathing on the other side of the door.

"Princess," he whispered. "Are you all right?"

"I'm fine," she whispered back. "Good night, Cowboy."

She could almost feel the tension on the other side of the wooden panel. She had known what memories it would conjure if she called him Cowboy. She felt her body rouse as she remembered their lovemaking.

"Princess." His voice was hoarse. "Open the door."

She turned and pressed her forehead against the cool painted surface. Her hand was on the knob. She would have turned it, except she heard Maddy call to him.

"Is Belinda all right?"

"She's fine, Maddy. Just a little tired, I think."

"I'm a little tired myself. Good night, Faron."

"Good night, Maddy."

Belinda waited and listened. A moment later she opened the door. But Faron was gone.

I should have opened the door right away, as soon as he called. I should have invited him inside. I want him here with me. I don't want to be alone tonight.

All she had to do was go downstairs and find him. All she had to do...

Belinda stripped and found her nightgown. But she didn't put it on. Instead, she slipped naked between the sheets. And dreamed of a certain cowboy making love to a woman he called Princess.

She must have been more tired than she had thought, because the next thing she knew, Faron was knocking on the connecting door between their rooms.

The connecting door!

Belinda scrambled into a sitting position on the four-poster bed and clutched the sheets to her naked body as the door opened and Faron stuck his head inside.

"When I didn't hear anything moving in here I

thought I'd better make sure you were awake. The convoy to the church leaves in about an hour."

"I can't believe you put us in *connecting* rooms!" Belinda said.

The sheet slipped on one side as she clutched it tighter, and Faron was treated to a glimpse of a pink aureole. "I've made no secret how I feel about you, Princess."

"What will your family think?"

"My family will mind their own business."

A call from downstairs drifted across the tense silence between them.

"Faaaarrrooon! Your eggs are done," Tate yelled.

"See you at breakfast, Princess." He grinned and pulled the connecting door closed just before the pillow Belinda had thrown landed against it.

If Belinda had thought the Whitelaws would act any more civilized at breakfast than they had at supper, she was sadly mistaken.

There was raw egg dripping down the front of the refrigerator, and the shell lay cracked and broken on a red tile floor dusted with a fine layer of flour. To her chagrin she realized she was sorry she hadn't been a part of the juvenile food fight.

"Coffee?" Tate asked as Belinda stepped into the kitchen.

"Yes, thanks."

"You look absolutely gorgeous!" Tate said.

Belinda froze as every male eye in the room turned to stare at her. She had put her hair up in an elegant twist and was wearing a sheath that outlined her figure, even though it concealed her from neck to knee.

Faron was surprised at the surge of protectiveness

that arose when Belinda became the object of all eyes. He slipped an arm around her waist and said, "And she's as nice as she is beautiful."

The warning was there. Unspoken but irrefutable. *She's mine and I protect what's mine.*

It was Charlie One Horse who diffused the tension in the room. He walked over to Maddy and said, "I 'spect I gotta vote that this here is the purtiest woman in the room."

Maddy blushed prettily and for a moment the glow in her eyes made her look exceedingly lovely.

Not to be outdone, Jesse announced that Honey was the sweetest in the room, and Adam countered that Tate was without a doubt the cutest one there. Until the only woman in the room who hadn't been complimented was Candy Baylor.

She stood by the stove, spatula in hand, staring at Garth and waiting.

But he offered not a word of praise to the young woman. At last he turned to Tate and said, "We'd better get moving if we're going to be on time. I'll go get the car."

He turned on his heel and stalked out the screen door, letting it slam behind him.

Candy's face paled as she stared after him.

There was a moment of awful silence before Belinda said, "It's hard to tell which needs a dipping worse, him or the floor of this kitchen."

Faron was at first stunned that Belinda would take on his eldest brother and then amused by the way she had chosen to do it. His grin soon found company, and the tension eased as everyone finished their breakfasts and divided into groups for the trip to church.

Belinda noticed that Candy avoided going in Garth's car, and she couldn't blame the woman. It wasn't until Garth had refused to play the game this morning that she had realized there was more going on between the couple than met the eye.

The christening was held before the church service began. Belinda sat in the first pew with Candy, Madelyn and the rest of the Whitelaw family. Faron stood beside his sister, Tate, and held her son, Brett, in his arms.

Belinda overheard Faron speaking to Tate as she handed the baby into his care.

"Thanks, Tate, for wanting me to be Brett's godfather even though—"

Tate had hugged him fiercely, the baby caught between them. "You're my brother, and I love you. Nothing—*nothing*—is going to change that."

Faron's eyes were moist when Tate let go of him.

Belinda was sitting at an angle where she could see Faron when he stood before the church altar. The love there, the exquisite tenderness on his face as he looked down on the child in his arms, moved her to tears. She listened as Faron promised to stand in the stead of the baby's parents in the event it was necessary, to be godfather to Brett Patrick Philips.

After the church service, the Whitelaw family was surprisingly subdued, perhaps awed by the dignity of the christening ceremony, as Belinda had been herself. But the celebration that afternoon, a picnic in the backyard under a spreading live oak, was as rowdy as any drunken brawl she had seen in the diner where she had worked in Casper. Only none of them was drinking anything stronger than iced tea.

"Having fun?" Faron asked, when he caught up to

her halfway through the afternoon. She was dressed in cutoffs, a T-shirt and tennis shoes. Her hair was in a ponytail. She looked about fifteen, and he felt like a teenager with the biggest crush of his life.

She grinned and threw a Frisbee at him. "I'm having a ball!"

Faron caught it and pitched it back to her. They played for a while until Faron threw the Frisbee as far as he could beyond the crowd. When Belinda ran after it, he ran after her. When he caught her, he picked her up and threw her over his shoulder.

"Where are we going?" Belinda asked with a breathless laugh.

Faron didn't answer, just kept on walking.

"Faron? Put me down, Faron." Belinda started wriggling on Faron's shoulder, but he grabbed her legs and pinned her against him.

As soon as Faron entered the barn, Belinda knew where she was. It was dark and cool inside. It smelled of horses and hay and the pungent odor of manure. A horse nickered from one of the stalls. Faron carried her to an empty stall and shifted her off his shoulder until she was standing in front of him.

"Here we are," he said.

Belinda just stared at him. Her heart was pounding with excitement. All she did was take one step toward him and Faron gathered her close in his arms. He lifted her legs and wrapped them around him. She clutched at his shoulders and buried her face at his throat.

"You feel so good, Princess."

Faron backed her up against the stall and found her breasts through the T-shirt with his mouth.

"Faron? Are you in here?"

"Damn, damn, damn," Faron muttered. "What do you want, Garth?"

"Candy will be here in a minute to check on that foaling mare."

He had forgotten about the mare. "All right. Thanks."

Belinda was too caught up in the passion of the moment to realize they had been interrupted. Faron unwound her legs from around him and tried to stand her up, but her knees wouldn't support her. He picked her up in his arms and headed out of the barn. Garth had conveniently, considerately disappeared.

Belinda hid her face against Faron's shoulder. "Looks like our timing was a little off," she mumbled.

"Don't I know it," Faron muttered.

"Hey, you two!" Tate called. "We're going to play a game of softball. You want in?"

Faron looked down and met Belinda's rueful look. "Sure. We'll join you."

They spent the rest of the afternoon in a game of softball, then tossed the Frisbee again until it started to get dark. Madelyn kept an eye on the babies and generally supervised activities.

As they were clearing away the picnic table, Belinda watched the various couples begin to pair off. Again, her eyes sought out Faron. He was walking toward her. She felt her belly tighten as he stalked her. She stood and waited for him to come to her. He didn't stop when he passed by her, merely paused long enough to whisper in her ear.

Belinda shivered when he said, "Tonight."

CHAPTER EIGHT

FARON WAS IN the kitchen, waiting for the house to get quiet, waiting for the right moment to go to Belinda. He hadn't *asked* if he could come to her, he had *told* her he was coming. He wished he could know for sure that when he knocked on her door this time, his Princess would let him in.

"What are you doing down here so late?"

Faron turned and found himself confronted by Charlie One Horse. The half-Indian codger was more than a hired hand. He had been part father, part mother and longtime friend to the Whitelaws. He had been a source of wisdom and knowledge all of Faron's life.

"Female problems," Charlie muttered.

Faron's lips curled in the semblance of a smile. "How did you know?"

"Only reason a man wanders the house at night in-

stead of going to bed where he belongs." Charlie concentrated on retying the beaded rawhide thong on one
of his black braids so Faron wouldn't see the concern
in his eyes.

"As long as you're here, I could use some advice,"
Faron said.

"I'm listenin'." Charlie crossed to the refrigerator,
opened the door and stood there looking inside.

"I'm in love with Belinda Prescott."

"So? What's the problem?"

"Her first marriage—her marriage to my father—
was a disaster. I don't know if she's ever going to let
another man get close to her."

Charlie took out a container of strawberries and set
it on the counter. He got a fork from the drawer, then
stood at the counter eating the ripe red berries. "Time
is the best salve to heal wounds of the heart."

"I don't have a lot of time," Faron said in a tormented
voice.

Charlie One Horse forked a huge strawberry and
held it up so he could examine it. It was a "double," a
strawberry that should have been two and had ended
up one. "You'll just have to be patient. Show her that
you love her. Once she realizes what love is supposed to
be, she'll come to you like a filly to a hand outstretched
with sugar." He stuffed the strawberry into his mouth
and began munching.

Faron couldn't deny Charlie had given him good advice. But it seemed too little, too late. He could feel time
running out. Tomorrow they would be headed back to
King's Castle. Next time a corporate buyer showed up,
he might not be so lucky. Next time the man might make
an offer he couldn't—and Belinda wouldn't—refuse.

Faron crossed the room and laid a hand on Charlie's shoulder. "Thanks, Charlie. Good night."

Charlie just grunted because his mouth was too full of strawberries for him to speak.

Faron headed for the stairs, then detoured to the parlor. He wasn't quite ready yet to face Belinda's possible rejection. He slumped down into his regular chair in front of the fireplace, thinking he was alone, only to discover that Garth was there before him.

"What are you doing sitting in the dark?" Faron asked.

"I could ask you the same thing," Garth responded.

Neither man gave a reason why he was there. Neither needed to. As Charlie had noted, only a woman kept a man from his bed when he ought to be sleeping. They sat there staring into a fire that was no more than glowing embers. Occasionally Garth drank from a glass of whiskey he held in one hand.

"Did you find the peace of mind you were looking for when you set out for Wyoming?" Garth asked at last.

"It was worth the trip to find Maddy," Faron said. "She's a feisty old broad." Faron thrust his hands through his hair and tried to smooth it back down again. "And I love the land, King's Castle. I don't know how to explain it. It's so different from the canyons and gullies on Hawk's Way. There's something about those endless rolling green prairies that feeds my soul. I'm going to miss it when it's sold."

"So don't sell."

"What?"

"Don't sell the place. Keep it."

"Belinda Prescott might have a few words to say about that. She wants to move into town."

"So let her go. Buy her half of the place from her."

"I—" Faron didn't know how to explain to his brother that a great deal of what he found so captivating about King's Castle was the fact that Belinda Prescott lived there.

Garth shrugged when Faron made no effort to explain himself further. "It was just an idea. So what did you find out about Wayne Prescott?"

"He wasn't a very noble character, my father."

"You knew that before you left," Garth pointed out.

"He abused Belinda."

"I'm sorry to hear that."

It was the first time Faron had ever heard Garth utter those words. It brought a lump to his throat to realize that his brother understood Faron's anger and frustration without him having to say more.

"I don't have to ask if you love her," Garth said. "It's written all over your face when you look at her. Are you sure you're doing the right thing to get involved with her?"

Trust Garth to go right to the heart of the problem. "It's right for me. I'm not so sure about how she feels."

"Does it bother you at all that she was Wayne Prescott's wife?" Garth asked curiously.

Faron took time to seriously consider Garth's question. At last he said, "Only because he treated her badly."

"So what are you doing down here? I never thought you were a coward."

Faron took enough umbrage to say, "I'm not the only Whitelaw sitting alone in the dark. What's the story between you and Candy Baylor?"

"None of your business," Garth said brusquely.

A slow smile grew on Faron's face. "Well, well, big brother. How the mighty have fallen."

"What's that supposed to mean?"

"You figure it out. I'm going upstairs where I hope there's a lady waiting for me. You can sit here alone in the dark all night if you want. But I suspect there might be a lady somewhere waiting for you, too."

"She'll have a long wait," Garth retorted.

Faron laughed. "Good night, Garth. Sleep well."

"Get out of here and leave me in peace."

"I'll leave, but I doubt you'll have much peace until you seek out a certain blond-haired, gray-eyed woman."

Faron had just reached the doorway when he heard the loud splintering of glass against the stone fireplace. He was almost sorry he would be leaving tomorrow. He would give his eyeteeth to be around to see his cynical, misogynistic brother finally fall in love with a woman.

As he climbed the stairs, Faron was aware of the silence in the house. When he reached Belinda's door he knocked and then turned the knob. It was open, and he let himself in.

There was a light on beside the bed. Belinda wasn't there.

"Damn." He should have known she wasn't ready yet to hear what he wanted to say to her. He shouldn't have pushed so hard. He had frightened her so badly she had run. But where the hell had she gone?

Faron felt like throwing something. He settled for slamming one fisted hand into the palm of the other. He clenched his back teeth and stared out the window into the distance. He would just have to take Charlie One Horse's advice and be patient. Belinda couldn't go far. And he would be here waiting when she returned.

Faron crossed to the connecting door between the two bedrooms and yanked it open. He stomped across the threshold and stopped short. His jaw fell agape.

There, sound asleep in his bed, lay his golden Princess. She was wearing a filmy nightgown with a delicate lace trim that cupped her breasts. Her hand pillowed her head and one knee was drawn up so that the nightgown revealed the length of her from her toes to the top of her hip.

He sat down carefully beside her on the brass bed, but even that slight movement woke her. She turned lazily onto her back and looked up at him through half-closed eyes.

"Hi," she said. "I've been waiting for you."

Faron's heart began to gallop. "I'm glad you're here."

Belinda slipped a hand around Faron's nape and drew his mouth down to hers. Just before their lips met she said, "I like your family, Faron. I wish…"

"What do you wish, Princess?"

"I wish I had waited…to find you."

"I'm here now, Princess. And I'm not going anywhere."

Belinda took the initiative in their lovemaking. Faron made it easy for her. He responded to the barest touch of her fingertips. It was as though he could sense what she needed, what she desired. She urged his mouth down to hers. The kiss was gentle at first, tentative, but Belinda's need was great, and there was an answering fire in the Cowboy.

Faron encouraged her by showing her how much pleasure he found in her kisses, in her touch. She found his leashed passion as seductive as an aphrodisiac. She slowly undressed him, one piece of clothing at a time, indulging her need to feel the textures of his body. The crisp hair on his chest. The hardness of muscle and sinew. The petal softness of his eyelids and the shell of his ears.

"Take off your nightgown, Princess."

Belinda hesitated a moment, then reached down and pulled it up over her head. Finally she was as naked as he was. His eyes adored her. Then his hands and mouth followed where his gaze led. Where Belinda touched him, he touched her. Shoulders. Ribs. Stomach. Hips. Buttocks.

Faron hadn't known he could find such pleasure with a woman. He wanted desperately to speak of his love. But he knew he must be patient. He had to wait until she was ready to hear the words. He had to show her that he loved her, so there could be no doubt in her mind how he felt. She had to know that he would cherish her. That he would never abuse her as his father had.

Faron's body tensed as Belinda's hands surrounded him and urged him close. Her hips rose and he impaled her. They rolled once and she was above him, her hair a cloak that tantalized him by half hiding her breasts.

Belinda felt free to love Faron in ways she had never loved her husband. She had an unbelievable sense of her own feminine power as she caressed him. His eyes glowed with the warmth of his need and desire. Her body tightened in response to his guttural groans of pleasure. His urgent kisses made her feel wanted and loved.

He rolled her under him once more, mantling her body with his own. "Come with me, Princess. Reach for the stars."

Belinda did. She reached for the happiness she had

never allowed herself to even dream of having. She let down the barriers she had put up to keep herself safe from a man to whom she had been a possession. And allowed herself to love a man who treasured her because of who she was.

Faron caught Belinda's cries of exultation with his mouth. He revered her with his hands, with his mouth, with his body. He brought her to the pinnacle, and they rose beyond it together.

Faron wasn't expecting the tears. "Princess? What's wrong? Did I hurt you? Are you all right?"

"I'm fine," she managed through a throat that was constricted so much it prevented easy speech. "I don't know why I'm crying. You were wonderful. It was wonderful."

He gathered her in his arms and held her while she cried. Belinda had a pretty good idea what was causing the lump in her throat. It was the pain of knowledge. Of regret for the years she had foolishly wasted. It was fear of the course she was determined to embark upon. And hope for the future.

Because now she could no longer deny to herself what she felt. She was in love with Faron Whitelaw.

That should have been the end of the fairy tale, and the beginning of the rest of her life. She would simply accept the handsome cowboy's proposal and they would live happily ever after.

Only the Cowboy hadn't proposed. He hadn't even said those three little words, "I love you."

Eventually the constriction in her throat eased. She grabbed a sheet and dabbed at the corners of her eyes. "Faron?"

"Hmm."

"I'm sorry for falling apart on you like that."

"Can you tell me about it?"

"I..." Belinda should have been able to tell Faron that she loved him. That she was hoping they would spend the rest of their lives together. But memories of times when Wayne had taken her tenderest emotions and ridiculed them came to mind. And kept her silent.

It was one thing to say she was going to forget the past and go on with her life. It was quite another to be able to do it. Apparently the wounds were deeper than she had believed. It might take a little longer for them to heal completely. "It's nothing you did, Faron," she said at last.

"Was it something my father did?"

Belinda's hand played across Faron's chest, winding in the black curls that arrowed downward toward his navel. Her fingertips skimmed across a male nipple, and she watched in fascination as it peaked. "I don't want to talk about Wayne. I want to make love to you."

Her fingertips skimmed down the front of him until she cupped him in her hand. His response was immediate and totally gratifying. Belinda grinned. "My, my, Cowboy. What have we here?"

"Don't play with fire, Princess, unless you're ready for the heat."

Belinda's laugh was cut short when Faron's hand slid down the front of her in imitation of her own intimate exploration. He slipped a finger inside her, then another, and Belinda arched up as his thumb sought out the sensitive nubbin that was the source of her desire.

Faron's mouth caught the cries of passion as Belinda arched up under his provocative caresses. But she would never again be a passive partner. She sought out the places on Faron's body that she knew drove him wild. The crease at his thigh, the dimples above his buttocks, the point where taut belly slid into crisp curls.

They taunted each other, refusing to be the first to give in to the sensual teasing. They laughed when they had the breath to do so. They kissed, their tongues entwining, their teeth nipping tender flesh.

And they loved. With their hearts. With their souls. With their whole beings.

But he never said, "I love you."

Neither did she.

When the sun dawned and sent the first rays of light across the tangled sheets, they were still wrapped in each other's arms. Neither wanted the fairy tale to end.

A knock on the door sent Belinda searching for her nightgown. Faron slipped on his jeans and buttoned them halfway.

"We don't have anything to hide," Faron said.

"What if it's Madelyn?" Belinda hissed. "I don't— I'm not ready to face her like this." She yanked her nightgown on, then raced for the door between the two rooms.

She was halfway there when Faron caught her and swung her back into his arms. He kissed her hard. "We have to talk, Princess."

"Later. Let me go, Faron. Please."

He let her go and she disappeared, closing the door silently behind her. Faron answered the persistent knock and found Garth at the door.

"This better be important," Faron growled.

"I thought it was. There was a call on the office phone. Somebody wants to buy King's Castle, but he needs to take a look at it tomorrow. Here's the number where you can reach him."

Faron grimaced. "All right. I'll be right down."

Garth took a look at the disheveled state of the bed and arched a brow. "Take your time, little brother. Take all the time you need."

Before Faron could protest, Garth was gone.

A second later Belinda was back in Faron's room. "Who was it?"

"Garth."

"What did he want?"

"A corporate buyer tracked us down. He wants to take a look at King's Castle—tomorrow."

Belinda sank down onto the bed. "What are we going to do?"

"*We* are going to listen to his offer."

Faron's reference to the fact it would be a joint decision wasn't lost on Belinda. "I... I suppose we should."

"Then we'll have to make a decision whether or not to sell."

The last thing Belinda wanted to contemplate right now was the sale of the ranch. Because once it was sold, Faron would be returning to Hawk's Way. Now that she had seen it, she knew there was no way Faron could prefer King's Castle to the comforts to be found here.

Furthermore, his family lived in Texas. She had seen how close Faron was to his brothers and sister. Family was important to him. Faron couldn't possibly contemplate living the rest of his life in Wyoming, separated from his family except for visits on holidays. Belinda knew how hard that was, and she wouldn't wish it on anyone.

Belinda tried to imagine Faron offering to bring her

back to Hawk's Way as his wife. Naturally, Madelyn would have to be part of the package. However, Belinda couldn't imagine Garth Whitelaw accepting Wayne Prescott's mother into his household. And she could never abandon Madelyn. Which meant Belinda could never live here, either.

"I'll meet you downstairs after you've had a chance to get dressed," Faron said. "And we'll give this guy a call."

"All right," Belinda said.

But when Faron tried to draw her into his arms she stepped back. "I need to get dressed," she said. She turned from him and walked away.

Faron didn't know what had gone wrong, but he had a pretty good idea it had to do with selling the ranch. But he would be damned if he could figure out whether his Princess wanted the place sold—or not.

CHAPTER NINE

IT WAS A toss-up who heaved the bigger sigh of relief when the corporate buyer made a ridiculously low offer. Faron tried to look disappointed. Belinda matched him furrow for furrow in her brow.

"King's Castle is worth too much simply to give it away," Faron said. "Unless you're anxious to get moved into town before winter comes."

"A few months won't make that much difference," Belinda replied. "Besides, we'd be making the man a thief if we accepted his offer."

The unspoken result of their decision not to sell King's Castle was a commitment to continue the improvements they had begun. But the changes they made now went further than simple repairs to put the ranch back into shape to sell. What Faron suggested to Belinda were modifications that would transform King's Castle into a viable, profitable ranching operation.

"Can we really afford to make these kinds of investments?" Belinda asked.

"They'll pay off in the long run," Faron said. It was as close as he could come to saying that he hoped there might be a "long run," without actually saying it. Because he feared saying it would put Belinda on the defensive. He wanted her to realize that they worked well together, that they made a good team, and that they could be happy making a life together on the ranch.

First she had to learn to trust him. He wasn't going to take the chance of pushing her too fast. So he had to keep his distance from her. Because if he took her to bed as often as he wanted to, it wouldn't take her long to figure out that he was playing for keeps. He wanted a chance to build good memories with her of life at King's Castle, to replace the bad ones that had made her want to flee the ranch.

Belinda searched out Faron's gray-green eyes and was forced to drop her gaze or be singed by the need she saw there. Ever since their return from Texas there had been a palpable sexual tension between them. She kept waiting for Faron to act on it, to tease and taunt her as he had in the past. But he exercised a restraint that she wouldn't have believed possible.

She had no doubt that he desired her. It was there in the subtle electrical charge that passed between them whenever they brushed against each other. She saw it in the fierce light that came into his eyes as he gazed at her when he thought she wasn't looking. But she was confused by the signals he was sending.

He obviously wanted to be her lover. But he seemed to be waiting for her to make the first move. It was a novel idea to Belinda, who had never been allowed that option with Wayne. At the age of twenty-eight, she decided it was high time she tried her sexual wings.

She tried subtle things at first. One evening she was working at the computer station beside the rolltop desk while Faron sat in the swivel chair and examined the printout she had just made of feed projections for the winter. She stopped for a break and said, "My shoulders really ache. Could you rub them for me?"

The look in his eyes was priceless. He was a sinking man going down for the third time. "All right. I guess I could do that."

He dropped the printout on the desk, stood and crossed the few feet to where she was sitting. Belinda had her hair in a braid. "Would you mind undoing my braid first?" She saw the flush high on his cheekbones and felt a flutter of feminine satisfaction.

He took his time unraveling the braid, and when he was done his hand tunneled up underneath her long golden hair and massaged her scalp. Belinda's head rolled forward and she exposed her nape to his caresses. She could feel the strength of his hands where they worked to relax the muscles in her shoulders. She was feeling languorous, but there was a rising tension in her breasts and belly.

The moment came when he had to decide whether to continue what he was doing or escape the sensual torment caused by her request. She felt his lips on her nape, soft and slightly damp. A shiver chased down her spine as she felt his warm breath where he hovered over her.

Abruptly he stood up and said, "I need a cup of coffee. Can I get you one, too?"

She turned slightly toward him. He was standing and she was sitting and her eyes were level with the blunt ridge that stood out starkly against the fly of his jeans. She stared for a moment before she reached out a finger and traced the length of his arousal. Down. And then up.

She heard him swallow.

"Princess..."

She dropped her hand and said, "Yes, I'd like a cup of coffee. Thanks... Cowboy."

She turned back to the computer and began typing again. She could feel him standing there a moment longer, then heard his swift tread as he escaped the room and the sexual tension between them. Belinda couldn't help smiling when Faron was gone, pleased with the success of her plan. At this rate he wouldn't be able to hold out for long.

She was surprised the next morning over the breakfast table when he said, "What would you think about having a party to meet the neighbors?"

"That sounds like a wonderful idea," Maddy responded.

Belinda grimaced. She hadn't seen much of her neighbors since the disastrous party nearly six years ago when Wayne had publicly accused her of being a cold woman in bed. It was shortly after he had begun taking the heart medicine that had made him impotent. He had been drunk and had taken out his anger and frustration on her in the most publicly humiliating way possible. She wasn't sure she was ready to face any of those people ever again.

Maddy's enthusiasm was hard to stop. "I'll take care of the invitations," she said. "It's about time we had some music and laughter around here."

"But Maddy—" Belinda protested. "We're too busy to take time for a party."

"Nonsense. Rue and I will take care of everything. All you'll have to do is show up." She turned and beamed a smile at Faron. "I'm looking forward to showing off my grandson."

What could Belinda say to that?

Faron could see Belinda was less than enthusiastic about the party, but he didn't know why. But he decided that if she didn't want to confront her neighbors he wasn't going to force her into it, no matter what Maddy wanted. "We don't have to have a party, Princess. Just say the word and the plans will stop."

Belinda met Faron's concerned gaze, and if she hadn't already been in love with him she would have fallen for him then. He could have no idea why she didn't want to confront her neighbors. Yet he had been aware enough of her distress to respond to it, and in such a way that her needs and desires came before his own.

She smiled and reached out a hand to cover his where it lay on the table. "The party's a good idea. It's high time we said hello again to our neighbors."

Faron's hand turned under hers, and he lifted her hand and brought it to his lips. "Whatever you want, Princess."

What Belinda wanted in that moment was to go upstairs to bed. She blushed furiously at the thought, causing Maddy to chuckle and Faron's lids to droop lazily as he met the stark look of need in her eyes.

Abruptly he dropped her hand and stood. "Got work to do in the barn. See you later."

A moment later Maddy and Belinda were alone at the table.

"I'll be surprised if our neighbors accept an invitation to a party at King's Castle," Belinda said to Maddy. "I hope you know what you're doing." Belinda kept her eyes lowered to hide her pain as she admitted, "I'm afraid to face people after the insulting things Wayne said in public about our personal life."

"I don't think anyone ever blamed you for the way Wayne acted the last years of his life. It was plain to see that he wasn't well."

"I hope you're right," Belinda muttered. But she looked forward to the coming party with a feeling of dread.

The days before the party passed with unbelievable speed. Too soon Belinda found herself dressing with care for a party she had no desire to attend. When Faron knocked on her bedroom door to ask if she was ready to go downstairs she opened the door and said, "I can't go down there."

Faron stepped inside Belinda's bedroom and closed the door behind him. He took one look at the distress in her eyes and folded her into his arms. "What's the matter, Princess? Don't you know I'll protect you from the dragons?"

Just having him offer his support made her feel better. But Belinda knew these were dragons—of the past—that she had to face on her own. Yet there was no reason why she couldn't do so with Faron by her side. She stepped out of Faron's embrace and said, "I'm all right. I'm ready to go downstairs now."

But it suddenly dawned on both of them that they were alone in her bedroom with the door shut behind them. Faron grinned. "How about a kiss for luck?"

"Whose luck? Yours or mine?" Belinda quipped. Her apparent nonchalance was a sham. She felt breathless with excitement that was fed by the avid look in Faron's gray-green eyes.

"Ours," Faron replied. "Have I told you how beautiful you look tonight?"

"No."

"You look absolutely breathtaking, Princess." He reached out and waited until she placed her hand in his. Then he drew her toward him until they were standing only inches apart. He cupped her jaw with his hand and raised her face to his. She no longer kept her lids lowered to hide her feelings from him. Blazing in her eyes was a need more than equal to his own. He lowered his mouth to hers and sipped of the nectar he found there.

His chest was tight with unspoken feelings. "If you need me tonight, I won't be far from your side."

He reached past her and opened the door, then took her arm and put it in the crook of his. "It's time to face your court, Princess. And if any of them dares to offer insult, it'll be off with his head!"

That brought a smile to Belinda's face that was still present when they reached the bottom of the circular staircase.

Most of their neighbors were already there, curious about Belinda and Faron and the reason for this party. Their looks were speculative as they eyed the widow and the roguish cowboy, but not unkind.

A young woman about Belinda's age, with brown hair and brown eyes and a vivid scar across one cheek, was the first to approach Belinda.

"Do you remember me?" she asked.

"Of course I do," Belinda replied. She remembered being appalled at the time that such a beautiful young woman should be so horribly scarred. She had been curious about what had happened, but had never gotten to know the woman well enough to ask. "Your name is Desiree."

The woman smiled and Belinda realized that the scar wasn't so visible after all. "That's right. I can't believe you remember it after all these years."

"I remember it because you were so kind to me that night after..." Desiree Parrish had been the one who had finally stepped between Belinda and her husband.

"I only wish there had been more I could do to help," Desiree said. "I'm so glad you had this party. I've been hoping we could be friends."

This time it was Belinda who smiled. "I could use a friend or two."

"Maybe you'd like to come over next week and visit."

"Or you could come here," Belinda offered.

Desiree shook her head. "It's hard for me to find a babysitter. Would you mind?"

"Just name the day," Belinda said. "I'll be there."

The two women parted company knowing they had planted the seeds for a growing friendship.

By the end of the evening it was plain that everyone was more than willing to leave the past in the past.

True to his word, Faron stayed close by throughout Belinda's ordeal. She wasn't even aware that she was judging him, comparing him to his father.

She watched to see if he talked too loud and drank too much.

He didn't.

He nursed the same whiskey most of the evening, and while she occasionally heard his deep laughter, he was never boisterous.

She watched to see whether he told off-color jokes.

He didn't.

Whether he flirted with the ladies.

He did.

He had a way of making each woman feel special, while still making it clear that he intended their relationship to be strictly platonic.

Whether the neighbors respected him as a rancher and a businessman.

They did. Several times she caught him in discussions with the neighboring ranchers. He was as willing to take advice as he was to share his knowledge.

Whether he made snide or cruel remarks about their personal relationship.

He didn't. While he was never very far from her, he did nothing to indicate their relationship consisted of anything more than the legal connection between them.

But Belinda was mistaken if she thought her neighbors didn't see the attraction between the widow and the bastard son. What she would have discovered, if she had been watching, was that her neighbors were more than willing to accept such an alliance.

They already knew her to be a dedicated and caring rancher. Although Faron might be something of a rogue, he knew the ranching business. With a spread as large as King's Castle, it was important to have someone in authority who knew how to conserve the land.

Toward the end of the evening, Faron approached Belinda with another woman beside him. "Belinda, I think you know Pearl Teasdale. She was just telling me about a problem I thought you might be able to solve."

Pearl was a robust woman of forty-five, with gray hair she was proud of and calluses she had worked to earn. Her brown eyes were straightforward and her voice was slightly nasal from a deviated septum. "I was just telling Faron that Mrs. Webster had to resign as chairman of the Christmas pageant committee at the church when she found out she's expecting her third, only it's her third and fourth—twins, you see. So the doctor wants her to take it easy.

"Anyway, I was wondering if you might be willing to take the job as chairman and plan the pageant."

Belinda had been in the pageant as a child, and knew how much it meant to the children who participated. As a young woman, she hadn't been involved in the pageant, even though she had continued attending church.

"I—" She hesitated.

"Please say yes," Pearl urged. "We could really use the help. And Faron told me how much you love children."

"He did?" Belinda arched a brow. How could she argue with the truth? She would love spending time with the children. It was something Wayne had not allowed. "All right," she said. "I'll do it."

The smile on Pearl's face was blinding. "Wonderful!" She quickly called over several ladies, including Desiree, and they all began chattering about schedules and costumes.

Faron felt warm inside when he saw the way Belinda's face glowed with pleasure. There was light and laughter in her eyes. He frowned when he realized that he wasn't the only one admiring her. There was a bachelor or two among the assembled males, and Belinda was a beautiful, very eligible woman. He wanted to lay claim to her before some other man got ideas. However, he couldn't lay his claim in public when he hadn't made his intentions clear in private.

Faron was startled when he heard Maddy's quiet voice beside him.

"So, are you going to give that girl a child of her own?"

Faron's eyes hooded. His mouth flattened. "Don't interfere, Maddy. Everything in its own good time."

"Don't wait too long," Maddy warned.

Faron scowled. Maddy's warning reminded him too vividly of his fear that Belinda might finally decide she couldn't take a chance on marriage again. Maybe it was time to let Belinda Prescott know his true intentions. He stalked right over to her and easily maneuvered her away from the crowd of women.

"Excuse us, ladies. There's something I need to discuss with Belinda."

"What is it, Faron?"

He dragged her all the way into the kitchen before he stopped. He spied the pantry and hauled her inside the small room and closed the door behind them. The pantry was lit by a bare bulb, and they were surrounded by canned goods and preserves. He pressed her up against the closed door and kissed her with all the pent-up desire he had been saving for just such a moment.

"Faron, stop. What are you doing?"

"Kissing you. Loving you. It's what you want, isn't it?"

Belinda had been teasing him for weeks. It would be foolish to pretend she didn't want him now. She did. She kissed him back with zest and passion. She felt the zipper coming down on her dress and a moment later she was naked to the waist.

"You're not wearing a bra," he said as his hands reverently cupped her breasts. Belinda stepped out of the dress and laid it across several jars of stewed tomatoes.

"You're wearing a black garter belt," he said with a blissful sigh. He sounded a little shocked but pleased when he informed her, "Princess, you're not wearing any panties."

Belinda couldn't help the small giggle that escaped. "You sound like a teenage boy who just hit a home run with his girl," she teased.

"I feel like a kid in a candy store," he said. "I don't know what to taste first."

His mouth latched on to a nipple and he suckled strongly. Belinda arched toward him, but bit her lip to hold back the cry of ecstasy that sought voice. There was a very real danger of discovery here, which only heightened her excitement.

Faron dropped to his knees and his mouth began a foray across her belly and down into the nest of blond curls below. His fingers and tongue indulged in a sensual feast that left her quivering. She would have fallen down if she hadn't been clutching his shoulders.

When he stood and kissed her again she could taste herself. The room smelled of sex and heat and desire. He didn't bother to remove his trousers, just unzipped them and shoved them down enough to free his aroused shaft. He lifted her and with one thrust sank deep inside her.

She wrapped her legs around his hips, her arms around his shoulders and buried her mouth against his throat. Her teeth closed on flesh, but she was unaware of the marks she was leaving as she felt herself driving toward the peak of ecstasy. His fingers bit into her, holding her tight as he thrust within her.

Their mouths merged, tongues thrusting, but they couldn't breathe and kiss at the same time. Belinda hid her face in Faron's shoulder as their bodies climaxed.

He pressed his mouth to her cheek to cut off his guttural cry of pleasure.

They stood there for scant moments panting, until Belinda's legs dropped down to support her.

She heard Faron's chuckle and smiled. "You're a crazy man, Cowboy," she said huskily.

"Then may I never be sane," he answered in an equally throaty voice.

To their chagrin and amusement there was a quiet knock at the pantry door. "You might want to rejoin your guests to bid them good night," Maddy said.

"We'll be there in a minute, Maddy," Faron answered her.

Belinda felt the door opening behind her. "Wait—"

A hand slipped inside bearing a damp towel. "I thought you might need this."

The door closed, and they heard Maddy walking away.

They took one look at each other and burst out laughing. Belinda put a hand on Faron's mouth. "Shh. We'll be caught."

He took the towel and put it to good use on her and himself. Belinda stepped into her dress and turned so he could zip her up. "Do you suppose they'll know what we've been doing?"

Belinda's hair had been left down tonight, but it looked considerably more windblown than when they had entered the pantry. Faron did his best to smooth it. Then he turned her around to face him, took one look at the sparkle in her eye and said, "They'd have to be blind not to know."

Belinda caught a glimpse of the satisfied smile on

Faron's face and pursed her lips. "It might help if you wipe that grin off your face."

He shook his head. "Uh uh. No can do. Feels too good."

Belinda gave up and joined him. "I suppose it does."

They returned to the party at intervals as though they had long ago gone their separate ways to do errands that had only just been completed. If their neighbors suspected what Belinda and Faron had been doing while they were gone, they were too polite to say anything about it.

OVER THE WEEKS and months that followed, Faron and Belinda were seen often in each other's company. At church. At the feed store in Casper. Riding the borders of King's Castle. At the Grange dances. Though no words had been spoken between them to declare it so, they were a couple.

Belinda radiated a new self-confidence. She worked with several ladies who had taken part in the Christmas pageant in the past to make sure that she didn't forget anything. And she loved working with the children. They were delightful. Open and loving and honest. She felt an undeniable yearning—which she fought—for a child of her own.

She made love to Faron as often as she could and in as many ways and places as they could devise. She couldn't help feeling that she was living on borrowed time. That the magical fairy tale they had created simply couldn't last. She was too happy, and she couldn't help feeling that there had to be a villain somewhere— every fairy tale had one—who would strip away her happiness.

As Christmas approached, she asked Faron to save some time to help her set up the tree. They decided to do it the third Saturday afternoon in December.

The boxes of Christmas decorations were kept in a room on the third floor of The Castle. Faron hadn't been up there before, and he was amazed at the history he saw in the items stored there.

"A lot of families must have lived in this house over the years," he said. He picked up a *McGuffey's Reader* and paged through it. There was a handmade wooden wagon and a rocking horse that would have been about the right size for a child of four or five.

Belinda picked up a reticule, a purse once carried by a pioneer woman, and donned a silk bonnet. "What do you think? Am I ready for a trip into town?"

"You look ready for a kiss." He lowered his mouth to hers and their lips met in the tenderest of kisses. "Belinda, don't you want to be a part of this? To preserve King's Castle for future generations?"

"I—I thought that's what we were doing."

Faron's voice was harsh when he responded, "Are we? Or are we just fooling ourselves, playing games until a buyer comes along and snatches all this out from under us?"

"That's not fair, Cowboy," Belinda retorted in a heated voice. "If anybody's playing games here, it's you. What is it you want from me?"

Maddy's voice filtered up the stairs. "Faron? Belinda? Are you up there? There's someone here to see you."

"We'll talk about this tonight," Faron said. He didn't give Belinda a chance to argue, just grabbed her hand and headed down the stairs.

When they arrived downstairs they found a man slightly older than Faron waiting for them. He had chestnut brown hair and cold blue eyes. He was about Faron's height, but heavier in build, with a bigger chest and shoulders. He was wearing faded jeans and a ragged shirt and his boots hadn't seen polish in a month of Sundays.

"Hello," he said, extending his hand to Faron. "I'm Carter Prescott. Your brother. I'm here to take this place off your hands."

CHAPTER TEN

"I SHOULD HAVE known that Wayne Prescott had more than one bastard son," Faron said bitterly.

"I'm not a bastard," Carter said in a frosty voice. "Wayne Prescott was married to my mother."

Both Faron and Belinda turned to Madelyn for confirmation. She nodded slowly. "It's true. Wayne was married once, a long time ago. The marriage ended in divorce, but as far as I know there were no children."

Carter smiled cynically. "I was conceived after the divorce papers had been filed and born shortly before the divorce was final. There was no love lost between my mother and Wayne Prescott. She didn't see any reason to let him know he had a son."

"Why have you waited until now to come forward?" Faron asked.

"I wouldn't have said anything even now, except I

want this place and I thought I'd have a better chance of getting it as a Prescott."

Faron forked all ten fingers through his hair. "Damn. I'm not sure what the legalities are—whether you're entitled to a portion of King's Castle under the will or not."

"I don't give a damn about any inheritance I might be entitled to."

Faron frowned. "Then why are you here?"

"I want to buy King's Castle."

Faron looked skeptically at the man standing in front of him. Carter Prescott didn't look like someone who had the kind of money it was going to take to buy a ranch the size of King's Castle. "Do you have that kind of cash?"

Carter's lips curled into a wry smile. "In the divorce, my mother took Wayne Prescott for half of everything he owned. Over the years I've made a few investments." He shrugged apologetically. "I'm rich as sin."

Faron turned stunned eyes on Belinda.

"I'm willing to pay you what the place is worth," Carter said. "Money is no object. Name your price. I'm just looking for some roots, and I think I might find them here."

Faron couldn't argue with that sentiment. He had felt it himself. But this was *his* place. Carter Prescott would have to find his roots somewhere else!

"I think Belinda and I need to have a discussion in private. Would you mind giving us some time alone?" Faron said.

"Sure." Carter turned to Madelyn and took off his hat to introduce himself. "If I'm not mistaken, you're my grandmother."

"I am," Madelyn said. There was a distinct chill

in her voice that surprised Faron. "I never liked your mother," Madelyn said to Carter.

Carter smiled ruefully. "Not many people did, ma'am."

That defrosted a little of Madelyn's ice, but she couldn't embrace this new-found grandson when she believed he was determined to ruin the happiness of the other.

"I could use a cup of coffee," Carter said.

"Come with me." Madelyn turned and marched toward the kitchen without looking back.

Carter settled his Stetson on his head and followed resolutely after her.

Of all the forms the villain in Belinda's fairy tale had taken, it was never that of a handsome young man. "I can't believe this is happening," she said.

"It's happening," Faron said. "Let's go into the study where we can sit down and talk."

Belinda was too nervous to sit down. Once Faron was settled in the swivel chair in front of the desk, she jumped up and began pacing.

"With the money from the sale of King's Castle, you and Maddy will both have the security you wanted," Faron began.

Belinda looked at him with stricken eyes. That wasn't what she wanted to hear from Faron. She wanted to hear that he loved her and wanted to marry her and that together they would spend their lives making King's Castle what it once was.

But she couldn't force him to stay if he wanted to go. And with Hawk's Way calling to him, how could she ever have hoped he might want to stay?

"I suppose it makes sense to accept Carter's offer," she said tentatively.

"Is that what you really want to do?" Faron asked.

"I'm willing to go along with whatever you want to do," Belinda countered, her eyes lowered to hide the grief she felt at the loss that was to come. "So I guess we sell."

Faron's tone was grim. "If that's what you want to do, then that's what we'll do." He kept his eyes lowered to the hands fisted in his lap.

Neither one of them realized they were sacrificing what they most wanted in deference to the needs and wants of the other.

"Do you want to tell him our decision now?" Faron asked.

"Not yet!" Belinda didn't know why she felt so frantic, only that she did. "Let's wait until after the pageant tonight."

"Postponing the inevitable isn't going to change it," Faron warned.

"I know. Please, Faron. Just wait until after the pageant." She could keep her fairy tale alive for a few more hours. It wasn't over yet, and she didn't plan to give up her dream until she absolutely had to.

Faron didn't know what else to say. "We'd better finish getting that tree up. You've got to be at the church early tonight to set up for the Christmas pageant."

When Faron and Belinda entered the kitchen, Madelyn and Carter were engaged in a rousing argument.

"What's going on here?" Faron asked.

"I was just trying to talk Carter into attending the Christmas pageant tonight. Without much success, I might add."

"Oh, please come," Belinda said. "It's so moving."

"That's what I'm afraid of," Carter muttered. "I don't care much for that sort of thing."

"But it's Christmas," Belinda said. "Everyone loves Christmas."

Faron took one look at Carter's face and realized his half brother was the exception. "You don't have to come if you'd rather not."

Madelyn wasn't about to let Carter off that easily. "I'd appreciate the chance to show off *both* my grandsons. Surely you won't deny me that."

"All right, Maddy," Carter said. But it was plain his heart wasn't in it.

"The children have worked so hard. I know you'll enjoy it," Belinda said. "They do a wonderful job."

The more Belinda said about children, the more rigid Carter's face got, until she realized she was only making it worse by going on and on. She didn't know what Carter Prescott had against children and Christmas, but it was clear his opinions were long-standing. Nothing she said was going to change them.

In the awkward silence that ensued Carter said, "By the way, did you make a decision about selling King's Castle?"

Belinda and Faron exchanged an uneasy glance.

"We want to think about it a little while longer," Faron said.

"Goodness. This is no time to be worrying about business," Madelyn interjected. "Look at the time. If we don't get busy, we'll be late getting to the pageant."

Belinda was so excited, she and Faron left early for church. Carter promised to follow later with Madelyn. It had begun snowing, and while Belinda was glad for the hope of a white Christmas, she was worried that the threat of a bad storm might keep some families away from the pageant. She was proved wrong when she arrived at the church and saw the pews were already beginning to fill.

She rushed around setting robes in place on shoulders, making sure the shepherds had their staffs and the angels had their halos. At the last moment there was some confusion about whether it was all right to use a female doll to represent the baby Jesus. Belinda did some fast talking and got the youngster playing Joseph to agree to the deception.

Belinda watched the program from the sidelines, nestled in the curve of Faron's arm. "The children are so precious," she whispered. Unspoken was the wish for some of her own.

Belinda watched Faron watching the children and saw his eyes soften with tenderness as a six-year-old Mary nestled a baby doll Jesus in her arms. She watched them light with laughter as an eight-year-old shepherd scattered live sheep down the aisle of the church. And watched them glow with what she would have sworn was love as he turned to her and squeezed her hand while they sang "Silent Night."

When the pageant was over and all the children had been divested of their costumes and bundled into coats, Belinda and Faron looked for Carter and Madelyn. All they found was Maddy.

"Carter left," Madelyn said. "He said he would meet us back at the house."

"But why?" Belinda asked.

"I think it was too hard for him to stay any longer," Madelyn said mysteriously. Belinda never could get any more of an explanation from Madelyn all the way home. At last Belinda realized there must be a lot of people like herself and Carter who had pasts they would rather forget. She felt a little guilty for forcing Carter into a situation where he had been forced to confront demons he might rather have left resting in their dens.

When they got back to The Castle, they found Carter settled in front of the fireplace with a brandy. There was no sign either in his face or his greeting that suggested a reason for why he had left the church.

"If you're comfortable, Carter, I think we'll just leave you here for a while. Belinda and I need to talk privately with Maddy," Faron said.

"I'll be fine," Carter said. "Don't worry about me."

As Faron and Belinda ushered Madelyn into the study, she demanded to know what was going on. Faron refused to say anything until Madelyn was seated in the swivel chair in front of the rolltop desk.

"Why all this hush-hush secretive business?" Madelyn demanded.

"Belinda and I wanted you to hear that we've decided to sell King's Castle before I inform Carter about the deal."

"What!" Madelyn rose with a vigor that denied her age and her ailing heart.

It was apparent from her ruddy complexion and the outrage in her voice that even though Faron and Belinda were willing to be so foolish as to give up their dreams, Madelyn was not.

"I absolutely refuse to leave this house!" she said. It was more of a shriek, actually.

Faron and Belinda stared at the agitated woman who stood across from them, her hands twisting a lace handkerchief. Madelyn was having trouble catching her breath.

"Please sit down, Maddy." Faron was seriously concerned that she might make herself sick. He tried to get her back into the swivel chair.

Madelyn eluded him and marched around to stand beside the desk with her back to the wall. "Don't coddle me! I won't sit down until I hear from your own lips, Belinda, that you would even consider something as horrendous as selling this house out from under me!"

"But Madelyn, I thought you understood that was why Faron and I were making all these improvements," Belinda said.

"Well, I didn't understand!" Madelyn said in an imperious voice. She turned her irate gaze on Faron. "As for you, young man, I'm gravely disappointed in you."

Faron felt the heat on his cheekbones and wasn't sure whether he was feeling shame, embarrassment or anger. Actually, it was a combination of all three. "What is it you're most disappointed by, Maddy? The fact that I would court your son's wife in front of your nose? Or the fact that I'm willing to make Belinda happy at your expense?"

"You young idiot! Don't you see that selling King's Castle isn't going to make anyone happy? Least of all Belinda!"

"You're wrong. Belinda told me months ago that she wants to live in town. She just got through telling me she wants to sell this place."

"Foolish man! Belinda was willing to move into town to take care of me. She would never leave King's Castle if you decided to stay here with her. Ask her!"

Faron leapt up from his chair and turned to face Belinda. "Is that true, Belinda? Would you stay at King's Castle if I stayed here with you?"

"Since that isn't going to happen—"

Faron grabbed Belinda by the shoulders and shook her. "Answer the damned question!"

"Yes! I'd never leave this place if you were here with me. But Faron, that isn't possible, don't you see?"

"Why not?"

"Do you mean to say you'd be willing to leave Hawk's Way? That you'd be willing to spend the rest of your life in Wyoming?"

"I'd move to hell and set up housekeeping if you were there with me. I love you, Princess."

Belinda stood stunned. "Why didn't you ever tell me so?"

Faron shrugged sheepishly. "I didn't want to scare you away. What I want, Princess, what I've wanted for what seems a very long time, is to marry you and work this ranch and raise children here with you."

Belinda thought of the risk involved in committing herself to another man. What she discovered was that her love for Faron, and his love for her, took all the fear out of taking such a risk. Faron wanted only to make her happy, just as she wanted to please him.

"If that was a proposal," she said at last, "I accept."

Faron threw his arms around Belinda and hugged her so tightly she squeaked.

"Don't squeeze the girl to death," Madelyn chided.

Faron reached out and included Maddy in the hug. "You conniving old woman. I don't know what you're complaining about. You got exactly what you wanted."

Madelyn grinned and chortled. "I suppose I did at

that. Now. What are we going to do about that young man in the parlor?"

"We have to invite him to stay for Christmas," Belinda said. "We can't send him off alone."

Madelyn's eyes narrowed speculatively. "No, we can't do that, can we?"

"You're not matchmaking again, are you, Madelyn?" Belinda asked when she spied the look in her mother-in-law's eyes.

"Who? Me, dear? What makes you think that? However, Carter did mention while we were having coffee in the kitchen that he owns a ski resort in Vermont. It's located in a town not far from where Fiona runs her bed and breakfast. Two relatives should get to know each other, don't you think?"

"Carter's not related in the least to Fiona!" Belinda protested.

"No, they're not related, are they?" Madelyn murmured. "How fortunate. But I do foresee a slight problem."

Belinda knew she shouldn't ask, but did anyway. "What problem?"

"Carter doesn't like cats."

"How did you find that out?" Faron asked, amazed at how much information Madelyn had pried from her newest grandson in the little time they'd had together. "About Carter and cats?"

"Oh, we were discussing conservation. Carter's working to save the mountain lion, even though he doesn't like cats. I don't suppose Fiona would be willing to give up Tut…"

"Madelyn—"

Belinda's warning was lost as Madelyn headed for

the parlor. "I'll just go get Carter and send him in here so you can give him the bad news."

When she was gone Belinda looked up at Faron and shook her head. "I don't think there's any help for it. I suppose I'll have to call Fiona and warn her what's coming."

Faron grinned. "What, and spoil all Maddy's fun? From what I know of your sister, Fiona can take care of herself."

"At least it looks like our fairy tale is going to end happily ever after," Belinda said as she gazed up at Faron with adoring eyes.

"What do you want for Christmas, Princess?"

"A baby."

"You've got it. But I think I'll go ahead and give you the gift I had planned." Faron opened the top right hand desk drawer and reached into the back of it. He pulled out a small velvet box and opened it. "This is for you, Princess."

Inside was a topaz surrounded by baguette diamonds. "It's the closest thing I could find to the daisies we picked that first day we spent together." He took the ring from the box and placed it on her finger. "Now you'll always be wearing flowers, Princess."

Tears blurred Belinda's vision. "It's beautiful. Thanks, Cowboy."

ALL THINGS CONSIDERED, Carter Prescott took the news that King's Castle had been taken off the market pretty well. "You know I could go to court and challenge the will," he pointed out. "I could tie up your assets so you'd have a hell of a time making ends meet."

"You could," Faron said, a muscle ticking in his jaw.

"But I'd fight you every step of the way. And I have some considerable assets at my disposal."

Carter measured Faron's determination and apparently decided Faron meant what he said. Carter smiled wistfully. "I envy you, brother. Guess I'll have to keep looking for those roots."

"I wish you luck finding them," Faron said. "You'll always be welcome here. In fact, we'd be pleased to have you join us for Christmas."

Carter shook his head. "I don't think so. I don't want to intrude. In fact, I'll be leaving tonight."

"So soon?" Belinda asked. "I know Madelyn would like to spend more time with you."

Carter shook his head. "If I stay here much longer I might get to liking this place too much." He reached out his hand to Faron. "Goodbye, Faron. It was a pleasure meeting you."

Faron shook his half brother's hand. "I wish we had more time to get to know each other."

"Maybe I'll be back this way again sometime."

Faron and Belinda walked Carter to the parlor where they found Madelyn. She was distressed that her grandson had chosen to leave so soon, but didn't try to change his mind.

Carter hugged his grandmother. "I'm glad I met you, Maddy. I'll see you again sometime." But the way he said it didn't sound like he thought it would be anytime soon.

"Maybe sooner than you think," Madelyn said with a smug smile.

Belinda shook her head. Once Madelyn got an idea in her head it was hard to get it out. Somehow the old woman had gotten her mind set on matching Carter and Fiona. Belinda decided the best thing to do was to stand back and watch the fur fly. Considering how Carter felt about cats, that was a definite possibility when he met up with Tut.

The three of them stood at the door and waved as Carter drove away. It didn't take long for his pickup to disappear in the flurries of snow.

"Now that our company's gone, I think I'll go to bed," Madelyn announced. "I'm feeling a little tired tonight."

Faron and Belinda looked at each other anxiously.

"Are you all right, Maddy?" Faron asked.

Madelyn grinned. "Now don't you worry about me. I plan to be around long enough to dandle a couple of great-grandchildren on my knee. I just thought I'd leave you two alone so you could get started." Madelyn winked, then turned and headed up the stairs.

Faron and Belinda stood stunned for a second before they burst out laughing.

"I can take a hint," Faron said. He lifted Belinda into his arms and headed for the parlor. He set her down on the rug in front of the fireplace and joined her there. The only light in the room came from the fire and the colored bulbs on the Christmas tree.

They didn't speak, just sat and held each other, listening to the fire crackle and the wind howl as it blew snow against the house. The aroma of spruce pervaded the room, bringing the vast reaches of King's Castle inside for Christmas.

Faron kissed Belinda's cheek, and she snuggled back into his arms. "It's nice holding you like this," he said.

"It's nice being held."

"Would you like to get married on Christmas Day?"

"That would be nice," Belinda said. "Maybe we could get your family and mine both to come here for the occasion."

"I suspect we might be able to talk them into it."

"I love you, Faron."

He smiled. "You know, that's the first time you've said that to me."

"Is it, really? I've thought it a thousand times."

"I hope you'll keep on saying it."

"I love you. Love you. Love you." She punctuated each pronouncement with a kiss.

Faron slowly lowered Belinda to the rug in front of the fireplace. "Your eyes are lit up like the Christmas tree," he said.

"I can't tell you how happy I feel. Maybe I can show you."

She slowly began covering his face with kisses while her hands roamed his body seeking out the places she had learned would bring him the most pleasure.

"Let's make our baby here, now," she murmured. "Love me, Cowboy."

Faron didn't need more invitation than that. They wasted no time undressing each other, and soon their bodies lay entwined like two golden stems in the firelight. Faron spread Belinda's legs with his knees and settled himself in the cradle of her thighs.

"How many children shall we have?" he murmured as he kissed his way up her throat toward her ear.

"At least a boy and a girl."

He grinned. "I knew a family that had six girls before they got a boy."

Belinda flushed. "I think I could be happy with just girls. Or just boys."

Faron's hand slipped down past her belly to the nest of curls below. She was already wet, and he didn't wait, just slid himself inside her. Then he lay there, waiting to see how long he could stand the pleasure before he had to move.

Meanwhile, Belinda was busy playing with the curls on his chest. She found a male nipple and laved it with her tongue. Faron jerked, and the friction of their bodies moving together wrought a soft cry of pleasure from Belinda's throat.

"Don't move," Faron begged. "I'm trying an experiment here."

Belinda lifted her hips and Faron groaned.

"What kind of experiment?" she asked.

"I wanted to see how long we could just lie here joined together like this."

Belinda grinned like a cat with a bowl of cream. "Not long, Cowboy."

She shifted again and Faron fought back a guttural sound in his throat. "Princess, I'm serious about this."

"So am I." Belinda reached down between their two bodies and touched him where they were joined. Her hand slid down and gently cupped the sac below.

Faron wasn't able to stay still under her onslaught. "All right, if that's the way you want to play, I'm game."

He reached down between them and found the heart of her desire. In moments his caresses had her undulating with pleasure.

"What do you say, Cowboy? Ready to cry uncle?"

"Not until you do, Princess," Faron replied.

Faron latched on to a nipple and suckled hard.

"That's cheating," Belinda rasped.

Faron was too busy to answer. Belinda threaded her

hands in his hair and urged his mouth up to hers. "I want to be your woman, Cowboy. I want to have your baby."

Faron answered, "I love you, Princess. I want to make love with you tonight and tomorrow and the rest of our lives."

Their loving was like a prayer, a litany to happily ever after. As their bodies succumbed to the demands each made upon the other, their souls entwined once and for always.

With the woman he loved in his arms, Faron said a prayer that the weather would hold good over the winter so they would have enough feed to manage without buying more. And that his new wife would present him with a daughter in the fall, along about harvest time.

Belinda said a prayer that she would be a good and loving wife, and that she would present her new husband with a son in the fall, along about harvest time.

And just like in a fairy tale, both their prayers were answered.

* * * * *

SPECIAL EXCERPT FROM

♦ HARLEQUIN
ROMANTIC SUSPENSE

*After a suspicious death on her team, environmentalist
Emma Copley knows someone needs to investigate.
When the authorities won't, she decides to do it herself,
despite Beau Kingston's warnings. He may have a
financial incentive to stop her investigation, but he
certainly doesn't want her hurt. Can they trust each
other long enough to find the real culprit?*

Read on for a sneak preview of
Deadly Texas Summer,
the latest thrilling romance from Colleen Thompson.

She looked up at him, her expression stricken. "You don't
believe me either, do you? You don't think I can prove
that Russell was on to something real."

"I'm reserving judgment," he said, keeping his words
as steady as he could, "until I see more evidence. And
you might want to consider holding back on any more
accusations until you've recovered from this shock—and
you have that proof in hand."

"Oh, I'll find the proof. I have a good idea where, too.
All I have to do is get back to the turbines as soon as
possible and find the—"

"No way," he said sharply. "You're not going out
there. You saw the email, right? About Green Horizons'
safety review?"

She gave him a disgusted look. "Of course they want to
keep everyone away. If they're somehow involved in all

this, they'll drag out their review forever. And leave any evidence cleaned and sanitized for their own protection."

"Or they're trying to keep from being on the hook for any further accidents. Either way, I said no, Emma. I don't want you or your students taking any unnecessary chances."

"I'd never involve them. Never. After Russell, there's no way I would chance that." She shook her head, tears filling her eyes. "I was—I was the one to call Russell's parents. I insisted on it. It nearly killed me, breaking that news to them."

"Then you'll understand how I feel," Beau said, "when I tell you I'm not making that call to your folks, your boss or anyone else when you go getting yourself hurt again. Or worse."

She made a scoffing sound. "You've helped me out a couple times, sure. That doesn't make me your responsibility."

"That's where you're wrong, Dr. Copley. I take everyone who lives on, works on or sets foot on my spread as my responsibility," he said, sincerity ringing in his every word, "which is why, from this point forward, I'm barring you from Kingston property."

Don't miss
Deadly Texas Summer
by Colleen Thompson

Available March 2020 wherever
Harlequin Romantic Suspense
books and ebooks are sold.

Harlequin.com

SPECIAL EXCERPT FROM

H HARLEQUIN
INTRIGUE

Sheriff Jamison Wyatt has never forgotten Liza Dean, the one who got away. But now she's back, and she needs his help to find her sister. They'll have to infiltrate a crime syndicate, but once they're on the inside, will they be able to get back out?

Read on for a sneak preview of
South Dakota Showdown *by Nicole Helm.*

Chapter One

Bonesteel, South Dakota, wasn't even a dot on most maps, which was precisely why Jamison Wyatt enjoyed being its attached officer. Though he was officially a deputy with the Valiant County Sheriff's Department, as attached officer his patrol focused on Bonesteel and its small number of residents.

One of six brothers, he wasn't the only Wyatt who acted as an officer of the law—but he was the only man who'd signed up for the job of protecting Bonesteel.

He'd grown up in the dangerous, unforgiving world of a biker gang run by his father. The Sons of the Badlands were a cutthroat group who'd been wreaking havoc on the small communities of South Dakota—just like this one—for decades.

Luckily, Jamison had spent the first five years of his life on his grandmother's ranch before his mother had fully given in to Ace Wyatt and moved them into the fold of the nomadic biker gang.

Through tenacity and grit Jamison had held on to a belief in right and wrong that his grandmother had instilled in him in those early years. When his mother had given birth to son after son on the inside of the Sons, Jamison had known he would get them out—and he had, one by one—and escape to their grandmother's ranch situated at the very edge of Valiant County.

HIEXP0220

It was Jamison's rough childhood in the gang and the immense responsibility he'd placed on himself to get his brothers away from it that had shaped him into a man who took everything perhaps a shade too seriously. Or so his brothers said.

Jamison had no regrets on that score. Seriousness kept people safe. He was old enough now to enjoy the relative quiet of patrolling a small town like Bonesteel. He had no desire to see lawbreaking. He'd seen enough. But he had a deep, abiding desire to make sure everything was right.

So it was odd to be faced with a clear B and E just a quarter past nine at night on the nearly deserted streets. Maybe if it had been the general store or gas station, he might have understood. But the figure was trying to break into his small office attached to city hall.

It was bold and ridiculous enough to be moderately amusing. Probably a drunk, he thought. Maybe the…woman—yes, it appeared to be a woman—was drunk and looking to sleep it off.

When he did get calls, they were often alcohol related and mostly harmless, as this appeared to be.

Since Jamison was finishing up his normal last patrol for the night, he was on foot. He walked slowly over, keeping his steps light and his body in the shadows. The streets were quiet, having long since been rolled up for the night.

Still, the woman worked on his doorknob. If she was drunk, she was awfully steady for one. Either way, she didn't look to pose much of a threat.

He stepped out of the shadow. "Typically people who break and enter are better at picking a lock."

The woman stopped what she was doing—but she hadn't jumped or shrieked or even stumbled. She just stilled.

Don't miss
South Dakota Showdown *by Nicole Helm,*
available March 2020 wherever
Harlequin Intrigue books and ebooks are sold.

Harlequin.com